LANDFALL

LANDFALL

BOOK III OF THE BOOK OF BERA TRILOGY

SUZIE WILDE

unbound

First published in 2023

Unbound
Level 1, Devonshire House, One Mayfair Place, London W1J 8AJ
www.unbound.com
All rights reserved

Text design by PDQ Digital Media Solutions Ltd

A CIP record for this book is available from the British Library

ISBN 978-1-80018-148-9 (paperback)
ISBN 978-1-80018-149-6 (ebook)

Printed in Great Britain by Clays Ltd, Elcograf S.p.A

1 3 5 7 9 8 6 4 2

Women are great but this book is dedicated to the male of the species, as the skern might say. There always have been good men, and I've loved a few of them. You know who you are.

With special thanks to Rory Bremner for his generous support of this book.

Author's Note

Some readers of *Obsidian*, Book II of the trilogy, requested an explanation of skern and Drorgher, so here is a brief glossary of terms adapted from Norse mythology.

Skern is my term for *fylgja*, literally translated as 'follower'. It's a form of twin spirit, and in some of the sagas it takes the form of an animal, which can reflect the character of its human twin. You'll have your own idea of Bera's skern but the word can also mean 'afterbirth', which gave me the idea of them cleaving in the womb.

Valla is *Völva* in Icelandic, which is a witch or seer. They can sometimes read Fate, but I gave Bera greater purpose.

Drorgher is *draugr*, a revenant. Only careful burial rites keep the walking dead away, which is true of many cultures. The various forms of prevention in the books are all taken from real practices, from knocking a hole in the wall and taking out the corpse feet first, to filling its mouth with a stone so that it cannot bite its way free of the shroud.

My debt to Celtic and Norse mythology, to ancient sites and to the Icelandic sagas is clear. Weaving it all together is the warp and weft of fiction.

HIRAETH

Hiraeth is a Welsh word for an emotion that has no direct translation because it's so personal. Always poignant, it's to do with homesickness, or grieving for something that may never have been known. The word tugs at a yearning within me that I cannot name. It's certainly to do with loss and never belonging; it's a call from deep time, the long dead and the sadness of being exiled from a home I have never found.

1

Hefnir was dead.

Bera told Heggi to keep heading out to sea and went up to the bow. She was weary to the marrow of her bones and had no more to give a man who refused his skern.

Beneath the hull of her beloved boat, sea creatures were returning to the empty sea; shimmering and flicking quicksilver flashes that should have made her glad and proud. Instead, she scried the fear inside herself that was summoning her from beyond the sea rim, almost hearing a command bound in stone...

'Papa's alive!' Heggi shouted. 'He made a noise!'

Bera comforted him by checking. Her husband's face was waxen and his eyes crusted with oozing poison and death, and yet... a breath rattled like a chain underwater and the hope of healing made her own chest ring. She raised Hefnir's head and put a spoon of water at his cracked lips. It dribbled down into his beard. Still deep in the poisonous world of wolfsbane but not yet in the dark.

'Lash the tiller, Heggi, and come and help.'

'The wind's dropped.' Heggi kneeled beside her. 'Will Papa live?'

'He's fighting and he's strong.'

'What can I do?'

'Stay with him, talk to him. Give him something to live for.'

'He doesn't care about us.'

'He might, when he wakes.'

He won't. Her skern lay on the deck like a puddle. *The misery around Hefnir is of his own making.*

Despising her husband gave Bera energy, and a Valla's duty was to heal. She hoped Hefnir's gaze was inwards, to repair his faithless

3

heart. He also needed food. She found some smoked meat, which she chewed, rolled into a ball and then tried to push into his mouth. There was no getting past his teeth, so she threw it for the gulls.

He had not taken another breath.

'His eyes make me feel sick,' said Heggi.

Bera spat on a cloth and wiped them. 'Come on, Hefnir, you are aboard the *Raven*. This boat is more powerful than we knew.'

'He can't hear you.'

'Hearing is the last sense to go.' Or so Sigrid had said when Bera's mother lay dying.

'I'm here, Papa,' Heggi tried.

Bera was holding her breath, as if the gasp of needing air would force it into his lungs. Hefnir, whose wide-ranging life across distant seas had narrowed to this boat deck, was choosing death. Then it came, the shuddering of bones that loosened the chains that bound him to this earth.

'It must hurt, though,' Heggi whispered.

He took his father's hand and gasped. On the underside of his wrist was a rough black tattoo, like a strange wheel with three turning spirals.

'The Serpent King had this tattoo,' Heggi said.

'Don't touch it!'

He dropped the hand. 'I wasn't going to.'

'I would rather touch a snake. In Iraland, believers in Brid have to earn it. Hefnir did but Egill did not.'

'What did they have to do?'

'I hope we never know, Heggi.'

'What is Brid?'

'Brid is three women in one and her believers send away their skerns.'

We must never go to Iraland. Her skern shivered.

'Will this Brid come and take Papa, then?'

Bera asked the Vallas to return Hefnir's skern to him, but it was not the old belief that had banished them. Her ribs cracked with the memory of such rending and her own skern paled.

With no twin spirit, he is losing the battle.

4

'Mama?'

A whale spouted a loud hiss and spume of spray. Then silence. It was as if the whole world was waiting for Hefnir's next breath. Bera pressed a finger to Hefnir's neck. Nothing was outwardly different… but then she sensed a change.

'Watch, Heggi!'

Whatever it was that made him Hefnir, left. Something only seen slantwise, but real and alone. Her skern shook his head, trembling.

Heggi looked back at her with wide eyes and nodded.

'I wanted you to see the leaving. Your Papa has gone.'

'Did his skern come?'

'At the last,' she lied.

Bera scooped some seawater into a bucket. 'Time to tend to your father.'

'For burial at sea?'

'It's a kind of crossroads here, at the meeting of whale roads. I will send Hefnir to the deeps, properly.'

Heggi soaked a cloth and dabbed his father's hands, but then backed away. He had suffered enough. Obsidian had nearly killed them all.

'It's all right, boykin. Get out the land anchor and any spare rope.'

Bera washed the ash from Hefnir's face. He looked younger, though scratched and bruised. He had been kind to her on that first day in Seabost. She had no idea how old he was and for a moment was sorry that he would see no more summers. They had shared so little.

'There's no time to stitch him into the blanket,' she said. 'We'll weigh him down with the anchor.'

'Good.' Heggi held it up. 'It's the old lore of smiths: iron to heart.'

Bera was surprised he knew that.

Once it was lashed in place they got the body where the hull was lowest and rested it on the rail. Heggi kissed the shape of his father's brow beneath the makeshift shroud and Bera blinked away tears, deeply moved by his forgiveness.

'Swap with me, Heggi. You take this end, it's lighter.'

'I'm taller than you and stronger.'

'But a Valla must be at his head to preside over death.'

Especially with no skern. Hers was on the rail, swinging his long legs morosely.

Heggi broke down. 'I thought he was going to live, Mama.'

Hope is the cruellest thing.

'Be brave, boykin. We will roll him overboard together. It's a proper ending for your father.'

A Valla must say the right words but what could she say to a follower of Brid, if that was his belief. Horrified, she thought perhaps he believed in nothing anymore. Did that mean he would return as a Drorgher?

Names are power.

Bera placed her hand on the brow. 'We send Hefnir, son of…?'

'Hersir.' Heggi straightened proudly.

'We send his body to the deep. Let him feel no more pain or fear on his journey to his ancestors, and may he rest in their hall.'

And stay there.

'Ready?'

They got the body poised. A swell was coming in from the east. Perhaps the earth was shivering from all the shocks it had suffered.

'Third wave,' said Bera. 'One, two…'

The hull dipped and they let the body roll overboard. Pockets of air held him for an instant before the weight took him down.

Bera felt lighter. That part of her life was over – and loss brings freedom, as she now knew. She told Heggi to brace the sail and pushed the tiller hard over to head north and east.

2

Waves rolled in, making the *Raven* yaw. Bera concentrated on helming, pointing the boat up towards the crest then glancing away safely before it broke over them.

'I feel sick.' Heggi's face was the colour of goose droppings.

'Keep looking at the skyline.'

'I am.'

His teeth were clacking. Poor boykin. Bera worried he might listlessly roll overboard with seasickness.

'Come on, let's sing.' It was the last thing she felt like doing.

'My throat's raw.'

'It will help the burns to get salt air into our lungs.' Bera started to croak, 'In the bones, in the bones...'

'Feel the east wind in the rigging...' Heggi's dry warble ended in a coughing fit. 'It's like fire when I sing.'

Bera rubbed his back. 'We're like a pair of old crows.'

'Ravens.' Heggi managed a smile.

'Last verse.' Bera counted three and they tried again.

> *In the heart, in the heart*
> *Feel the pulsing of the whale roads...*

Heggi was beating his heart with his fist to stop it hurting so much. Bera had done it so often herself that her feelings were beaten deep inside her chest.

There was a weight pressing down on them; the volcanic clouds had left behind a lingering greyness. But then a small gleam appeared.

7

'Look, boykin, the sun's trying to come out!'

He pointed upwards. 'A patch of cloak.'

'It's a scrap of blue sky.'

'No.' He looked bereft. 'We're supposed to shout "Seabost!" and all punch our chests.'

She had never belonged in Seabost.

The wind whipped up, the sail cracked and the clouds were chased away, giving them the first unsullied light they had seen for months. The sun's warmth blessed their heads with a promise of summer, food and hope. Bera gloried in being aboard the *Raven*, her father's finest vessel.

Ottar's boatbuilding skills made the hull sit lightly in the water so from distance she looked as airy as a sea bird, flying above the waves. From stem to stern, she had been planed and smoothed by his own hands. She thought back to his workshed at the boatyard: every tool cleaned and sharpened at the end of the day, put in its place to come to hand next morning. Who had taught him? She had never asked. Never asked how he chose which planks to use where; why he built like he did. Ottar may have mistrusted women but his boats had a womanly shape and he loved them. Perhaps he felt too much to be able to show it.

Like you.

They were now cleaving the waves cleanly and Heggi's colour improved. They were healing with the sparkle of the sea and flash of fish and swoop of bird, dizzy with life. A wild joy burst through Bera – to be living – and in the sureness that everyone she loved would be alive back at the settlement. Her baby girl, Valdis.

'When we get back it will be all right, Bera, won't it?'

She smiled. 'You can go straight up to the forge to your Ginna.'

'I hope Rakki's up there, too, with his pup.'

Bera hoped their dog had made it back with Faelan. She turned to her skern. 'Is it too late to be an ordinary woman, to love and marry and tend my garden?'

You are not and can never be ordinary. Nor can your daughter, the next Valla.

Heggi elbowed her. 'Are you asking your skern about Rakki?'

8

'Look! The Stoat!' The tall skerry marked the entrance to their beach.

'Home!' Heggi's voice cracked.

The Stoat slowly grew closer, white with birds and their droppings. Bera was amazed that so many had already returned to their breeding grounds, but Heggi did not turn his head to look.

'Let's name all the different breeds we can see. I'll start. Herring gull, black-backed gull and crow-beak.'

'They're all gulls.'

It became important to Bera. 'All right. Skua, skar, sooty tern, sea-mew.' She was making the naming a charm so that their home would not have been destroyed. 'Come on, help me.'

'I'm not a baby.'

'Can you see any puffins?'

'Stop it, Bera,' Heggi shouted. 'You made us leave Rakki behind in Smolderby. And Faelan – and he was drowning.'

'We would have drowned otherwise.' Guilt throbbed behind her eyes.

He can afford to be angry now you're out of danger.

A gull swooped to snatch a fish from the water, mobbed at once by a gang of other birds, squabbling and remorseless.

'It's not fair.' Heggi blew snot out of his nose.

'Point away when you do that.'

'Still not fair.'

'Nothing ever is. It's what calls us to action. We have to chart a course through whatever the Vallas deal us and ride the waves of Fate. It doesn't mean it's an easy passage.'

'I hate you and all your Valla stuff!' Heggi kicked the rail.

'Are you going to sulk or help?'

'Two of us can't roll the *Raven* up a beach.'

'Where can I put in to, then?'

Her skern tapped his nose. *Think of a lamb on a ledge.*

'I know!' Heggi's moods passed like cloud shadows. 'That inlet where Faelan keeps his skiff!'

'It's too narrow.'

'I'll guide you in! You can do it, Bera.'

He wanted to shine and she did not have the heart to refuse him. Bera tried to remember what Ottar had said about getting a boat into a channel that had steep sides and little sea-room. The Stoat already loomed over them and still she could not remember. From here, the entrance looked like a crack. She would have to be workmanlike as her father had taught her, she decided, and stood off the inlet to plan.

Heggi took over the helm while she looked for anything they could use to get ashore.

'Keep well off till we're ready,' Bera said. 'There are sure to be rocks near the entrance.'

'I know. I was in the skiff, remember, not you.'

Bera rummaged through the stern locker. To her relief, Egill's curricle was there under a greased cloth. It was for one person and as light as eider down. She rested the rim on her head so that it lay on her back like a shell and kept a hand free to steady herself as she made her way to the rail. She collected a long line from the mast, tied it to the high prow and fed it back to the curricle.

'You're not going to row that thing ashore, are you?' he asked.

'No, Heggi. You are.'

Bera took over, and summoning all her boat skills, she squeezed the *Raven* into the narrow inlet, keeping her eyes on the craggy steep sides, carefully judging when to nudge the tiller and when to let the boat go with the wave surge.

The channel widened – and there was no skiff alongside the steps.

Heggi sank to his knees. 'Faelan must be dead, and Rakki.'

'Well, then, their spirits will be here, protecting us.'

Only me, your twin spirit, as ever. Her skern was a comforter around her neck.

How she pitied Heggi. As a plain being he would have no such comfort until his own skern returned at the point of death. Bera wondered if Vallas needed their twin to bear the load of duty. Her beads were heavy on her neck. What if unseen skerns dwindled away if folk lost their belief in them?

Her skern shivered. *They may, in Iraland.*

Too awful a thought.

Bera steadied herself. 'Right, Heggi. Get ready to lower the curricle. Then you'll just have to be brave.'

Heggi scrambled up, his eyes gleaming at being a hero.

'The wind's holding us off the landing steps so paddle hard and take the line across. If there's a mooring ring—'

'There is.'

'Good. So take a turn and then bring the line back here.'

'Will it reach?'

'It has to.'

Bera held the boat off the cliff with an oar while Heggi lowered the curricle. He stepped onto the tiny thwart, then nearly tipped straight over. He held on, sat down and untied the paddle. Then he rowed in a tight circle, throttling himself with the rope tied to the *Raven*, which he had forgotten to cast off. Bera made a gasping snort. Without looking at her, Heggi untied the line and pushed off. In clear water the curricle tipped and turned but then he got the hang of it and made for the steps.

You can laugh now.

'He's doing well.'

Heggi had taken a turn round the large ring and was on his way back, cleverly pulling hand over hand on the outward line instead of paddling. As he clambered back aboard, the sun dipped behind the cliff and they were in shadow.

'The line will hold us off the rocks,' said Bera.

'How do we both get ashore?' Heggi asked.

'We'll sweat it.' Bera stood at the bow, took a turn round the king thole pin and gave Heggi the end. 'I'll heave and you take up the slack. Ready?'

The first attempt failed but then they found a rhythm and the *Raven* drew closer to the steps. The wind fell away and the last few pulls were easier. With hands trembling from the strain, Bera took a few turns round the mooring ring. They were back.

The steps were slippery with eel grass that no one had cleared. They slithered their way up on hands and knees, making their tattered clothing more ragged and foul-smelling. When they reached higher ground, it dipped and swayed under Bera's feet. Her legs felt boneless and she realised it was land sickness, missing boat movement.

And fear, sweetheart.

Heggi bent over, retching. They had not eaten for so long that he spat out only a thin yellow bile and groaned. Bera rubbed his back, hoping the eruption had not destroyed their stores.

'We'll soon have some food, boykin. Sigrid's best puffin stew.'

'Rakki will never be able to hunt again, even if he's still alive.' He stumbled off ahead.

Not the kindest thing to say.

Bera trudged behind, holding her Valla necklace and asking her mother to help. She never did, but now the obscure darkness in the unending line of Vallas that she had glimpsed in Obsidian was a bigger fear. What Fate had they woven? Better to think of all the folk who had chosen to stay with her here on Ice Island; of building the settlement with Faelan's help and Dellingr. Their smith was her rock.

'Let them be there, let them be there,' she repeated at each step.

Heggi waited for her at the small rise where the homestead would be seen. No smoke was coming from any of the huts. No animals, no one working in the fields. Even from a distance the place had a forlorn emptiness. The only sound was a plover's lament.

'Will there be bodies?' Heggi asked in a thin, high voice.

Bera only hoped there were no Drorghers if no one had lived long enough to bury the bodies.

'We need to get down there before sunset.'

3

The home village must have looked like this after red-spot, when those who could walk had left the sick behind. The unburied dead would have joined the band of Drorghers preying on anyone left alive to steal their skerns.

Bera stopped in the blackened yard. 'Let's search.'

'What for? No one's here.'

'They may have left a message and food.'

'We hadn't grown any.'

'Faelan gave us some, remember? Sigrid would leave some. She knew I would return.'

'We nearly went to Iraland.'

'Heggi, stop this! We were going for the wolfsbane remedy. I promised to come back here, and they trust me.'

'I don't care. I'm going up to the smithy,' Heggi declared.

'If she's…'

'If Ginny's dead, I want to be with her alone.'

Bera hesitated. 'You must be back before dusk.'

He ran. It was better to find out the worst alone.

Bera wondered what lay ahead for her in the longhouse. Her scalp was not prickling but the rawness from its brymstone scorching might mask its warning.

'Not even a riddle to help me?'

Her skern rubbed his eyes. *I can't see far ahead.*

She entered under the low lintel of the byre, hoping to be soothed as ever by the calming low breaths of a gentle cow. Dear Feima.

Get it over with.

Cold stone and dirty straw; a pail half-full of grey water with a bloated rat floating in it. No orderly leaving, then. She took a deep breath and went through to the hall. No pile of bodies, no dead babies but the hearth was lifeless and the embers cold. The table had two beakers on it. Bera lifted one, leaving a clear ring in the ash that covered the rest of it.

'Oh, Sigrid!' Bera was suddenly six again and Alfdis dead. She pictured Sigrid, her mother's best friend, stomping about squarely, fussing about getting her out of salt-stiffened boat rags and into clean clothes and making her eat a stew, and caring.

Bera went through to the pantry. A stool was kicked over in the dust and a rat scuttled away. She went over to the underearth bin and knelt down. Days of promise, when they had dug this. She lifted the heavy lid to the sweet ripeness of cheese and smokiness of dried meat. Bless Sigrid! Bera reached inside, found the rough string that held a linen parcel together and brought it up. Something clattered back inside but it would keep.

She untied the stiff cloth and bit into the cracked and yellow cheese. Bera wiped dribble off her chin, wanting to chew but making herself suck gently, to get the most flavour. It was better than any of the sweetmeats she had eaten at the Abbotry; better than anything in her life before. She kissed the linen, which smelled of summer.

'It's beeswax from Faelan's hives.'

What about Heggi?

Bera had one last nibble and then tied it up and slipped the parcel into her apron. She went outside to see if he was coming.

The whole homestead was too quiet. It had the same prickling fear as the ruined huts. Those huts, and using their stones, had started it all. Guilt made her hot and visible, as if she was a beacon in the landscape. There was a clatter of footsteps and Heggi came round the corner. It hurt Bera that Rakki was not racing towards her, barking a demented greeting.

'You've got to come up there, Bera,' he panted.

Bera held up the parcel. 'I have cheese.'

'Yes!' Heggi dipped through the rail and grabbed it. 'I'm starving!'

For once it was true. He took the whole lump of cheese and there was ham beneath, which Bera managed to seize. They watched each other eat like wary dogs until the scant rations were gone.

'So what is up there?' she asked.

'Valla stuff.' Heggi paled.

Bera looked up. 'Not long before sunset. Do we have to go now?'

'I think so.' He took her hand as they climbed.

Was it for his sake or hers? Neither spoke until they were near the forge.

'Is it inside?' she asked.

'Behind, nearly on Faelan's land. Near the ghost fence.'

Bera pulled him round. 'Why did you go up there?'

'I thought I heard a bark.'

She hugged him, understanding, and they went on. Lapwings were calling over and over, and Bera was waiting for her scalp to prickle a warning if they got too close to the ghost fence.

Heggi stopped. 'There.'

Bera walked closer. Bare soil made a small mound with three large stones placed unevenly on top.

'It's a burial, up here on the boundary, done in a hurry. Did you find any marker, Heggi? A rune stone or stave?'

'I'd have told you!'

'Yes, and you were right to bring me, boykin. So quickly fetch two spades from the forge; Dellingr can't have taken everything.'

'You think they're alive?' Heggi's face shone. 'Resettled?'

Bera tried to find reasons to hope. 'I only see one grave, don't you? They must have moved on.'

'Only we don't know where.' He cast about him. 'Up at Faelan's farmstead?'

'Enough talking. We must stop this body walking before sunset.'

He is terrified it is Ginna.

Heggi sped off to the forge and Bera moved the stones, ready to dig. He came back with one spade and a shovel.

'It's all that was there.'

The new earth of the shallow grave was easy to scoop away, although they were both sweating by the time the outline of the small corpse appeared.

Heggi backed away. 'I don't want to see who it is.'

15

'Dearest boykin.' Bera searched for some comfort. 'If it is Ginna, you can make sure she will be at peace.'

'What if she's already a Drorgher?' he whispered.

'Then we'll find out.' His lips were white. 'I can finish this alone now, Heggi, but stay close and keep vigil.'

He moved away, casting a long shadow. She had to work fast, but gently, to uncover a female body, curled as though sleeping, with arms protecting the only grave good: her head, cleanly severed from the neck. This body would not walk.

'Is it Ginny?' Heggi called.

'No. It's her mother.'

Dellingr had helped Faelan bury their dead and had done the same for his wife, except he had not put a stone in her mouth. Bera found one to fill it and flinched as she pulled the sharp teeth apart in a mouth that had been so often wet with hate. Now she felt only sadness that Asa had let jealousy win; that she always refused to be a friend to her, as she had been to Sigrid.

'There was no peace for you in life. Rest now, Asa.'

Bera spoke Valla words of protection as they shovelled the soil back into the grave and then replaced the stones on top. They hurried away, threw the spades into the forge, and stayed clear of shadows.

'Do you think that was the only grave, Mama?' asked Heggi.

'They would have buried folk together.' Bera hoped it was true.

'Is it wrong to be glad it was Asa?'

'I think you're really only glad it wasn't Ginna.'

'I secretly hated her mother.' He kicked a stone. 'She kept saying I was like all my family – bad blood. The Serpent King.'

'Don't speak ill of Asa now she is dead, Heggi!' Bera had to swallow the sourness, too.

They reached the meadow and Bera bent low, casting about.

'What are you doing? The sun's going down!'

'Trying to protect us, so help.' She picked a few plants. 'I'll bunch this mugwort. Look for some rill.'

'What does it look like?'

The plants you have won't be at their strongest yet.

'Never mind. Let's go.'

16

They ran back to the longhouse, where Bera spotted some rue, and slammed the door behind them. The silence was eerie; her scalp gave no warning, but the hall should have been full of busy folk. She told Heggi to make sure every door and window was fastened with a sprig of rue in each hasp while she looked for tapers. There were two, with a few sticks to set a poor fire. The night would be very dark. Finally, Bera lit the mugwort and waved the smoke into every corner to protect them from any evil that was already inside. She put the bunch in one of the beakers and hoped it would smoulder till dawn.

'Will it work?' Heggi whispered.

'Back home, Mama used to do it every night, according to Sigrid.'

'You were overrun with Drorghers in Crapsby.'

'And I kept them away.' Bera was firm.

Her skern studied a long nail. *Might be the time to see what Sigrid says.*

Bera took a taper and headed for her billet.

Heggi ran after her. 'What are you doing now?'

'My skern just hinted about Sigrid and she left my wedding chest for me.'

'So?'

'I'm hoping there's a message.'

Bera undid the hasp and pushed up the lid. The smell of the wood took her back to the night she was taken to Seabost.

'Are you thinking about when you married Papa?'

Her skern gave a dry laugh.

'My father, Ottar, made this chest for me.' That part was true.

Bera took out the few clothes that had come to Ice Island and groped all round the bottom of the chest, certain there would be a slate, but there was not even a button.

'Hold up the taper.'

'I am.' Heggi scowled. 'What can I wear? It's all women's stuff.'

'The tunic and leggings.'

'They're too small.' He pulled his shoulders back. 'Anyway, those leggings are a girl's colour.'

Bera was bone-weary, hungry and afraid. 'They will fit. Put them on!'

'No.'

She waved them in his face. 'You smell awful!'

'You smell like a cow.'

'And you smell like a dead stoat.'

'Stinky walrus!'

'Mangey bear!'

Bera tickled him, he shoved her away, laughing, and then they got into the clothes.

'Is there anything else to eat?' he asked.

'We'll check the underearth bin again.' She remembered the clinking sound.

They hurried back to the pantry. Bera put her head and shoulders right inside until her fingertips touched a rough-edged coldness.

'What is it?'

'I can't…' She finally got her fingers underneath. 'Pull me back, Heggi.'

He got hold of her waist and tugged.

'It's a message from Sigrid.'

'Let me see!' Heggi snatched the slate.

'Don't lose the marks!'

There was the S rune but the rest was scrawled in a hurry, with many of the runes overlapping.

'It looks like a forest.' Heggi put the slate on a bench.

'Sigrid says…'

Told you.

'There's your Bera rune, look.'

'Bera… something… home.'

'What home?' he asked.

'Show me. "Sigrid… tells Bera to go home." And this one, pointing upwards. North?'

Heggi groaned. 'She can't mean go back to Seabost?'

'This is typical Sigrid, to not be plain! She'll have worried about spies or some such.'

He swept away the marks with his sleeve.

'What did you do that for?' Bera took the slate and glared at it.

'I don't know. I—' He blinked away tears.

'My fault, boykin, talking about spies. I'm sorry.' She slipped the slate into her pocket. 'Come back to the hearth. We need rest before we set out tomorrow.'

Bera checked the big wooden door again. If Drorghers were to come, they would pour in through the place they remembered. She made a full hammer sign on it, made the sprig secure and was pleased to see the mugwort still glowing.

Heggi was shivering before the peevish fire.

Bera pulled a shawl over them. 'We'll cuddle up and pretend Rakki is keeping us warm.'

He curled up in a tight ball and Bera cursed herself for upsetting them both. She tucked herself into his back and was surprised to fit. He was going to be as tall as his father. And uncle.

Don't think about the Serpent King or you'll never sleep.

A chill was seeping up from the ground and she tried to get the shawl under them.

'Stop wriggling, Mama,' Heggi grumbled.

She nestled into his neck and let his dear smell comfort her, matching her breathing with his. Her young second. She wanted to tell him how much she valued his companionship and help, far beyond his years. She must say it. Just in case.

'Boykin?' she whispered.

Like a puppy, he was in a sudden deep sleep, but she spoke into the darkness.

'I love you.' Bera prayed she had done enough to get them through the night undisturbed.

4

Sleep would not come. Bera missed the reassurance of low voices round the hearth, coughs, snores and the soft stamp of animals in their pens. The stone hall was colder and darker than the wooden halls of home and the turfed roof and mud walls smelled like the grave. Buried alive with no taper to hold the shadows back. Obsidian had stolen her strength and the sureness that would let her recover. How she envied Heggi, who could sleep anywhere.

Her skern was at her ear. *Rest.*

When she closed her eyes she was back at the gate of Hel, swathed in smoke and death.

The mugwort fumes present the past and future.

Bera was looking down on a rain-drenched valley, with two camps of armed men waiting for a signal to start fighting...

'My signal?'

There is our belief... and others. That is what blinds me.

'They are blinded by fear. Deep time, ancient and dark...'

A knock.

Dread tore Bera from her vision. Drorghers only knock once.

It was so long since she had faced them that she wondered how she had ever dared. Obsidian and getting too close to Hel had surely weakened her.

'Mama?' Heggi's breath was coming in panicky gasps. 'Was Asa...'

'You saw her body.'

'Yes, but she hates you and me. What if she's out there with no head?'

A louder knock.

'It's all right,' she whispered. 'That's the second.'

'So is it a living being?'

'We didn't see anyone.'

The door banged a few times, louder. Bera and Heggi clutched each other, his heart hammering against her own. She was blind again, lost in a darkness that had its own weight.

'Mama?'

'Sh!'

'But—'

'It can't get in.'

'I k-keep thinking about the S-S-Serpent King.' His stammer returned with the memory.

'Turn your mind away, like I do.'

'No, but would a sword stop him? What if he followed us— ' There was a low, snuffling grunt. 'That's him outside!'

'Sh, boykin. How can it be?' Bera kissed his hot forehead.

'He might really have a dragon body now he's dead!'

'He doesn't know where the homestead is.' Didn't, she corrected herself silently.

'Maybe he can track us, like an animal. Listen! He's crouched down now, snouting under the lintel.' Heggi pulled the shawl over his head.

'He is dead, boykin. You saw it.'

All the hairs rose on the nape of her neck. There was the long, indrawn breath of a creature scenting its prey. Bera pictured the Serpent pouring under the door like smoke. She steeled herself to stop it getting inside.

'Wait here.'

'No, M-Mama, don't leave me! What if it's a trick? What if you go to the hall door and he gets in through the b-byre or something?'

'You have your dagger.'

'It's too d-dark!' It wasn't, but he was rightly terrified.

'What if you hid in the chest?'

Heggi groaned. Being locked in a small space was his worst fear. Until now.

'All right,' he said, 'but don't shut the lid.'

They held hands crossing to the billet and Bera groped for the chest. She helped him in, kissed him and lowered the lid, leaving an edge of the shawl outside.

'Stay in there, no matter what. If anything comes near, slip the shawl away.'

Dim outlines of hearthstones, table, the rail of the byre, comforting and familiar, guided her to the door. Perhaps it had gone.

Face your fear.

'I am.'

Bera took out the sprig of rue and tucked it into her beads. Then she slid back the wooden bar and pulled open the door. Nothing, only an empty darkness in the covered way. Then, from low down, a pair of inhuman green eyes.

Then the creature was on her, knocking her down. Licking her face, a blur of joy. Rakki. Her dog was all teeth and tongue, leaping away, back on top, off, twirling in a halting circle, then back to her. Bera sobbed, tugging at his rough hair to pull him closer. She pushed her face into his neck; her jaw clenched. Dogs knew love all right and never mistook those tears for sadness or its fierceness for cruelty. Her dear, dear Rakki lay panting beside her and then she took in properly what the brymstones had done. Guilt squeezed her heart in its tight fist. His poor face was scorched and scabbed, and one hind leg was gone.

'When you lie down in the snow, your dog will die beside you,' she said aloud.

'That's not quite what I used to say.' His voice was raw and Bera's stomach lurched to hear it.

She still couldn't see Faelan but her words had been meant for him; he had to be with Rakki. She ached with sadness and the need for his forgiveness.

'I let you down, Faelan, as a dog would not.'

He stayed hidden and silent.

'How did you know Heggi and I were here?'

'I waited for you after your folk left.' Every word rang with pain. What apology could ever be enough?

'Faelan, please come closer. Let me see you.'

'A face like mine belongs in the shadows.'

He pulled out a firestone, lit a brand and put it into a sconce behind him, so that all she could see was his outline. Rakki raised his head and set off with a click of claws. Then distant barks and shouts of joy.

Bera got up. 'Heggi's come out of hiding.'

'Good.'

There was a chasm between them.

'I—'

'You—'

They began together.

'Sorry. You go on,' she said.

'It… hurts me.'

In her mind's eye was his smooth, clear face; his eyes that crinkled when he smiled, which he did a lot. That long, raven's wing of hair. What burns did he suffer after she left him to drown?

You're too scared to look.

'Were you up at the farmstead?' she asked.

'Helped your smith bury his wife. Hates me more now for making him hack off her head.'

'Didn't you see us up there?'

'Too much work. Rakki stays close but today he took off, like old, and didn't return.' His voice was freeing up.

'He must have trailed us.'

'Found him here at the door. When I couldn't rouse you I feared… something else might have got in. I went back to Miska to get my axe.'

'Dear Miska! Riding her seems another lifetime. Is she still lame?'

'Dellingr fixed her.'

He rubbed his jaw, which rasped. Perhaps he had grown a beard to hide the scars.

'Sigrid left a message for me,' Bera said. 'Why do that with you here?'

'She said I would leave.' He coughed. 'There were tremors, ash falling. My workers all left.'

'Why not you?'

23

'You know why.'

Tell him you longed to see him. Her skern brought warmth to her lips, but she swerved away from the feeling.

'What did you tell Sigrid?'

'About Smolderby? The truth. What happened after you left me, anyway.'

Bera hoped he could not see her blazing face. 'I'm sorry.'

'Sigrid was sure you would end up in Dyflin,' he said.

'Whereas you trusted I'd keep my word.'

'Has Hefnir gone there, or is he aboard the *Raven*?'

'Hefnir is dead.' Bera's voice was flat. 'So where are my folk?'

'Following Dellingr. He wants to trade in Smolderby.'

'The fool!'

'I tried to make them understand the damage but pedlars had lured them all summer, saying eruptions have happened before and folk always gather in Smolderby so the markets and livestock get going fast.'

'How can it?'

'Many hands make light work. They all yearned to be settled, Bera, with more food…'

Her stomach rumbled. 'Have you brought anything?'

'Miska's packs are full, though I doubt Heggi will manage a morsel?'

Her laugh was almost genuine.

Faelan led his mare into the byre. While he unstrapped the packs, Bera pulled her fingers through the mare's tangled mane and Miska nudged her when she stopped. Bera kissed her long nose, which had the softest skin, like silken velvet.

'I like this bit best,' she said.

Faelan kept his head down. 'She likes being kissed on her muzzle.'

'That's a good word for it, nuzzle.' Bera kissed her again.

'It's muzzle,' he said, 'but I like your word better.'

She carried the packs through to the hearth where Heggi and his dog were curled into each other, fast asleep. Bera gently nudged him.

'Faelan and Miska are here.'

Heggi rushed to meet Faelan, who was coming in with a sack. He threw it down and they bear-hugged. Bera wished she could be as open.

'Is that stuff to eat?' Heggi asked.

'Logs.' Faelan laughed. 'Not enough to fill your belly.'

'You're the one called Wolf!'

Faelan growled and lunged at Heggi, who cuffed him and they raced off, with Rakki barking. After a great deal of noise, they returned with some furs and blankets, which they threw down around the hearth. Even on three legs Rakki managed to keep up but then he got a fur to his liking and curled up in it.

'Faelan says Ginny misses me,' Heggi said, snuggling into his dog.

'And Valdis?' She kept her voice level.

'Both babies are hearty,' Faelan said.

Bera got the fire blazing and her fingers and toes tingled. Faelan unwrapped the parcels, with only the good side of his face lit by flames. Was he still hiding, or did the heat hurt his burns? Then she and Heggi crammed their mouths with food, and Faelan's lopsided smile as he watched them made her happy.

He reached back to a leather knapsack. 'And best of all...' He held up a glass jar full of sunlight.

'Honeycomb!' shrieked Heggi, dribbling.

Bera passed him a small horn spoon before he tipped the lot into his mouth and then took a spoonful herself.

'That,' she said, 'is the best thing I have ever tasted.'

'Soothing for burned throats, too,' he said.

'Will you not eat?'

'It's all for you.'

He was always generous, but perhaps he could not eat without pain or messiness and did not want anyone to see. Like poor Thorvald. There were many kinds of bravery.

'You can't hide forever.'

Heggi elbowed her. 'Leave him alone.'

And, just like that, she finally wept: grief, death, loss, exhaustion, every feeling she had packed away. Bera rolled onto her stomach and hid her face. Rakki got under her arm and lay still – and the others stayed close, without questions, and she quickly came back to sit on her heels, dizzy but soothed.

'Mama.' Heggi passed her some ale.

Rakki laid his head on her lap and she bent over to kiss his neck, that smelled of the sea and newly baked rusks. Faelan passed her a linen cloth and she blew her nose.

'Hefnir?' he asked.

With his son listening, Bera had to agree. 'I hoped to save him.'

'I am sorry for the loss of your husband, Bera, and of your father, Heggi.' Faelan got to his feet. 'I'll stay in the byre with Miska and keep watch, so you get your heads down.'

Bera longed to tell him that she did not love Hefnir. Now he would keep his distance and she would never know how they might have been together.

At some point in what was left of the night, Bera fell asleep. She awoke with a start, retching; the smell of blood and sharp male sweat was in the air…

Her head clasped under the foul armpit of the Serpent King, the sound of a belt buckle, and then he was a real dragon, whose immense black and shining claw sliced her in two…

Bad dream.

The revulsion was vivid. 'Why am I dreaming about him? And I stopped him, that time in Seabost, and Sigrid hit him with a skillet. We even laughed.'

All in the past. Not my subject. Her skern was drumming his heels on the hearthstone. *But thinking about the Serpent King gives him power.*

'Where's Heggi?'

All boys cross to the men's side.

'So he's with Faelan.'

So he's safe. He touched her brow. *Rest. Go fishing…*

Bera was lazing in the sun on her own small boat in their home fjord; the soft rattle of water, a line drifting from the stern…

'No!' She sat up. 'I feel as if I'm at the end of something, not the beginning.'

You need to plan.

'I know, so tell me what lies ahead.'

You never listen.

'I do.'

You don't.

'You can't see, can you?'

I'm afraid.

Bera went outside, glad to see Miska cropping the new grass. The mare looked up, her brown eyes full of trust. Bera rested against her neck; its smell of leather, oatmeal and honey chased away the nightmare. She wanted to ride her but was stopped by the return of the others.

Faelan's hat had a wide brim and he was talking to Heggi, hiding his face. They had been fishing without her, which hurt.

'A fresh day meal!' Heggi raised their catch.

They had collected driftwood and Bera got the fire hot enough to cook. Faelan gutted the fish outside, and when it was cooked, Bera did not shame him by watching him eat.

'Bad dog!' Heggi yelled at the fleeing Rakki. 'He stole my last bit of fish skin, the crispy bit. I was saving it for best!'

Bera laughed and Faelan gave his last piece to Heggi, which he bolted, grabbed a whole flatbread and chased after his dog. It felt like an ordinary day, and she liked it.

'Did you go out in your skiff?' she asked.

'It's gone. Stolen, I think.'

'Any workers left up at the farmstead?'

'No one.'

'Dead or…?'

'They all left as soon as I set off with you; Dellingr made sure to tell me.'

'He never liked you,' Bera said, then wished she hadn't.

He jabbed the fire. 'The ash cloud scared them away. My workers told Dellingr that my mother predicted ruin if it was ever bear-shaped.'

'Did she?'

'A smith has value, so they lied. Or Dellingr did.' He shrugged. 'My mother only ever said that Bera would save us.'

In another time his mother would have helped her become a great healer, knowing and growing the plants in Ice Island and its seasons. Would she have wanted her to marry her son?

'What are you thinking?' he asked.

'I was wondering if Sigrid meant us to stay here. Her message told me to go home, but where is that?'

He turned away, when she wanted honesty. Did he want her to stay? Would he come with her if she left?

You need to be honest if you want honesty.

'A mark at the end pointed upwards. They can't have gone back to the village I grew up in!'

'Crapsby?'

She started. 'Did Sigrid call it that?'

'They weren't happy about us leaving, even Sigrid. The Seabost folk blamed your upbringing, especially Asa, who said she never wanted to stay here.'

'They all chose to stay with me because leaving with Hefnir was unthinkable after the hard passage over.'

He faced her. 'You are a better leader than that, Bera. They settled here because you gave them belief.'

The green flame of burning driftwood was like poison. 'I was wrong. The land tried to kill us.'

'My mother said the land called you when it was most sick. You, Bera, not her.'

'She was dying.'

'She was right. You healed it. Tell me about your home village.'

He wants to comfort you, so let him.

'I don't deserve it.'

'Why are you frowning?' Faelan asked.

'My skern is being annoying.'

The skern stretched thin with indignation and snapped into a scuttle.

Bera gave in. 'We lived at the end of a narrow fjord, at the edge of the Ice-Rimmed Sea.' And she was there, with a Seabost brute, seeing for the last time her father's boats, golden in a dawn mist; the rainbow over the waterfall; her mother's rune stone. 'Perhaps it did shape me. But now Sigrid and I are the only ones to remember how it was.'

'You are very close.'

'Sigrid raised me. At least… Well, things happened.'

Heggi roared back in again. 'He's just as good on three legs.'

Rakki did a twirl to prove it, limped over to Bera and sank down, panting.

'Don't tire him out, he's getting old now.' She stroked the grey hairs under his chin.

The dog looked up at her with more trust than she could bear. She had left him to the brymstones, too. What gave most pain was that he would forgive her anything.

Heggi flopped beside him. 'Are we staying, then?'

Bera glanced at Faelan. 'We haven't decided.'

'It's the leader's decision,' Faelan said.

'Oh no, we don't do it like that,' said Heggi. 'Papa did all the trading stuff but our folk decided everything else in the mead hall.'

Bera stood up. 'Well, we have hearth, hall, folk and dog, so let's start.'

5

There was only one decision to be made: stay or go. It was always this question, and always the same answer.

'You have to take your hat off,' Heggi told Faelan.

'Why?' Bera felt his awkwardness.

'Faces must be seen to fairly decide.' It could have been his father speaking.

'It's all right.' Faelan pulled his hair over one side of his face. 'I've grown it long, so I can use it to track.'

Heggi yanked a handful. 'It feels like real hair.'

'Ouch! It hurts for real, too.'

'Could you track the others, then?' asked Bera. 'They have no boats, so how far could they have travelled overland?'

'They will be slow with all the carts but they should already be in Smolderby by now.'

'But it's in ruins!' Heggi groaned.

'Maybe they have rebuilt it,' said Bera.

He sniffed, refusing false hope.

'The countryside isn't ruined,' said Faelan. 'Remember the old mute crone who gave Bera the salve? She nursed me and Rakki, after... after I took his bad leg off.' He looked at Heggi. 'Would you like to ride Miska?'

'Can I!'

'Better ask her,' he said.

'Come on, Rakki, let's go.'

Bera's mind scratched with her dog's exhaustion. At least she could protect him here.

'Let Rakki stay with me.'

Heggi thought about it. 'He might get under Miska's hoofs anyway.'

It pleased Bera that he was not putting himself first. When he left she tackled Faelan.

'How long are you going to keep your scars hidden?'

He lowered his head.

'Please let me move your hair away.' Bera's heart was thudding against her ribs.

Tell him you're frightened of seeing the scars, too.

'Faelan? If you forbid me, I won't. I'll always try to keep looking away, for your sake.'

'It's not for my sake!' He groaned. 'Oh, Bera, can't you see that my ruined face will hurt you? This... horror... will make you blame yourself even more.'

'I have to live with what I did. Let me see your wounds.'

'Leaving me behind was the only decision you could make. I would have done the same.'

'Would you?' She shook her head. 'I don't blame you for not trusting me.'

'Please, Bera. Let it alone.'

'Hiding makes it worse, can't you see that? You've no idea what I picture! Egill told me her father was struck by brymstones and his whole body melted like a taper.'

'I can't push this rotting face at you. I can't...' He was frightened.

Bera understood. 'You haven't looked at your scars, have you?' She reached out but he shrugged away. 'Faelan, I can heal. Your mother grew plants at the farmstead. Could she store her potions?'

'Certainly.'

'Then we are going up there. Now.'

Heggi was watching Miska crop the grass. 'I had a bit of a ride.'

'Did you?'

'I could have done.'

Faelan loaded the lighter packs onto his mare and let her pick her own way through the scrub.

'This is the shortcut you and I did, Bera,' he said.

'We were both on Miska.' Bera shrugged. 'I could see nothing from behind your back.'

His elven beauty had made him seem a shape-changer in that dusk. Bera blushed, thinking about how afraid she had been riding to his dying mother, too late to save her.

You enjoy a thrill of fear.

'The Valla passion is still a danger.' Perhaps it was safer to have him wounded and earthly; less likely the Vallas would take him from her as they did whatever she most loved.

The river was low enough to cross on stepping stones. Rakki tried to catch a wagtail on a steep rock, lost his balance and fell in. He shook himself as though he meant to go swimming but no one laughed. He was a puffin-hound no longer, which hurt.

'Papa would have killed him once he'd lost his use,' Heggi said.

'He would have had to kill me first,' said Bera.

'I know.'

Faelan let Heggi get ahead. 'I had to cut off Rakki's leg, Bera, it was worse than useless.'

'It would hurt, too,' she said. 'I am sad about the hopes we had for the settlement. We decided to start our new life straight, on a level, with no thralls.'

'I pay my workers. Paid,' Faelan said. 'Vikings killed my father and sold my mother and me as slaves. Now, on Ice Island, all folk hear the laws spoken aloud so that all are on a level. No slaves.'

Heggi turned. 'Who does the work, then, with no thralls?'

'We work for the common good. You saw it at the whale-stranding.'

'Do children make laws?'

'No, but when they have experienced life, understand what is important, they are allowed to make decisions.'

'I make decisions now.'

'Luckily you are outnumbered,' said Bera, ruffling his hair.

Heggi rubbed his head, making it even more caffled.

'Miska and I used to visit the law-speaking,' Faelan said. 'I'd make sure the crone was faring well, take plants from my mother.'

At her name, the mare trotted over and nudged him. A man good with animals was always to be trusted.

Heggi stroked Rakki. 'What about dogs?'

'Dogs and horses are like young children,' Faelan said. 'They need our guidance so that they feel safe and then we owe them respect for their work.'

'I like the straightforward character of a dog,' Bera said.

Heggi covered Rakki's ears. 'I don't think he'll catch as many puffins this summer.'

'No need to. It's our turn to feed him, because we love him anyway.'

Faelan went on ahead and then started casting about for something, screwing up his eyes. Heggi also stopped, but he was looking back towards the forge huts.

'We'll bring them home, boykin. And then you and Ginna can have your betrothal feast.'

'If she still wants to,' he muttered.

Bera remembered how Heggi used to go on tiptoes to kiss Ginna.

'You'll be—' She was about to say 'taller than her now' but managed to stop.

Unusually tactful.

Faelan was urging Miska to walk on and Bera set off again. Heggi lagged behind, kicking stones.

'You can comfort Ginna about losing her mother,' she called back. 'You share that now.'

'Except I don't have a father, either.' He glared as if she had killed Hefnir.

Bera had not caused it, not even by being a Valla. She had never loved Hefnir; had felt only passion. One day, perhaps, Heggi would understand the different kinds of love and that even for ordinary folk, Fate could snatch away the ones most loved.

Miska's eyes were wide, ears back, and she was snorting and stamping. Faelan kept his voice low to soothe her. When Bera offered to help, he told her to stay clear.

'Go on up with Heggi. Something just spooked her.'

He stroked the mare's arched neck and led her away. Bera went on at a slant, checking that Heggi was following her. A puff of decay made her nostrils twitch and quickly became a stench. She looked

33

down to see if she had trodden on a stinkhorn but then her mind was flooded with dread.

'Stay back, Heggi!' Bera spread her arms, though he was below her.

Pain crackled through her head, neck, shoulders, backbone, legs in a bolt of unseen evil. Her face prickled and a wave of sickness made her buckle. The ghost fence! Miska must have sensed its horror before touching it. The world spun and went black…

She stood above a rain-drenched valley with two camps of armed men waiting for her signal…

'Mama!' Heggi was beside her. 'Mama? Are you hurt?'

She rolled onto her back to let the earth's wild energy steady her. Instead, it chanted in the drumming of her blood…

Chaos is coming. Chaos is coming. Chaos is coming…

'Who is Chaos?'

Her skern had no answer and paled to nothingness.

'I'm so sorry.' Faelan pulled Bera to her feet. 'My eyesight is still bad and I must have missed the safe pass in the fence.'

'I'm sorry.' So his poor sight, too, was her fault. Had this started whatever Chaos was, or had it been much earlier?

'We're not far enough yet,' said Heggi.

'We are.' Bera felt it. 'The evil is spreading.'

The shock of the ghost fence had summoned her to Valla duty and forged a warning inside her. Whatever Chaos was, she must stand against it. How soon would it come? She looked towards the ancient ruins, past their failed homestead, on to the black shore and out to the Stoat, guarding the bay. Scrying the land.

'When we first settled I thought the land was empty because I couldn't see anyone. But you were up here all the time, Faelan.'

'I found him,' Heggi put in.

Faelan patted Miska. 'Are you thinking some may remain? The land is not destroyed, thanks to you, but the crops will die, left untended. Your folk headed for Smolderby, trusting your smith, who promised them the old magic of iron.'

The words rang in her head; the linking of the ancient lore and Chaos.

'Dellingr needs to find himself again,' she said. 'There is plenty of iron in Smolderby.'

'It's dangerous,' Heggi said. 'I want to get Ginny out of there.'

'Sea paths are how we move best.'

Faelan rubbed his jaw. 'They had no boat.'

'We can afford a few days to get the *Raven* ready. And ourselves. Don't look like that, Heggi, you're half-starved. We need what remains of your stores, Faelan, and I shall make salves to heal your face.'

He turned away. 'It's too bad.'

She let that be. 'Until we sail, we dare not let the *Raven* be stolen by pirates.'

'Look.' Faelan presented an empty sea. 'I haven't seen one boat since my return and most trade between Dyflin and Smolderby.'

'That boat is part of me, Faelan. My mother and father, my protector. My past.'

'Mine too,' said Heggi.

Bera held him close. 'So your duty, Heggi, is to guard her.'

His face flushed. 'I'll go right now! Come on, Rakki.'

Faelan pointed out a narrow rift. 'If you follow that it will take you straight down to the inlet.'

'I know. Rakki and I found it when we first settled.'

'Do you remember the pass through the ghost fence?'

'Better than you, fellow!' Faelan swiped him with his hat.

Bera touched her beads. 'Be back before sunset and be sure to stay hidden, boykin. I'd rather lose the *Raven* than you.'

'And Rakki,' he said, setting off.

'And your daughter,' said Faelan softly.

The guilt of Valdis. He had no idea that the thread that should bind a mother to her child had snapped the moment she left her behind with Sigrid.

No. You are linked in the chain of Vallas. A long line of mothers.

Who would understand that she feared her daughter? As soon as the next Valla was born, her mother's death was certain for she was no longer needed. It was a matter of the Valla's choosing when that would be.

'Don't look so worried.' Faelan swung her up onto Miska. 'Heggi won't see any pirates.'

'I know. He's fretting about Ginna, so I'm distracting him. Pedlars might come but he can outsmart anything.'

He has a natural cunning.

Her skern was cheery, but his words plunged Bera back into swirling ash and smoke, her rasping breath burning her chest and a sword in the Serpent King's throat. Evil, cunning and Heggi's uncle. Bad blood.

Faelan used his long hair to track the safe way through the ghost fence. Miska carried Bera, who did not argue. Was her tiredness natural or did Chaos bring sickness? She fought lethargy and when Faelan stopped before a long stone wall, she jumped down.

Moss and lichen sprang from every cleft and cranny.

Bera stroked it. 'This looks healthy.'

'My mother planted her healing garden where foul air would not come.'

'Does the wall go all round?'

'I'll show you before I start gathering stores.'

'How much can we take to the boat?' Bera asked.

'As many trips as my poor Miska can manage.'

He threw open a rough wooden door and Bera caught her breath. She entered a sheltered garden where low hurdles made of birch-brash protected neat rows of healthy plants. And her skern, lounging against a rosemary bush, the picture of health.

Order and calm.

'It's beautiful, Faelan.' Bera silently thanked his mother.

Every leaf – broad, narrow, spiked or round – every shade of green, sparkled with dew. These were remedies, so the few flowers were tiny and only served to make the green greener. It was what she had craved without knowing it, like the first thaw when the barren white glitter of snow gives way to soothing green pasture. Her eyes were moist and when the stinging stopped she realised that she had been worrying at them ever since the eruption. Healing energy pulsed through every stalk and stem and all were a balm, so that

Bera understood a garden could keep mind and body well simply by being.

Faelan gave her time to herself. She properly understood, in her bones, that this was her achievement. Without stopping the chain of eruptions these leaves would be dead.

Perhaps he noticed a change in her face. 'If poison rains follow, Bera, the leaves could yet wither and yellow.'

'I sent the ash cloud far out to sea.'

'Don't forget it's happened before.'

'At the ruins?'

He nodded.

'Before me. And all things recover with time.'

'Except this.' Faelan gestured at his face.

'Even the burns. Heggi and I have wounds that may not show, but we can heal each other here.'

He flinched and Bera realised it sounded as if he was left out. She kept getting it wrong. A loud drone led her to a row of skeps on a long trestle. Clouds of bees were in flight, or pushing past each other in the tiny doorways, or dancing in circles, and it thrilled her to see so much life. Faelan kneeled close to them and mumbled something.

'What are you doing?'

'I am telling them you are here,' he said. 'My mother always told them what was happening with the family. I told them when she died. And when I returned, that I was changed.'

As a Valla, Bera understood the importance of choosing the right words. As a woman, she could be carelessly hurtful. She went to look more closely at the plants to hide her guilt. There were few she recognised.

'All the main herbs are over here.' Faelan took her elbow.

'What are herbs?'

'You may have another name. It's when any part of the plant can be used to cook with for flavour or as a natural remedy.'

'I recognise some of them.' Bera looked around her. 'We use the leaves, seeds and roots, too. What's in this bed?'

'These are special.' Bera liked the way he touched the leaves with care despite his damaged hands. 'They came over from Iraland.'

'Traded or raided?' She was sharp, thinking of Hefnir.

'Smolderby, Dyflin, all trading towns, grow rich. The men who trade… well, you saw them. The best are dangerous and cruel, but we need them.'

'Like the Serpent King?'

He moved away. 'He trades in flesh. In Dyflin, the biggest slave market of them all.'

Bera caught up with him. 'He is dead!'

'A dead King may be more powerful.'

A monstrous dragon's claw cleaved through her. It was happening somewhere ancient and dark, only this time the horror was put into her mind by Faelan.

Her skern shrank away. *Deep time.*

'There's my mother's remedy store,' Faelan said. 'It's always in the shade and cool.'

Behind it, the river tumbled down a series of rockfalls that threw up a rainbow mist. Bera wanted to lift her face and freshen her thinking. Faelan told her to choose remedies to take aboard but when he left she went straight to the falls. The droplets felt cleansing, but her face was grimed on the inside.

She returned to the store, desperate to find a remedy against the Serpent King or the monster he had become.

You only need yourself, not some jollop. Her skern swung from the store's lintel. *Remember: no one is all bad.*

'I wish I was as blind to the past as you.' Bera ducked through a low, thick doorway.

There were a few steps down into a dark cell that smelled of rotting apples. No, that was a memory of Heggi's cell and the Drorgher that waited there. This was the orderly store of a healer who kept her remedies fresh.

'Oh, to be such a woman!'

Then you would not be speaking to a skern.

Bera was expecting to find the potions in rough clay pots or horn beakers, but these appeared to be used only for mixing, alongside a few heavy pestle and mortars. There were some empty glass jars, all green, and the dark shelves were lined with them, and some wide pots topped with linen and tied with string. The farmstead must bring wealth to have so much glass and to use it for a quiet purpose instead of a show of power in the mead hall. They were all sealed with beeswax and marked with thin and scratchy runes.

She took down a jar and a pot, pulled out a three-legged stool from under the bench and sat. Its seat was made to fit a larger woman's sit-bones and made Bera feel like a child – and able to take this time alone without guilt. She breathed deeply in the soft air, fumed and moistened by salves and potions. Her chest felt less raw and she wanted to share it with Heggi, to put out the fire in his scorched lungs.

'I wish we could stay here.'

Yet always in a rush to leave.

'I have to be.'

Her skern held the jar to the light. *Depends how you look at it.*

'Do you mean the settlers got it wrong?' If they doubted her, and following Dellingr suggested they did, then they might have given up the settlement too soon.

Can't mend the past.

'Vallas weave Fate.'

Forwards, ducky, never back. He twirled the pot.

Bera took it from him. Sure enough, it contained a thick, greasy balm, whereas the glass jar held a pouring remedy. She put them back in their place and sat on the stool, thinking clearly.

6

The healing garden seemed changed, as if it had a message. Bera walked slowly, trying to hear it, asking her mother, Alfdis, to help. She touched the necklace that was her dying gift and held a pain that lay too deep to reckon, which she would pass on, with the heavy beads, to her own daughter.

When the Vallas decide.

Faelan's mother would have named all the plants. Bera pulled away some fleshy leaves to see the stem of one and noticed a slate marker in the loamy soil. She picked it up it and it became a lightning rod of connection to the woman who had created this garden with knowledge and love. A true healer: linked to the land, using its energy.

You can't read it though, can you?

A sulfur-yellow butterfly danced past her, heading for the open half of a stable door. Its sloped roof butted against a wall, making a small booth, hardly bigger than a larder. What was in it? She went over and leaned inside.

Her shadow fell on Faelan, who quickly pulled his hat lower.

'Your face is already hidden by the tied-bunches.' Bera moved to make it true, resting her elbows on the half-door.

Drying plants were neatly hanging from every cross-beam. It all spoke of his mother's orderliness: grow, pick, dry, mix into salves, store.

'This wall gets hot and the door faces inland, away from the salt sea breezes.' Faelan's voice was thick.

There are many kinds of hurt.

A lazy bee droned somewhere, drunk with nectar.

'I used to hide in here when I was young.'

'You still are.' Bera slipped inside. She crumbled one of the dried leaves into a potent-smelling dust. 'All the power of summer made stronger for winter use.'

Every leaf and petal of the bunches was brittle brown and their combined scent beat beneath the sun-warmed smell of Faelan's skin. The nearness of him was in the pulse of her blood. Could he feel it too? If he was blind, would he know it was her just from the scent of her skin?

No. She must not care for anything again for it was always lost. *Too late, dear one. It's always too late for you.*

Faelan had been speaking low. 'And after the horror of the ruins I needed healing.'

Could she feel any worse? 'Smolderby.'

'No. After the old eruption, when I was a child. When the wounds were only inside.'

'As opposed to the ones you have outside now?'

'Oh no, Bera! I do try to steer away from blaming you.' He hit the beam above his head. 'Fool with words! I should have said, for *sounding* as if I blame you.'

'How can you not? You may not claim the blood debt, Faelan, but it will always be between us.'

Bera moved away to hide her shame. The yellow butterfly was inside, a flickering taper in the dark. They stood at the edge of a ruined friendship and watched it without speaking. When it went back into the sunshine, Faelan came close and read the tag on the nearest bunch.

'Lungwort. Made into a tonic for coughs and colds.'

She backed away to another. 'Flamewort. A balm for ringworm.'

He followed. 'Starwort. Picked at night. Heals cuts.'

'Same as ours.' She moved on. 'And this one?'

'Feverfew.'

'That's an easy one.' She went further in.

He followed. 'Against fevers. And headaches.'

'And this?'

'Eyebright. For swollen eyes.' He was so close that she could feel his words on her neck.

41

'What's this one?'

'Good against clegs. And midges.'

'This?' They were deep into sweet-smelling shadow.

'Bee balm. To relieve melancholy.'

'Melancholy?'

'Sadness.'

Bera longed to reach out and stroke his poor cheek, to heal him. But savage desire made her honest. She wanted to be pressed hard against warm stone and taken right there, without shame or regret, by a man without weakness; a man like Hefnir. So, like her mother, the Valla passion was too strong. Bera was only safe with a wounded Faelan, and there would always be too many words.

'You see?' He turned away. 'None of these can mend melted flesh.'

'They can ease the pain. Come to the salve store with me now and let me tend your face.' Bera went ahead. She could at least heal skin.

Her skern was sitting like a cobbler on the empty bench.

Try thinking before you speak. You can both be hurtful.

Faelan stopped at the doorway. 'Where are all the remedies we're to take?'

'I couldn't tell what the pots hold.'

So she starts with a lie.

He moved to the pots. 'These are ointments for wounds, whereas the glass jars are tonics for ailments like stomach pains.'

New words for old troubles. Her skern brushed his nails on his scrawny chest.

'Now tell me why you really picked nothing.' Faelan was starting to know her too well.

'They are staying here because, for a while, so are we.'

He gave a long whistle. 'So Sigrid was right.'

'We will follow… but not yet.'

'Why did you change your mind?'

'I often leave before I'm forced to go. I sat in here and gave myself time.'

'For…?'

'I think the whole farmstead might be healing.'

'My mother chose the place and set it in the right aspect, protected by the ghost fence.'

'There are always losses to make the land safe again. This time I made them and sent the evil away to the south. It might have reached Iraland.'

'What are you saying?'

'Smolderby will be safe now. Before we can help others, we need to heal ourselves.' She touched his sleeve. 'Why take these remedies with us when your mother arranged them to be stronger here? She would want me to make you well.'

'You can't put me back the way I was, Bera.'

'Perhaps I don't want to. Be different. But I must see your face.'

'Don't say my mother would want me to.'

'She would.'

'No.'

'It would help us both.'

'No.' His undamaged eye was a dark stillness of hurt.

If he could not forgive her, she must try to make him trust her. Faelan would never smile with his whole face again but she wanted to see the long crease she loved that must still be graven on his cheek beneath his beard.

Bera had learned to say nothing when she greatly wanted something. She took hold of his hand, which fitted hers as well as she remembered. They used to walk in step, too, unlike Hefnir, or any of the Seabost men. They were in accord, their bodies. A small muscle ticked at the corner of his eye and their faces were as close as lovers.

Faelan pulled his hand away. She had hoped for too much and lost him. But then he touched the front of his hat. Was he hiding his face? He tapped the brim a few times, and a few times more, and then held on tight.

'Faelan, if you don't want to...'

He swept off his hat and pulled his hair away from the ravaged side of his face.

He looked so brave, so braced against hurt, that Bera wanted to hug him like a child, and tried not to show it. His seared flesh gave her as much pain as if it was her own; and she wished it were. The urge was strong to kiss every piece of scorched skin; the swelling that closed one eye and the patch of baldness at his temple where fire had burned the scalp.

She searched for the right words.

Men hate looking helpless. Her skern was peering too closely at a blister.

'Hiding the burns has stopped them healing properly. They need air. Can you see at all out of that eye?'

'I'm not blind, if that's what you mean.'

See?

'Well, if I get the swelling down that will help. How much of this side is burned? Is your beard covering a lot?'

'I'm not shaving it off.' He firmly put his hat back on.

'Please don't hide again.' Bera moved to the shelf. 'I can't read the runes on the pot lids.'

'They're my mother's signs.'

'Which ones are for burns?'

Faelan put two pots on the bench. Bera took off the linen covers and sniffed both.

'This smells like the salve the old crofter made me take. I used it on my leg.'

'What happened to your leg?'

'Oh. Midge bites.'

My arse.

'Let me see, Bera. Scars are stories.'

She did not want to see disgust on Faelan's face when he saw the real scar.

Exactly how he feels.

Bera rolled down her thick sock.

Faelan groaned as if it hurt him. 'No midge did that.'

'All right, a wolf did.'

'Then you are lucky to still have a leg.'

She agreed. 'But I am changed, Faelan. You, me, Heggi, Rakki, we're all different. You said it yourself, so we must tell each other what happened.'

44

'Rakki too?' He was teasing.

'You see? Even sharing this much has cheered you. You can tell Rakki's story.' She rolled her beads, finding comfort. 'It is a pressing need, now, to tell our stories, to heal.'

'Heal?' Faelan scoffed. 'Why would you punish yourself by hearing my story?'

'If we are to make the future our own, we have to understand the past by hearing our own story spoken aloud.'

He sat down heavily. 'Can we try some other healing first?'

Bera gently took off his hat and laid it on the bench. Faelan scraped his hair off his face and knotted it at the back of his head.

'I hope your mother's remedy works as well as the crofter's.'

'They shared herblore and swapped plants if they were better suited in the other's garden. The crone's grew stronger, always, in the croft's soil.'

Bera dabbed the cool balm onto his skin while he was speaking but as she lightly worked it in, Faelan sucked in his breath. She flinched away from his pain, but carried on, because it had to be done. Then she waited until his breathing calmed.

'How could they share herblore when the crofter couldn't speak?'

'She learned the signs on the lids, and they drew them in the air, with others meaning different things, too.'

'Their hands speaking?'

'She said hands are better than lips for saying what is in the heart.' Faelan tapped his chest.

'I wish your mother had taught me. People keep dying before I can learn enough.'

'Your own mother.'

'And father.'

'Ottar taught you boat skills.'

'True.' Bera touched his arm. 'I'll do the worst burns, now. There's lavender and marigold in here. It will sting a lot at first but soon the pain will go and the wounds won't go bad.'

Faelan groaned with the pain. 'Wolf bite,' he said through clenched teeth.

He needs a story right now.

Bera touched her amber bead that was like the pack leader's eyes, and told Faelan how the wolf had saved her, and how she knew his thoughts and had made a promise to save his pack. She worked on through his gasps, and described the grey tower and the well with a ring of small skulls, but she kept to herself the terrible nature of Obsidian. And then it was done.

'The lavender will make you sleepy. Don't fight it. Sleep is the oil on the storm swell of care, as Ottar used to say.'

'Grand.' He winced. 'What happens to the *Raven*?'

Bera gasped. 'Do you mean we are staying?'

He tapped his head. 'I can't think straight with this, but we're safe enough inside the ghost fence. So – what about the boat?'

'I'm going down to Heggi, my second, like Thorvald was to Hefnir. I should treat him like a man.'

'But he's only—'

'Don't say it, Faelan. Life has made him grow up fast.'

'So let him be a boy again with Rakki. Let's give him a breathing space, Bera, for as long as we can.'

He was as kind as ever.

Bera climbed up to the bluff that looked down on the narrow inlet, feeling that her old self was there, before Obsidian. If she were, would she tell that Bera to stay with her daughter?

Attend to the future.

'It began with her birth, my body tearing apart, the land tearing apart. It was a sign. Our future was destroyed that day.'

It's never a single moment. Her skern stroked her cheek. *Valdis will love you.*

'She won't know me! Sigrid is the only mother she has known.'

Bera crawled towards the edge of the high bluff, hearing the low booming of the sea far below. Sheer drops frightened her but she faced her fears.

And go too far.

Out on the sea paths, striping the waves with drilling fins, were so many sharks and starkwhales that her heart sang, for the big hunters had returned. Clouds of seabirds made air and water white as they preyed on all the teeming creatures beneath. The wrinkled whale roads led far beyond the Known World.

Don't look towards Iraland.

There was the decaying, earthy stench of stinkhorn, somehow linked to Chaos, and she scried...

A darkness on the sea rim that spread like a stain: shadow-boats in a war fleet of the dead with long bones for oars. They were coming to take her through Norgrind, the corpse gate to Hel...

Starting back, Bera reached out for Rakki but that had been the day of the lost twin. The sea rim was empty and the day bright but nothing good ever happened on the bluff. Was the shadow-fleet real? It was a warning of something.

'How can we hide the boat?'

Ask Heggi.

A cold nose pushed into her hand. Her dog turned a circle on the spot, made sure she was watching and did another, displaying his mastery of twirling on three legs.

'You're the best dog, but I have no cheese. Where's Heggi?'

Rakki led the way. If he tumbled Bera pretended not to notice, sad that even an able-bodied dog's life was too short. He made for a group of thorn trees, bent like hags against the wind. With vivid curses, Heggi finally emerged, red-faced but grinning.

'I got a bit stuck.'

'How did you know I wasn't a pirate?' Bera picked some twigs out of his caffled hair.

He rolled his eyes. 'Because Rakki wouldn't bring an enemy, would he?'

'Did you see any longships?'

He shook his head. Bera doubted he could have seen much through the thorns.

'Let's get down to the landing.' She walked fast. 'Listen, while we're alone – Faelan is in pain, not just his face. Have you noticed he's limping?'

'No.'

'I think it hurts more than we know.'

47

'Well, he's hiding it. It's what men do.' Heggi assumed the air of a raider.

'So do women.' Bera poked him. 'Stop walking like you've wet yourself, I want some sense.'

'About Faelan?'

'What if we stayed long enough to get stronger before fetching the others. What do you say?'

He threw a stick for his dog.

'Heggi? We will sail straight to Smolderby.'

'You know there's too many folk there. How will I find Ginny?'

'Her father wants to work iron so he will be in the smiths' quarter.'

Rakki barked and Heggi threw the stick again. 'Sounds like you've decided everything, as usual.'

'Let the poor dog rest. The problem with staying is the *Raven*.'

'I'm guarding her, aren't I?'

'Not from pirates, boykin, and the longer we stay the greater the chance one may pass by close to shore.'

Heggi drooped. 'And the *Raven* would be gone.'

'Not only that. Raiders would know someone is ashore and come looking. So how do we hide her?'

'I'm starving. Have you brought any cheese?'

'Am I a walking pantry?' Bera froze. Coming from the east was a blood-red sail. Was it the shadow-boat she had scried?

Her skern squinted. *It's crewed by the living.*

'It must have been behind the skerries,' said Heggi. 'What shall we do?'

'Put out to sea so they won't find the settlement.'

'I know!' Heggi yelled. 'We can hide the *Raven* right now!'

Bera checked distance as they ran. The boat was a way off but coming fast with a full sail. Not a dragon boat, but not Northmen. An unknown boat brought well-known trouble, as Ottar would say.

They slipped the lines and took an oar each, taking a stroke one side or another to keep the boat mid-channel. The wind picked up at the entrance. They did not want a sail to be seen so put their weight into rowing hard against the choppier water. Bera's whole body soon screamed with pain, her stomach worst of all, and Heggi complained of hurting. Only he had been in Faelan's skiff, so he was scanning the shoreline for a place to hide.

'How much further?' she asked.

'There's a rock like a walrus out to sea and then… There!' He pointed to a wall of rushes.

'We won't get the *Raven* in there!'

'It might have grown a bit. Or we might be in the wrong place.'

Bera reckoned the other boat was on the same heading, and closing. 'All right, we'll have to risk it. Take it slow and steady and when I say ship oars, don't take another stroke.'

'Never do,' he grumbled.

They turned in and pulled hard, finding a narrow opening. The prow nudged aside the tall rushes and they pushed through – but then held fast. Bera felt as trapped as a lamb in brambles hearing a wolf howl.

'Have they seen us?' Heggi squeaked.

'They soon will, stuck here.'

The strangers might not respect Valla power, so she might be forced to fight to save her father's precious boat and her son.

Doubt attacks both mind and body.

'Hel's teeth and buckets of blood!' Bera seized a long boat knife from the mast, went forward and slashed at the reeds, cursing them even more colourfully than her father would have done.

Heggi laughed. 'You've changed, Mama,' he said and began clearing with a boathook.

'Push!'

They were slowly getting upriver. When Bera stopped and looked astern, there was a slice of sea showing through the reeds the width of the *Raven*.

'If they are only traders they will keep well out to sea and miss it.' Bera fixed on the gap, using Valla will to keep the boat away.

Rakki flumped down beside her with a deep sigh. It grew hotter inside the cloaking grasses. Sweat tickled Bera's face and flies settled to drink it. Tiny midges arrived in a blood-sucking cloud.

Heggi swung his arms about and slapped his cheeks. 'I hate them!'

'Quiet! I can see them!'

The longboat had reduced sail and slower boat speed meant they might notice the carved swathe of rushes. There was buzzing, droning and then silence. A plop made them jump. A river creature going hunting. Then nothing, only clear sea and sky. They waited.

Heggi made a long fart noise with his lips to annoy Rakki.

'Be quiet!' hissed Bera.

'They'd be in here by now.'

The stillness reassured her, too. 'Why did Faelan bring the skiff in here?'

'Oh, we used to catch things in pots and snares.'

'You spent a lot of time with him without my knowing, didn't you?'

'You had the baby and that.' Heggi bit his thumbnail. 'Asa used to shout if she saw me and Ginny together.'

Bera flinched, feeling again the sharp teeth of Asa's mouth as she filled it with stone.

'Can we get ashore upriver?'

'There's a jetty somewhere.' Heggi waved airily.

Bera sent him off in the curricle with a line. 'If it's too far, we'll run out of rope.'

The small round boat easily slipped through the rushes and was gone.

Rakki leaned against her legs, never going to be left behind again. Bera's mouth was bone-dry and she dipped a bucket into the river. The water was brackish, so she tipped it over the dog to cool him. There was a flagon aboard that she should have filled. She fetched it and gave it a shake. The water would be stale but she wet her lips and then poured some into her cupped hand for Rakki.

Heggi clambered onto the deck. 'It reaches.'

He took a long swig, spat it out and then they began to haul the boat towards the jetty with the last of their strength.

7

As days passed without any sign of strangers, Bera stopped fretting. She vowed to ride the waves of Fate, as Vallas must, to make her folk safe in Smolderby. Until they set sail, she would enjoy being an ordinary woman, with a man going about his duties and Heggi recovering the freedom of youth, happily wearing Faelan's cast-offs. His mother's garments were too big for her, but Bera was pleased with her alterations. The only concern was that Faelan himself seemed to be shrinking, as if his body were curling around some pain inside him.

'Does it mean we should leave now?'

You need a threshold of earth, water and air. A waterfall, perhaps?

Before seeking Obsidian, Bera had sensed some timeless vastness in that place that had studied her as a spider would a fly. Yet she had been given answers and now she must brave it again. She also decided to fill the *Raven's* water barrels up there, to store the waterfall's pure energy.

Faelan brought them by cart. 'I must leave you and Heggi. Bathe if you like. Miska and I will be back by noon.'

He was pale. Bera thought about him bathing there, his slender body like a water elf. If he had been naked now, she would be able to count his ribs.

She ran her thumb along a ridge of a sea-glass bead, a favourite. 'Heggi? Did you and Ginna used to come up here, before?'

'Before' meant life before Obsidian for them all. They were in a strange time now, between lives.

'Ginny and I tried once but there was too much snow.'

Bera was glad. It had been her secret place, and Faelan's, who still did not know that she had wanted him to take her then and there

51

in fierce Valla passion. Heggi and Ginna were too young for such dangerous feelings.

You can't hold back nature, and the boy's almost a man.

'His voice may have broken but he lacks a man's understanding.'

He is his father's son.

'Hefnir. Exactly.'

Heggi tugged her sleeve. 'So are you?'

'What?'

'Coming to the pool. Rakki wants to swim.'

'Don't turn into an elf.'

Heggi's eyes narrowed.

He whistled for Rakki and set off through the mossy rocks. Silence closed in and Bera's awareness sharpened. The distant drumming of the falls plunged her back into fear yet promised some deeper insight or recognition. Afraid to go on, she dared not go back and miss it. Her feet were iron, welded to the earth.

It's further on. Her skern made long strides.

Bera willed herself to keep walking towards the ledge that ran behind the falls. It was where she had heard a wolf howl and seen the man she called Crowman. It was the beginning of understanding that the Vallas also held darkness.

'I'm not going. I want to be a simple wife and mother.'

Silliness. You're playing with dolls.

She growled and chased him. Following the throb of the waterfall, Bera scrambled up rocks as she had done before. How high she was! The mist was cold and she shut her eyes. Her ears rang and the two visits became one; she was looking at herself then and now. Time was odd again. Dizzy, Bera was drawn towards the plummeting water. She took slow steps towards the edge and leaned out. The plummet pulled her like iron to a lodestone, feeling her weight shift; she would be falling, free as air...

Like stone!

Bera flung herself back, pushing hard against the rock wall. She waited until her heart slowed, then trod with care on slime-wet stone. The ledge brought her into a green twilight behind the thundering falls. It was a threshold behind a threshold, with all that power. The torrent of shivering glass made her giddy, like looking up into the blackness of the Abbotry where ravens flew unseen. Here, there were no cawing echoes, but the deafening force of water. Light not dark, but still a warning of danger.

Gaze into the water.

Her hand went to her beads. They were blood-hot and she watched the hairs on her arm rise.

The green wall is a looking-glass.

A long line of her Valla ancestors stretched away to a distant pin-prick of the eldest.

'It's like Obsidian!' Bera pushed her thumb-pads against her eyes, against their darkness.

No, dearest, this is clear water made from the purity of ice.

Rushing to the sea. Her hand found the ridged bead and she let her sight slacken. There was her mother Alfdis holding her granddaughter. They were gazing lovingly at each other – with no Bera between them in her rightful place.

'Valdis! Mama's here!'

Neither turned; a pain as savage as a wolf bite.

'Am I going to die?'

So will we all one day. But watch and listen.

Bera heard…

The sail creaking as the *Raven* clipped along a starlit sea path that soared into the sky as Bifrost, the Shimmering Road. Veiled by billowing white ghosts of the North Lights, her ancestors chanted:

'We travel light years in a single moment, from deepest black through blood-red, scorched by the blue flash of an exquisite trail of dying stars, we are in space and time, and in that place, the ultimate reach, lies the power of three; and the youngest will behold the eldest and the scantling mote shall split.'

The Vallas were moving away into the green twilight…

'I need to remember! Stop! What does it mean?'

Her skern stroked her cheek. *It's the ancient echo coming from deep space.*

'The time of peace is over. The time of war has begun. Chaos is coming!'

*

Bera's eyesight played tricks as she picked her way back to the pool. She was shivering amongst the hard glitter of Bifrost's stars, with the dread of where she must go.

'We have to leave.'

The mere thought of Iraland is weakening me. Her skern was wrapped round her for comfort. *They don't believe in skerns there.*

'Then I must never lose sight of you.'

Faelan and Heggi were loading the cart with barrels and flagons, which seemed too ordinary a task.

'You were ages!' Heggi said. 'We've been working really hard while you've been messing about. Even Rakki.'

Her mind was full of other voices. 'I was scrying. A kind of scrying.'

Faelan turned, his face bloodless. Had he heard them?

'I need to talk to Faelan,' she said.

'I'll do all the work myself, then.' Heggi gave an overdone sigh. 'I thought I was supposed to be your second?'

'You are. But a time is coming, when—'

Faelan crumpled to the ground.

Bera rushed to him and put two fingers to his neck. The beat was thready. 'Help me get him home, Heggi. He has worked himself too hard.'

'Will he be all right?'

'He has to be.'

They dragged him over to the cart where Miska breathed softly on her master's face. Faelan rallied and tried to get up.

'Stay there.' Bera passed him a flagon and made him take a long drink.

Afterwards, Faelan got himself up on the cart but Bera grasped the reins and let the mare take them home. Heggi stayed with her in the byre while Bera settled Faelan near the fire. He shuffled into his bedroll, more ill than she supposed. Whatever Chaos meant, it had already brought frailty. She had a sense it preyed on weakness and went to look for a wholesome remedy. Bera liked the idea of his mother nursing him, and thought he would heal sooner.

She returned with some mead. 'All the goodness of your bees in there, and I think your mother will have mixed in a cure.'

'M-mead warms.' He took some sips. 'So, so sorry, B-Bera. You want to leave. Written on your f-face.'

'The ancestors told me the time of war has come. I think it's a meeting of enemies. I saw the exact place, Faelan.'

'Not here! I can hardly stand, B-Bera, I've no f-fight.'

'Rest.' She put a hand on his fiery brow. 'I've had visions of a rain-filled valley. Now I know it is in Iraland.'

He turned his head away. 'The place brings nothing but trouble.'

'We shall stop at Smolderby for our folk, but must then go on to Iraland.'

'Yes, you'll need Dellingr, of course!' He hammered his chest. 'How can I fight? Damn this!'

'Stop, Faelan.' She caught his hand. 'It's Fate and we need to be whole to face it. It's the long days of summer so healing will be faster.'

He rolled his whole body away from her.

Bera went to the store to find a salve for his chest. She wished they were back here together that same hot day for ever and ever. No, she dared not love him. She had to protect Faelan in every way, and everything she loved was taken from her.

Her skern trailed after her, sneezing. *Or are you afraid love will make you lose your powers, like your mother?*

'She died, didn't she?'

After their meal, Bera looked at the glum faces around the hearth. Even Rakki had his head on his paws, downcast. She gave the dog a scrap of cheese and wondered how to cheer the men. Once, this hall would have held all the farmworkers and others after a stranding or homecoming. Bera remembered the mead hall in Seabost, having to make her mark as a stranger. Her skern had made her hold the Valla beads and she spoke from the heart: of her mother dying and baby brother put out for wolves by Ottar. She had saved herself by speaking truth and linking to their own losses.

Try the blue bead.

She held it up, looking for some meaning. 'When I gaze...'

'Oh no,' moaned Heggi. 'She's going to make us go off again, isn't she?'

'"She"? Who is this "she"?' snapped Bera. 'You will show me some respect, Heggi!' Rakki tried to climb into her lap. 'Now you've upset the dog.'

'No, you have!' Heggi glowered.

Faelan coughed. 'This is my fault. You are both angry with me, not each other.'

'No, Faelan, it's not—'

Heggi kicked over his stool. 'Why do we have to go anyway? Rakki's better here and everything!'

'What about Ginna?'

'I bet she's dead. Everything I love is dead.' He stamped to the door. 'Come on, Rakki.'

'It's late!'

'It's bright-nights.' He spoke as though to an idiot.

'Do not go past the ghost fence!'

The door slammed.

'He has lost so much,' said Bera, 'we all have. I can't lose him now.'

Faelan struggled to his knees. 'I'll take Miska...'

'Then I will have you to worry about as well.' She swung a shawl round her shoulders. 'Bank up the fire and rest.'

As she walked, Bera thought that the blue bead had reminded her of a warning; something glimpsed of wolves and the grey tower.

It's a perfect globe.

'That's it! I saw this world of ours in Obsidian! It was beautiful, hanging in black space, like the ancestors keep saying. Is it to do with the echo? You said something about Deep Space. Will it help me stop Chaos?'

Her skern stretched out a bony arm in the direction of the ghost fence.

'Heggi!'

He was too far to hear and then her breath caught, for in the gloaming a figure was closing on him, the set of its small back reminding her of Asa. Bera ran. Was her corpse become a Drorgher after all? She dodged roots, jumped over rills and then fell into a shadowed dip. When she got up the figures were gone. She started down the slope again, her breath like fire in her chest.

A creature barrelled into the back of her legs and she was poleaxed.

'Rakki!' She tried to get up. 'Go back to Heggi!'

The dog sat on her. And then Heggi laughed.

'You are funny, Bera.'

There was no Drorgher. Was it her fear alone that had shaped the horror? Relief washed over her. She breathed in the sweet grass and thanked her mother, the Vallas, whatever, for keeping her boy safe.

'I could strangle you with my bare hands,' she said, sitting up.

The other figure appeared.

'Hello, Bera,' said Ginna.

'You walk just like your mother.'

'Ginny walked back for days!' Heggi reproved her.

'I'm sorry.' Bera rubbed her face. 'You look famished, poor girl. Are the others down at the homestead?'

'I left them in Smolderby.'

Bera was aghast. 'You came alone? Is Sigrid alive? Both babies?'

'They were when I left,' Ginna said. 'And Papa.'

It was a carefully guarded truth. Bera hurried them back to the farmstead, before nightfall, wondering what Ginna was not telling them.

8

Ginna's face drained of all colour when she saw Faelan. It was not lost on him.

'Am I so changed in a few short weeks, Ginna?'

'I-I thought Bera's healing…' She was a poor liar. 'I came to fetch you.'

'And hoped I'd be here,' said Bera, winking at her.

Heggi wrapped himself round Ginna. His smothering love was a danger but Bera held her tongue.

Faelan gestured to the bench at the hearth. 'Sit. Eat. And then tell your tale.'

Bera brought some stew and sat beside her, slapping Heggi's hand away from reaching across for some bread. While Ginna ate, Bera worried at the message slate in her pocket, impatient to hear how their folk were.

'It was brave of you to come and we must hear your full story. But first I want to talk about your mother.'

The spoon was poised at Ginna's mouth; perhaps she was expecting hostility.

'You should know that I said some Valla words over Asa's grave.'

'To keep her in the ground,' said Heggi unhelpfully.

'To give her peace.'

Ginna put down the bowl and looked at Bera straight. 'Papa would not let me see her. He said a sudden death is not for any woman except a Valla. And you weren't there.'

It was a rebuke.

'But properly done,' Faelan said. 'Your father buried her as our custom directs.'

'Anyway, Bera was off saving everyone,' Heggi said. 'So was I.'

Ginna passed him the stew.

She has his measure and loves him for it.

Her skern was right, but it was simple for them. If Bera could split herself and be wherever needed she would do it. At this very moment she would rather be both on the sea paths and also with her folk. Perhaps it was as the Vallas said, that the mote should split.

'Does that mean I am the mote?'

I thought you knew what the ancestors intend?

'Some of it, but some words have no clear meaning. I have to stay on guard or Fate could snatch someone I love.'

Heggi elbowed her. 'Ginna just asked you something important.'

'My skern was speaking, go on.'

Heggi's eye-roll was directed at Ginna, who frowned at him. Perhaps she was not trying to heap guilt on Bera by speaking honestly.

'No one would tell me how Mama died. You would have talked straight to me, Bera, if you'd been here, even if it hurt.'

'I would have, yes.'

'So can you tell me now? What did she die of, Bera, please?'

Bera looked at Faelan, who gave a slight shrug.

Heggi glared at her. 'You gave him that look. If he's told you about Asa, you have to tell Ginny.'

Faelan shook his head. 'I'm sorry, Ginna. I am the last person your father would tell.'

'Would it help to know, sweetheart?' Bera took her hand. 'I wish I had not seen what happened to my father.'

'Mama was so sad after you left, even Sigrid could not cheer her. We all thought she would be glad you were gone. I'm sorry, Bera.'

'Oh, Ginna, I would have expected her to be glad if I died.'

'And me,' said Heggi.

'Don't say that, Heggi.' Ginna was angry.

Bera gave her some ale. 'Start at the beginning, sweetheart. Why did you leave the homestead?'

Ginna twisted her apron. 'Faelan knows. His men said the volcano was about to blow.'

Faelan cursed. 'Bunch of old women.'

'There were pedlars,' she went on. 'Sigrid said they were spies, and that we'd all be knifed in our beds, or poisoned, like before.'

Bera groaned. 'Not this again.'

'She got everyone worked up and then when Faelan returned, my father...'

'Couldn't wait to leave,' Faelan said. 'Dellingr hoped I never would, for certain.'

'We rested at the old crofter's hut. She's very kind.'

'I hope you didn't raid her stores,' said Faelan.

'We added to them. Papa liked her and made sure of it. But some of the others – your workers, Faelan – they made fun of her muteness. They threw her in the trough and when she called for help they mimicked her noises.'

Bera's heart clenched. 'I hope Dellingr dealt with them.'

'He gave them sore heads and threatened them with the old magic, with iron from the croft. They ran off with some pedlars and then we moved on alone.' Fear tightened her voice. 'To Smolderby.'

'I'd bash them with the anvil,' said Heggi. 'Then curse them forever!'

Ginna was fixed on her story. 'The land was covered in ash. It was choking, horrible... There were burned bodies when we got into the city. Flesh melts, it goes black and I will never get the smell out of my nose.'

Faelan touched his scars. He had been there, in the firestone hail. What sickness might the stench of decay bring to mind and body? Bera was without hope. How could any of them forgive her?

'Don't say any more,' said Heggi.

Ginna turned on him. 'This is why I've come, you fool. I have to tell you!'

Heggi's cheeks flushed red but he said nothing.

'We rebuilt a hut near other smiths,' she went on. 'They smashed it down. Three times Papa got it finished, and three times they took it apart. No one spoke. They watched him do all the work and then destroyed it while we slept.'

'Why would they try and break him?' Faelan said. 'Trades always keep together, protect each other and they need to rebuild. They need a man like Dellingr.'

Bera thought the worst was coming. 'What happened to your father?'

'Nothing, then. Sigrid told the wives that he had a new kind of magic and they got to like her. You know how good Sigrid is at making friends, folk trust her. So Sigrid asked them why they wanted us gone and they said there were some pirates, before we arrived. They told the Smolderby lot to listen out for anyone speaking like us.'

'How do we speak?' asked Heggi.

Faelan said, 'You have an accent.'

'No, you speak funny sometimes, not us,' Heggi said.

Bera leapt up. 'Are we in danger because of the way we speak now? Did I save Ice Island and all the lands linked by fire for it to come to this!'

'It's about power and money,' said Faelan. 'The Serpent has many boats supplying traders with whatever makes them rich and kept plain folk fed.'

'It's true,' said Ginna, 'and they fear the Serpent too, so they will do anything he asks in Smolderby.'

'The Serpent King is dead!' Bera shouted.

Ginna dabbed her eyes with her travel-grimed apron.

'Use this.' Bera sat down and gave her a fine linen cloth. 'It's Faelan's mother's. I'm shouting at Fate, Ginna, not you.'

'We killed him, Ginny,' said Heggi.

'Well.' Ginna pulled at the cloth. 'One of his dragon boats has joined a war fleet, to take the Serpent King to Iraland.'

'How can it be?' Bera was afraid, thinking of the shadow-boats of the dead that she had seen from the bluff.

'They told Sigrid one of his crew made it to the Abbotry to get aid.'

'Left him to rot more like!' Heggi said.

'Even if he lives, he is only one man,' Faelan said.

Bera was trying to make sense of it all. 'But Heggi and I know the Serpent is dead...' She saw long bones for oars. Was war a battle of the dead? Was this Chaos?

Ginna's knees were pulled up and she rested her head on them, rocking. It reminded Bera of poor, mad Egill, and she held her close.

'Can you go on, sweetheart?'

'This is the worst bit.' Ginna looked up. 'Someone in Smolderby did betray us because the pirates came back – and they have taken Papa!'

'Not Dellingr!'

'They need a good smith for – some special purpose.'

'The babies? Sigrid?'

'Them, too.'

'Taken them where, Ginny?' asked Heggi.

'Iraland,' said Bera. 'For the time of war has begun.'

The Vallas had stolen her folk and freedom to send her to Iraland. What sleight of their ancient hands had taken the Serpent King there? Their lives had intertwined so often: if Chaos was their final battle, then she would fight to win.

'I hid and watched,' said Ginna. 'Papa fought and they could have killed him, so they must be keeping them all alive, Bera.'

Heggi rubbed his head. 'Why?'

'A tavern woman told Sigrid it was to get Bera to Iraland. The traders are to tell you to follow as soon as you enter Smolderby.'

'We would have been there before you if we had come straight from the Abbotry.' Bera pushed away more guilt, thinking. 'How did you get away?'

'Same woman. She told me to hide behind some barrels at the tavern. She came back with one of the crew and said I had to… to let him…'

Heggi drew his knife. 'I shall kill him!'

'She works there,' Ginna said. 'Her friend stabbed him in the back.'

'Were they whores, then?' asked Heggi with a swagger.

'Put the knife away, fellow,' said Faelan.

'Did the man… hurt you, in any way?' Bera asked her gently.

Ginna's mouth twisted. 'He was too drunk. It's all right, Heggi, truly. He flopped on me and then he was dead.'

Heggi hugged her. 'You're tiny. He could have crushed you.'

Bera finally understood. 'I think they were always going to let you escape, Ginna. That swine took advantage, but they want us to go straight to Iraland now.'

'It was still really brave,' said Heggi.

Bera agreed. 'The whole journey was. Brave and clever girl.'

'I owe the old crofter everything,' Ginna said. 'I went straight back there and she fed me and soothed me after… and losing Papa. Then she walked with me to beyond the stunted forest, even though it hurts her. It slowed me down and I was so afraid you might have got back and left before I ever reached you.'

'I hope she got home safely,' Faelan said.

Kindness was an underrated virtue in a man, thought Bera, and dogs could always pick them. Rakki put his head on Faelan's lap while he had a fit of coughing.

'As you see, Ginna, we are all still healing. Faelan, how long will it take us to reach Dyflin?'

'How fast do you want to go?' He drank. 'Folk often break the journey.'

'Is there land on the way?'

'There are islands and small skerries. Cronan told me they used to put an ermite on each, all alone.'

'What do they eat?' asked Heggi.

'Air?' Faelan shrugged. 'But there is an island with only pigs living on it.'

'How did they get there?'

'Dropped out of the sky,' said Faelan gravely.

Ginna laughed and it occurred to Bera that he meant her to. He caught her looking and gave his special, lopsided smile. At some point since her return this smile had taken over from the ready smile he gave to everyone. This one was now hers alone.

Any smile hurts him now.

Faelan was too ill to set off, though he denied it, and Heggi declared that Ginna needed Bera's care, which was true. The Serpent's crew were sailing in the same stream of Fate that would take her to a final meeting with the Serpent King, and so Bera determined to be patient. The Vallas had woven her folk into the pattern and only time would reveal what that was.

Midsummer was the season to store food. Faelan's mother had got ready clean crocks from the year before, as women did to safeguard their futures. With Ginna's help, Bera salted, dried or pickled what they did not eat at once and she liked feeling part of a long line of good, plain women. Preparing the stores was a secret promise to her future self, should the Vallas allow.

After a few days, Faelan was strong enough to slaughter a pig and he showed Heggi how to joint it. Bera salted and barrelled a half-pig to take with them, in case they were stranded. Then she admitted to Faelan that she had added the rest to his underearth stores.

'I hope that's because you plan to return here.' But his sad smile matched her feelings. 'If we do return, war makes many changes.'

He was overtired, so Bera sat beside him at the hearth to keep him still. They watched the flames, sitting so close together on the bench that she could feel the heat of his thigh. Then a log fell with a lisping sigh.

'It's the Serpent King!' she cried. 'I keep hearing his fork-tongued lisp behind me.'

'Do you?'

'I did just then.'

'Bera, the sword in his throat will hold him after the birds have stopped picking his bones. It formed the cross of Brid.' He put a hand over his own cross, lying under his shirt.

'Brid won't keep him in the ground, I can tell you that!'

'My wooden cross was protected by Brid. It was not even scorched.'

'Stop it!' Bera jumped up, then sat down again. 'Sorry.'

'What is the matter?'

'I don't know.' She beat her forehead. 'What if… I lose my power? If you doubt me?'

'Not possible. But fear makes you angry.'

'So Sigrid tells me.'

'Fear brings out the worst in us all, I mean.'

'I have always had to face it.' Bera thought about her folk sleeping safe while she was outside, sending Drorghers away.

'Tell me what hold you think the Serpent still has over you.'

'I saw your face while Ginna told her story and you fear him too, Faelan. How can we stop him?'

He touched her chin. 'You know what we're doing?'

What she wanted him to do was kiss her on the nuzzle.

Muzzle.

'My mother taught me the beliefs of our island,' he said.

Bera heard Iraland. 'Tell me one that might help.'

'If you want power over something you must know its name. Plants, animals, everything.'

Told you.

Bera brightened. 'Our own plantlore says if you know the true name of the plant you can channel its power.'

'It's the same, isn't it?'

'So what did they call the Serpent King at the Abbotry?'

'Bera, you saw his full dragon body. He would not keep a plain man's name.'

She thought about the disgusting, winking eye in the Serpent's armpit. 'But you might have heard it earlier from somewhere.'

'I know you hate that I had dealings with him.'

It startled Bera. 'Did I say so?'

'Your feelings are always written plain on your face.'

'So did you trade with him for yourself or the Abbot?'

'Both.' He let the word lie without trying to squirm away from the fact.

Bera took a breath. 'Faelan, I need to find out his true name. Because of the Vallas' last words. We are going to war.'

'Did they tell you what war means? It makes lies the truth. Black becomes white and evil turns into bravery. If you need a true name, Bera, you won't find it in war.'

She thought of the long bones as oars. 'They say Chaos is coming, and if that means the Serpent King is raising an army of the undead, we must all be afraid.'

9

Each evening they would go up to the pool. A hot spring came from deep underground to fill it and cold water poured through a V-shaped rock to form a spout. The warm bath and then the freezing shock made Bera feel fully alive. If they began to talk, it bored Heggi. He would go off with Rakki, and Ginna would promise to keep them away from the ghost fence. Her boy was well protected.

Then Bera would return to the still part of the pool, enjoying the slide of her feet on the shine of polished rock. She would shut her eyes and listen to the gentle birdsong, slowly wafting her hands through the soft slip of water, hoping to be followed by Faelan. He always did.

The shimmering light of bright-nights was especially intense there; some quality existed between the mountains and the sea that held back the shadows. Her skern quietened as colours faded and yet got more penetrating. They were ringed by deep blues that gradually paled to the silver-blue of the sea. In this secret place, between worlds, they began to be trusting friends, stripped of shyness in speech and skin. Faelan's face was pinkly healing, with new hair on his temple. Bera did not hide her leg, where the wolf bite was a sickled hollowness.

One night, he turned her wrist over, drawing his finger along a forgotten, childhood scrape.

'So tell me this scar's story.'

The white line was hardly there but he must have noticed it before, and his gaze was thrilling.

'Sigrid's son, Bjorn. Fish hook.'

'Too short a story. Do you miss him?'

'I miss his friendship, but he started to nag about marriage.' Bera wanted to share a dishonourable secret. 'He shamed me, Faelan. He wrote a love poem.'

'Was it a good one?'

'Very bad.'

They laughed, not unkindly, and her shame was gone.

It was Faelan's turn. 'When I was Heggi's age I was in love with a girl.'

'Were you betrothed?'

'Too young. And then... my m-mother and I were taken by pirates. The girl never m-made it to their boat. I've never said that aloud before.'

Bera put a finger to his lips. 'We have them in our hearts.'

'As I said, hands can sign what's in our heart, Bera. That is where the truth lies.'

'Teach me.'

So it was here that Bera learned to speak without words. Faelan began with easy signs, like eat and thanks, but they gradually created a shared signing and she found that her hands could contain more meaning than her lips if she let them. And so it was that although she learned the sign for love, neither of them risked making it their own.

Sigrid's message slate was still in her pocket. Bera would roll it like a worry-stone, and its blankness made the reproof worse. It grew bigger in her mind until she could ignore it no longer and she told the others they would have a special supper.

When he joined them, Bera was pleased to see that Faelan's beard had gone and they enjoyed their meal.

Tell them.

Bera stood at the hearth. 'We have thrived here, but midsummer has passed.'

Heggi pulled a face. 'Watch out. I know what that voice means. And she knows we're not going to like it.'

Ginna elbowed him, hard.

'I don't care,' said Heggi. 'I'm not going.'

'We have to,' said Bera.

He stomped to the door. Ginna slipped out after him with the dog.

Faelan watched the flames dance. 'I have pretended to myself that we could stay here forever, Bera. All of us, the animals too.'

'Did you tell the bees?' She tried to stop the wrench in her heart.

'I know you mourn Hefnir, but I can't stop thinking… that in another life…'

'Don't!'

It surprised her, the pain of that other life they had glimpsed here. And she feared it, too, for wouldn't it leach away her powers?

'Of course. Stupid. Who could have such thoughts, looking like this!' He jabbed his finger against his temple, hard.

'No, Faelan, not that, please. That's never it.'

'Hefnir dead is harder to fight than Hefnir alive – and I'm not the man I was.'

'You are so, so wrong.'

'Well.' He faced her. 'I'm going to say it, anyway, Bera. This time together has been the happiest I have been my whole life.'

It was what she had wanted to hear, but from the man he was at the pool, not spoken like a rebuke, blaming his brokenness.

'I'm not built for happiness, Faelan.'

'But I've watched you here! You've been happy!'

'And that makes me fear more. Can't you see? It was a relief to put down the burden of larger duty and be a plain woman with smaller cares. But the Vallas are calling and I always must be strong enough to answer.'

She ran outside to Miska and Faelan knew her well enough not to follow. He would be at greater risk if she said out loud that she loved him. Perhaps this was why she dared not make a sign for love; it held too much truth.

The Vallas already know. Her skern's voice trembled at her ear.

She held the ridged sea-glass bead and looked up towards the waterfall, to address the Vallas.

'I understand more now. Faelan grew more ill when my love for him grew stronger. You warned me of Chaos and war, so hear this. I will turn to my duty and away from love. You will spare him. That is my pact.'

Before dawn, Faelan and Heggi brought the *Raven* round to the landing. They carted the water barrels down and Miska made a last trip with a day meal, pans and bedrolls. Heggi and Ginna were happy to stay aboard.

Back in the hall, Faelan said he wanted to make the farmstead as secure as possible but Bera knew he had done that. The set of his mouth was unusually determined and she recognised a need to be alone, which she shared. There were words of farewell that Bera had to make.

'I'll lock the healing garden,' she said.

As she passed through the green space she whispered her thanks to Faelan's mother, then stood before her skeps. The bees would not be drowned for their honey now and she was glad about that.

'The garden is yours alone now, bees. We may not return, so work together for your own sakes and be strong.'

Loss swept in like a sea fret. Visiting the two herb stores would be unbearable. Bera left but when she shut the door behind her, her hand would not turn the key. The garden would grow wild, all his mother's careful patterns spoiled. The past became vivid: the woman's Fetch appearing too late to save her. Did his mother bring all the beliefs of Iraland here, as Faelan had said?

No one better to ask than a skern, he said grimly, *except those folk send skerns away.*

'I have to go to Iraland. You know that.'

To war? I fear it will be their belief that kills us all.

Faelan helped her onto the boat. The others were trying to keep Rakki from the pork barrels. Bera looked around the rest of the boat.

'Where is Miska?'

Faelan was staring inland.

Bera spoke softly. 'It's because we have a long passage now, isn't it?'

'She's never liked change, gets afraid. I don't want…' His voice thickened.

A terrible thought struck her. 'Is this why you went back alone?' Bera pulled him round. 'You didn't…? You couldn't!'

'Of course not.' His lips were white. 'I led her through the ghost fence, to let her join the others, to be free in their roaming.'

'Won't she keep looking for you?' Bera asked.

'The gap is closed.' He picked up a strongbox and left.

Bera took the others to get the sail onto the yardarm and quickly explained. They gazed at the high pastures.

'Miska was all he had left,' Ginna said. 'I keep willing her to appear on the landing.'

'She trusted us,' said Heggi darkly. 'Like Rakki does.'

'Trust shone deep in her eyes,' Bera agreed. 'How much Faelan must love her to set her free.'

'She might still follow us,' said Heggi.

'She can't.' Faelan went to the helm, looking grim.

They slipped the *Raven*'s lines and it was too late.

As soon as they were out to sea, Heggi declared he was hungry. He doubled over, dangling his arms. 'My stomach thinks my throat's been cut.'

Ginna pulled him up by his fringe. 'What does that mean?'

'No food going down, stupid!'

They cheerfully cuffed each other and Bera was grateful for their liveliness.

'I've packed a day meal somewhere.'

'I bet you were hiding it from me,' said Heggi.

He was right.

Bera took her time getting the meal so that she could watch Faelan's helmsmanship. He was not as strong as Hefnir and responded to the *Raven* much as she did herself, through instinct, a supple understanding, whereas her husband was heroic, good in storms, putting his own body, bone and sinew into wresting them on course. Light touch or firm, Ottar's boat responded. Bera could never love a bad helmsman.

Careful.

She took the parcel over to Faelan and unwrapped it.

'Come over here, you two!' she called.

Heggi and Ginna swapped parts of their portions that the other liked best. Faelan had been standing longer than he should, so Bera quickly finished eating and took the helm.

'Now you can eat with both hands,' she said.

He gave her a dark look, grabbed some bread and went off to the prow to eat it. Heggi did exactly the same.

'I didn't mean his wounds,' Bera said. 'I would have said it to anyone.'

Ginna said nothing and her tact made Bera feel more clumsy and unkind. But soon the usual joy swept over her; the excitement of being on passage, always forward, never back, seeking the unknown. Bera let herself feel it instead of trying to scry the future. This was the right time of year. Her father's sleek longboat creamed through a dark blue sea that made the limitless sea rim a looking-glass for the cloudless sky, with teeming sea beasts below matched by countless birds above. She was a better person if she gave herself up to this freedom. No more doubt about where home was: her true home was here, aboard the *Raven*.

Yet Iraland is the lodestone that pulls you. Her skern was moaning in a bucket.

The land had drawn Egill, who had loved it; Hefnir for the wealth and trade; the Serpent King to gain evil power. Herself? The crackling energy of the passage to Iraland was a lightning bolt to a faint heart. A trial was coming – and more than accepting it, Bera welcomed it.

Heggi and Faelan lifted their gloom by playing a board game. Bera was grateful and wondered why Heggi needed it with Ginna close. Perhaps being on a passage had brought back his father's death, or the memory of being forced onto the Serpent's dragon boat. They were all orphans now, except for Ginna, and she would do everything possible to protect her father. As would Bera now her respect for Dellingr was restored. It drove her onwards.

She let the boat speak, loving the speed as they surged down the front of a wave; the judder of the steer-board like the pulse of blood in her veins. Ottar always said that if a boat looked right, she would sail right, and it was true. The *Raven* tracked effortlessly and they were as one. If only she had told her father how proud of him she was for his boatmanship, for his determination to save them all and his bravery. She looked at the sun to make herself sneeze and give a reason for tears.

Only Ginna noticed. She was staying close to Bera, watching her closely, and after a while she asked if she could learn how to helm. Bera was about to refuse, claiming it would be dangerous, but then she recognised that she was hugging the skill to herself.

'I've remembered another of Ottar's sayings: "Knowledge is power that will not grow less if I share it with you."'

'I like that.' Ginna repeated it. 'I'll remember it now.'

'Trouble is, he used it about Valla power, saying my mother held on to her secrets.'

'Did she?'

'She died.' Bera was not ready to share with Ginna her feelings for her family, or the Vallas. 'Now – helming. Get here in front of me and take hold of the tiller like this. Don't tug, let the *Raven* choose her path. That's it, gently nudge. Better, but you're still gripping it. You'll wear yourself out. Feel the boat-song.'

'I don't know what that means.'

'All right, we'll both steer together and then you can take over when you can feel it.'

Bera described what she was doing so that Ginna could recognise and use the wave train, see a wind shift, let the boat respond to a light touch, and then how it felt when she got it right, coursing down the waves. When she thought Ginna was ready, Bera secretly let go and nudged the tiller if they began heading off course.

'I can hear the boat-song, Bera! Heggi, look at me helming!'

They clapped her and then Ginna drove into a wave and splashed them and even Faelan laughed for the joy of it.

At sunset the wind dropped and Bera left her to it. Being able to see Ginna's wide-eyed, open-mouthed concentration filled her with a new pleasure of teaching. The power of knowledge had grown in the sharing. Bera had struggled alone to find her Valla power but that was no reason to hug the hard-won knowledge to herself; how much better to share it with someone. Not Ginna, of course, she was not of the blood.

You have your own small Valla to teach.

72

'Valdis. She is lucky to have a mother to teach her.'

Long may it last.

Ginna was speaking. 'It takes my mind off the other stuff, too.'

'Sailing?' Bera guessed. 'I used to go out fishing and leave trouble all behind.'

'But it's still there, on land, isn't it?'

Bera held the girl's back. 'That pirate did hurt you, didn't he?'

'Not like that. I was trapped, Bera, I couldn't move, I couldn't breathe. I keep thinking what if—'

Heggi barged in, dodging around them, itching to take over. Bera wanted Ginna to stay in charge, talk about her fear, so she told him to help Faelan.

'I'll stay here and give practical advice,' he declared.

Ginna laughed, the best remedy.

'See that smudge on the skyline?' Bera said. 'They may be land clouds.'

'It's how sailors navigate,' said Heggi importantly. 'I tend to use the flight of certain birds.'

Bera went forward. One end of the spare sail's lashing had come free and she retied it. See a job and do it on a boat. She hoped Heggi would also be cheered by sharing knowledge. Surely Ottar felt it when he built a small boat and taught her to sail it, for all he moaned about women's lack of skill.

Faelan called her over to the game board, which he had chalked on the deck. It was big, about one ell square, she reckoned. She was not surprised to see that a cross made four sections, with the middle part dyed red.

'Hefnir used to play board games in winter,' she said, 'but this looks different.'

'This is called King Maker. It was devised long ago in Iraland.'

'Tell me it's not about the Serpent King!'

'Ermites taught me. Shall I show you?'

'I don't like board games.'

'They teach tactics, a war game.'

'Tack-ticks?'

'It's... how to get people in a fix so they have to do what you want.'

'So tick-tacks is a ploy?'

'It's the Art of War.'

Bera sat down. 'Teach me.'

Faelan explained that the highest value gaming pieces were walrus ivory and ebony.

'Highest capture, too. The ebony are hardest to replace, so don't throw any overboard if you lose.'

Bera glared at him and held a glossy black figure to her cheek. 'I want this one and will call it the Warden.'

'Good choice. Except he's actually a Prince. The gaming piece, I mean.'

Bera didn't care, as long as she won. She listened closely to the clear rules and liked not having to unravel some Valla riddle. They began. When they moved gaming pieces their hands sometimes touched and then his special smile returned. But after four games Bera had yet to win and she glared at her captured pieces that were all commoners of hartshorn or bone. Faelan had the precious ones. When she lost again she kicked her pieces off the board.

'I hate this!'

Faelan collected them up and patiently put them back. It made her crosser.

'Go on, say it! I'm a bad loser!'

Heggi shouted, 'You're a bad loser!'

It made Bera laugh. 'I'll never understand, though, Faelan. It's not like any of Hefnir's games. Why can't I be all dark pieces and you the light ones?'

'Is life like that, Bera?' he said. 'Am I only one thing?'

'If they're all trying to topple the King, why don't the dark move like the light? It's confusing!'

'Some have weapons and others do not, so you have to gain them,' he explained. 'It grips you after a while.'

'Did Heggi understand it?' She was impressed. 'I need to get better at this.'

When she won a few bouts, Bera thought she had mastered the game.

He's letting you win, ducky.

She brandished the King at Faelan. 'I bet there are harder rules that you're not telling me!'

'I'm not hiding them, Bera. I thought it best to work up to them.'

'Don't treat me like a child! I hate rules!'

You hate losing.

'Why can't I go across in a slant?'

He laughed. 'That's what Heggi said. There's no game without rules. Learn to go round behind to make me move my King back into his fortress.'

'Move an old sheep knuckle into a chalk square, more like! All Hefnir's gaming boards were ivory and silver.'

Faelan picked up the King. 'This piece is narwhale tusk.'

'Shabby to use it for so petty a thing.'

Their sparring had become a challenge. It was closer than kissing, dangerous because it stripped away pretence. What could Faelan see in her eyes that she was hiding from herself?

'I am no match for Hefnir,' he said. 'Never was, but especially not now.'

'Don't say it's because of your face!'

'No. Because he's dead.' He got up. 'My turn to steer.'

Bera went forward, as far from him as possible, pretending to watch the track of the boat.

He thinks Hefnir will always stay a hero.

'He is wrong but let him think it. It might keep him alive.'

Sacrificing truth is a dangerous game.

The wind was astern and they were pointing down the face of waves, which gently lifted the *Raven*. The bow-spray made a rhythmic hiss as their boat met the regular wave train so perfectly that Bera's heartbeat slowed and she was in calm blue space. Her duty also tracked clear, and no storm clouds threatened, no war fleet darkened the skyline. She lost herself in the dance of the bow, the music of the rigging, the creak of tarred ropes. Bera became the *Raven*, parting the waves, flinging up spray like crystals against a limitless sky.

'Look, Bera.' Heggi waggled the passage marker at her. 'One side is days, like we always have, but the other I've made marks for our watches. I'm helming next.'

'It's neatly done.'

'Ginna says it's really clever. It tells when it's time to take over, too.'

'Show me mine?'

Heggi tapped his nose, touched a whittled notch on the marker and left. Bera strongly suspected it would show any watch-time he chose.

As an apology to Faelan, Bera offered to take over from him at the helm. He let her, as his.

'How well your father made this boat,' he said. 'Perfect balance, helm and trim.'

His kindness got under Bera's guard. He thumbed away her tears. 'It was the only choice with Miska. She had to come first, not me. I let her go because I love her.'

Was Faelan telling her he understood their future? Broken-hearted in bright-night, Bera steered on towards a cloud-shimmer on the skyline.

10

The wind fell away overnight and the boat speed fell to almost nothing. It was a polished silver sea, broken by regular plumes of whale-breath. Bera said it was a chance to eat a meal together and lashed the tiller on course. They gathered around the mast to share the rations. Ginna said she had seen a right whale and claimed the biggest piece of cheese.

Heggi glowered. 'I told you what to look out for.'

'I still saw it first.' Ginna waved the cheese under his nose. 'If you smile I'll share it…'

Instead of getting sulky he tickled Ginna and grabbed the cheese. Bera admired the way she treated Heggi. Had her parents shown her the pattern? Dellingr and Asa had been sweethearts since childhood, but Bera had never been an unfettered woman; her Valla duty meant she would never have so innocent a love.

Rakki gave a long, lonely sigh, so Bera picked through his rough fur for caffles. He was white-blond now, with the grey hairs of old age. It made him more loveable but the thought of losing him stabbed her. The dog rolled onto his back and looked pointedly at her, so Bera got to work. It was easy to spot the shiny dark fleas running across his pink stomach and satisfying to pinch them off and pop the bodies between her thumbnails.

'Bloodlust.' Faelan smiled.

He was joking, of course, but it made her think.

'Ottar never built warships and your King game is a mystery, Faelan. If I am to face war, I must know more.'

'Did Hefnir not say?' Faelan rubbed his chin. 'Not even the Tales of War?'

'Papa was a trader,' Heggi said, 'the best ever, but he never talked about trading, either.'

Bera spilled some ale. Hefnir had said nothing because he mostly raided and she did not want Heggi to follow his father.

She shook the drops off her apron. 'So tell us, Faelan.'

'I've been lucky all my life.' He gestured at his burns. 'Yes, even this. I could be dead. Rakki and me, we're two lucky beings.'

Rakki's tail thumped the deck but he stayed snoozing.

'The luckiest part of my life was that I was taken to Ice Island before the Great War of Iraland really got started. The outlying skirmishes were bad enough.'

'Was there lots of killing and blood?' Heggi was too eager.

'You've heard of bloodlust?'

He nodded, perhaps his bad blood was rising. Bera saw again the opposing armies but this time heard screams of women and children. Could that be right?

Faelan went on. 'Well, think of a raiding party, each member fighting through the red mist, drunk on death, and now picture them hundreds strong, charging at one another with axes and swords, with armoured battle hounds and trampling horses, hacking, cutting, biting; stumbling over chopped-off limbs and fallen heads.' He spat, then wiped from his mouth the foulness of war.

'Evil,' said Bera.

'The smell of blood never leaves you. I saw enough and heard the rest. It's a place where the Serpent King could excel, rising above the others in cruelty to exult in killing.'

'If he lived,' Heggi said. He was pale now.

'Did your father ever talk about being Chief Warrior?'

Bera had to get Heggi away. 'You and Ginna need to rest.'

'I want to hear more,' Heggi said. 'I can't sleep when it's so bright, anyway.'

'Come on.' Ginna yawned. 'Help me rig up a booth. It will be dark under there.'

She winked at Bera. Heggi, misunderstanding, grinned and followed her.

'Are you concerned?' Faelan asked.

Bera shrugged. 'That girl has more sense than I ever did. She's more like her father than her mother.'

You hope.

Faelan threw a bone overboard, taken before it hit the water.

'Are you jealous of Dellingr?' she asked.

'I'm wondering if Heggi's father gave him sense of what is right.'

'What is Chief Warrior?' Bera asked. 'When I first heard it, I didn't liken the words with war.'

'A kind of champion,' Faelan said. 'War is ugly, Bera, but men grow rich.'

'Hefnir also loved power.'

'They said in Smolderby that Hefnir wanted the Venerable Prince Abbot to know he had Obsidian and would bring it to Dyflin.'

'He lied!'

'Perhaps he trusted you to succeed, Bera? But the Prince Abbot's longship never got out of harbour before the eruptions began.'

'Egill did say Hefnir wanted Obsidian as a trading piece of great worth.'

'That's it. The Venerable Prince Abbot of all Iraland would have made the first person to bring him Obsidian Chief Warrior; that's why the Serpent King fought for it. Riches and power bring evil in the wrong hands.'

Bera tapped her blue bead. 'Obsidian was guarded because of its corrupting nature, Faelan. If this Prince Abbot person had looked into it his power would have destroyed our beautiful world.'

'You dared to use it.' Faelan sighed. 'What changes did it make in you, Bera?'

Shocked, she signed a heart-clutch of fear.

He understood. 'War, too, brings riches but demands sacrifice.'

'Then we must be ready, for the next war is upon us.'

Heading for the fair-weather clouds put more east in their course but Bera was certain they heralded land. Not Iraland, yet – they were still a good way north – but Faelan talked about it. He told them its other name was Wolf Island.

'His name means Wolf,' Heggi announced for the hundredth time.

'My mother liked the name,' Faelan told Ginna, 'but I'm no wolf. The west is ruled by real wolves who let no man enter.'

'They'd let Bera in,' said Heggi. 'She saved a whole pack.'

'One wolf bit her,' Faelan said. 'How close you came to death.'

Bera put the amber bead to her lips. 'You have to know who to trust and then keep your promises.'

'Or, if you don't have a tame Valla, build high walls, like Dyflin,' said Faelan. 'Rogue wolves roam the whole island. The ones too violent to join the main packs form snarling loose groups, like war bands.'

'Do we have to go there?' asked Ginna. 'With war and wolves? Perhaps Papa is on some other island.'

'No, Ginna, they mean us to go to Dyflin,' said Bera.

So do the Vallas. Her skern's voice was thin.

Faelan agreed. 'It's where the Venerable Prince Abbot is waging war, which is why he needs a smith.'

Heggi put his arm round Ginna. 'Sailors say that the western wolves are guarding the edge of the Known World. Beyond it is nothing.'

'If the Serpent's crew said it, they know nothing.' Bera brandished her necklace. 'I had a vision of a chain of eruptions that went right around the whole world, which was perfect, like this blue bead hanging in space.'

'And you saved it, Bera,' said Faelan, 'even its unexplored vastness.'

His dear face was veiled in billowing lights and the ancestors were speaking...

'*... scorched by the blue flash of an exquisite trail of dying stars, we are in space and time, and in that place...*'

'Mama?' Heggi's frightened voice, distant, but she knew this by heart, surely...

'*... the ultimate reach, lies the power of three; and the youngest will behold the eldest and...*'

'Mama!' Heggi was tugging her sleeve.

'Wait! I've forgotten that part! Come back!'

Faelan was studying her. 'Were you speaking with someone?'

'Ancient echo…'

Ginna passed the flagon to Bera and she was grateful, but their care had robbed her of something important.

'You went really white,' said Heggi.

'A warning, the Valla ancestors…'

'Ultimate reach sounds like it's under the sea,' said Faelan.

Heggi's voice wobbled. 'We watched the birth of an island, Bera and me.'

'Look!' Ginna pointed. 'There are islands being born over there!'

Bera could see nothing, but her sight was strange. Was this how the echo ended?

'I can't see them,' said Heggi.

'I did, truly,' Ginna said, 'but they've gone.'

'Islands can't just vanish.'

'Keep watching to southward,' said Faelan. 'I think Ginna had a vision.'

Why would they show Ginna? She was no Valla. Bera silently ran through the echo, trying to reach the end, 'Power of three, ultimate reach, power of three…'

'Sailors say that at midsummer, if the air is still like this,' said Faelan, 'and the sun is— There!' His voice caught in wonder.

He pointed towards a flickering brightness low on the sky rim that formed into golden buildings like the Abbotry, but more and bigger. Better.

Bera filled with joy. 'A golden city floating in the sky!'

Domes and towers. Even her skern was smiling again.

'But upside down!' Ginna clapped her hands. 'It's changing, getting bigger!'

Heggi ran to the rail. 'Some bits are still upside down but the underneath, look, is the right way up now.'

They were all enraptured by the vision, but Bera's true joy lay in their dear, excited faces. At last she could share this natural magic with no Valla warning or distant threat.

'You can see golden cities from over the rim of the Known World,' said Faelan. 'I never dreamed it would be so clear.'

'So is it real?' Ginna asked.

'The Abbots say it's a sign from the ermites that they have found Brid.' Faelan touched the cross beneath his shirt. 'Sailors say they are elven palaces. Did your father ever see it, Heggi?'

Bera said, 'Hefnir had many secrets.'

Heggi turned his wrist to her, his finger on the place where his father had the mark of Brid. If she ever found out how Hefnir had earned it, Bera vowed to protect his son from the knowledge – and from ever following.

The wind got up and at last distant islands appeared. Bera joined Faelan at the helm to share landfall.

'Are they skerries?' she asked.

'Bigger. You Northmen call them Southern Islands but others call them the Summer Isles.'

'And what do you call them?'

He gave her a look of quiet despair. 'Home.'

Bera wondered at his feeling but was also envious of it.

'We'll overnight at the first.' Faelan was gruff. 'Go ashore for fresh water.'

They closed the first island as the sun kissed its hills. The boat's slow drift through glassy water and herringbone wake reminded Bera of arriving at Egill's island so long ago. That frail being, with her halo of white hair, so hard to reckon. Her true friend? The mark of Brid had been on her wrist, too.

Her skern nestled into her neck. *Let the past go.*

'There may be lessons for the future.'

Scry the land.

These isles were the green edge of the Ice-Rimmed Sea and Bera matched the colours with some of her glasswork beads: from clear green, through shadowy blue-green, to duller grey-green and dried-pea yellow. Moss and stone; grassland and rivers. Bays. Inlets.

'Troles!' Bera gasped.

On top of the next cliff were huge figures, black against the sky. Waiting for them. Faelan steered closer.

'They'll hurl rocks!' Bera shouted. 'Ginna, get back to the stern. Heggi!'

Faelan laughed and she hit him. She hit him again and he only laughed more.

'Stop!' he begged. 'You don't feel any danger, do you?'

'No prickling,' Bera admitted.

'Because these fellows are made of stone.'

'Rune stones?' asked Ginna. 'So many?'

Bera was uneasy. 'But I do feel something. Some meaning.'

Faelan got back on course. 'We'll go up there tomorrow and see what you make of them.'

'Bera will know,' said Ginna.

Bera was touched by her trust and hoped she merited it. This was an older belief.

They chose a well-protected bay with silent, still water. Heggi lowered the curricle to take the lines ashore and Rakki hurled himself into the small craft, making it tip and twirl, barking to get at the puffins. Peace was gone.

'Silly old dog,' said Heggi.

The others took up the *Raven*'s oars, following gently, and when they were secure, Bera took stock. Heggi was skimming stones for a joyful Rakki to swim after.

'This is a right place.'

Ginna smiled. 'Like a right whale.'

They went ashore to stretch their legs. Bera wondered if Faelan was thinking about Miska and how she would love the soft grass. He went straight off alone without saying where he was headed, and he must know the island already. Once more she wondered how men managed to hide so much of themselves. The Serpent King, Hefnir and, in that way, Egill: what did they need to hide? The ring of skulls in the Abbotry well; was that part of the cult of Brid? Faelan shared that belief, so was it the believers, not Brid, that were the danger?

You so want to trust him. Her skern was perched on a rock.

'I do trust him in every other way.'

Islanders are good at hiding feelings.

When they reached the top of the bluff and looked into the low valley, Heggi let out a long whistle. It was a mix of the most colours Bera had ever seen, woven into a dense mat.

'My eyes hurt with it,' said Ginna. She ran ahead, leaping over rocks like a young deer.

Sigrid used to say that there was a stage, if a girl liked a boy but was too young to know it, when she would show off her fettle – like stream-jumping or climbing for birds' eggs. It cheered Bera to see it.

'Come on!' Ginna shouted. 'I want to roll in red!'

'Bathe in blue!' yelled Heggi, chasing.

'Yell in yellow!'

'That's cheating, Bera!'

'Look at your dog!' Rakki kept crisscrossing in front of her, nose to the ground.

'Perch in purple!' said Ginna, slowing.

Heggi laughed. 'Plunge in pink!'

'Your turn again, Bera!' Ginna took her hand as she arrived, panting.

Bera threw herself down onto the springy flower meadow. 'Time to roll!'

They leapt on top of her and rolled, tickling each other. Rakki clambered over them, licking their faces, so that they shrieked and laughed and then slowly stilled, drunk with the scent and fellowship.

Faelan woke them. 'How would you like fresh bread?'

Heggi wiped his mouth. 'I'm already dribbling. Is it far?'

'Depends how much you want the bread.'

Heggi, Ginna and Rakki set off, racing each other.

'Rakki's running again,' said Faelan.

'Lopsided. Are they going the right way?'

'No.'

Bera laughed with him, but their closeness felt charged and they walked on, Faelan deep in thought. She wondered if he was reckoning his own feelings. They stopped at the foot of a steep slope covered in tiny white flowers.

Faelan whistled to the others and they came over, Rakki trailing behind, limping but determined. Bera respected dogs for never giving in but it squeezed her heart. She let the others go on ahead and then kept pace with him. Rakki looked up at her with his old grin.

'Don't tell the others,' she said, 'but I love you, you know.'

His eyes told her he already knew, and returned it a hundredfold without asking her for more. Why was it so easy with a dog?

They were waiting for her to catch up. It was another place that kept dwellings hidden in its folds. The scattered huts below them mostly had grass roofs, but some were covered in long, thin sticks. It was a plain village but lived in by folk who made stone troles.

The thrill of the new is also fear.

'Most are thatched with reeds,' Faelan said. 'See the one with a stream rushing past it? That's the mill. The one next to it is the kiln to dry the grain.'

'We had a huge mill in Seabost,' Heggi said, setting off.

'It was much smaller,' said Ginna, 'and kept breaking down.'

'Hefnir's men were never there to fix it,' Bera explained. 'Now can you stop my son before he tells the whole village how much better Seabost is?'

Faelan led them into the village. Some women were heading towards a rough stone longhouse and they turned wind-shrivelled faces at the sound of their voices.

Bera cautioned the others. 'We are strangers, with war threatening.'

'I met one of them earlier.' Faelan turned to the women. 'These folk are going to the longhouse and will show us the way.'

The women kept darting glances as they walked. Ginna attracted most attention and when a woman put a hand to her red hair, it troubled Bera.

'Say something,' she told Faelan, 'or I might start a fight.'

'They are my mother's folk, Bera.'

Heggi grabbed her. 'Look, those reeds are held in place by old fishing nets with stones tied to them. That's clever.'

Is the fear in your head or heart?

'I'll know when we are inside the longhouse. The stones will tell me.'

The threshold was silent. Faelan stopped them at the door, letting the islanders stare, scrying their faces like rune stones.

'Welcome, son of the Summer Isles,' said a short, clean-shaven man with hair as black as Faelan's. 'And welcome strangers.'

'He looks like a thrall,' hissed Heggi.

Bera clapped a hand over his mouth.

The man led them to the hearth and the fellowship of ale and song, which was shared the world over, began. He invited them to spend the night in the hall and Bera was now sure they would be safe, although a boy was sent to watch the *Raven*.

They met singers and skalds and shared some work songs from the whale roads that Ottar had taught her. Faelan blossomed, belonging to these folk who revelled in the words and rolled them round their mouths like Bera might a cloudberry. And so they sang and drank far into the bright-night.

Bera remembered trying to belong in Seabost, desperate to recite a poem that would be worthy of Hefnir. Then and now, she could never match up to her mother, nor would Alfdis help, even when Bera found she was gripping her beads.

A kind of sadness settled on her, an almost pleasurable feeling of longing for something she could not name. The faces around her had a wistfulness that felt familiar; perhaps she did belong. These islanders also lived by the sea's harsh laws and fickleness. All seafarers were chasing something better over the sea rim, often dying for it, like Sigrid's husband Bjarni who famously drowned seeking a narwhale. The sea endlessly called them; yet the songs spoke of yearning for home. Bera understood. Whether sailor or woman left ashore, they all shared the knowledge of loss, and always would. A crone stroked Bera's arm and half sang in words she understood: 'The only safe boat is a burned boat.'

'My father built them strong, and the whale roads are singing out there. Listen.'

She joined her small crew, where Faelan was heaping some furs as bedrolls. Other folk were dozing round the hall. Bera tried to sleep. Although it was darker here than on Ice Island, she missed the cradle-rock of the *Raven*. Pale light slatted through small, high windows, whose rough sacking covers swayed in a slight breeze. Could a Drorgher get in? Perhaps this earth could be dug all year and the corpse beheaded with a stone in its mouth, as Faelan had shown her. Like Asa. How had she died?

Hush, sweetheart. Sleep.

Terror swept in when she drowsed…

A monstrous group of longstones surrounded her, towering over her. There was intent in the rough granite, with yellow lichen giving expression to their malice. Her breath was rasping with fear. They tilted, teetered, toppling towards her with crushing weight…

'Bera! What is it?' Faelan's face was above her.

She pushed him away with both hands.

He sat back quickly. 'I'm sorry, you cried out; I was worried.'

He had been as solid as the longstone, as a drunken Hefnir, as the body-press of the Serpent. She turned her back to him and came face to face with her skern.

Unfair.

'Should I fear Faelan?'

Do you want to?

'What sort of answer is that? I don't want to fear anything.' She yawned. 'I shall go to the stone circle tomorrow and reckon the place.'

Today, sweetheart, he said, rocking her back to sleep.

The others came with her and stood in awe. There were three stone circles, one inside the other. The tallest stones were in the outer ring. Bera recognised several of them from the stippled markings in the lichen and could not shake off the foreboding of her dream. One of them had a wound that oozed blood, which, close-to, became a crack with brown granite streaks. Long, straight lines of stones made the place special but she could not reckon the whole pattern.

'Does anyone know its meaning?' she asked.

'The longstone circles were made before time,' said Faelan. 'They were old when the first ermites came, my mother said.'

Heggi threw a stick for his dog and then ran after him, whooping, with Ginna. It was very silent when they were gone.

'My scalp is prickling.' The dream did hold a warning.

'A warning.' Faelan echoed the thought. 'The stones were too dangerous to be left standing, so the early islanders buried them. They should never have been unearthed.'

'Things that are buried should be left in the ground.'

Faelan nodded. 'I'll be with the others.'

He understood her need to be alone. In order to know this longstone fully, she must show it respect.

It was twice the height of any other. Bera reckoned it to be roughly the length of a narwhale. The granite had a rippled, blue-grey sheen, as if it surged out of the ground like the sea beast through the waves. The sides were flocked with patches of yellow lichen and there were notches like scars, and she pictured the clumps of mosses and lichens as barnacles. Yet again she lamented killing the narwhale, hearing again its females' sad cries as they went out to the whale roads, but for the first time she remembered, with shame, that she had felt triumph in its death.

Touch it.

'No!'

This is not a living creature. Not as such.

Bera hesitated. 'It stung me before – the narwhale tusk, on the killing beach.'

She put a hand to the longstone's crackled surface. It was surprisingly warm, so she turned and pressed her weight against it.

'It soaks up light and stores its power.'

That's part of it.

Bera went to the shadowed side to say a prayer to the narwhale, whose death had begun a chain of events that had brought her here. Its tusk had power and she felt it in this stone, too.

A flash of something.

She whipped away: a distant echo of spilled blood somewhere here. Dark and old, like Hel.

Sacrifice.

'There was death here,' she told her shivering skern.

And in Iraland. The Long Dead.

Bera hurried back to the sunlit face. She knew the ancients held darkness, and rested her cheek against the unyielding stone. It was like trying to be close to Hefnir.

It's not about what's there but what's not there.

'A riddle.'

It soaks up event.

Like thresholds. Bera willed the stone to tell her its purpose.

Yet it cannot speak.

'All right, please explain.'

Mortal folk always look at things, instead of the spaces in between. It's where things happen. It's where we skerns are, and Fetches, and others. You Vallas should know why liminal places are important: it's where you find yourself, right up against the edge so you can't miss us.

'Just tell me where to stand.'

In the middle.

Bera went through the stones, trying to judge where the exact centre might be, with the lines and circles fanning out around her. It was hard to reckon, with some gaps wider than others. Perhaps some stones were missing. Her skern was in the wrong place, tapping his foot, but she gave in and could instantly feel the vibration. She stood for a while as if on the *Raven*, turning her face to the wind. Here was the very centre of the land's energy, but also the hopes and future of everyone who had ever lived on this island. She was a needle charging on its lodestone.

So start spinning.

Bera's arms lifted of their own accord as the energy filled her. She found herself slowly turning, like the needle would do in a bowl of water, turning north, east, south, west, until she fixed, pointing True North...

'Chaos is coming, Chaos is coming, Chaos is coming...'

She could see the pattern but she kept spinning round and round, faster and faster, until she could touch the four quarters of the Known World, through fire, air, water; she was the flickering shuttle of the Vallas' dark weaving and could not stop what had to come.

'The ultimate reach...' Utter blackness.

Someone helped her sit. Two Faelans.

'Did you faint?' he asked.

Bera covered her eyes. 'Stop the stones whirling.'

'Here.' He gave her a white flower. 'Bridwell. Press the petals between your eyebrows. Up a bit.'

She needed to regain her balance in every way. The coolness helped, and Faelan did not pester her with questions. When she opened her eyes again the world was still.

'See the long lines of stones?' she said. 'They make a cross.'

'The sign of Brid.' He touched his wooden cross.

'More powerful than that. The cross fixes a pattern that is older than we can imagine. It is a force outside time that connects to the universe. It's what I saw when I held Obsidian. It's where the Vallas weave our Fate.'

Faelan picked at the grass, thinking, and it was her turn to give him time. His fingers were covered in red, pearly burns. Bera wondered if his wounded and slight body could ever feel as shielding as Hefnir's. The thought surprised her. She dealt with everything alone.

Her skern tapped his bony chest. *And me. Tell him.*

'This is more powerful than ordinary war, Faelan. I don't yet have all the knowledge. But the stones want blood.'

11

It was only an island hop in fair weather but Faelan told them a boat could easily be caught in rip tides in the narrow channel between the islands, so they would take the longer route and stay outside. When Heggi and Ginna were together at the helm, Bera asked him how he knew so much about these small islands.

'My mother loved to speak of them.'

She was surprised. 'I thought you came from Iraland?'

'My mother's mother did. We were taken back there when my mother was seized by pirates.'

'We?'

'I was b-born here.'

Bera could understand the gut-tug of belonging yet not belonging. His eyes had revealed it when they first sighted the most northerly of the isles but she had not recognised it then.

'They took her to be a slave,' he went on. 'She b-bartered for my life.'

'What did she trade?'

'Her b-b-body.' Rage made him stammer. 'Slaves with a b-b-b-baby inside cost more.'

Bera dropped her voice. 'You know Heggi's birth mother killed herself when she was taken?'

'Perhaps she could not face life without her son.'

It was a point of view Bera had not considered. 'I thought her love for Heggi wasn't strong enough to live for, to fight for.'

'That's because you love him, don't you, Bera? Even though he is not your own son.'

'I would die to save him.'

The boy himself arrived and flumped next to his dog, who put his head on his knees and went straight back to sleep.

'I'm tired.'

Faelan prodded him. 'You're supposed to be on the helm.'

'Ginna wants to do the next bit on her own,' said Heggi. 'What were you talking about?'

'These islands.' Bera pushed a boat rag back into his pocket. 'Faelan said his mother taught him all the safe passages.'

'It was my lullaby,' Faelan said. 'Islanders can say the landmarks before they first go out to sea.'

'Fishermen always do,' Heggi declared. 'And traders, like my father.'

Raiders, like his father, had to risk sailing unknown shores. Bera looked at Faelan's clenched jaw. Had Hefnir taken islanders as slaves? Heggi himself had noticed the likeness to some of their thralls. Was he forgetting his father's nature, making a story for himself to live by? She, too, kept shutting her mind from how much of Hefnir might appear in his son as he grew older. Better that than become the Serpent that was in his mother's blood.

They ran the *Raven* onto a shallow, sandy beach and rolled it up to the seaweed tideline.

'There's more difference here between high and low water than at Ice Island,' Faelan said.

'Let's use a land anchor in case,' said Bera.

They planned to leave the next day, so Heggi announced he and Ginna were off on a long skime and would need rations.

'Skime?' Faelan asked.

Ginna laughed. 'It's like looking for something you don't know is there.'

'Ah.' He thought about it. 'Or longing for something you've never had.'

'Don't get lost,' Bera said. 'And don't let the wretched dog get lost either. Or hurt.'

'Leave enough for us to eat anyway,' teased Faelan.

They went off hand in hand, with the dog gamely leading the way.

'I don't know how old Rakki is,' she said. 'I can't bear to think of him dying.'

'You and I have seen so much death.'

'Yet there's something about an animal you love…'

When he did not respond she found him worrying at his face.

'You can't rub out your wounds.' Bera took his hand away. 'And I don't just mean the ones outside.'

'I want to see where we once lived.'

'Wait. You have never talked about a brother or sister. What happened to the baby forced on your mother?'

'A wolf took it.' Faelan dared her to comment. 'Are you coming?'

He set off without waiting.

'I expect you want to be alone, then, Wolf,' she muttered, and then called after him, 'I'll stay near the boat, keep watch.'

He disappeared over a ridge. Bera shrugged. She liked being alone to think.

For a while she simply sat at the top of a cliff where she could keep watch over the *Raven* and gaze westwards. She lifted her face to the sun, which she fancied was stronger here, even when clouds scudded past it. The sky was full of birds; most she recognised but some were new to her, with strange cries, and she wanted to learn their names. Far below her the ledges crawled with black and green crabs with heavy claws that dragged beside them. Sleek seals slid from offshore rocks into the fish-full waters. Time and again their glistening heads would pop up, listening for the cry of their own youngsters, expecting to be fed. Plentiful, easy nature.

This is you thinking, is it?

'I listened instead.' Bera snubbed her nose at her skern. 'And now I'm going to take stock of the island.'

You are hoping to find Faelan.

The wildflowers were arranged differently here: there was a distinct pattern, with backlit grass making a bright green border and background. The wind ruffled the sward, making the pattern shift, and perhaps this constant breeze kept all the plants short. A swoop, and a sea eagle had some creature in its talons, and away. Kill or be killed, but with clear rules and only to keep starvation away. Clean.

Soft rain fell from somewhere. There were the same clouds, some grey, but none looked dark enough for rain and they were distant. Bera saw a line of rainbows, bridges across the sky, which melted away as quickly as they had appeared. It was a reminder of home, and the leaving of it.

She had never been here before but felt she knew it. 'I feel that the land knows me, too. Like it's been waiting.'

Watch. Her skern put a sharp fingernail between her brows...

She saw an unending line of lives stretching far, far into the deep past, beyond when the stone circle was made by men. The rainbow bridge stretched into night and became the white road of stars, Bifrost, beloved by sailors. Then the past folk streamed past her across the bridge. Like the chain of Vallas, it was a long line of mothers, too: babies born and babies lost; of possible lives and lives to come...

'Is belonging only for ordinary folk?'

Her skern was stifled by too much past. *It shows the dullness of repetition.*

Bera walked on, sinking into springy moss and soft grass. Nothing was dull. The clouds burned away to leave a blue sky that went beyond the edge of the Known World. As if it was the first day of spring, she took off her boots and leggings to feel the upwelling energy and crossed a crystal stream. The small stones were sharp and she stepped carefully, watching tiny fish scatter away. Although her feet turned pink, Bera was shocked to be able to feel them when she reached the other side.

It's not meltwater. Her skern was in the middle of the stream, looking down his long legs.

'You look like a heron.'

Thank you.

'It wasn't a compliment.'

There were healing plants wherever she trod. The dew had soaked down into the earth so she threw herself down and rolled, crushing the leaves and dizzying herself with their scent. Then she lay back and shielded her eyes from the sun.

Her skern settled round her neck and fear returned to clamp her guts.

'How can I keep you close in Iraland?'

Hush, sweetheart. We are here now.

Bera breathed deep into her stomach and held it. Her heartbeat slowed. Could she stop time or slow it to the timing of her breath? To stay here, where the land felt as if it was imagined by some earlier Vallas; women who created land out of a single wish for peace? Was that what she had been shown to take with her to Iraland?

There are no skerns there to tell me. It was a lament.

She rolled onto her side to find peace in the wide expanse of water. The seas were running from the island, streaks of white spreading out towards the skyline. Bera made them a sign of moving forward, suggesting everything she might be and might achieve. She had found hope.

Heggi and Ginna came back with shining faces that suggested the island had also given them a glimpse of a brighter future. The young couple might have already grabbed it of course, but Bera refused to believe her boy was old enough.

'This is a magical place,' said Ginna.

Bera agreed. 'And the weather is so settled now, after that mist. I think it's a perfect summer.'

Ginna lay beside her. 'The most summeriest of any summer.'

Bera laughed. 'There's deep winter so maybe this is deep summer.'

'No, wait!' cried Ginna. 'There's deep winter... and so it's high summer!'

'Yes! The highest summer we've ever known!'

Heggi shook his head in disgust. 'Girls.' He whistled for his dog. 'Let's you and me find Faelan.'

Bera pulled Ginna to her feet and they chased after him, laughing. Soon some instinct made them slow and they came to a dark lake. Dense mats of huge round leaves patched the surface with pointed spikes, golden in the low sun. Faelan was sitting on a rock, staring at the still water. There was something intense about him that Bera did not want to disturb, and she put a finger to her lips.

He had a pale cloth spread on his lap, which he carefully folded and dipped in the water three times, like a ritual. He wrung it out and then held it to his scars. Bera made them wait until he had completed it three times and then they went down to join him.

Rakki arrived first and Faelan shoved the cloth behind him, like Heggi hiding a piece of stolen cheese. When Bera arrived she reached behind him and pulled it out.

'Whatever works, Faelan. Every place has its own powers. I'll put salve on again later.' She sat beside him and gave him back the cloth. 'Does the water itself have properties?'

'I was shown a long time ago.' His voice was small. 'I... think... it's the right lake.'

'I don't guard my knowledge, Faelan.'

It caused him to face her. 'Oh no! I'm not guarding... I didn't want you to think I doubted your skills.'

'Your mother had different knowledge, so help me learn.'

'Oh, not now,' groaned Heggi. 'It's boring.'

Ginna punched him.

'It must have been before I was five.' Faelan worried at the cloth.

Before the pirates took them. Bera had an urge to hold the cloth against her own face to take on his hurt.

'Go on.'

'You must soak a piece of clean linen in the lake, wring it out and press it on the wound.' No one told him they had seen it. 'This water is twice as potent because it holds Brid's white flowers, which are a sign of rebirth.'

'The leaves are like what we ate off in the Abbotry,' Heggi told Ginna. 'Platters, they call them.'

'Swanky.' She smiled at Bera.

'You should see the flowers when they open right out,' said Faelan. 'They are the size of swans.'

'A good try, Faelan,' said Bera, 'but it's another tale to make fun of us Northmen.'

'I believed it.'

'You were only five!' Heggi scoffed.

'The flowers are real, though,' said Faelan. 'They call them water lilies. A sign of purity, like Brid herself.'

'As long as it slakes my thirst.' Heggi squatted down and cupped some water into his mouth.

His wet dog bounded into the lake and then splashed over to the others.

'Watch out!' Bera stepped away too late.

Rakki shook himself to his great satisfaction and grinned at the shrieks and drenching of everyone else.

'Bad dog!' said Bera, kissing him.

'Who, Faelan?' Ginna scanned the empty landscape. 'Who are the folk who call them water lilies?'

'I should have said "called". I don't know if there was another settlement, after.'

Bera wanted to be alone with him. 'Shall we see who gets to the boat first? One, two…'

Heggi set off at once with Rakki. Ginna shrugged at Bera and followed.

'Don't go yet, Faelan.' Bera took a linen cloth from her pocket, which she folded. 'This is one of your mother's.'

'Yes.'

She followed the same ritual she had seen him do.

'Your wounds have healed, Bera.'

'Only the ones you can see.' Keeping her back turned, Bera held the cloth against her heart.

Every loss.

Faelan was a warmth behind her, but, with an instinct for unhappiness, did not presume.

All the losses of her life included her daughter. Her fault: she had wanted to leave her with Sigrid. There was not enough water in this lake to cure her shame. She could not speak of that to anyone. There were too many demands on a Valla. If only she could be a plain woman, a good mother. It was so clear to her in the islands that she was mourning the life she could never have, beside the man she might have loved.

I dare you.

Bera took Faelan's hand and intertwined her fingers. The pump of blood. She quickly let go, failing her skern's dare, and was grateful to the sensitive man who never pressed her to explain anything.

'Come,' Faelan said. 'One last task.'

He led her to a bent old hagthorn tree that had pale scraps of cloth hanging limply from its branches like long flowers. He tied his piece beside the most threadbare.

'They face the weather this side,' he said.

'Why would that help?'

'They rot quicker. "When a rag has gone to dust, so all hurts will heal... and must." Or something.'

His wry smile was touching, and Bera tied her rag next to his, with no belief it would work.

They put out to sea again without getting the lines ready. They could do all the checks underway, and Faelan said their passage luck would hold. Of course, it did not. The weather could change in a heartbeat and a Valla should give warning. As soon as they reached the Pinch the wind stiffened and the *Raven* butted into choppy waves. Bera took the helm while the others got the sail set and then a squall hit from another direction.

'I should have seen this coming!' The wind whipped away her apology.

You've grown dull with wanting to be ordinary. Her skern went off to glower from a bucket.

The sky became a wan yellow, as if it was seasick. For all the boat's clean lines and Ottar's skill, Bera could find no steerage in the quartering seas. It was heavy work to stay roughly on course and she was not surprised when Ginna turned green.

'Get her to leeward, Heggi,' she shouted. 'Hold her tight at the rail.'

'I know!'

Faelan hauled himself on handholds to the helm. Bera thought he would take over, like Hefnir, and prepared to fight, but he stood close and his quiet presence was heartening.

The storm passed overhead with clouds like fists. They watched crackles of lightning fork into the sea.

'I'm glad Miska isn't here.' He meant the very opposite.

'You steer,' Bera said. 'I'll make sure Ginna eats something.'

The skies cleared and the *Raven* picked up speed. As soon as they were out of the Pinch Heggi wanted to steer.

'To Midway Isle!' he whooped.

Faelan pointed at a group of tall rocks that stood off a coast.

'They mark the entrance to a dangerous whirlpool. When we get there, watch out for their waves. If they get steep enough, boats never get inside, for Blue Men surge up in the crests and grasp the sailors.'

'And drown them?' Heggi's voice throbbed with eagerness.

'I would like to drown,' groaned Ginna.

Bera rubbed her back. 'Eat. I promise you will feel better then.'

A rope snapped.

'The yardarm!' Before it crashed, Bera rushed with Faelan to take down the sail.

'We'll have to put in at a skerry to fix it,' he said.

'Then take them ashore,' Bera said. 'Ginna will feel better on land.'

'Why not you?'

'I want to mend it.'

You want to suffer.

It was her fault. Her father had taught her to do proper checks before setting out. She had been lulled by the peace of the Summer Isles.

Your fears are centred on Iraland so you miss the present threats.

The others jumped ashore and Bera began cutting out the frayed parts. Hefnir must have re-rigged it because the rope was horsehair, which made her hands bleed when she spliced it. She cursed it all.

'More time lost, too. What if the war has started in Dyflin?'

I don't want to go at all.

'The pirate boat's large crew could make running repairs, or keep rowing if the wind dropped. They might not have stopped at all.'

Bera dipped her hands in a bucket of seawater and they smarted. She shook them about and found she had summoned the others. They pushed the boat from the shallows and clambered aboard.

Ginna's colour was back.

Heggi was grinning. 'I named it Pig Island.'

'It's true, what Faelan told us,' Ginna said, 'but now the pigs don't trust men and run away!'

'Good,' Bera said.

Heggi talked over everyone. 'Rakki would have caught one but he had a lie-down in the shade.'

Bera felt a clutch of some small fear.

Old age.

'Pigs can eat a grown man whole,' said Faelan. 'Rakki had more sense than to get near.'

Bera smiled her thanks for his taking the dog's side, as ever.

'My watch,' he said. 'I'll take us through the Maelstrom.'

'We faced it in the White Sea,' Bera said. 'It can't be here as well.'

'We call it a whirlpool.'

Heggi beamed at the idea. 'Perhaps it's bigger! It might be so big that every bit of land, every shore, every isle, gets sucked down into the Skraken's maw!'

Bera was pleased that his lust for destruction was because he had never been close to it.

They were soon nearing the tall rocks marking the start of the troubled waters.

'Say more about the Blue Men,' said Heggi.

'They thrive on stories,' Faelan said. 'I hope you have a good one, Heggi, because if the Blue Men don't like it, they will swamp our boat.'

'I'm not very good at them.' Heggi rubbed his chin.

'Are there Summer Isles stories, Faelan?' Bera asked.

'They are coming back to me,' he said. 'Listen to the waves. Each one has its own tale. It's as if my mother is whispering to me.'

A memory flashed, of sitting beside Alfdis as she told the beads... the sea-milled glass and the drowned Valla...

Heggi patted her hand. 'Listen. It's Faelan's story for the Blue Men.'

'This is not your Maelstrom, Bera, but this one is nearly as dangerous if we get it wrong. Folk say you can hear its drumming roar from as far as the longstone circle when it's at full spate.'

A throb began in Bera's ears. 'We should have been through before it starts to run but the squall and mending delayed us.'

Faelan agreed. 'And there's a way to go yet.'

'What is its name?'

'You want power over it?' He shook his head. 'The trouble is, no one knows. But there's a story about it.'

'Tell us, please,' said Bera.

'It starts like all stories, with a king and his beautiful daughter.'

Heggi smirked at Ginna, who elbowed him. Bera thought of Bjorn's idiotic doting and liked Ginna all the more.

Faelan went on. 'The King of the Summer Isles had a daughter as fair as the driven snow. Many men wanted to marry her but she refused them all. Then one day a Black man came.'

Bera started. 'A dragon body?'

'No, no, with real black skin that glowed like an ember pulled from the flames.'

'Like the Warden in the tower,' said Bera. 'So beautiful.'

'Anyway, these two fell madly in love.'

'Of course,' Heggi and Bera said together.

They held the crook of their little fingers and made a silent wish.

'That's for luck,' Ginna informed Faelan.

He nodded. 'Your man's name was Brecken. He asked the king for her hand in marriage…'

'And the king said no!' shouted Heggi.

'You want to tell the story, Heggi? Then I can get on with steering.'

Heggi flushed red. 'Kings always say no.'

'And always to three suitors,' said Ginna.

In stories, everything comes in threes. Powerful lesson to remember.

'Who are my three?' Bera asked, but her skern only pointed at himself.

Faelan steered through a steep wave and then carried on. 'The king decreed that Brecken could only marry her if he could keep his boat in the whirlpool for—'

'Three—' Heggi began.

Bera shoved him. 'We know!'

'Brecken accepted the challenge, saying' – Faelan raised an eyebrow at Heggi – 'three days and three nights would be easy. But he had no plan, so his men refused to go with him and the islanders told him all he could do was pray. He sank to his knees on the beach, mocked by the sucking of the deadly whirlpool. But an old crone was gathering driftwood on the shore…'

'There always is!'

Ginna clapped a hand over Heggi's mouth.

'… and she told him this' – Faelan put on a crone voice – '"You must anchor in the centre of the whirlpool." Brecken was aghast, saying, "I will be sucked to my death." "No," said the crone, "for you must lay three anchors, with ropes made from three things. The first will be hound's hair; the second horsehair and the third maiden hair."'

Bera gave Faelan a hard look, suspecting it was not the hair from a maiden's head. He winked and carried on. 'Brecken gave the crone a gold coin. She told him that islanders could make the hound's hair rope and the horsehair rope but only in his own kingdom would he find the maiden-hair rope.'

The waves were growing steeper with the Blue Men's impatience.

'Is it much longer, Faelan?' asked Bera.

'No. He returned to his kingdom and asked the maidens to make him a rope made from the… er, hair of maidens.'

'Was it red?' Ginna held up her plait.

'It just had to be from maidens,' said Heggi, smirking. 'Ones who had not lain with any man.'

'I know full well what a maiden is,' Ginna said. 'Thank you.'

Faelan was squinting. 'Is the water very ruffled over there?'

Bera wondered if his eyesight would ever heal; the white water was obvious. Would the Blue Men let them pass?

'Please get to the end,' she said.

'I'm enjoying it,' said Heggi, suspiciously keen.

'Brecken sailed out at slack water and put out his three anchors. When the whirlpool was in full spate on the first night, the hound's hair rope snapped. On the second night, the horsehair rope snapped.'

'So the maiden hair one was strongest!' Ginna raised her arms, the winner.

'Sadly not,' said Faelan. 'On the third night the last rope snapped and poor Brecken drowned.'

'No!' Bera cried.

'That's all wrong!' Heggi joined in. 'Stories must end happily for the lovers!'

'A Valla drowned,' said Bera, 'whose twisting hair was made by sea-change into a narwhale tusk.'

The others stared at her.

'I needed a very short story for the Blue Men,' she explained. 'Feel them swirling the *Raven*.'

'That wasn't the end,' said Faelan stiffly. 'Brecken's faithful dog pulled him to the shore, where the king's daughter found him. She vowed to make the lying crone pay the blood debt. She saw her admiring Brecken's gold coin and drew her sword. "Wait!" said the crone. "Go to his kingdom and ask. If you do not find the answer you can return and kill me."'

Heggi frowned. 'Then what?'

'Then nothing. That's the story.'

A poor ending brings worse trouble.

'I can hear the whirlpool sucking,' said Heggi.

Bera looked across to the shore. The grey crags were frowning but the seabirds gave no warning cries.

'It's the suck of waves off the cliff, Heggi, and our own dear dog has told me the true ending. Brecken's faithful hound got his master ashore in time for his true love to breathe life back into him and he killed the wicked king and they all lived happily ever after.'

'Even the dog.' Faelan smiled.

'Especially the dog, who never ran out of bones.'

The Blue Men laughed with them, jostling playfully as they passed into the Corrybrecken before the flood. Heggi whooped as the *Raven* cut through rippling white water. Bera let Faelan stay at the helm to share her love for this boat. It was the most generous thing she had ever done.

I hope he's not completely blind. Her skern was making the bucket his only friend.

They passed Midway Isle during the night and the greyness of Iraland appeared on the sea rim at dawn. When Faelan took the helm from Bera she asked how his story really ended. His eyes glittered in the dim light.

'The king's daughter went to Brecken's homeland and asked why the maiden-hair rope had broken. It was from one maiden alone, who was his own true love. When she heard he was dead, she plunged a dagger into her heart, saying, "I sent him to his death. I am with child, so my hair was not pure."'

What message was he giving her?

'Same as the Valla turned into a narwhale tusk. Love and death, Faelan.'

He stopped her leaving. 'The point is, was the baby Brecken's? If it was, he would have known she lied.'

While others slept, Bera had time to ponder this and was sure the baby could not be Brecken's. So he may have blithely gone to his death, trusting his faithless love, or he knew she had been unfaithful and wanted to drown. Either way, she wondered if two people could ever find the complete trust that she had for her dog and the *Raven*.

The others woke when the coast was plain and gathered around her.

'Iraland!' Ginna was breathless; with fear or hope?

A low moan rolled round the bucket.

'There are so many river openings,' said Heggi. 'Let's go upriver!'

Faelan took the helm. 'Wolves are everywhere, Heggi, unseen until they attack.'

'Rakki and I will fight them.' Heggi waved his knife.

'Don't risk your faithful hound,' said Ginna.

She kissed him and Heggi allowed her to sheath his knife, smiling.

Ginna would be the making of Heggi and Bera did not need Valla skills to see it. She wished this sweet girl was her daughter, not Valdis, and flushed with shame.

You don't fear Ginna, that's all. Her skern was at her ear. *She will not be the next Valla, bringing your death.*

Bera brushed him away like a midge. She wondered if smiths passed on their skills and feared their sons? It seemed unlikely – and Dellingr had lost his son in the terrible passage to Ice Island. The smith had been her rock; the only person who could draw out her Valla power with the lore of iron. She loved to watch his strong, skilful hands working it. A father's hands that she could trust. But on Ice Island there was nothing to work. She had made him less the man, snatching him from where he belonged to settle in a land where no one belonged. And it had killed his wife somehow. He would be right to lose all trust in her.

'We must go straight to Dyflin,' she said. 'I took our folk to Ice Island so now I must protect them.'

'We are.' Heggi gave Faelan the look of men together on a ship of fools.

Before Bera could remonstrate, Ginna hugged her. 'I miss Papa so much, Bera. He knows you will come.'

Faelan held his wrists together, signing to Bera. Her folk might already be slaves – but surely she would feel it?

What of the shadow-boats, a dark stain on the sea rim, and the stinkhorn stench of decay? Bera realised she had been expecting utter darkness. Instead of which, this sunlit land was a piercing green that hurt her eyes if she looked at it straight.

Her skern was singing mournfully, back in his bucket:

> *There is terror by day as well as by night,*
> *Comfort in darkness and danger in light.*

A jutting headland forced them out to sea again and when they looked back the rock was snarling.

'Like a giant wildcat,' Ginna said, and put Rakki on the alert.

Bera needed no skern's verse or savage headland to put her on guard. All the peace and renewal of the Summer Isles was leaching away. And then they drew near the coast and joined a group of trading boats heading towards Dyflin. There was a pall of soot in the air and the reek of a city carried towards them on the wind. Bera steered to follow the knarrers, who would know the safe channels.

At the next headland, a high wall stretched away into the distance. Something monstrous and earthly must be kept behind so solid a defence.

'Is Sigrid safe?' she asked her skern.

The bucket was silent.

Bera yearned to turn the boat round, yet the duty she owed as a Valla and woman lay in Dyflin.

'What's the wall for?' asked Ginna.

Faelan said, 'To keep wolves out. They couldn't stop the sea wolves, though.'

'Vikings?' Heggi lit up.

'Traders in slaves. The women were especially beautiful here, but now it's a barren land of hags. The others have long since been sold.'

That was why Hefnir made no distinction between trading and raiding where a woman had the same value as a fine brooch and could be stolen and sold. Or an add-on to a boat deal, like herself.

'And the biggest slave market is here in Dyflin.' He had silenced Heggi.

'We won't get snatched, will we?' Ginna asked. The freckles were vivid on her face.

'We are free women,' Bera said.

Faelan rubbed his nose. 'Yes, and so all those poor women supposed.'

Bera felt a flash of anger for the slaves, and then for herself. Had she treated her thralls as free women in Seabost? At the start, she had been in awe of them. She had to concentrate on steering, for there was a jostle ahead with other boats of all shapes of hull and sail coming up from the south.

'And those,' Faelan went on. 'See the wide ones, there? They're full of slaves from all the cities that border the river Seven, and there are many. They'll be sold for more money here.'

'How do you know so much?' Heggi asked. 'You were only a child.'

'The men I served on Ice Island talked about their wealth.'

Bera remembered the woman stroking Ginna's hair. Like beaten copper, high value. Was she putting the girl into danger for the sake of saving the others? One of them was her father, so Bera would have to try and keep everyone safe. At this moment, it meant attending to the *Raven* before turning into the entrance.

'Lower the sail.'

When Faelan and Heggi got in place to row, Rakki curled up at his boy's feet, secure in the stops. Bera envied him.

Then, from behind the opposite headland, an immense vessel appeared, bristling with oars. Its dragon prow, with jaws wide open, was as tall as the tree it had been carved from and the noise and speed was like nothing Bera could have imagined. As it turned into the channel, Heggi stopped rowing to gape at it and Faelan shouted at him to keep rowing.

'Wake coming,' Bera warned. 'Hold tight, Ginna.'

'Easy oars,' Faelan commanded.

Heggi slowed and braced Rakki with his feet. Bera marvelled at how cleanly the dragon boat drove through the water with not a splash, despite so many oars on the stroke. These were proper seamen.

'We won't roll,' she said.

Faelan gave Heggi the stroke.

'Why are there so many aboard?' asked Ginna.

'Part of the war fleet,' said Faelan.

How wrong it was to admire something deadly. Ottar would have, and Bera thought this war was already making her more like her father than she wanted.

'They have fifty or sixty men aboard,' he said. 'Ottar should be with us, Bera. They build them here.'

Perhaps you should use both your parents if we are to survive. His reedy voice was unsure.

Boats of all kinds filled the channel. Most were longboats without bossed shields, like Hefnir's fleet of seaworthy trading ships. Others, heavily stacked with goods, were coastal broad-beamed knarrers that were wallowing in the crisscross wakes as they headed out of harbour. Several boats looked like bigger versions of Egill's black-pitched curricle, with ten or more rowers, but a few were painted blood-red, with striped sails and strangely hatted crew. Bera studied every dragon boat but there was no sign of her folk. It was a real threat now. How could she save them?

Faelan told them all the Known World came here to trade.

'Or be traded,' Bera said. What if her folk were already gone from Dyflin?

The wide channel opened into a harbour thronged with vessels. The war fleet was anchored in the whole eastern quarter and smaller dragon boats lined up towards the quay.

Heggi whistled. 'I can't count them all!'

'We don't have words for that many,' Ginna said. 'How will we ever find Papa?'

Faelan glanced at Bera. They both knew the high-value smith would be the first to be sold. Sigrid and the babies second. What would happen to the chain of Vallas if Valdis was taken away? Was this to be Bera's punishment for abandoning her? At least she was sure that she would feel the world tilt if the small Valla had already been sold.

They coasted in through the rafted lines of trading vessels, keeping to the westerly lanes. Ahead were the grey stone walls and turrets that made the city a fortress, and outside them a quay stretched into the distance with small trading boats tied up alongside. They cruised along the lines until they came to three longboats that were roughly the *Raven*'s size, so they went alongside the outer vessel and tied up. Heggi took more lines ashore to make the boat secure and then quickly came back aboard.

'Dyflin's not like Smolderby.'

The south-westerly wind had prepared Bera for a bigger and smellier city but not its deafening bustle. The broad quayside was a commotion of folk on a mission – like kicking an ants' nest. Busy people streamed around booths, livestock pens, barrels, sacks, boxes and crates; they ducked under stretched nets and sails and barged the folk mending them. All were about their raucous business: calling out their wares, swearing, laughing, bartering. Fishwives sang. Snarling dogs fought pigs for scraps. Geese and chickens squawked indignantly out of their way. Bands of filthy urchins ran amongst them all, yelling. The stink was worse than the noise and the danger worse than the brutes of Smolderby.

'I want to go home,' said Ginna.

Heggi put an arm round her. They could not, must not, and had no home.

Bera had to give them hope. 'Let's take stock before we go ashore. We might be in and out.'

Faelan did not look at her.

'Can we eat first?' asked Heggi.

Bera agreed, so that they would not have to enter a tavern too soon and be seen by the Serpent's crew. Rakki hung about with a heart-rending droop until Bera gave him some of her cheese and then he stared fixedly at Heggi with the same success.

Faelan took a long swig of ale, then wiped his mouth. 'Let's get this done. We need to get ashore while the tide's high. It must be a long climb up that ladder at dead low.'

Bera frowned. 'Rakki must come with us. Heggi, tie a rope to him, or he'll be off after rats. The place is running with them.'

Faelan showed Ginna how to cross other boats. 'Step over here, look, where the hull is lowest, but be sure to ask for permission first.'

No one was on the inner boats, so they were quickly up on the quay. Bera checked the mooring lines, wanting to leave in a hurry. Theirs could not be slipped, and she was anxious.

'What happens to the *Raven* when the tide goes out?'

Heggi tapped his nose. 'We're tied to the other boats and I took a line to the quay as well.'

'It's as slack as the other lines,' said Faelan.

'But it's not a slip.'

Heggi paled. Perhaps he was also remembering trying to cast off with the enemy thundering down the jetty and what had happened to Ottar. Bera hid her tears by remaking the knot.

Faelan led them along the quayside, finding gaps in the crowd and always making sure the others were keeping up. Then he stopped dead. Beyond him, a group of children were standing in a long roped line, the only points of stillness.

Bera pulled Ginna closer. 'They look lifeless.'

'Blank with shock,' said Faelan.

Then they began to be passed down onto a skiff.

'What's happening?' asked Ginna.

'They'll take them out to one of the big vessels,' Faelan said.

'Were you that age?' asked Heggi.

'Younger.'

Faelan's face was anguished. Perhaps it made a memory sharper to see a past self in the present, but the set of his shoulders armed him against any comfort.

'So… was Faelan a slave?' whispered Ginna.

Bera nodded. 'As children always will be.'

They scrambled to catch up with him and then got into step with the crowd, walking quickly, keeping their heads down and never staring at the strange folk, not even at a man as tall as a trole with flame-red hair. Heggi gawped, but Bera moved him on fast. There was running and there was walking: this was a mix of both and she hated being carried along like a log into the maelstrom. Poor Rakki was struggling so she tugged at Faelan's tunic and he understood and cut across to the booths that lined the city walls.

There, the flow became more leisurely as folk bought and bartered. Bera listened closely but the coarse drawls and twangs were hard to understand, even when they were Northmen. The others, small and dark like Faelan, made no sense at all. The Northmen replied, so they must have some common tongue. Bera hated not understanding and it put them at greater risk. She glimpsed her skern in a bronze bowl but it was her own reflection. She felt alone, her skills and skern dwindling in this place.

'What's all the broken glass for?' Heggi asked a trader.

'To make bracelets.' The man made every s into sh. 'From Saxony, mostly.'

Bera touched her beads unthinkingly.

The trader sniffed. 'Some o' them stones are worth a bit. Not much, not all, but I could give you a price.'

'They're not for sale.'

'Everything's for sale, girlie,' he said, licking his lips.

Faelan stopped her hand. 'He's not worth it, Bera.'

'You're right.' She walked on. 'We dare not make a scene anyway.'

'Where's Saxony?' asked Ginna.

Heggi wafted a hand northwards.

No idea, mouthed Faelan.

Bera ruffled Heggi's hair, her boykin again, and her mood recovered.

Faelan told them goods were coming into Dyflin from all over: from the Golden Horn to the Marsh Lands. Bera had heard the names in Seabost. There were walrus tusks from the utter north of the Ice-Rimmed Sea; soapstone from the Southern Isles and drab goods Bera had never seen before, like tin plates, cups, platters and beakers from the west. There was finely worked silver from the east and the best thing: a shining cloth that was the colour of buttermilk.

The trader, as thickset as Ottar, held it out to her. 'Feel it. Go on, 'old it up to yer face.'

It was a butterfly kiss on her cheek.

'It's the exact colour of your hair,' said Faelan, a catch in his voice.

Bera thrust it back on the stall. Could they all see how much she wanted it and how much she wanted to hear Faelan speak like that again?

'It's called silk,' said the trader. 'All the big traders cross the Midworld Sea, to cities where more people live than the rest of the Known World put together.'

'He's even more swanky than you.' Ginna poked Heggi.

'Under that Sea is where the Skraken lives,' Heggi boasted. 'His head, anyway.'

'Swallowin' its own tail.' The trader kept his eyes on Bera. 'Sometimes it screams in agony and then it gulps 'ole ships down. Worth it, though, for that silk. It's why the price is 'igh.'

'The Skraken's stomach is in the Ice-Rimmed Sea,' said Heggi. 'It's what he keeps ripping open, so it's actually much worse where we live.'

Fear broke the silk's fascination and Bera pulled Heggi away. 'Don't tell strangers where we're from.'

'Why not? Anyway, they can tell by looking at us, like Faelan said about your hair.'

It was true. Their skin colour, hair, height, proclaimed them Northmen.

'Faelan looks like he belongs, though, so they don't stare,' Heggi said. 'Till they see his burns, anyway.'

'I hope he didn't hear that!'

Faelan and Ginna were moving to the next stall.

'You watch. Even ugly folk gawp at him.'

Bera felt a deep pity that Faelan would despise. 'Let's keep up.'

It was a stall of carved tokens on leather thongs. Heggi joined the others, bartering with the trader. Bera hung back to study the tokens. Besides the familiar Thor hammers and Brid crosses were many of the Skraken, forever eating its own tail, a symbol of eternal life. She thought about that. Did its constant pain mean life always renews in torture? Did the Vallas know this and was that why it was the bracelet her mother wore? Or worse, did the Vallas cause it? They were as sharp and indifferent as a knife blade, as Obsidian had shown her. She could clearly picture the huge metal Skraken on the raven-hall door at the Abbotry. The believers of Brid might tell folk they would never die but that could mean suffering without end. There were worse things than death, as any Drorgher could tell the living.

Each row of strange, carved gods made her more afraid. Bera's head throbbed under the weight of so much other belief that further sapped her Valla powers. Where was her skern? Would she miss his uncleaving here?

'Let's go,' she cried, panicked. 'Can't breathe.'

Tall, rangy dogs loped along the quay, all ribs and claws, looking as if they never ate the scraps they scavenged. A pig was pushed off a mess of blood by a dog the size of a horse. It caught Bera staring and glared at her with cruel marble eyes.

'It's yours. I don't like rotten meat anyway.' Bera caught up with Faelan. 'Those dogs remind me of Blind Agnar's dog: grey as hoarfrost and shaggy. His old hound was sweet-natured, though, so what are these?'

'Wolfhounds. Don't go near them, Bera. They're bred to kill.'

If you couldn't trust a dog, what remained? This was the most threatening place she had ever been.

They reached the city gates without seeing the slave market. Bera wondered what to say to the guards to let them enter but there was such a stream of busy people going through that they were swept inside like flotsam. The whole town behind the walls was rising to a mound, and they began to climb. Instead of longhouses, jetties and bleached walkways, there was a scrambling heap of mean houses that lined poky streets. Stinking ginnels between the rough quarters steamed with blood and dung.

Bera needed sweeter air. 'What's the fastest way up?'

'That wider throughfare.' Faelan gestured. 'There should be a two-room quarter.'

She set off before Heggi could ask what it was and stay longer in the stench. Rakki was the only one of the group to look cheery. Faelan led them to larger houses, with post-and-wattle fences. A few plots had vegetables and chickens grubbing about but many of them were covered in weeds and rotting bed litter and the women held up their skirts from the mess between fences.

'It smells marshy,' Bera said.

'There's a mire ahead,' said Faelan. 'We'll have to cross sides.'

'How?' Ginna asked.

Heggi cast about. 'Cross what? Why?'

Bera felt a scream building. She had to be alone to find her skern and restore them both, and to plan, away from this mad scramble in a place she could not read, which was sucking her down like drowning. Her scalp prickled and she was suddenly certain that her folk were at the slave market now, about to be sold.

'Just go, Faelan!'

'We have to get across these plots and the only way to do that is on woven pathways.'

Bera set off.

'Wait, Bera! They're made by each homeowner, who has a price, or won't let you through at all if he doesn't like your face.'

'Better hide yours, then,' said Heggi, nudging him.

Bera and Ginna rounded on him but Faelan laughed, just like Ottar with Heggi. And with Egill, too. Again, Bera was baffled by the unfathomable rules of male understanding.

The first wattle pathway was guarded by a woman with a face like tanned leather. She spat out something bright red. Not blood but a plug of leaves. Whatever her price was, Faelan refused and they had to go back onto the throughfare.

'Pay,' said Bera. 'I don't care how much, we need to get to the market.'

'You'd need a treasure chest.'

'Then you should have brought that strongbox.'

'It's my mother's and safer hidden aboard,' he said quietly. 'Let's try this scabby-looking pathway.'

A thin woman with wild hair was beating a blanket hung on a line. She ignored them until they were close and then threw down her stick.

'Strangers must pay.'

Bera understood her. 'We have little of your coin.'

The woman had a good scratch under her armpit. 'Can't come through here, then.'

Faelan showed her two coins. 'The boot-faced woman back there wanted three. Take these or nothing.'

'Why should I take less than her? Besides, it's dearer on market days.'

'I reckon those blankets are full of lice and fleas, the way you're itching,' said Bera. 'No wonder, if all you do is sunning and beating.'

'What do you care?' The woman set about her scalp like a dog.

'Here's fleabane,' said Bera. 'Boil the leaves in water, let it cool and then stick your head in the bowl. Use a lice comb afterwards. That's worth letting us pass.'

Faelan walked on. 'I'm in awe of a Northwoman's apron.'

After all the wicker pathways, the mound was finally ahead but the way was blocked by a crowd of men. Instead of the trading bustle of the quay, there was a watchful stirring, like bees sensing a wasp near the hive.

Bera pulled them back into an alley. 'It smells like a tavern. If we are to find them, we'll have to pass.'

Faelan looked at Ginna. 'We'll try another way. Let's hope the Serpent's crewmen are too drunk to know you.'

Heggi stuck out his jaw but Bera knew he was frightened. They set off through alleys that never saw the sun, with the stench of ale, piss and vomit throughout the ruins of a shantytown. There was no need of a tavern when every shack was a brewhouse. Easy women and drink were everywhere, so they kicked and elbowed their way through reeling drunks without drawing daggers.

Ginna's face was whey. 'Can Papa still be there, Bera?'

'We are so close, dearest. This was a test and we shall be rewarded by saving Dellingr and all our kin.' Bera tapped her beads.

At the top, they froze. It was a market like no other. Raised above an eager crowd were rows of women and children, roped apart, their fight gone. Only babies were allowed to be with their mothers and Bera scrutinised those lines, desperate both to see but also not to see Sigrid with two babies. She guiltily scanned the rows again. Many of the women being sold first were protectively holding their obvious bellies, not merely rounded but near birthing.

'I can't see them!' she cried.

Faelan moved closer. 'Those children at the quay. That was a glimpse of my past. This is so much bigger.'

'At least they allow mothers to keep their babies.'

'Allow?' His mouth twisted. 'Look at these women, Bera. They are sold first: two for the price of one. Traders want women already with child so pirates make sure they are before bringing them to market.'

'Make sure ...?'

'Not just one man.'

Rape by many men in the name of trade. It made her father adding her to a boat order seem kind. And Sigrid had two babies with her. What might these types do to Valdis? The thought seared, at last; she had to save her daughter because she was her flesh, not as the next Valla.

'This could be my mother and me, Bera, and all the other wretched souls over the years. It would be your husband doing the selling.' Faelan spat. 'Did you ever think the thralls were people, who cooked your meals and cleaned your home?'

Bera kept her eyes on the line of women. 'Growing up, we did all the work, so when I arrived in Seabost they sneered at me. I was jealous of one very beautiful thrall. Hefnir almost certainly did buy her – but he may have also done the selling.'

'The last stopover before Dyflin for traders coming up from the south is a walled city. I told you about the river Seven. It brings to that city such a choice that only the best are captured. Their cost is high, so prices are raised here. Look at them, Bera. Young and strong, beautiful. These will fetch the highest price – and have the shortest life.'

Misery. Still more lines of women were led out as others were sold and taken away.

'I can promise you, Faelan, that I will never, ever, own another slave.'

'Your husband owned you too.'

'Your anger is not with me, then?' More than anything, she wanted Faelan's understanding.

'How could it be?' His voice was soft.

Bera's only plan was to rush and grab Sigrid when she appeared. There was an even greater jumble of voices and faces here than at the quay. They spoke in a mix of high and low notes, coming from the nose or the throat. Some wheezed, others drilled or barked. She hated not being able to place people; like arriving on Ice Island, wondering who to trust. There, at least, they were able to make themselves understood. How could she save her own folk if she had none of their words? Could she rely on Valla skills when this place of non-believers had made her skern shrink back? She felt small and lost as a woman and mother.

'I'll get closer,' said Heggi.

'No!'

'I've got Rakki.' He was gone.

'I'll fetch him.' Ginna slipped between the men in front.

'That copper hair…' Faelan said, following.

So quickly it was all worse, and she had to wait when she was the one who should act. Had her skern taken her few remaining skills with him? Bera roared one of Ottar's finest curses and a woman glared at her, outraged.

She held her hands up in apology. 'I didn't mean you were a raven-starving bitch, or… the other bit.'

The woman moved away, muttering. Bera had forgotten that Dyflin folk could probably speak some of the North tongues in order to trade. Or be warned that fights were brewing.

Faelan was back. 'It's all right.'

'Where are they?'

Bera scanned the buyers, who began jostling and craning to see the new goods being led up onto the mound. It was men this time, and her scalp flared. Heggi barged into her with Ginna.

'Papa,' she sobbed.

There was no mistaking him. Her smith was being led by two squat men, like a bear being brought to the ring. Dellingr was in chains but the others were roped together, hobbled like the women, so no doubt he had fought to free himself. She willed him to look their way but his face was granite.

Faelan caught her arm. 'Don't rush up there.'

'I'm not a fool!'

He was right, of course. Her only plan. All she had ever wanted was a man who would truly know her. But instead of seizing that damaged face and kissing him till their lips bled, she punched his chest. Wrong time. Wrong place.

'I wish I had Miska,' said Faelan. 'We could have ridden in and snatched him away.'

'Would you risk her to save Dellingr?'

'The smith is important to you.' He added something else but it was lost under the crowd's cheers.

A woman nudged Bera and shouted something, her eyes glittering. She made the shoulder to stomach cross of Brid. Bera, afraid to be different, did the same and the woman jerked her chin to where a box on long poles, effortlessly carried by four boys, parted the crowd.

'The Venerable Abbot of All Iraland,' said Faelan.

The claim of following Brid made her feel sick. Bera thought of the shrivelled Abbot in Ice Island who had wanted her dead. This more important figure must be even older – so old, perhaps, that the box contained only bones and dust. There was one small peephole for whatever was inside, so she could not see.

'How many coins do you have left, Faelan?'

'On me? Enough for food.'

'And in your mother's strongbox?'

He frowned. 'There's no time for us to get back to the boat.'

'I'll run. If I'm too late, follow wherever they take him.'

'You can't buy a smith with what's left!'

'I'll think of something else to offer. It's only a start, to make them listen.'

'That's no plan at all.'

Heggi stepped up. 'I'll go with you, Mama.'

Bera was about to refuse but she thought if he stayed, he would make some madcap attempt to save Ginna's father.

'I must stay near Papa,' said Ginna.

'Do not let your father see you. He will die trying to keep you from slavery.'

Ginna nodded. 'That's why I haven't run to him already.'

Heggi untied his dog's tether and knotted it onto her belt. 'Rakki will protect you.'

The dog pressed against the girl's legs, knowing his duty.

'No, no, this makes no sense,' Faelan said. 'I must go and you stay here.'

'I am more likely to be sold than you. Tell me where it's hidden.'

He hesitated.

'You do limp a bit,' said Heggi helpfully.

Bera frowned. 'Trust me, Faelan.'

'I... feel guilty.'

Bera thought he was going to say something completely different. Faelan pulled out his Brid cross. It now had a key on the leather thong and he put it over her head, keeping his head close.

'Go deep into the bilge, beyond where Egill hid. The box is there and the money is under her brooches.'

She and Heggi set off. The crowd was thinning; many were following the Abbot. Bera stopped to try and catch Dellingr's eye. He was looking straight at her. She prayed he did not think he was abandoned and sent him her message of hope, and that she would keep his daughter safe. What his fixed gaze was saying, she could not tell.

12

They walked as quickly as they dared behind the lines of women and children, not wanting to draw attention to themselves by running.

'Why are we going the wrong way?' hissed Heggi. 'It took long enough before.'

'I'm trying something.'

All eyes were on a stoat-faced man dressed in mustard yellow. He began a low drone as he pulled a boy forward. Then folk began raising their hands and then their voices got louder and higher, and he shouted over them, spittle flying.

'What's happening?'

'Bidding for the older children.'

A pretty girl was next, aged about twelve. It was clear that traders put their prizes up first in each section to fetch the highest price while folk still had the coins to pay for them. Men were yelling over each other, wanting the child, and then they started brawling. Bera grabbed Heggi and they skirted the scuffles to get to the far side. From here they could see a wide track that led down to the quayside beyond the *Raven*. They ran.

Heggi whistled. 'Clever, Mama.'

'There had to be a fast way to load folk onto the slave ships.'

'I'm glad we won't have to go back through those stews.'

'What stews?'

'It means brothel.'

'Don't ever use words like that.'

'Papa used to.'

Her fear had always been that he might become his uncle the Serpent. Bera was now seeing too much of his father in Heggi but this was no time to bicker. When they reached the quay, Heggi complained of a stitch and sat on a barrel, rubbing his ribs.

'Get up!'

'I can't help it, they're growing pains.'

It might be true. He was taller than her now. 'Well, take some deep breaths as we walk.'

He did not move. 'You know about words?'

This was why he had stopped, his need to ponder. Thoughts rippled across his face like cloud shadows over grass. It was his way to worry at things; very different from his uncle's unscrupulous urges.

'Words like stew.' He went on. 'Why am I not to say it when Papa told me it?'

'Words are power. It's not only that you put them out in the world but your words become who you are. They get into your own head, as well as the folk who hear them, and they shape you.'

He looked blank.

'Come on. I will try to explain later.'

The tide was already lower and they would have to use the rusty ladder to reach the rafted boats. Bera went first, testing each rung.

'It's lucky I gave Rakki to Ginna,' Heggi said.

'We'll lower him on a rope later.'

No one was aboard the first boat but on the second, a blotch-faced man was resting his pot belly against the rail alongside the *Raven*. They asked permission to come aboard and he beckoned Heggi to cross where he was standing. When it was Bera's turn, he was close enough for her to smell his rancid breath. She hitched up her skirts to sit on the rail and he smacked his lips. Her fist itched to punch him but she swung round and landed on the deck beside Heggi.

'I'll kick him when we go back,' she muttered.

'In the balls,' he said with relish.

'Make sure he keeps his piggy eyes on you while I go below.'

Beneath the mast was the deepest part of the hull where livestock were penned on passage. Folk had to live on the open deck but the animals had some shelter down here. Not enough. As she crawled to the hiding place, tears tickled Bera's nose. This was a place of loss and grief, where Egill had hidden, keening, rocking to and fro in the smothering darkness, where despair turned into madness. She could hear wailing, now.

It's only the rigging.

Bera's courage grew, hearing her skern. 'I'm glad you're back.'

I fade ashore.

She squirmed along on her stomach, her skirts soaked in sour seawater. What possessed Faelan to put the box so far into the bilge? It was stifling and every strake, nail, block, dug into her. She pulled her sleeves over her fists and when she touched the stern she groped for the strongbox and clouted her head.

'Hel's teeth and buckets of blood!'

Only then did she realise that she would have to crawl backwards, dragging the weight, which was harder than pushing. Her clothing rode up, her apron hem tore on an unclenched nail and when she was back at the mast Bera was cold, wet and furious. She couldn't even scream because it would make the bloated, leering, wine-blotched idiot on the next boat even more interested.

Heggi was speaking to him and Bera stayed low to judge the situation. She wished his voice had not broken; it used to be easier to hear. Then another voice, male, came from near the bow; muffled words, but having the familiar rhythm of home.

'My father used to come…' Heggi.

'Why has your mother made…' The other.

Both their voices dipped at the end. This was wasting time! Bera put down the strongbox, got her rumpled, sodden garments in order and scrambled up onto the deck.

Heggi was leaning against the prow, talking easily with someone who had his back to her. Dark blond hair. For a moment the set of his shoulders reminded her of Bjorn, but that was ridiculous. And yet her son was smiling at this person with a Northman's hair.

'Can I help you?' she called out.

The man turned and she did not know him at all. His face was unmarked but not unremarkable. He was probably her father's age, she reckoned, but not as hard-worked. His brown face, blue eyes and reddish-blond hair in a long, plaited beard had the look of a sailor, of home. But he wore the style of cloak she had seen up at the mound, except this had a kind of hood lined with fur, which made him at least as rich as Hefnir.

'He saw us earlier,' said Heggi. 'He says he knows you.'

The sun was warm on Bera's head and her scalp gave no prickle of warning. Still, she was uneasy at this stranger who wore such a cloak on such a day.

'I don't know you. Or your name.'

'I'm here to help, not harm you,' he said. 'I've been watching for your ship.'

Bera scrutinised him for any recognition, but none came. He moved closer, palms out, like he might approach an uncertain animal.

'I think you need a friend,' he said.

'I have friends.'

He looked sideways at Heggi. 'A boy is no match for Dyflin folk.'

Bera would not be provoked into telling him who else was in her company.

'I don't need help.' Heggi was surly. 'I'm going back up there to Ginna now.'

'Wait, Heggi,' said Bera. 'This person is leaving first.'

The man looked at her wryly, then stopped at the rail. 'I've already removed the... er, obstruction to your crossing.'

He stepped over the next boats and up the quayside ladder. As soon as he was gone, Bera retrieved the strongbox. She bundled it in a blanket, tied it with rope that she crossed over her chest, with the box resting on her hip, so she could climb one-handed. Heggi helped her at the top.

'They must have sold all the men by now,' said Heggi.

'You wasted time with that man!'

'I didn't! You—'

'Faelan's following the buyer. Whoever has him, I will meet the price to get Dellingr home.'

Whatever kind of price it turned out to be.

There was no comforting presence of her skern. Did he fade ashore because other skerns were missing? If the Vallas had sent her here, knowing this, it was a glimpse of their dark purpose. But other needs were pressing and Bera went from stall to stall, not finding one that suited.

'What are we doing?' Heggi groaned. 'I thought we were going straight to buy Dellingr?'

'Faelan says the coins won't be enough, so I'm selling his mother's jewels.'

'You can't!'

'Watch me.'

The trouble was, Bera had no market skills. She was a Valla, used to dealing with the big things in life: weather, floods, famine, earthquake. Before she learned how to do it she was only a girl who went fishing. Trading was done by men in strange lands. Hefnir. She was sure she did not want to learn that sort of skill. It had to be easy bartering.

'I need to find that stallholder who wanted to buy my beads, to strike a fast bargain.'

Heggi stopped her. 'What with?'

She tapped the bundle.

'You won't get much for an old box!'

'I'll haggle a good price for what's in it.'

'What is in it?'

'I told you.'

'You don't know, do you?'

She winked. 'Nor does he.'

At last she found the right stallholder. He was dealing with two women, chattering in a spiky tongue, who picked and pulled at the bright things on his stall with beady eyes, like crows. When the trader saw Bera he stared at her neck, dabbing his chin as if he was wiping away dribble. She hardened her face, trying to look like Hefnir, and set the box on his stall.

Bera tapped the lid. 'I have better things in here than my beads.'

She hoped the other women understood her. Their greed might drive up the price.

'Let's 'ave a look at 'em, then.'

'I've had offers at other stalls.' Bera kept the box so he could not look inside. 'Let's see if you can do better.'

This was no game. She should have taken the coins out earlier and seen what else was in there. It was all the stranger's fault. Bera lifted the lid as if a viper was in the box and quickly passed the leather pouch to Heggi.

'What was that?' asked the trader.

'Small coin. The jewels are further down.' She made a flourish of taking out two small wooden boxes and setting them down on the stall. 'Look at the working on the lid, signing their precious content. So what will you give me?'

'Open 'em up.'

'No. That's the risk we both take, because I don't know what they hold, either. Make me an offer and you may be lucky.'

'More likely I'm buying a crock of shit,' he said.

Bera shrugged.

He spat a dark juice onto the quay. 'No deal.'

One of the women went to pick up a box. Bera snatched it away.

'You make me an offer first,' she said. 'We don't need a trader's profit.'

The woman shrugged, puzzled.

Bera pointed at her and rubbed her fingers and thumb. 'You pay.'

The other woman bared yellow teeth. 'They is thieved!'

Her breath could stop a bear. She barged into Bera and the first woman grabbed the box. Heggi tripped her but Yellow-tooth had seized the strongbox.

Bera's knife was out and at her throat. 'No deal.'

The woman snarled but gave it to Heggi, who put the small wooden box inside.

'Get away, both of you.' Bera kept her knife unsheathed.

The woman glared at her, putting a hand to the point of blood on her neck. Her friend dabbed it away with a rag, the two of them hissing like cats. The trader said something and they smirked, then linked arms and strolled away. They probably worked the market, bringing him whatever they stole.

'That was good,' said Heggi, sheathing his knife.

Bera tutted but could not help grinning.

'You got no clue,' the trader said.

He put a chunk of something into his mouth, plugging a cheek, and then started packing away his wares.

'Wait!' Bera banged the strongbox onto the stall.

The man sighed. 'All right, I'm feeling kind today, but no see, no deal.'

'This is never going to work,' Heggi muttered. 'Papa would have—'

'Enough.'

She took out the wooden boxes again and then found one in metal, which rattled nicely. There must be precious stones inside. Then there was a silver grooming set, which she would have liked to keep, having lost hers in Smolderby.

'Worth nothing,' the trader said. 'Let's see the tin.'

He went to take it but Bera prised off the lid and smiled with relief. Lying on blue cloth were some tiny pearls.

'How much for these?'

He gave her a pitying look. 'Why would I want baby teeth?'

Heggi leaned over. 'He's right, Bera. It's a tin of teeth.'

More precious to a loving mother than jewels. After disappointment came shame. Would Valdis, her poor baby girl, be teething now? Would Sigrid keep them in a tin for years? Bera winced at a gut-tug on the cord that links every mother with her child – and the long line of Vallas. And the string of beads.

'I bet they're Faelan's,' said Heggi.

'Like I said, crock of shit.' The trader shook out the boxes onto his stall.

'One bit of hair, one feather and a lump of rock.'

Bera put them back in the strongbox. 'I will go back to the ones who recognised their worth.'

'And offered you a good price?' He gave a nasty laugh. 'My arse. You only got one thing, girlie, worth anything.'

The beads burned her throat.

'You can't,' said Heggi.

Her mother's last gift. It fixed Bera into her place in the line that stretched far back to when the middle world was made and a woman spoke its Fate. How could she break that?

'Come on, I haven't got all day. I'm closing soon.'

The slave market might be over soon, too. Bera was demented by the yawning waste of time when she should be saving her smith. Had she lost her energy and purpose ashore? Was her skern's absence the cause or a sign of it? Was being such a poor mother to the next Valla weakening her?

'It's all right, Mama.' Heggi picked up the strongbox. 'Let's try somewhere else.'

'No.' What if she traded only a few of the beads? Bera tried to think of one she could bear to part with as she struggled to untie the knot at the back of her neck. 'I can't…'

A hand softly closed over hers. Slightly damp.

The trader picked up the barrow-stall and rattled away down the quay, without looking back. He must fear whoever had stopped her. Bera turned to face the man from the *Raven*. She went for her knife but he held his ground.

'You need no weapon,' he said. 'But you already know that.'

'I don't sense danger but you need to earn my trust.'

His face held only sadness. 'So I won't untie it, but may I…?'

Bera let him gently lift the heavy necklace and pass the beads along the cord, until he found what he was looking for.

'She kept it,' he whispered.

'The B rune,' Bera said.

'You're so like your mother. Like Alfdis.'

'Who is he?' asked Heggi.

'Look at his hands. He can't hide those scars under a fine cuff. He's a fisherman from the village where I was born.'

'Oh, Crapsby,' scoffed Heggi. 'I thought he was important.'

The man raised an eyebrow. 'So Seabost comes to Dyflin.' He ran a hand over his beard. 'Seems I can never escape the place.'

'Seems to me like you escaped everything,' said Bera.

'I had reasons. You may know some of them. I know my duty now, though, and you must never, ever, sell those beads.'

'Don't you dare tell me my duty! I've spent my whole life doing my duty so the rest of you can follow your own pleasures. My duty is to keep folk living long enough to enjoy them.'

'I thought Vallas tended to the future.'

Heggi tugged her sleeve. 'Aren't we in a hurry?'

'No need to rush away.' The man smiled. 'You were always going to be too late for your smith.'

Bera had sensed it, but his saying it made her furious. 'You know everything of course! So what about Sigrid? Where have you been all these years? Why aren't you up there now, protecting her?'

'Sigrid wasn't there, we looked.' Heggi screwed up his face with bafflement. 'And anyway who is he?'

'Where is she, Bjarni?'

'Safe.'

'How does he know?' asked Heggi.

'And the babies? My daughter?'

'Safe, all of them. I paid a high price for them with my own coin.'

'Bera, will you please tell me what is going on!' Heggi shouted.

'He was Sigrid's husband.'

Bjarni pulled lace cuffs over his hands. 'It was all a long time ago and in another place.'

'One day you will pay for all this,' said Bera. 'Now we have to find Dellingr and buy him back.'

'He was only there to drive up prices. He is... er, special and already taken. The Serpent's crew took him straight to the palace. He is working for the Venerable Abbot of All Iraland now. Preparing for war.'

Bera's scalp was on fire. A dog rushed at her, seized her sleeve and then capered round Heggi. It was Rakki, with Faelan behind, supporting Ginna. Heggi rushed to take over.

'I didn't need to follow,' said Faelan. 'The whole world knows where he's gone.'

Ginna's eyes were swollen. 'I couldn't get near him.'

'Your father is high value, sweetheart.' Bera swept some hair out of Ginna's mouth. 'They won't let any harm befall him before we rescue him.'

'Who is this man?' Faelan stood taller.

'I'm an old friend of the family.'

'He is a drowned man,' Bera said, 'but he has Sigrid and the babies safe and he will take us to them now. Won't you, Bjarni?'

13

It was agreed that someone should stay aboard the *Raven*, so that was Faelan. Heggi offered to go with him, taking Ginna.

'She keeps being stared at. I want her to feel safe.' A new thoughtfulness.

'It's the poking and pinching that's worse,' said Ginna.

Bera was grateful to lessen her burden of care. 'The tide is right out now and we would have to hoist poor Rakki a long way. He'd be best staying with Sigrid to look after the babies.'

'He'll be good at that,' said Heggi, with a last scruffle of the dog's ears.

Bjarni started off, impatient, and when Bera did not follow he crossed his arms and tapped his foot.

'You will get Papa back, I know,' Ginna said. She rushed at Bera and flung her arms round her waist, like a daughter.

Bera liked the feeling and would not betray her trust. 'I will find a way into the palace and save Dellingr. First I must make sure all is well with Sigrid. I'll return when the tide is high enough to anchor off.'

Faelan led Ginna towards the ladder. 'While we are waiting we can form a plan to help Bera and I promise you'll feel better to be doing something.'

'Why don't you have a mead hall meeting round the mast?' Bera called after them.

Heggi lowered his voice. 'You won't get her father back for ages, will you?'

'Fast as I can, boykin. Seize Dellingr and go.'

Bjarni sighed loudly.

Bera ignored him and went to the ladder with Heggi. He felt for the top rung. His hair was caffled, thick with salt and uncombed. She wanted to kiss it but he hated being a child and when she reached out he jerked his head away.

'Lice comb for you when I get back aboard.'

He snarled happily.

Bjarni did not wait. Bera caught him up and whistled for Rakki. He scurried from the ladder to her side, then back towards Heggi, back and fore, troubled by his pack splitting up again, as was Bera. He finally stayed with her and she slipped him a morsel.

'I wonder at you wasting time talking about nits,' said Bjarni.

'You know nothing of love.'

They carried on in silence. Bera thought about the B rune, and whether Bjarni had loved her mother or used her. Poor Sigrid. And poor Bjorn, trying be like his drowned father. If he had only known Bjarni was no hero. But what else was he?

'Now tell me your story,' she said. 'The truth – before we reach Sigrid.'

'She knows it.'

They reached the far end of the quay and were clear of the clusters of folk who were still drinking there. Bjarni said nothing even when the last pedlar was behind them.

'Well?'

'I didn't drown.'

'Is that it?'

'More or less. I chose where to fall in and let the others think I was taken by a shark.'

'The crew said you were given full honours.'

'They didn't even wait to see if I came up,' he said.

'So they lied. And poor Bjorn never felt he was as good as you.'

'A shortcut.' Bjarni gestured for her to go ahead. 'There's this narrow wynd to get through and then we're nearly there.'

It was not an open sewer like the ginnels but a foul-smelling drain ran the length of it. Bera held her apron over her mouth and nose. The tall huts on either side seemed to lean in on her, getting tighter as she went further and squeezing her uncomfortably close to Bjarni. Yet at the far end a couple of women were carding wool, and when they smiled at her she liked the reminder of simple days at home. Sigrid. Flooded with love, Bera wanted to run to find her second mother. Everything would work out.

They emerged onto a wide cobbled path that led up to a row of stone houses. A knife grinder had his barrow outside the first dwelling and was sharpening tools. He touched his cap as they passed. There was vileness, but also standing and wealth in Dyflin. And Bjarni had both.

Bera stopped him. 'You jumped ship. Then what?'

'I hid behind a rock. A stark whale or ice shark could have truly taken me.'

'Pity they didn't.'

He ignored the barb. Sigrid had probably given him worse.

'The boat sailed on and I got to the beach I'd chosen. It's a skerry where we used to overnight sometimes, where the narwhales mate.'

A narwhale and its precious tusk. It all connected. 'It's where Bjorn was killed.'

His eyes slid away. 'Sigrid told me.'

'Then what? You can't live on a skerry.'

'I didn't want to live.'

Bera waited.

'You want the truth, Bera?' Bjarni ran a hand through his hair. 'Your mother was the only woman I ever loved. When I lost her I could hardly breathe, so I decided to drown myself.'

'But you lacked the courage to do it.'

'You know now that it takes more courage to go on living, Bera, don't you?'

His quiet concern moved her, but she owed it to Sigrid and Bjorn not to yield.

'Courage like Sigrid's? You betrayed your wife, Bjarni. She lost you twice over.'

'I was a dutiful husband. I could not help loving Alfdis.'

'Did you love her so much?'

'Alfdis was the sun and moon to me.'

'I wish I could remember her.' Her hand went to her necklace.

Her skern held it. *Go on, say it.*

'Say what?'

Get it off your chest, to someone, about the fear you still feel.

'I don't.'

Bjarni nodded. 'Your mother would disappear like that. Alfdis spent more and more time talking to her skern.'

Bera liked him being matter-of-fact about it. They began to walk uphill.

'You still believe in skerns.'

'Of course.'

His belief and enduring love for Alfdis lets me speak.

'Were you as easy about scrying and skerns with my mother? Sigrid always hated "Valla stuff". Is that why?'

'It was the Valla passion she hated.' He stopped. 'It is good to talk about Alfdis.'

'Don't assume I have forgiven your betrayal. Not only of Sigrid but of my father!'

'Ottar…' He went on ahead. 'No matter.'

Let the past stay there.

'Is that your best advice?'

Here's more. Don't get bogged down in human frailty. Get yourself to the Long Dead.

Her scalp prickled at the thought of the ancient echo.

Into the Dark, the utmost reach.

'Where?' Chaos was coming, so was this how to stop it?

Bera ran after Bjarni. 'Where can I find the long dead?'

'No idea what you mean.' He rubbed his chin. 'There's a plague pit outside the walls.'

'With long dead in it?'

He shrugged. 'We're nearly home now.'

An odd word for these strange stone houses. 'Why do you choose to live up here? To have this climb every day?'

'So the shit runs down to the bottom. We get clean air. That's why we call them low-life in Dyflin, and I'm right at the top.'

'Top of the dung pile. Heroic.'

Near the top of the hill, Sigrid came out of a doorway. Her familiar, stout, bundled figure became a blurred smudge and Bera ran to her. Home was this woman. Sigrid's smell was different, scented by soap, but as soon as Bera got past the shawls and burrowed into her neck it was like being a child again. Sigrid rubbed Bera's back with her strong hand and made her feel safe.

Then she pulled away. 'You saw Dellingr, then?'

'I was trying to save him. I didn't know then that...' Bera found it hard to say the name to Sigrid.

'Bjarni.' Sigrid looked across at him. 'This is his home. I always said he would return to me.'

Bera opened her mouth at such a lie but Sigrid must have her reasons. The safety of her baby boy, perhaps.

'Where is Valdis?' she asked instead.

'In there.' Sigrid cocked her head towards the back of the hall. 'Fast asleep. I've weaned them now, her and Borgvald; it's what they do in Dyflin, soon as they can – off the breast and straight on to oatmeal. The rich do, anyway. That's what they give them here, porridge with a drop of brandy. Works a treat. Don't go and wake her.'

Bera's guilt returned and with it her irritation with Sigrid, who knew how to twist the knife.

'I'm going to see my daughter. Alone, Sigrid.'

'If you can remember what she looks like,' she said, just loud enough to be heard.

Bera hurried through to a billet with enough space for two cradles. The babies must be too big to share one now. She had only been away for a matter of weeks but missed so much. It mattered a lot, with the sweet smell of sleeping babies surrounding her, and she envied Sigrid. Borgvald was in the first cot and Valdis nearest a window. Bera tiptoed over but her daughter was awake, her eyes fixed on her mother, wide and dark as stones; a true Valla.

'Don't you ever sleep, small one?' Bera heard her own pretence.

She lifted Valdis, who shoved herself away from this stranger. Bera held tight and was furious to see the obsidian bead was back on her wrist. She ignored the screams of outrage and untied the knot.

Sigrid rushed in and Valdis held out her arms piteously. Bera put her back in her cot, kissed the red mark on her chubby wrist and then held up the bead.

Sigrid sniffed. 'She loves that bead, don't you, Disa?'

'That bead brought death to the homestead and I told you to throw it in the fire. But you put it on her again! And don't call her Disa.'

'I can see your mother in her. But she's cleverer than Alfdis, and you, at her age. Look at her listening to us. You know every word, don't you, sweet baby girl?'

Bera wanted to cry; the mix of anger and shame she felt whenever she was with her daughter and Sigrid, who was a natural mother not a pretend one.

'Let Valdis sleep, Sigrid.' She lowered her voice. 'What is going on with you and that man?'

'Don't start. Me and Bjarni are back together and there's no point raking over the past like you always do.'

'Believe me, there so much past I could have told him but I kept quiet.'

'Well, don't start on me.' Sigrid sniffed. 'We all have to get on with our lives.'

'Does he know who fathered Borgvald?' The baby boy began to cry. 'Is he hungry?'

'Poor Baba Borgvald, does he want his mama?' said Sigrid. 'That's not a feeding cry, Bera. It's to be picked up, but he'll have to learn he won't always get what he wants, like most men do.'

'In other words, I know nothing about motherhood.'

'Did I say that?'

'Stop it, Sigrid. I didn't come here to argue.'

Valdis joined in the wailing. Bera wanted to soothe her but she would probably fail and then Sigrid would gloat and the rift between them widen.

Sigrid took her hand. 'Come on, dearest, leave them to grizzle.'

Her kindness made Bera feel even more pitiable and she wanted Rakki. They went back into the hall where Bjarni was lying on a long bench, throwing pieces of cheese into the air. Rakki caught every one, delighting Bera that he was getting stronger and agile on three legs.

'Rakki's staying here to guard the babies,' she told Sigrid.

Sigrid glanced meekly at Bjarni, which troubled Bera.

'It's all right, he already agreed.' Bera took a stool to the hearth. 'I must get back to the boat before dark, so we need to plan. Where has this old Abbot Thing of Iraland taken Dellingr?'

Bjarni stopped throwing. 'You don't think you can march up to the palace and walk off with his smith?'

'I shall bargain with him.'

'He's war-mongering. You have nothing that is worth more than your smith.'

'She might, then.' Sigrid was eager. 'Did you come back with that obsidian?'

'No, Sigrid, I used it to save lives, not get rich.'

'That's you all over,' she snapped. 'Us settlers get herded like cattle while you're off saving the Known World. Onto a dragon boat, of all things! Me, on a boat, with that Serpent's crew like wild beasts, and sold as slaves!'

Bera closed her eyes and counted. The trouble was, Sigrid was right, and she missed out the dishonour of Bera being unnatural, unmotherly. An unwoman. Despicable.

Rakki pushed his nose into her hand and Bera obediently stroked his ears.

'I have something of higher worth,' she said.

'What, then?' asked Sigrid, bringing another stool over. 'What's higher?'

'Myself.'

A smile flickered across Bjarni's lips. Had she been played?

She took stock of the man and how Sigrid was with him. They hardly looked at one another; very different from how Sigrid had been with Borgvald's father. There was something bullish about Sigrid's face, her jaw set, daring Bera not to probe. What was she afraid Bera would say? Had Bjarni's wealth silenced the wife he had deserted? Perhaps she was grateful to him for taking her into his household, with two children that were not his own, but Sigrid could have said that, and had not. Bera knew her well, and she was steeled against something. Truly frightened.

Bjarni clapped his hands and a young lad, shaven-headed, appeared from the back of the hall. Of course he would have thralls.

'Fetch more logs in, boy.'

'Yes, sir.'

That was surprising: the thrall spoke with hardly an accent. He had wide eyes, the colour of Faelan's. When he made no move to obey, Bera expected Bjarni to be angry but he spoke softly.

'Why do you not go?'

'Sir, folk say they come in daylight now, out of the forest.'

Sigrid's hand went to her throat. 'I told you! I was washing the linens at the river with the others and—'

'The wood store is near,' Bjarni spoke over her. 'They won't attack unless you're wounded. Draw your sword and look as big as you can.'

'Are they so close?' asked Bera.

She would need to reckon the enemy. It was all happening too fast. She quested for her skern but something kept him away from here. Was Sigrid taking on the new belief? Rakki nudged her and she pulled at his ears again.

The boy looked uncertain. No thrall had a sword.

Bera guessed. 'Your son, Bjarni?'

'You mistook him for a thrall.'

'For good reason, with his hair shaved off.'

Sigrid violently rubbed her nose. 'I did it. He was crawling with nits.'

Bera scratched her own head.

'Don't tell me you've brought them.' Sigrid brandished a comb. 'That's your plan, is it, to give the Venerable Abbot nits and fleas?'

Bera laughed and they were friends again. But when Sigrid stood behind her to unplait her hair, fear was coming off her in waves. For herself, or Bera?

'I dealt with one old Abbot before,' Bera scoffed. 'They reckon I'm Brid.'

'Brid is honoured in Iraland.' Bjarni stood over her. 'Do not make light of the power of three, Bera.'

Rakki's low growl forced him back a little. The power of three was important somehow, but Bera was lulled by having her hair groomed.

'She's not saying there isn't a Brid.' Sigrid nudged her.

'But she isn't me.'

Bjarni stroked his beard. 'I wonder if we might use it, though?'

'If he bought Dellingr to work the old magic of iron, then I'll tell him only a Valla can deepen the power, not this Brid of yours. Ouch! Sigrid!'

'Have you put a comb through this since you left?' Sigrid kept tugging.

'I doubt if he will even meet you,' said Bjarni.

It made her more determined. 'So pay him. You're wealthy, he must need money to give Dellingr enough iron to work for this war.'

'I have already paid.' Bjarni stroked his beard again.

Bera clamped her lips together in irritation and stared at the fire instead. She didn't want to, but perhaps she had to pose as Brid again. Choosing to be Brid was at least a clear plan, but was it safe? If only she could ask her skern. The very fact of his dwindling was a sure sign that the muddle of old and new beliefs in Iraland was lessening her Valla power. She must decide and then act.

'Right, Bjarni. All you have to do is get me inside. Tell them I can scry, that I have seen the future that concerns the Abbot and the war. They can't blame you for bringing me, it would be your duty!'

'And what is the future?'

'She'll make something up,' said Sigrid. 'Like she always does, won't you, Bera?'

Bera swung round. Bjarni put out a hand to stop her and she grabbed it.

He pulled away. 'Did you think I was going to hit her?'

'He stopped you falling off that stool.' Sigrid's voice trembled.

'What are you afraid of, Sigrid?'

'Sigrid's scared of everything,' Bjarni said. 'Always was.'

'You've made her too scared to speak for herself, apparently!'

Bjarni made a calming gesture that made Bera's hands itch to hit him so she plaited her hair instead.

'Sigrid?'

Sigrid looked away.

'She feared Alfdis,' said Bjarni, 'and now she fears her daughter, who has grown to look so like her.'

'Sigrid loved my mother!'

Bera looked at Sigrid, expecting her to agree, but she kept her eyes on the fire. In the crackle of the flames was all the Valla passion that lay between them.

Bjarni spoke. 'Do what you must, sweetheart, and I will do all I can to help.'

'I am not your sweetheart.' The trouble was, she needed him.

He opened his arms wide, like an honest and generous host. 'Sing for your supper, Bera. Tell us all about Obsidian.'

'Bjarni knew Egill,' Sigrid said. A warning?

Bera told them the story of Obsidian, except how it ended.

'What really happened to the Serpent King?' asked Sigrid.

Bera glanced at Bjarni. Did he know the dragon boat had brought his body to Dyflin? Her stomach rumbled with unease.

'Have you eaten?' Sigrid asked. 'Stupid question, of course you won't have.'

Bjarni got up. 'I am ashamed of our poor hospitality. I shall get the boy to prepare a light supper. I was given some rabbits at the palace.'

As soon as he was gone, Bera went over to the bench and sat close to Sigrid, who was working her poor, chapped hands.

Bera took one and kissed it. 'Come back to the *Raven* with me now. You don't have to stay here.'

'I do, then. Besides, I shall never set foot on a boat again, not ever. You'll be off and what would become of the babies?'

'What is it you're so afraid of, Sigrid?'

'Wolves.' Her answer came too pat.

Bera let it go for now. It was, after all, Wolf Island. So it wasn't a war band that had scared the washerwomen but wolves, coming in broad daylight. Yet Sigrid was afraid of something besides that.

She thought of the wolf pack at the Abbotry and the debt their leader owed her. Bera held her amber bead, trying to link minds with the wolf. Instead, there was a scramble of love, and she returned it to Rakki tenfold.

'What are you rolling that bead around for?' asked Sigrid.

'Talking to Rakki.'

'You and that flea-ridden dog.'

'I let a pack of wolves run free on Ice Island.'

Sigrid swept some ash away with her foot. 'They call it a rout here. Leastways, the palace does, so Bjarni started.'

'A rout of wolves.' Bera stopped Sigrid's fidgeting. 'You were relieved to say that was your fear.'

Sigrid looked shifty. 'I need to strew some tansy.'

'What's it for?'

'Tansy? Bjarni uses it for ants and mice. I put some fennel round, too, mind. It's one of their nine holy herbs, to keep evil away.'

Bera wondered what evil stalked a land in summer. 'I'll keep asking, Sigrid. Do you fear Bjarni?'

'I'm not like you, Bera. I need a man.'

'What sort of answer is that?'

'Did you get to speak to Dellingr?' Sigrid asked.

'How could I? He was sold to the Abbot.'

'He wasn't sold, then. He was a gift, from that rabble.'

'What rabble? Bjarni told me the Abbot had bought him.' Or had she assumed it? 'Whose gift?'

'The Serpent King's crew of course, off one of his slaving boats, that took us. They want him made Chief Warrior.' Sigrid scraped back Bera's hair, replaiting it tightly. 'You've made a mess of this.'

'Ow, Sigrid, you're giving me a headache. How could the Serpent be their Chief when he's dead?'

'They're joining Brid. Or some such. Don't ask me, it's all over my head.'

'I should scry, I suppose.'

'You don't sound very sure.'

Bera dared not share her worry about dwindling Valla powers, especially with Sigrid, who feared what she most needed.

'I'm tired, Sigrid. I want to be like you, with only babies and a household to run.'

'Only, she says!'

'You know what I mean.'

'I know what you mean, all right. That Faelan. I saw it first minute I saw you together. "You can't trust someone as handsome as that," I thought.'

'Well, he's not handsome anymore, is he!' Bera kicked over the stool. 'Is he more trustworthy now, with a melted face?'

Sigrid gave one of her looks and carried the stool back to the hearth with a rigid back that was all reproof, then headed for the babies' billet. Bera refused to follow in yet another failure of motherhood, but Sigrid passed the doorway and went further into the hall.

Bera put her head on her knees. Her skern would tell her she picked fights when she felt guilty and she was most angry with whoever accused her of the thing she blamed herself for, which was usually Sigrid. She never remembered this in time. Vallas fixing on the future surely made them blind to their true characters in the present. Was it how Alfdis could so readily betray Sigrid, her childhood friend? She went to apologise.

Sigrid was in a dark, cool pantry, with a long wooden trestle running down the middle, a bench and shelves on one side, and a large buttery opposite. All spoke of wealth and plenty, and strangeness. There were some small green knobbled sheaths on the table.

Bera picked one up. 'What's this?'

'Peas, Bjarni calls them.'

Bera bit into it. 'Mmmm. Sweet. A bit stringy, though.'

'That's not the peas, that's the pod. You have to shell them like this, look.' Sigrid popped the top with her thumb and then slid her nail downwards. She opened it out gently to keep the peas in a neat row and showed Bera. 'There you are. Easy.'

Bera reached for the pod. 'Snug as bugs.'

She opened her mouth and slid the peas in with her thumb. They were cool and damp. She rolled them with her tongue and then bit down. Sweetness burst in her mouth and made her scalp tingle.

'More.'

Rakki was lying in wait and pounced when one dropped. Sigrid was deftly shelling them into a bowl and soon Bera was as good, so then she slipped a few peas to her dog and pocketed some for Heggi.

'I can see you,' said Sigrid, taking a pod from her. 'There won't be enough for our meal. The Abbot sent these down special with the boy. Most get by on bread and scrape.'

'Let me do it. I won't eat any more.' Bera picked up another pod. 'I like the noise shelled peas make, pinging into the bowl.'

They worked on, as comfortably as weaving together. There was so much worry ahead. Not only the war, too big to reckon as yet, but some closer thing that was keeping Bera alert.

'I wish my life was ordinary, Sigrid. Everyday, peaceful, you and me…'

'Pinging peas into a bowl.' Sigrid held up her thumb. 'And making our nails turn black.'

'Oh.' Bera glumly studied her thumbnail.

'You want peaceful.' Sigrid nudged her. 'Watch.'

She threw some empty pods onto the floor. A bustle of hens came scurrying in, like fisherwomen holding up their skirts to join a brawl. Bera scattered some, laughing at the rumpus of scuffles and squawking. Rakki was moping and she flung the rest into the yard for peace.

Sigrid put the bowl of peas into the shade and covered it with damp linen.

'How did Asa die?' asked Bera into the silence.

Sigrid picked up the empty sack, took it outside and shook it out in the yard.

Bera followed. 'Tell me, Sigrid.'

Sigrid picked up a broom and went back to the pantry, sweeping the last scraps outside. Bera stopped her following them.

'Why won't you tell me?'

Sigrid sniffed. 'She wouldn't want you to gloat.'

'Why would I? I keep saying, Asa had nothing I ever wanted.'

'Well then.'

'Oh, come on, Sigrid!'

'The truth? She hated you when you were there and when you left, she started hating herself.'

'Asa took pleasure in hating.'

'Not fair! And remember, in Seabost she nursed me back from the red-spot.' Sigrid knew how to hurt. 'She was the only one who ever came near the sick huts.'

'She lived next to them!' Bera took a deep breath. 'I was forbidden to risk sickness, as you well know. By Hefnir, my new husband, of high standing in his own home.'

Sigrid crossed her arms, unyielding.

'You are the most maddening person, Sigrid! You and Asa, always happy to pick me apart with gossip!'

'I thought you wanted to know how she died.'

'So let's have it, instead of trying to fill me with guilt.'

Sigrid turned, looking seawards, hiding her tears. All her bluster was to distance herself from the sadness of losing Asa.

'Oh, Sigrid. I'm sorry.'

'We never should have left Seabost.'

'We had to leave.'

'You did, and other folk. I mean Asa and me. It started going wrong for us both on the passage over.'

'You always said it's loss that makes you strong.'

'Well, maybe I was wrong. There are some losses that can't be borne, or too many striking at once.'

Ginna had said something like this about her mother's grief, the loss.

'Asa took her own life, didn't she?' said Bera.

'I'm only glad I got there before that poor girl saw her mother...'

'Hanging?'

'She cut her throat with one of Dellingr's knives. Made such a good job of it he had no trouble taking her head off for the burial.' Sigrid's voice was a flint weapon. 'He won't forgive you for that, Bera. Not ever.'

14

They brought the babies to the hearth to feed them while their own meal was stewing. Sigrid became her old self with Bjarni gone. Valdis refused to take her mash from Bera. Sigrid opened her mouth like a gaping fish every time she wanted Borgvald to take his next spoonful and then did the same with Valdis. Bera copied her, and to her amazement it worked. Did all mothers have to become idiots? They burped the babies afterwards and rubbed their backs. Valdis brought up some porridge and Sigrid handed Bera a cloth.

'You'd hate ordinary life.'

Bera wiped her shoulder. 'I could be a good mother, if I ever had time.'

'Oof.' Sigrid hefted her son onto a hip. 'Borgvald takes after his father all right.'

She pulled a glossy brown fur near the hearth and they lay on it with the babies, who began to sleepily cuff each other. Bera measured her hand against the bear paw.

'Do they have giant bears here?'

'In the mountains, maybe.' Sigrid shrugged. 'They have big enough gates, that side, must be to keep out something bigger than wolves.'

'All year?' Bera asked. 'Drorghers are midwinter.'

'They have Fetches in Iraland.' Sigrid picked up a pot. 'And nothing would keep one of them out.'

Bera thought about the Watcher on Ice Island. 'A person's Fetch comes at the point of death, doesn't it? More like a skern?'

'Aye, well, they sent away their skerns here, along with the old gods.' Sigrid hitched up her skirts and studied a knobbly blue vein. 'This drives me mad.'

'Don't scratch it,' Bera said. 'What old gods?'

'You know, our lot. And goddesses. They have new ones. Same as ours half the time, Bjarni says, with new names.'

'Like Brid?'

'She started it. Now they've taken a bit of this and a bit of that and made up a new faith. I reckon the old gods have gone off in a huff.'

Bera laughed. 'Dear Sigrid. You make Thor sound like a fishwife.'

'I don't, then.' Sigrid tucked in her shawls. 'But I'm telling you, all the talk of healing waters is an excuse. And whatever he tells us to believe, that Abbot is the worst. Three a year, just in Dyflin.'

'Three what?'

'Three women. They chop off their heads and toss them into the river to keep Brid sweet. They're big on heads here.'

Bera shuddered. That was why she kept thinking of the children's skulls in the Abbotry well.

'Does the water heal?'

'The Abbot says it does. He charges enough for it to keep him in that palace. And now it's war.'

Bera's lips felt cold.

'Listen to me harking on, and you not eaten,' said Sigrid. 'I'll get you something to keep you going.'

'Wait… do folk pay for the healing water?'

'And to dodge being a sacrifice.'

'Is sacrifice always death?'

'Ask Bjarni.'

Sigrid went off to the pantry and returned, hands full, and the boy followed, with logs. He threw them on the hearth and gave Bera a wide berth as he left.

'A man can choose what to believe,' she said.

'We say that, but not the Abbot. It's believe what he tells you or else.' Sigrid waved a stockpot. 'That's what this war thing is about.'

'I need to understand—' Bera changed tack when the boy came in with more logs. 'Wolves. Why are they coming in broad daylight?'

The boy said something to Sigrid.

She banged the stockpot onto its stand. 'He says the wolf's gone, taking a toddler with it.'

'Are folk hunting it?' Bera asked him.

He kept his eyes down, blushing. Sigrid handed Bera a flatbread and chunk of smoked ham. She bit into it and slipped a morsel to Rakki.

'I saw that!' Sigrid scolded. 'Wasting good food on a dog.'

The boy scruffled Rakki's ears as he left, and Bera liked him.

The flatbread stuck to the roof of her mouth, so she went to the trestle and poured herself some ale. The glass jug was shaped like a green fish, mouth agape, its tail the stem. Beautiful.

She returned to the rug where the babies were sound asleep. She was leaden with tiredness herself and lay beside them, liking their warm milkiness and small ronfling snores. What had babies to do with war? Her beads were warm and heavy, and she was...

Brid, with Valdis, the Abbot, two ravens. Chaos and sacrifice in the utmost reach. Stifling, under earth, not water, stench of decay...

Bera was startled awake by a drowned man, his skin tight over the bones of his pearly face.

'Meal not ready yet?' It was Bjarni.

They were alone together and the air was charged, as if Bjarni had shared the dream. Bera was still half in it and glad that Rakki was guarding her.

'Your lad did rabbit stew with peas.' Sigrid bustled in. 'It's ready, look, on the hearth, keeping warm.'

Her fearful brightness made Bera angry. 'You should be out hunting wolves, Bjarni, not filling your stomach.'

Sigrid used lifting Borgvald to glare without Bjarni seeing. It was certainly her drowned husband making Sigrid so afraid, and Bera had been given a warning that made the Abbot a greater threat. And why was the dream-Valdis smiling in so dark a place? Bera looked down at the real Valdis and her daughter's unsmiling gaze unnerved her; not only as a future Valla but a very present child with her own mysterious needs.

Bjarni poured some ale. 'I had business. Now let's eat.'

'Was your business with the Abbot?' asked Bera.

Sigrid kicked the bench over. It made a fireguard for the babies, who began tussling on the bearskin beside the long-suffering

Rakki. Bjarni's son hurried in, served the stew and went off with his own bowl.

Bera could resist the delicious smell no longer. 'So we'll go to the palace after this,' she said, her mouth full.

'The palace will be locked.' Bjarni delicately broke the bread. 'It's sunset soon.'

'Sunset?' Her spoon clattered. 'I must get back to the *Raven*!'

'All the city gates will be closing.'

'I'll run down to the quay.'

'Enjoy your stew.' Bjarni sucked the flesh off some small rabbit bones. 'While I was down there I advised Faelan to anchor off and he did.'

'You advised! He was supposed to wait!'

'Sigrid is so pleased to see you.' He dabbed his lips with a cloth. 'Stay here with us – and your daughter.'

Bera wanted to hit him. 'Are you accusing me of leaving Valdis?'

Sigrid stacked the dishes and took them outside.

'Here.' Bjarni opened his hand. 'Give them to the dog. I remember you always loved to spoil animals.'

'Rabbit bones!' Bera snatched them and threw them on the fire. 'They'd splinter and kill him. Stop wasting time and get me to the Abbot!'

'It doesn't work like that, Bera.'

'Have you tricked me?'

'I want you to rest and go prepared. It would not help Dellingr to barge in shouting demands.'

'I would not have shouted!'

Bjarni raised an eyebrow.

Rakki retreated from the screaming babies. Bera looked round for a plaything but there was only the poker. She waved it about and they stopped crying. Valdis happily watched it, to and fro, and raised her mother's spirits.

'Run to the palace, Bjarni,' said Bera, 'and tell the Abbot to see Brid at dawn.'

'The guard will certainly pass on that message.' He left at once and took the bad dream with him.

The die was cast: she would be Brid from dawn.

Bera tickled Borgvald, who chuckled and grasped her finger with surprising strength. He was a dear, simple boy; no burden of a Valla future for him. Poor Valdis. Had the obsidian bead given her a glimpse of the chain she was bound to, with all that meant? Would she be needed in the utmost reach?

'My good, good baby.'

Valdis smiled and tore Bera's heart open. She picked her up and walked around, softly singing her mother's Raven Song, right to the end.

'... *the feathers oars that tipped the waves as they flew across at speed*,' she finished, and still no tears.

Bera whispered nonsense, glad no one could hear. This smiling daughter was a sweet, ordinary child, not the next Valla who would supplant her mother.

'There's the girl, Disa.'

Bera touched the baby's nose and blew a cloudberry. Valdis chuckled, so she did it again, willing Sigrid to come back in and see her being so natural a mother. Bjarni was maddening, but he had given her time to recover with the ones she most loved and prepare herself for the Abbot. She would be without her skern, for sure, in such a place and needed to plan how to rescue her smith. Would the Abbot make demands of Brid? Who could help her?

Did Bjarni have influence? Who was he, and why so rich? There were signs all round her of a household as costly as Hefnir's in Seabost. The hall was smaller, but many of the wares, like the glass fish, were finer.

Heggi was born to such wealth but there was no going back. Dear boykin. She pictured her first glimpse of him: his shock of white hair that was more a mix of oatmeal and honey blond now. She could almost smell it, and she ached to be back aboard with him. Bera prayed to her mother that she could one day feel as deeply for her birth child. She lay Valdis next to Borgvald, who did not stir. What a stupid risk to name her a mix of Valla and Alfdis, making her stronger than a mere Bera, surely?

Sigrid returned with more ale. 'Where's he gone to?'

'The palace.'

'Good. I need to talk to you.'

Bera waited while she filled their glasses. 'Were you there when I was born?'

'Course.'

'Was it... bad, like the birthing of Valdis?'

Sigrid snorted. 'No earth tremors. Your brother, mind... Well. Least said, soonest mended.'

Bera sat beside her. 'You want to tell me about Bjarni.'

Sigrid rolled her thoughts round her mouth with the ale. 'I need him, Bera, for protection, but he's changed so much.'

'He frightens you.'

Sigrid sighed. 'He doesn't hit me like he used to, but... I don't know... how did he get here?'

'Fishermen don't swim. I noticed that about his story.'

'He paid some pirates with a narwhale tusk.'

Bera's fingers tingled. 'There's a special magic in narwhale tusk and I felt it. I think he lied to his crew about losing one that time and hid it on the skerry.'

'Trouble is, Bera, I need your help as a Valla.' Sigrid made sure they were alone.

'Tell me.'

'Bjarni. I think he's dead.'

Bera let out a breath. 'He's no Drorgher.'

'You said it yourself.' Sigrid's eyes were sharp. 'Fetches.'

'Faelan did say sailors can return as husbands even though they had drowned.'

Sigrid made the hammer sign and crossed herself. Both beliefs. 'Did they father children, Bera, these drowned men?'

'You don't mean...?'

'No!' Sigrid shuddered. 'Have you felt his hands? And that boy's. They're like cold wax. What if his son is a Fetch thing?'

'Rakki likes him.'

'Bjarni wasn't burned, Bera, was he? So how do we really know? They might have any kind of walking dead here.'

Bjarni did have a cold, damp touch. Unpleasant, but was it unearthly? No skern to ask.

'Look, I'll work out how to protect us,' Bera said. 'Find out what they do to return drowned men to the sea.'

'Who can you ask?'

'I'll scry.' Bera was firm. 'I had to find my own Valla powers after my mother died, didn't I? Whatever a Valla believes, will happen.'

'That's the danger,' said Sigrid. 'My neighbour says the war's about wealth and power, same old thing, but this time it's split into two: our old beliefs and their new one. And that's joined lots of small leaders into two great armies.'

Two beliefs. Was that bringing Chaos?

Bjarni slammed the door. 'Don't waste candles, Sigrid, we shall go early to bed. We rise before dawn, Bera, and wait at the palace gates.'

Sigrid lit tapers without a word and they took the sleeping babies back to their cots. She pulled out some blankets from a chest.

'I'll sleep in here with them,' Bera said.

Sigrid's eyes were huge with fear. 'He'll be waiting for me.'

'No Fetch would worry about waste, Sigrid.'

But Bera was shaken. Was she wrong, and poor Sigrid sleeping beside a Fetch? Was any belief worth a war? If it wasn't, was it a belief worth having? Far from finding comfort from Sigrid, she had learned things that disturbed her more. It might be dangerous to claim Valla powers in such a place as this, before she knew what was at stake.

Bera fretted, missing her skern, missing the others, trying to scry the darkness. Blankets tangled, trapping her in worry when she was already overtired and would need to be sharp. The night dragged on, with odd shouts from outside, the howling of wolves. She gave up and kept watch over the babies.

Just before dawn, Sigrid came in with a light. Bera roused herself, wondering how to be Brid, alert to the Abbot's beliefs, but also true to her Valla self if she was to save Dellingr. Or simply stay alive.

15

The palace lay beyond the wealthy quarter on another high point of Dyflin, far from the slave market and quay. Bjarni was bragging as if he had built it.

'It was the first fortification, so has walls within walls.'

How close belief was to war in this land. No wonder Hefnir and the Serpent vied to be Chief Warrior.

They came to a flight of wide stone steps and Bera stopped dead.

'You could carry a longboat up there sideways on!'

Bjarni looked smug and began to climb, with Bera trying to keep up by taking two steps at a time. A gust of wind blew the hair from his neck, and she studied the skin. There was none of the mottling she had noticed in drowned fishermen but the corpses were quickly burned, so she had no idea if it passed off with time. In daylight, she could not believe he was a Fetch but Bjarni troubled her and she wished she did not need his help.

At the top was a stone arch with two oaken doors. One of them had a small door cut into it.

'That's a man-door,' said Bjarni grandly. 'We call them wickets here.'

The heavy ring on it, as Bera expected, was a serpent, eating its own tail.

'My mother had a bracelet like that,' she said.

'I gave it to her. As a sign of our everlasting love.'

'Your fisherman's lust.'

He banged the silver ring three times. 'Remember, in the palace you're Brid. So don't talk like that.'

'It was my idea.'

A slot at the level of a man's face slid back. Bera went on tiptoe but there was a grille, too, so she couldn't see the person speaking in a different tongue. The wicket opened and a man stepped out wearing a metal jacket like the Abbotry guards. What had Egill called it?

'Armour,' she said.

'Of course. The war is looming.' Bjarni gestured her ahead.

Bera was inside the palace.

The garden attacked all her senses with too much all at once. She was giddy with the jumble of colours and shapes and rubbed her eyes, then sneezed so hard she stumbled.

Bjarni put out a hand. 'Steady. You must get used to the perfume. This is the rose garden.'

'It smells like ensence. I'd think it would kill an old man.'

'The scent of a rose makes the blood run hot.'

Bera did not like his look; the closeness in her dream of his pearly corpse.

'Faelan's mother had a garden that was practical and neat. She grew herbs and plants that could be eaten. Their simple flowers fed her bees. What are all these for?'

'For this.' He spread his arms. 'This overpowering effect, which you feel, is to disarm.'

'I think it's to swank about this crumbling Abbot not having to grow plants to eat.'

'Swank?'

'It's a good word. Showing how much he has when others have so little.'

'You think paupers would be admitted? Look at the beauty, Bera! Wasted on the poor.'

'You were poor once! You're not now, but this garden isn't yours, so stop bragging.'

'I love beauty.' He smiled. 'But the first garden is to render an enemy defenceless should they storm the gate. So many roses give off a perfume that muddles the senses.'

'It would only work in summer.'

'Wars only happen in summer.'

She thought about why. 'All right, say more.'

'You lose all sense of direction and possibly belief – but if you are a friend and take the time to become accustomed to it, it's a form of sensuality.'

'Why do you use long words when we have good, short ones?'

Bjarni touched the gold brooch on his rich, wolfskin cloak.

'Swanky.'

Bera would not let him see she was awed, so she walked unsteadily to a rose with dewy petals like deep-red velvet. She pulled a stem towards her and yelped. A drop of blood bloomed on her finger that she quickly sucked away.

Bjarni came closer. 'They are beautiful but have vicious thorns.'

'If you say "like a woman" I will punch you.'

'Steady.' He took her arm. 'I'll show you the right path.'

'I don't need your help, thank you. So let go!'

He held up both hands, smiling. 'So like your mother.'

'Stop talking about her.' Bera could see no path through the tumble of roses. 'Just point the way.'

'It's through the white arch.'

There was a long hedge of single white flowers, alive with bees, and Bera could not see a gap. Her pressing duty was to save Dellingr, so she gave in. Bjarni turned her right round and took her elbow. As they passed underneath the mass of blooms, a single scent stopped her. There was a pink rose at the foot of the arch with softly ruffled petals. Bera plucked one and brushed her cheek, breathing in its headiness.

'The most expensive rose,' said Bjarni. 'Men have died to bring back the damask: the flower of love.'

'Don't start that again.' Bera took some deeper breaths and found the dizziness was gone. If this was meant to make her lovesick it had the opposite effect. She was clear and keen. 'I don't have Valla passion. My mother did, but I am very different.'

'A warrior,' he agreed, 'which is what we most need.'

'We?'

He moved to let her pass. Bera expected to go inside a kind of Abbotry, with a dark hall full of ravens where a ruin of a man would be guarded by armoured warders. Instead, she found herself alone in a walled garden. She followed a shingle path and stopped. Two huge ravens were perched on the back of a long seat, greedy for the titbits they were being fed by a slim youth with his back to her. He was dressed in glossy black, like his birds: a raven master like Cronan, except he was straight-backed, not twisted like her old guide.

Bera stepped forward into a shaft of early sunlight.

'Good morning,' she said to make him turn.

The youth's smooth face was white against his clothing, and he bashfully kept looking to one side of her, even when he smiled showing all his teeth. No gaps. He was too young for a raven master, possibly only a raven boy.

'They love cheese,' he said. 'I smuggle it out of the pantry when cook isn't looking.'

Bera smiled, trying to meet his eyes. 'Dogs like cheese too.'

She dived into her pocket and held up a morsel. In a black flurry, one of the ravens was on it with its cruel beak. The other tried to snatch it and their wide wingspan cast her in shadow. They beat the air, squabbling, and then went off, shrieking. Bera was on her knees. What would Brid do? She opened her arms and got up, as if in ritual.

The raven boy came closer. He met her outstretched hands with his, so that they made a cross of their bodies, and then pulled her to him, heart to heart. She had no idea what would happen next.

He let her go and bowed, keeping his eyes down. 'I have heard stories about you my whole life. I am the Venerable Abbot of All Iraland and I welcome you, Brid.'

Bera let out a long breath, surprised at his standing but overjoyed not to have to prove herself as Brid. The first lie to get her into the palace had worked. Now she had time and a friendly Abbot to deal with, not a sinister old man but a youth hardly more than Heggi's age. No wonder Bjarni had got rich: he was probably giving the lad all kinds of advice to feather his own nest. A youth would be easily led, so it was time to convince him that he should only listen to her – especially when it came to smiths.

The Abbot gestured at the bench. 'Let us converse.'

Whatever that meant, it was clear she was to sit beside him.

He gave two short whistles. 'A summons for Brid's ravens.'

They swung in from behind and settled heavily at the back. Bera slid sideways, to keep a wary eye on them. This close, their bodies were the size of geese. She wanted to scry the Abbot's eyes and reckon him, but the birds had a habit of ruffling the feathers on their necks and darting their heads forward, putting their savage beaks too near her head.

Brid would not cringe. 'They are very beautiful.'

The birds considered Bera with dark, unforgiving eyes.

She rummaged in her pocket, hoping some crumbs were left.

'Do you always keep wee gobbets in there?'

Bera laughed. 'I've always done it, ever since I was small. Not for myself but to give to any animal I meet.'

She flinched, being stupidly truthful.

The Abbot smiled at her ear. 'Brid is indeed the woman for strays.'

Bera was riding the wave of Fate. She found a piece of flatbread, kept her hand in her pocket and looked at the nearest raven. Was it cruel or clever? Its eye was obsidian. She heard an echo of Cronan's ravens, cawing as they took the word up into the darkness of the Abbotry tower, *'Obsidian! Obsidian!'*

Up into the uppermost reaches of the tower. Utmost reaches?

The raven was making pretty turns of its head to lure her into looking into its gleaming eye. Was it to trick her into scrying and reveal herself a Valla, or was its own cunning mind reckoning her? Well, she was a Valla who had dared to look into Obsidian…

'And in that place, the ultimate reach, lies the power of three; and the youngest will behold the eldest and the scantling mote shall split.'

The scantling mote!

How could she have forgotten? Whatever it meant, hearing it here must surely be a sign from the ancestors that it was safe to be Brid.

The Abbot was smoothing the other bird's back. 'Ravens belong here. They have lived beside the Abbot since time began. It's foretold that when the last raven leaves the palace it will be the end of all Iraland. But, of course, you know that.'

'And it shall never end,' said Bera quickly.

She was sure her panic would show on her face. Luckily, the Abbot was only ever studying his birds or the top of her left ear. She put a hand to it in case there was a spider or something caught in it. Then Bera gave her attention to the clever ravens.

Cronan's birds had seemed plain black in darkness, and she became fascinated by all the colours within these sunlit feathers: like the inside of an oyster shell, or a rainbow. Some feathers, in shadow, looked as if a knife had scratched lines on a rune stone. She broke the bread inside her pocket and the birds sidled closer. Their armoured claws clacked and clenched the wood.

The Abbot got up. 'They greet their mistress.'

He went to the arch and called for Bjarni, who appeared at once. Had he been listening? The men went off, using words Bera could not understand. She decided to make a test of her own.

When their voices were distant, she stood up and stepped back, facing the ravens. She palmed two pieces of flatbread, praying the birds would not fly at her before she was ready. She forced herself to be calm, rolled the food to her fingertips and then showed them. They turned their heads away, unimpressed by stale bread.

Bera carefully reached towards their beaks. 'There, my sweethearts,' she cooed. 'Be good and gentle, you two, and come to nice Brid, who has tasty titbits for you.'

It worked. To her delight they took the bread with one precise peck each. She still had all her fingers, not even a drop of blood. The rose had hurt her more. The test was certain, and she felt warmly to the ravens. In sunlight their eyes were a deep, warm brown. Almost amber, like the wolf. Wise creatures, not cruel.

She softly sang to them:

> The raven made twelve pairs of rope from the twists
>   and turns of its bowel;
> its claws were long and thin and sharp and made six
>   pairs of trowel;
> the beak was a black and shiny ship that cut the
>   Ice-Rimmed Sea;
> the feathers oars that tipped the waves...

Grief surprised her and she faltered. Someone was behind her.

'Your mother's lullaby.' The ache in Bjarni's voice matched her own and she thought perhaps what Ottar called lust might have been love.

'The ravens passed the Vallas' test, Bjarni. I am Brid.' He frowned. 'I mean, I undertake the pretence with their blessing.'

The Abbot was back. 'I have much to discuss with B-Brid. Return at noon.'

Bera glanced up but clouds were hiding the sun. 'How far off is noon?'

'I'll show you,' said the Abbot. 'Come into the next part of the garden.'

'How many gardens are there?'

Like all the men she had known, he gave no answer to a question he chose not to hear. Except Faelan, who also looked her in the eye straight. Bera followed the boy Abbot under another arch. It was covered in coils of green leaves and yellow flowers.

'This smells better than the roses,' said Bera. 'Sweeter, anyway.'

'Honeysuckle. Look at the bees now, suckling the honey.'

'Where are the skeps?'

'Hives are kinder. There are ninety hives at the furthest point of the garden, beyond the fish tanks. Tens of thousands of busy lives – and my beekeepers don't have to drown them to get the honey.'

'I've always hated that.'

'I'll show you them later.'

There won't be time, she vowed.

They walked along a path of glinting white stones bordered by herbs. Bera was thinking of Faelan and the healing garden, and kindness and kinship; of Miska and Rakki, and poor Feima, when the Abbot touched her arm. He pointed ahead at a rune stone set at the meeting of three paths.

'It's to tell the time. I devised it.'

'Did you ever meet Egill?' she asked, wondering if his boasts were as hollow. Once again, her words were like frost-smoke in the air. She followed him.

'I call it a sun dial. It uses shadow to tell us when to pray.'

'Are your gods not to be spoken to at other times?'

'You are Brid made flesh. Or do we also have that wrong?'

Bera flushed. 'Of course. I wondered what other gods you pray to.'

'And I wondered that since Brid was unexpectedly here, we might be wrong about setting times.'

She was certain they were testing each other, and she was too close to her smith to risk losing him now.

Bera went to scry the sun dial. It was the height of Dellingr and as broad, all the way to the ground. There were three rings at the face, heart and groin height. The Abbot left her to study it for herself and, unwitnessed, she hoped it would give some guidance.

The stone was man-like in more ways than height: as unyielding and silent. Where was the pliant space for scrying? Its 'nose' was a bronze stick that cast a long shadow between straight lines. It led her gaze right down to the lowest ring, at the 'groin'. An erect serpent reared out of it. Bile scorched her throat. Could she never escape the Serpent's violation?

'This is too mannish and not womanly.'

The Abbot pointed at the rings. 'There are the three marks of Brid.'

'But that's Yr.'

'Are you ill?'

She shook her head. 'I'm saying the rune.'

'Ah. I now understand that you, as Brid, come in many guises to many lands and must learn their teachings.' The Abbot smirked and pointed in turn to other runes. 'This is a symbol for man and this for woman. The divisions are shown in the middle circle where the year contains three hundred and sixty days, and three plus six plus zero equals nine, which is a holy number. As you know.'

Bera was feeling sick. Her counting was one, two, many.

The Abbot tapped his brow. 'I was interested in your raven lullaby. It contains the twelve and six numbers, divisible by three. Three is dawn in the summer and the ninth hour after that, when Bjarni will return, is what we call—'

'Indeed,' she interrupted. 'Do the serpents belong to me or the other gods?'

'The serpent is your emblem of healing,' he said, surprised.

'Ah. My water snake,' Bera lied, remembering the ring of small skulls. 'I know of the holy wells.'

'We shall go there next.' The Abbot seemed very keen to keep moving. Distracting her.

'I would rather see my most important...' Bera struggled for the word. '... thing to help me heal. My smith at the forge.'

'You are the silversmith.' The Abbot turned a bracelet at his wrist. 'But I suppose Brid could make the smith's iron more potent...'

'That's it,' Bera pounced. 'The lore of iron in a perilous time.'

'You sense the imminent threat. War is upon us and we need strong magic.'

Bera was completely alert. War had saved Dellingr's life, but forging weapons was trapping him here. She drew herself up.

'Readiness is all, if war is not to destroy us. I will work with my smith.'

16

The fire risk kept the forge well away from the main parts of the palace but it was still within the gated walls, not at a crossroads. So Bjarni was right, Bera would have to use shrewdness not force to free him. But instead of planning, she found herself thinking about a time that was not long ago, but was the difference between being a child and a woman. It was so clear to her now that she had made Dellingr into a kind of hero, when he was only a man. It wasn't his fault. She was the one who had taken him out of Seabost to a place where he had no iron to work. She had demanded he must stay as their smith and that had cost him his wife and son. So she must be loyal. But to whom? What kind of man would Dellingr be here?

'You are very pensive,' the Abbot said, regarding the tall buildings. 'Is the palace deficient? The entire edifice is a shrine to Brid.'

Bera had no idea what the words meant. She tilted her head in what she hoped was a Brid-like way and was saved from answering by Dellingr. He stooped to get through the low lintel of the forge and straightened, wiping his hands on a grimy cloth.

'Our smith is come to greet us.' The Abbot skipped towards the forge.

He's a dangerous child. Her skern popped out of a fire bucket, failing to hide his delight about appearing again.

It must mean belief and the power of iron was strong here, which meant her smith remained true to the old lore. Bera's heart lurched with the memory of her first sight of Dellingr in another time, another place. This time he did not smile.

Bera's mouth was dry. They had parted badly; he hated Faelan, and he was a respected smith here with weapons to make. He may not want to leave his iron and smith lore. Would he betray her and deny her as Brid? Would the Abbot be made to see she was a mere woman?

You're a Valla, not a mere woman. You see the danger in wanting to be 'ordinary'? You have a duty and purpose.

'I know. I'm working on it.'

Her skern drizzled back into the bucket.

The Abbot stood beside the smith, not reaching his shoulder. Neither of them looked at her directly.

'This meeting was prophesied when I became Abbot, aged nine. We three: Abbot, Smith and Brid. It was foretold that we shall meet when the final battle will wage at the Blood Moon to gain victory.'

Dellingr's face was carefully blank under all the soot.

'Who is the enemy?' asked Bera.

'It was foretold most recently that my smith would join the enemy side and make the weapon that would kill me.'

'That's not possible!'

He held up a hand. 'It's not my own skin I am protecting, Brid, but our faith. So only you can save Dellingr by making sure the enemy never takes the field.'

'Wait. You bought Dellingr to be sure of killing him?'

'He was a gift.' The Abbot shrugged. 'I have had years to plan and I am ready. We have traded for weapons and our smith has been making weapons to add to the armoury.'

'Dellingr hasn't had time!'

'Oh, Dellingr is not that smith.' The Abbot stressed his name. 'He replaces our last smith, who was then quickly dispatched.'

'Dispatched?'

'Beheaded,' said Dellingr flatly.

Now she understood why he was staying so carefully blank: he didn't want to give this madman any cause to behead him. Or her? She had misjudged the Abbot, his youth blinding her to the threat.

'The ravens foretold that the one I should fear would first appear a true friend,' the Abbot carried on. 'But we revered that person as the closest living incarnation of Brid, before she came among us.'

'There is only one Brid.' Bera was frightened by how certain the lie sounded. Would Fate take revenge?

Had Dellingr felt it, too? His eyes held something she could not read, his lips tight.

'Indeed.' The Abbot looked as if he had won the King-Maker game. 'But that sacred blood is shared.'

'I share my blood with no one.'

Bera does.

Guilt struck her like a sword. But her skern was warning her, not scolding. Something bad was coming.

'You may not know this yourself, perhaps,' – the Abbot smoothed his downy upper lip, enjoying her discomfort – 'but it was also foretold by the ravens that the man we revered, the only man who can kill me, is the brother of Brid.'

Bera's mind was tangled with too many lies to work out who her brother might be. Brid's brother. Was it Dellingr?

Steady. Whatever it takes to free your smith.

'I have no living brother,' she said.

Dellingr frowned slightly.

'Well, the ravens know he's dead now,' the Abbot said, as if she were stupid. 'He must be raised at the Blood Moon and in that moment, before his band of dead can join him, you must marry him.'

Bera needed time to listen, to think, to react as Brid. Was it all going wrong because she had lied?

Don't listen to two cheese-eating birds!

'And then he cannot kill me!' The Abbot had a peculiar smile. 'As your husband-brother, he will be yours for a year and a day. What is more, we shall grow strong, and prevail in the Holy War.'

Bera wanted to run. 'My brother died as a baby!'

'If a smith may speak,' Dellingr cut in. 'The lore of iron would make handfasting the only way to safeguard the bind, and must be done on my anvil. To avoid war.'

Bera gaped at him.

'Wouldn't you agree, Brid?' he pressed.

Your smith is giving you a sign.

She thought about all the ones she had failed to save. All of the past had led her into this trap: bound to a rotting corpse and marching to war. How could she have let her guard drop? Who was the dead man? Bjarni? Was Sigrid right and was he a Fetch pretending to be her brother for power and more riches?

'No man may marry the three-in-one,' she said.

The muscles in Dellingr's jaw were tight. Without seeing the trap, she had somehow made it perilous for them both.

'Are you saying we are wrong about Brid?' The Abbot's soft voice was dangerous.

Her skern held up three bony fingers.

'The power of three redoubles the three-in-one,' she made up on the spot. 'It must be the lore of iron that binds.'

Dellingr stood taller. 'And Brid's own smith must do it.'

Bera was thinking fast. 'Leave me here with our smith and we will carefully plan how to stop the war.'

The Abbot smiled up at the sky. 'Oh, we do not want it stopped; we need to win. My council will have gathered by now. I shall affirm the prophecy of Brid, since we now have her among us.'

That's the sound of a trap being sprung.

It seemed being Brid was as fettered as being a Valla. Everyone used her for their own purpose, devising their own version of what being a Valla or Brid was all about. She thought of the *Raven*, drifting at anchor, then Faelan and Heggi and, yes, Ginna who she now loved. Freedom to sail back to the Summer Isles. All islands, on all the sea paths. All lost.

Dellingr coughed a warning that she should speak. He was again her strength and stay. She needed a real prophecy, and hoped the Abbot would not question it.

'The ancestors have spoken to Brid.' Bera crossed her fingers.

They spoke to a Valla. There is danger here...

She'd faced it already. 'And in that place, the ultimate reach, lies the power of three; and the youngest will behold the eldest and the scantling mote shall split.'

Hers was the only voice; the Vallas had not joined her.

'And we will triumph!' The Abbot spun round and skipped away.

Bera was dizzy with relief, until her skern drummed his heels loudly on the bucket.

A game of deceit is dangerous for both players.

'I glimpsed my dear Ginna at the market,' said Dellingr. 'Thank you for keeping her safe.'

'She is brave and strong but losing you has brought her low.'

'I fought and was in chains as punishment for trying to escape. What do we do now?'

Bera looked round. Eager spies could easily be close. 'Let's go inside the forge.'

She strode ahead, impatient to talk, and blinked in the cobwebby gloom. The smell was familiar and welcome: hot metal and coals. Male sweat. Motes of ash and dust blew with each whump of the bellows wielded by a boy. He stopped blowing.

Dellingr blocked the light. 'Fetch some wood.'

The boy passed Bera with a sharp smell of fear. He ducked beneath some sacking cloths to avoid Dellingr and went out.

'Not like you to mistreat a bellows-boy,' she said.

'It's not me he fears. It's you.'

'Brid, you mean, not me.'

Dellingr put a finger to his lips and checked outside.

'He's gone.' He turned back to her. 'Even in this place, I am so glad to see you, and I have an idea.'

His teeth gleamed in the dark and, as always, she wanted to keep that smile. It was fond, like a father's. But she was caught being Brid, which trapped them both into some weaving of Fate that was so over-complicated the pattern couldn't be seen.

Dellingr dropped his voice even lower. 'I know Hefnir is dead, as is Asa. So I can marry you.'

The fool means it.

Bera wiped the sticky sweat from the back of her neck. 'I am here to save you, Dellingr, not marry you.'

What did he really feel about her? She always wanted him to be proud of her, like a father.

'You could say I'm your brother that you thought dead.'

'I'm not Brid, though, am I?' Bera clacked some tongs in his face. 'I'm Bera, with a real family to love.'

Dellingr grabbed them. 'Clear off and leave me, then!'

'I can't! Because Ginna loves you and I love her.'

Their anger came in growls and hisses, staying quiet, like animals at bay.

He rubbed his face with rough hands. 'I thought, Asa thought, you had feelings for me. Then, in Ice Island, I wasn't sure. Sigrid said being a Valla would always come first but that it also made a Valla woman, like your mother—'

'Passionate? I've heard it all and when my father said it, I believed it. I think it's you men who decide what we are. You see what you want to see and make up rules to excuse your own lust.'

'Then forget all that. Bera, you know the partnership we had, the smith's ancient magic and Valla skills. We made the other stronger. Together, we can defeat any enemy.'

'Have you heard about war? It's axes hacking through flesh and bone, not a board game!' The sound of one axe would be in her head forever.

'Your father,' said Dellingr softly.

Bera was filled with the same feelings as she had had in Seabost for this man. She had tested him through so many trials and he had earned her trust. He was loyal and kind, and trying to do what he thought was best to save her from the believers of Brid.

'We have been through so much, you and I,' she said. 'Asa was your only love and now Ginna needs her father back. As for me, I shall never marry another.'

'Give me a chance to help, Bera.' Dellingr slung away the tongs. 'War is coming, whether we like it or not, so we must join forces.'

'And we shall, but not by marriage. Ginna and Heggi yearn to be betrothed. They could never marry if we made them brother and sister.'

'I will not force marriage on you, Bera,' Dellingr sighed, 'or ruin their lives. So tell me what I can do.'

'Has the Abbot told you anything about this "brother"?'

The boy came in backwards, carrying logs. Like every bellows-boy, his sacking tunic was covered in spark holes.

'Bank the fire.' Dellingr jerked his head towards the door and Bera followed him outside.

The sun came from behind a cloud and blinded her. 'Do the walls go right round the palace?'

'Up to the slave market, that side. They're so thick, they have guardrooms in them, so they say. There's a lake, and all, but come over to the anvil, we might be watched.' Dellingr made a show of testing a dagger-blade. 'Look. We both know you're not Brid and this brother isn't real. What matters is that if you marry me you can't marry a dead man, whoever he is. That's all there is to it.'

'I won't be forced!' Bera touched his arm. 'Oh Dellingr, I will not destroy the happiness of our children, I've told you. But greater by far is that I must stop the war, even if it means— Oh.'

'What?'

'I've begun to think I can. What if men's beliefs shape action?'

He rubbed his hands on his apron. 'Go on.'

'What if I do as they say and there is no war because they believe Brid has done it?'

There will be recompense.

Dellingr scoffed. 'You think you can bring a corpse to life and marry it?'

'Of course not. But I can say I have, and who will doubt Brid? Then no one will fight.'

'Lies, Bera. Lie upon lie.'

'Once it's done we go off, together, and make a new home and be straight again.'

He hammered his feelings onto a piece of dented armour.

'Now.' Bera was brisk. 'Do you know my brother's name?'

'I can't get the hang of their tongue.'

'Try.'

'It's something that isn't Chief Warrior. They've made up his name, too, to mean something or other, to fit.'

Bera moaned as if in pain.

'Dellingr, I need to have his name to have power over him! But if you really don't know it, do you know why he is the Abbot's enemy?'

'It started when Hefnir wanted to be Chief Warrior of All Iraland and promised to come back with Obsidian, which the Abbot wanted above everything.'

'I know all that now.'

'Have you brought it then?' His eyes widened. 'The Abbot would declare himself Chief Warrior and we could be on our way home.'

She shook her head. 'Even if I had it, Dellingr, I would give it to no one, especially not a dangerous child.'

'Bera, it would solve everything.'

'Obsidian brings ruin! It is a looking-glass that reveals darkness. I looked into it and I think the first Abbot did too. It drove him mad, and I think it scrambled my mind for a time.' She looked at him. 'Perhaps forever. All I want is stillness, if I am ever allowed it.'

'We are a long time dead, Bera.'

Long dead, chanted the skern.

'I still don't know where I'm to find this corpse.'

'Are you being Brid now?'

She tugged her hair in frustration. 'No, I'm asking you as Bera.'

'I'm very confused.'

'That's because these are not our own stories, but nonsense made up by folk who want power. How can I scry here to find out how to stop it?'

He touched a finger to his lips.

'I'm frightened, Dellingr,' she whispered.

'So let me—'

Bera held up her hand. 'Listen. I am wondering what evil can be hidden in the madness of war. Chaos is coming.'

'Do you know what that means?'

'I shall find out and deal with it. As Brid, Bera, whoever, and set you free.'

Dellingr checked the trueness of another blade. 'One tale is that Brid is a warrior and she has a son who is killed by her dead brother. His uncle, I suppose that means.'

It reminded Bera of Heggi's uncle; the truth of his bad blood. 'I killed the Serpent King, Dellingr.'

The smith clapped her back. 'Warrior maiden indeed! Was it the sword I made for you?'

'Don't praise me! I only did it to stop Heggi taking the blood debt, and you've made me more like Brid!'

'Heggi's not your son.' Dellingr raised his hands. 'All right, you love him just the same. I meant, it isn't part of the Brid folklore.'

Bera began pacing. 'I don't want to talk anymore. I don't want to kill. Where is this "brother"? Can I go and make peace with him?'

Dellingr rubbed his face, spreading the black smears as far as his ears.

'Thing is, they're not sure. He went missing looking for something. Remember I haven't been here that long, but back on the pirate boat they talked about the dead coming back to life in a special place on a special day.'

Her skern waved from the anvil. *Long dead.*

'Drorghers?'

'No, it's one person on one day of the year.'

Long dead.

His anvil was marked with different runes on one side. 'The Abbot said it was soon, but not where.'

Long dead, long dead, long dead!

'They are pressing me to make… weapons as fast as I can. Look out! The Abbot is back here with someone.' Dellingr picked up a sword and elbowed her.

Her skern was pointing at a lake where tall bulrushes stood stiff in the breeze. A tumble of some climbing plant scented the air, which was full with birdsong. Above the lake were flashes of emerald and jade as tiny wings and bodies flashed in sunlight. The bright blue of one came closer, in a big circle, then hovered in front of her, turning its head so that one huge eye and then another could scry her. A dragonfly. A full dragon body. The long dead.

'This person coming back from the dead. It is the Serpent King, isn't it?'

17

Bera went to the anvil, asking the Vallas and skern to help her scry.

'I need to keep him dead.' She rested her cheek on the cold metal, gazing past her skern's spindly legs. 'Where is this special place? When is this special day?'

Nothing. Was this a punishment for taking on another belief, even as a lie?

Dellingr hissed. 'Get up, he'll see you. Vallas can't use the old magic anyway.'

The Abbot came round the corner of the forge with Bjarni, who was as silent and waxy as a drowned man.

'We have consulted and my council of Abbots agree with me,' the Abbot declared. 'Once your brother is restored to the living, I must handfast you both here. There will be a feast.'

Dellingr gave Bera a warning look.

Bjarni looks so sour because he thought this handfasting charade would be you and him.

The Abbot had asked her something. 'Brid?'

'My... um... they speak of "the long dead". Is my brother long dead?'

'No, that sounds like a riddle. I'm good at them.' The Abbot tapped his chin in a show of thinking. 'So clever of you, Brid, to make it hard. Oh, I know! It's what we call a barrow.'

Her skern sulked. *He already knew the answer.*

'As I told you, Bjarni.' He kept his gaze skywards. 'The barrow is where Brid's brother lies. The ultimate reach is where he must be woken at the coming Blood Moon, before the war begins.'

'Then my smith must come with me.' It was Bera's last chance to save Dellingr.

'Brid' – the Abbot smiled at a cloud – 'you declared yourself the three-in-one. My smith has secret work to do, which is more safely done within both city and palace walls. He stays.'

'We would be safer still aboard the *Raven*.'

The Abbot looked pitying. 'How could he work metal?'

'We need' – Bera crossed her fingers – 'to discuss our ancient magic over water.'

'I have a voice!' Dellingr thrust the sword into the earth. 'I choose to stay where I belong, in my smithy, with the song of anvil and hammer. It's where any smith belongs, between fire, iron and water.'

Dellingr had rediscovered himself and was in earnest. His home, his love, was fire and iron. Bera envied his strong sense of belonging.

Your home is the sea path.

'Yet to be at sea is to be forever restless.'

That's precisely why you belong there.

It gave Bera an idea. 'Most Venerable Abbot Thing—'

Her skern winced.

'Ah.' The Abbot coughed. 'Bjarni has persuaded me, and my council agrees, that henceforth I shall be known as the Warrior Abbot. To match our warrior maiden, Brid.'

He's up to something.

Bera was playing her own long game. 'Most Warrior Abbot, I request that since Dellingr has chosen to stay here of his own accord, he should be reunited with his daughter, Ginna. He will work better knowing she is safe and beside him.'

Dellingr looked at her. Straight to the heart in respect and trust. 'Brid is right, and I thank her. I need Ginna with me to aid my work and strengthen the magic.'

The Abbot swept an arm to include all the unseen palace folk.

'We have waited a long time for Brid's return to our shores and we are glad that we could... predict her wishes. Bjarni, you must accompany Brid to keep her safe.'

Bera fumed as they passed through the grounds; with so many guards about she was unable to tell Bjarni what she thought of his wanting to marry her. As soon as they were out of the palace she let rip.

'I was there to plan Dellingr's escape, not be bound to you! You're disgusting and old, and probably dead, and how can anyone ever trust you!'

'Bera, we are at the sharp end of life in another homeland. I am the one person you can trust.'

'Would you let me board the *Raven*, then, not lock me in with Sigrid?'

'You must do whatever you need to keep our own life and beliefs safe.'

'Our own?' Bera stopped him. 'Which "our" would that be?'

'There is only one home.'

'Which you abandoned, of course.'

'I stand by what I said: I shall support whatever decision you make.'

'You would let me sail away, then?'

'If that is what you intend then I will not raise the alarm until you are safely gone. We are all in your hands and if you say our future depends on your leaving Dyflin then I believe you. But, Bera, if you are your mother's daughter I don't believe you would abandon your duty: to Sigrid, to Dellingr and, most importantly, your own daughter.'

'Valdis would be with me.'

As they walked on, Bera was thinking hard. She felt giddy with longing to get aboard the *Raven* with all the ones she loved and go north, leaving this mess of lies and muddled beliefs behind. But the weight of duty that the Vallas decreed was to stay here and keep them safe.

Bjarni stopped. 'What's the matter with Sigrid?'

Sigrid was coming uphill, waving a shawl. When Bera waved back she started to run, waved again, doubled over and stayed there, with her hands on her knees. Borgvald was screaming and they hurried. Sigrid straightened when they reached her, fanning her red face and gasping. Bjarni took the baby and began to soothe him, which surprised Bera by working.

'He's not hurt,' said Bjarni.

'Not him.' Sigrid was panting. 'Hunted... high and low.'

'What is it?' Bera shook her.

'Only went… Borgvald woke, I dashed…'

'Where's Valdis?'

Sigrid's face was red. She started to wail. Bera couldn't breathe for fear that the Abbot had ordered her baby to be stolen to make sure she would do his bidding.

Sigrid sank to her knees. 'I'm so, so sorry.'

'Where's her baby?' asked Bjarni, dangerous.

'I don't know. Gone.'

'Look at me!' He really had no knowledge. 'Who took her?'

'I was only in the market two heartbeats…'

Bera ran. Was this the worst punishment for being Brid? All the way to Bjarni's house she bargained with the Vallas. 'Let her be safe. I'll do whatever you want but don't let her be dead, I beg you. Mama, help me. Just let her please, please be alive and I can save her.'

She stepped through a silent hall. Overturned beaker, broken glass, a stool, scattered kindling at the hearth. Violence. The Abbot would surely want Valdis alive but not the Serpent's crew, who must have claimed the blood debt. They would have followed Bjarni and Sigrid to his house. What a fool she was! Her foresight was gone, along with her skern. With mounting dread, she went into the babies' billet. And there was the empty cot, overturned, her blanket in a pool of blood.

Bera screamed. 'You murdering bastards!'

She rampaged through the hall, searching for her baby. She even looked in the buttery, knowing it was madness. Then the others were back.

'She's gone, Bera,' Sigrid said. 'It's not my fault. I left her fast asleep with the dog guarding her.'

Bera wanted to slap Sigrid, who stepped closer to Bjarni and took Borgvald from him.

'I had to go to the market, Bera.'

'It's odd the dog has gone too,' said Bjarni.

'He will be guarding her, of course, wherever they have taken her.'
Bera held her mother's bead, praying it was true.

'Or is she dead already?' Bjarni said. 'You can't ever trust a puffin hound.'

'I trust Rakki with my life.'

Sigrid rubbed her nose. 'He was all right before, Bera, I know that. Perhaps losing a leg changed him, being here, I don't know. Bjarni's right, though, and I'd never leave Borgvald alone with any dog. They're pack animals, aren't they? Once they've scented blood.'

'But you left Valdis!' Bera's anger was building behind her eyes, enough to splinter a Drorgher into shards. 'How dare you blame Rakki for your fault! Gossiping at the market, not protecting my baby!'

Sigrid used Borgvald as a shield. 'Bjarni's only saying it's odd that he's gone too.'

'I'm saying he's likely eaten her.' Bjarni spoke as if it was nothing.

Bera wanted to cram her Valla beads down his throat until he choked.

There was the pattering of claws on stone, the drag of a lame animal.

'Rakki!' Bera spun round.

He wagged his tail at her voice but then swayed, cowered, his muzzle covered in blood.

'That's guilt!' said Sigrid. 'Plain as you like.'

'Stay there, boy.' Bera moved towards him so that he would not have so far to try and walk.

Bjarni stepped back, pulled up Rakki's head, sliced his throat and let him fall.

Bera roared, slamming into Bjarni to get him away. She knelt beside Rakki and tenderly moved his head to close the deep gash. His puzzled eyes stayed open, so bright, surely he was still alive. Perhaps she had healed him by closing the wound. She stroked and kissed him, speaking softly, so he would know how much she loved him.

'Rakki, my sweetest baby dog. Good boy. Best dog ever.'

Sigrid touched her back. 'He's gone, Bera.'

'No, Sigrid, look! Can't you see his chest move? He's still breathing.'

'It's over, sweetheart. Rakki's gone.'

Bera pushed Sigrid away. The Vallas had taken another thing she most loved but her broken heart kept its forlorn hope. She put her head on his chest, desperate to feel a heartbeat but there was nothing. How could he die, between one beat and another? The shock of it. No warning, no bracing. Those bright eyes had no life behind them. No scratch in her brain of his thoughts. Too late to tell him that she trusted him with her whole heart. This loss had cracked her open. It would kill her.

Bjarni was unmoved. 'The villain's dead. He will have left her somewhere, but we can follow the blood. At least you know the pirates don't have her.'

Bera could not make her voice work, or her legs.

Sigrid got her to her feet. 'Let's wash your face, it's covered in blood. We'll look outside for Disa and give her a proper burial.'

There was a thin wail.

Bera ran into the billet, pulled away the jumble of blankets and lifted the overturned cot. Valdis was smothered, red-faced and glaring. Relief on top of despair made her giddy. Bera picked her child up, snuggled into her neck and drank in her smell.

Sigrid was fussing. 'Now Disa's got a bloody face.'

'Get away from us.'

'I can't see where she's hurt, though,' Sigrid lifted an arm.

'Of course she's not hurt, thanks to Rakki! You caused this by being absent, Sigrid. And your vile husband should have stayed dead!'

'It's all his fault,' Sigrid quickly agreed.

'He will pay the blood debt, right now.'

'What blood debt? It's only a dog, Bera.'

Bera thrust Valdis at her and marched out. The full reckoning with Sigrid would come later, but she did not think they could even remain friends.

Bjarni was gone, leaving Rakki's body in the hall. He looked so small in death that Bera's heart cracked open again. She covered him with a blanket and went looking for his killer.

Outside, there was a murmur of a mob somewhere but no sign of Bjarni. She heard her name and Heggi appeared round the corner of the house.

'Heggi!' She couldn't let him see his dog.

'There you are, Mama!'

'What are you doing here? Is the *Raven* at—'

'I came to see him; I must have sensed it!' He set off the way he had come. 'They're all talking about it, all of Dyflin. Quick!'

Bera followed him through a twitten into a yard filled by a jostling crowd. Heggi jinked through but folk got in Bera's way as they craned to get a view. What was it? Had Chaos come? Someone whistled for quiet and gradually folk grew still. Heggi, somewhere inside the crush, was speaking.

'I trained him from a pup.' It was his proud voice. 'He's the best puffin hound. You should see him hunting, even on only three legs now. One single night he caught sixty-four puffins. He's the bravest dog, too, so old bears and wolves never scare him.'

Bera wanted to die with the pain of it, could not stand to see what she now suspected was in the middle of the eager crowd. She had to bear witness and barged her way through. At Heggi's feet lay the body of a wolf. Rakki had saved her daughter's life at the cost of his own.

18

Bera ran, not knowing where she was going, not able to stop the pain. She should be telling Heggi and helping him deal with the awful knowledge. It was the most cowardly thing she had ever done but her legs obeyed her heart, not head. She was six again and running from her mother's death. Then she saw Bjarni. Her hand went to her knife and she slid it into her hand. This time she would claim the blood debt at once, and laugh while she killed him, because all she could taste was injustice.

'Bera!' He looked pleased to see her, the fool. 'I was wrong to blame your dog and you must take whatever revenge you choose but I beg you to first let me speak.'

He waited for her to say something but there were no words now. Nervously, he went on. 'I know I've only made matters worse, losing what little trust you placed in me.'

Trust. The gaze of love that could never lie with words. The precious gift of a dog. Where would she ever find a love like that again? She would give unquestioning love to her children but where would she receive it?

Bjarni was still speaking. Something about burning. Burning Rakki. But there was no need as dogs had no skerns. Or were they skerns themselves? No, only as close as a person's skern. So would they follow the dead? She tried to beat away the thought of Rakki being taken by Drorghers and made to hunt with them, punching the side of her head.

'Don't, Bera, please.' Bjarni went to stop her, then dropped his hand. 'I have caused your agony and it fills me with sorrow. I will tell you, not to lift the blame from myself, but perhaps it will help you, I want to tell you that Sigrid and I reckoned the wolf bites on Rakki and we think he was in agony and would not have lived, so really I...' He ran his hand through his hair.

She should kill him.

Bjarni's hand dropped to his side. His jerkin had been done up on the wrong button. There was something touching about it. No Fetch would have the buttonholes wrong. Stop it, stop it. This man killed Rakki. His weaselling had made it worse and yet there was sincerity in his face.

'So tell me, as a Valla. Say the word, Bera, and I will arrange it.'

One single word was impossible.

The way Rakki died was agony. The injustice! He was always and would ever be her hero. This was a particular pain. Her ribcage simply would not open wide enough to take in air. Besides, she did not deserve to breathe freely because after all, she was the one who had left poor Rakki to guard her daughter, while she was off doing 'her duty'. She almost spat. Sigrid was right about Vallas.

'Bera, please come back. I'm offering to burn him, even though folk here say it's heathen, so we must be careful no one sees you, as Brid would never oversee such a ritual.'

Brid demanded sacrifice, she remembered. Was Rakki a victim of Brid, not the Vallas at all? Bera felt trapped between two warring, ruthless beliefs. Or had she started all this on Ice Island by lying about being Brid to save her own skin?

He took one step. 'There is so much at stake! It isn't your child, after all, it's just a dog.'

He may as well have said 'just an arm'.

Her father had once met a man, a fighter, who had lost an arm to an axe. It wasn't the one he used to kill and eat, so he thought he could master it. But he kept falling over, not knowing its weight had been holding him upright every day. Now she knew how it felt.

'Oh, Bera. Say something.'

The longer she said nothing, the harder it was to start. Her body was shutting down and she started to shake. Ottar... axe... Rakki's throat... She must be strong, it was far from over. War was coming that she must stop. There was only one place she wanted to be, where she would be safe. Onboard with Faelan, who would understand it all and comfort her. But then would Heggi kill Bjarni?

It restored her voice. 'We will bury dear Rakki properly, as we do on Ice Island. And you will go down on your knees to Heggi and beg forgiveness. I spare you, for I see there is no evil in you – but no honour, either.'

They returned to the house, where Heggi had dug a grave. They carried Rakki's small body together and curled him for his long sleep, as if he was before the hearth.

'Rest now, dear one,' was all Bera could manage.

Heggi fell to the ground, sobbing like the toddler he had been. His misery was harder to bear than her own and doubled it. Sigrid looked wretched but Bera could not forgive her, so she wordlessly took Valdis, got Heggi to his feet, and left for the quay. She thought Bjarni might try and stop her but he shrank back from the door and let them pass.

Bera kept returning to it in her thoughts. Would the Abbot make him suffer by letting her go? No, he knew Bera had to take Ginna to her father. Trapped by love and duty, with failing powers and numbed by grief.

Heggi wriggled his fingers. 'You're hurting, Mama.'

Bera let go. 'I should have been there, boykin.'

'I wish we had never come here. I wish we were still in Seabost and I was up on the cliff with my best dog.'

She stopped so that Heggi could burrow into her for comfort but the baby was in the way. A few folk pushed past them, cursing them for blocking their path to the quay. Bera moved nearer the wall and they walked on.

'Don't go back to that house,' blurted Heggi. 'Ginny says Sigrid—'

'Is punishing me.'

'Yes!' Heggi's eyes were wide. 'I've wanted to tell you for ages.'

'I expect she heard Sigrid and Asa moaning. But it goes a long way back, to my mother and Sigrid's husband.'

'I hate him. I wish he'd stayed drowned.'

They carried on in silent grief. There was a nook in the wall ahead where Bera found some privacy and a place to sit. She hugged Heggi without Valdis being crushed.

'Oh, my poor boykin. I loved him, too.'

'Everyone did because Rakki was so good.'

Except it was the dog's spirited unruliness that Bera loved so much. 'I used to envy him, you know.'

'Rakki? Say about it.'

'The way he would run along the shore, grinning. How well he could swim!'

'After skimming stones...'

'Chasing everything with no thought of a cliff edge or getting into trouble with farmers or fishermen...'

'He was so brave.' Heggi's voice wobbled.

Neither of them could go on. Bera kept tight hold of Valdis, as though she could be snatched at any moment.

Heggi rubbed his eyes with a cuff. 'Why did you envy Rakki?'

'Oh, I wanted to be him sometimes.'

'Well, you are brave.'

'I'm not brave inside.' Bera wanted to be truthful. 'Oh Heggi, I'm so weary. From the day I was born, I've been yoked to my Valla duty, trying to be as good as my mother, never knowing the true care and friendship shared by others.'

'Did you have to, Mama?'

'I don't know.' She was forced to consider it. 'I believed, oh, that not being an ordinary woman would be rewarded one day. That I'd be allowed to see you and Ginna grow up and have children of your own.'

'Have you always been like this?'

'Like what?'

'Feeling all this. You've never said any of it. I don't think you've ever said as much about anything as you have since Rakki died.'

She missed the dog's sweet scratch in her mind. Now there would only be silence and injustice forever.

'I made a bargain with the Vallas that if Valdis lived, I would carry out whatever they have planned.'

Her daughter chirruped at her name.

'So you're leaving us.' Heggi's lip trembled.

There was a shout from above them.

Bera put an arm across Heggi and pressed back against the dwelling as a bucket of slops was emptied. She placed a muslin cloth over her baby's face so the stench did not poison her.

'Let's get you to Ginna.'

At the top of the city gates they turned to let the sea breeze cleanse them before going down to the quayside to signal to the *Raven*. They found Faelan waiting by the ladder with a larger curricle below. The relief of seeing him took Bera's words away but their faces would be enough to tell him the news was bad.

Faelan asked no questions. 'I thought we might need to get away at speed.'

He shimmied down the ladder and Bera passed him Valdis, then she and Heggi got aboard with care. Faelan let Heggi row them out into the harbour, with a nod when Bera thanked him with the sign. And then there was the *Raven*, which would be Bera's own balm.

Ginna took the line from Heggi, her face stiff with disappointed hope.

Her skern poked a bony finger into Bera, his return no relief. *She trusted you to bring her father.*

'Let's get aboard,' said Faelan. 'Then hear each other's news.'

First, Valdis had to be fed. She screamed and struggled but Bera kept hold of her instead of giving her to Ginna. When she was happily eating, Bera told them that Bjarni would be taking Ginna up to the palace to stay with her father.

Heggi stuck his knife into the deck. No one complained.

'He needs you, Ginna,' said Bera. 'The Abbot is forcing him to some secret smithing, so I want you to try and keep him away from danger.'

Ginna snapped. 'What you mean is, I'm the ransom to make sure you do as you're told!' She put a hand over her mouth and burst into tears.

'Shh, small one.' Bera took her in a bear hug. 'You belong with your papa, but you are right that the Abbot agreed as a safeguard that I must return.'

'And listen, Ginny.' Heggi sheathed his knife. 'Me and Bera are really sad, too.'

They kept the tale of Rakki's death short and then Heggi and Ginna wanted to go off together. Too dangerous ashore, and Bera was terrified that a life could be lost in a blink, so they agreed to stay in sight at the prow, while Faelan and Bera kept to the stern with her drowsing baby.

As soon as they were alone, Bera lost words again. Something had broken loose and Faelan saw it.

'Have you ever properly grieved for your mother?' he asked.

'Did you?' she countered.

'I mean cried, Bera. Sobbed so hard snot runs down your face.'

'Probably.' She shrugged. 'Or Sigrid stopped me.'

'Bera, when I first met you I thought you were confident and strong. Then I thought you were hard and cold. No' – he held up a hand – 'you know I understand why you left me. But now? I think you have a choice to make.'

'I didn't choose to feel like this!'

'I know that. But you weren't braced for Rakki's death and I think it opened that box inside you, the one you told me you shut away on the passage to Ice Island. I believe you made the box a long time ago, in fact, when your mother and baby brother died, so nothing could hurt you as much again.'

Bera perched on the edge of a barrel before she fell down. Her legs began jigging uncontrollably and she pressed her hands on her knees to stop them. Her apron was stiff with blood. Precious blood. The backs of her hands were freckled like an old woman's, with coursing veins that had risen in the heat. Blood, going on pumping. She turned them palms up. The lines and creases made runes that some old women said had been put there by the Fates. If so, she could not scry them. Did not want to.

'The pain's been carved into them,' she said. 'Before I was born, by Vallas.'

Faelan rolled another barrel to sit in front of her, knees touching, and then reached for her hand.

'My mother could read palms. I'm not sure I have the gift but let's take a look. Now, this is the life line…'

He drew a finger along it. Bera smiled, expecting the commonplace prediction of a long and happy life.

It was too hot to wear a hat and his hair was scraped off his forehead, so his face was in plain view. He met her gaze. The sun had browned his cheeks, apart from the pink burns, so that his eyes were even bluer and starred by small white lines. There was the smile-crease that she loved, and the small mole above his lip.

He looked away. 'Sorry.'

'Don't hide.'

Faelan sighed. 'You can hide but still wish to be seen.'

'You mean, to see beyond the burns.'

He gave a small nod.

'That's why I was scrying your features, Faelan.' Bera gently pulled his chin round. 'Did you become afraid of what I should find beneath the surface?'

'I never know what you're thinking.'

'Yet you understand better than most.'

'Talking to me might help us both, then. If you trust me.'

Bera took a deep breath. 'I'm afraid that if I open that box inside to let out my feelings, what else will come? Ottar always said if you dig one shovel of shit, the whole heap will fall on you.'

Faelan laughed. 'He's probably right! That's the risk, Bera. But it always helps to share the load, whether it's hay or shit, you halve it. Struggle on alone or share – but it means sharing everything.'

Bera opened her hand. 'What did you see on here, Faelan? Is there a line for my daughter? She and I are the same body, so will the choices I make change her?'

He rubbed his chin. 'I'm not sure what you mean?'

Love – and death.

Mother – and Valla.

Bera knew now that she would gladly give up her life for her child, and if Valdis did die it would be the end of her anyway, and of the Vallas, too. Was that written in her palm? But Chaos was coming unless she could avert it – and no one would be safe if it did.

Use your silent bargain.

What silent bargain? Her skern was annoyingly smug again, amongst believers.

'Bera?'

She sidestepped a little. 'If I feel like this about Rakki, who began as Heggi's dog, not mine…'

'You think grief can kill? I think it can, Bera, but you are the strongest person I know.' He took her hand but did not look at it. 'This says we can be even stronger together.'

'Hefnir once said that too.'

'He didn't mean it. He wanted Obsidian.'

'Chaos is coming, Faelan, and whatever that means, the Abbot is summoning it. He thrives on war, it's plain. So I will do whatever the Vallas demand to bring peace. I will find a place where we can safely settle. Only then will I be able to drop my guard. When I'm home.'

It was too hot to think, even out at anchor. Noises reached them of gathering war, shouts and hammering rising with the heat. Bera worried that Valdis was running a fever, her cheeks were so red. Please, not red-spot. She kissed her brow, and a memory returned of her mother doing the same for her, snug under furs, telling her that lips could tell a fever better than hands. Alfdis must have cared. Perhaps she was wrong about not learning anything from an unloving mother who died too soon.

Was she getting it all wrong? Ginn's going to the palace troubled her but her skern had given no warning. The girl kept her distance from Bera, which hurt, but also seemed cross with Heggi, although it was too hot for anyone to be as close as usual. Perhaps Ginna was hardening herself to leave him, which Bera understood.

And so they rested, until Bera saw Bjarni waiting on the quayside. Even at that distance she could not bear to look at him. The sight seemed to spark Heggi's anger at Bera, blaming her for Rakki's death. He kicked the slop bucket towards her and then nearly threw it overboard, except Faelan was too fast.

Ginna looked wretched.

'Be brave, sweetheart,' said Bera. 'There will be danger but I promise to return for you and your papa.'

'I'm coming with you in the boat,' Heggi said.

Memories of Bjorn's hot-headed rush to his death filled Bera with fear. All for the narwhale tusk that began it all.

'Ginna needs Bjarni's protection, Heggi,' she said. 'Your anger about Rakki will make things worse for her.'

'I forgave him!' Heggi spat.

Faelan held his shoulder. 'Best say your farewells here.'

'Heggi's hurting,' said Ginna. 'He's angry with everyone.'

'I'm not!'

Bera pitied her boy. It was at moments like this that he would always go off to recover his good spirits with his dog. She quickly turned her own thoughts away from Rakki and tried to mend the hurt.

'Heggi, we all need to blame someone. I blame Sigrid, but one day I must make peace with her. She says Fate was ruling Bjarni.'

Heggi mumbled something about Vallas that Bera supposed was the ripest Ottar curse.

'I'll go ashore with Faelan.' Ginna took his hand. 'He might be away awhile, so you must look after Bera and your sister.'

Clever.

Bera fell in with the pretence. 'Yes, Faelan needs to buy more food.'

Heggi slumped, his anger gone; he was too dejected to argue. Bera recognised the child he had so recently been: the one who stole all the attention when it was Ginna leaving and Ginna going into danger.

Faelan towed the curricle round from the stern. The couple spoke in low voices, foreheads together, until it was time to part. On impulse, Bera took both their hands.

'Now what did Sigrid show me about handfasting?'

Their dear faces were lit with joy and it delighted Bera to so easily give them this. Faelan nodded, understanding.

'There. Left to right and right to left. It doesn't seem much, does it, and not our custom, but they believe it binds, in Iraland, so... there.'

'Our arms make the rune for beginnings,' said Ginna.

'And fertility,' said Heggi. 'I love you, Ginny.'

'And I you. I always have.'

Bera's tears stung. Joy, grief, it was all the same in this moment.

'You will be together now for a year and a day,' Faelan said.

Ginna hugged her. 'You are my betrothed mother now, Bera.'

'It seems right that a Valla should do the binding of two people before the making of a new life.'

Heggi opened his mouth.

'No, you may not, boykin. You are not of age. I meant finding a place to belong and living there, all of us.'

'Now I am happy to go to papa and tell him.' Ginna kissed the baby's head. 'Goodbye, Disa. Thank you, Bera. Heggi and I have been true to each other no matter what, but all our hope lies in the future.'

She was already a young woman, unlike her betrothed, who might have a deeper voice and leg hair but was still too young to recognise from Bera's stare that he should also make a vow.

Faelan helped her into the curricle. 'Ginna, this handfasting makes an open pledge of your feelings and intent. None of your kin are here, but tell Dellingr that I stood witness for you. Tell him he and I are joined in this as much as the troubles we face, and we should be friends.'

Ginna nodded. 'He will be glad.'

Bera caught Faelan's eye. He doubted it, too.

'I'll ask Bjarni how close the war is getting,' said Faelan.

He took up oars and they were gone. Heggi moved further along the rail to be alone as the curricle weaved through the anchored boats in the harbour. Bera lost sight of it, then saw it tie up at the quayside. The two slight figures met the taller man and they were swallowed up in the throng.

Heggi stayed watching long after they were gone. If Asa had lived, she would never have allowed him near her daughter. Death also brought freedom. Who said that?

Not me. Her skern was on a barrel, letting his glum legs dangle.

'I wonder if freedom brings death?'

Then we should be too afraid to ever say it.

19

Bera dragged herself through the first few days, her head pounding with unshed tears, but the nights were worse. It was hard to sleep but when she did begin to drowse, she felt the ice-cold clutch of her dying mother's hand, the whistling rush of the Serpent's axe and the thud of her father's head on the jetty. The last would wake her: the death of Rakki. Then she would lie there, listening to drunken fights across the water, blaming herself for every failing, even a childish unkindness.

Why did the Vallas not show her how she should act? She slapped her cheeks in punishment, furious that she had been tricked into claiming to be Brid.

That's your own trap, there.

'Why is the Abbot making me wait so long?'

To frustrate you and bind you to his own belief, perhaps, so you will obey his purpose without question. I can't tell at the palace.

If she began to cry, she would never stop. In any case, she did not want to wake the others. Heggi had his own burden and Faelan might be too tender; might open her up to something she did not want to face. Not yet. Lying alone with trouble brewing and no plan, she missed Rakki's warm body curled beside her. He was the one being who knew her through and through; who saw through her and loved her just the same, trusting her. He would have given his life for her, as he had for Valdis.

Sleep.

'He trusted that when the time came I would ease his going, cradling him.'

Like a skern. He stroked her brow.

'I failed him.'

She did not deserve his comfort. Bera got clumps of her hair by the roots, pulling the pain away from her mouth to stop the scream inside.

One night she caught Heggi doing exactly the same and was flooded with guilt.

'Is it Ginna?' she asked, softly.

'What if that Warrior Abbot makes her…'

'What?'

'You won't let me say the word.' He pulled at his caffled hair again. 'Dellingr will protect her.'

Heggi knows all the power lies with the Abbot.

'And he rightly blames me for letting her go.'

The loss of Rakki was worse by day; odd things hurt, too, like hearing his particular way of drinking and eagerly turning only to find a pail of water but no dog, or the thump of his tail on the deck when Bera unwrapped food, which she then could not swallow.

Heggi's shoulders were tight but his face was a hard blank of the man he was becoming; cutting off sensation before it reached his neck. His pain was festering and Bera's attempts to release it were met with anger. When she played with Valdis, Faelan tried to distract Heggi by teaching him some knots.

'I know all this.' Heggi tied a slack knot. 'Ottar showed me when I was a boy.'

Bera drew a breath to say he was still a boy but events had made him grow up – and time was doing odd things for her, too: both stretching and shrinking.

'I hate not knowing where she is,' he mumbled.

'You need to picture her.' Bera understood. 'Shall I tell you about the forge?'

Heggi threw down his cord. 'It won't be in my mind, then, will it?'

Bera wondered where the closeness of the handfasting had gone. She had hoped it would join not only Heggi and Ginna but Dellingr and herself in a way she could manage, and Faelan need never know about Dellingr's offer of marriage. But still, they were three people swilling about, no comfort to each other.

She tried to hearten them with one of Ottar's sayings. 'Things always get worse and then they get better.'

'Cheery,' said Faelan.

'How could it get any worse for me?' Heggi stomped to the rail and glowered at any passing bird.

What worsening might mean was an extra burden for Bera but the only feeling she could allow was duty.

Duty isn't a feeling. It's a decision.

'But I need a sign! I hate being stranded out here, waiting for someone else to move us forward.'

A gathering cloud of black birds above the city began and ended each day. It was a warning, but no summons came from the palace nor vision to form a plan. The only one who moved forward was Valdis, who began to crawl. She was so fast that Faelan made a barricade of barrels to keep her safely penned. And seeing her son and daughter play bear hunt made Bera laugh. She laughed so easily that it shocked her, and Heggi's gawping face made her laugh more, and then Faelan joined in. Tears streamed down their faces and Bera got hiccups, so they howled loudly, joined by Valdis; was she happy or sad? Both? Bera's own feeling was too huge to know, but the iron bars of her ribcage burst open and she gulped in lungfuls of sea air.

Afterwards, they played with Valdis, who chuckled joyfully. It was a glorious sound and Bera wanted more of it. But then a splinter went into her daughter's knee and she felt a sharp pain in her own. The baby's eyes widened but she did not cry, and bravely raised the place to be kissed better.

'Brave girl, Disa.'

After that, only her mother would do. Perhaps the feelings of a natural mother did not have to be learned but simply allowed to be. Had Alfdis known this? Or was she always the Valla? What lessons could she teach her granddaughter?

Ta-dah! Silent bargain. Power of three.

'But I must go and be the Valla.'

Bera called the others to the mast. 'I am going to the palace.'

'Me too,' said Heggi. 'I want to be closer to the forge.'

'You can't see it from outside, and you are not to go in.'

'Ginny will know I'm there.'

Faelan pushed back his hat. 'Did you have a sign?'

Bera shifted. 'I'm sick of waiting. I shall make something happen.'

'What if it's the wrong thing? How will you get in? Will you risk going to Bjarni's house?' He looked pointedly at Heggi.

'I am going to stop the war, one way or another!' Bera stepped away. 'Let's not row, Faelan. I have checked the tide to go in, and the market is busy enough to give us cover.'

Faelan's jaw was set as he got the curricle ready and started to row them to the quay. He had not looked so angry since his fight with Dellingr on Ice Island. She had forgotten that he was slow to anger but then he blazed; could the two of them ever find peace in a new home if they could escape? He handled the curricle with ease, giving Bera time to study every boat they passed for signs of the Serpent. Too many had flags and pennants with snakes, skulls and dragons on them, and she felt evil growing. She thought of the wrist tattoo that Egill, Hefnir and the Serpent King had somehow earned; what did it mean?

Widdershins is never good. Her skern was already dwindling with so many unbelievers around them.

The war fleet was in the main harbour, gathering more warships every day, but even here shield-embossed dragon boats were starting to outnumber ordinary traders. As they neared the quayside Bera wondered if Bjarni had shaped the young Abbot, or been shaped by him. Where had his wealth come from and what would he do to keep it? Had he even summoned Chaos to come?

Heggi started off as soon as they landed and Bera told him to wait while Faelan tied up. Then she was caught between the two: Heggi scuffing ahead and Faelan angrily following behind. It was dangerous to split up. At least Valdis was safe in her bundle as Bera threaded through the raucous life at this end of the market. Trestles laden with quicksilver fish were surrounded by women who sang at fast-gutting pace. Their knives flickered like sunlight on water and they were surrounded by squabbling gulls, cats, chickens, pigs and vermin, attacking the thrown guts and each other.

Bera was braced for the sight of town dogs but when a rat scuttled through some barrels she pictured Rakki's little face, screwed with determination to be as fast on three legs as he had been on four. Her throat ached, like swallowing a pebble. She held both hands over her heart and pressed.

'Grief is a dagger.' Faelan was beside her. 'You don't need to be strong with me, Bera.'

'But I do need to be strong.'

She was determined to put grief aside. In any case, she did not deserve Faelan's comfort. He had never complained about leaving Miska behind and that sweet mare had been with him far longer.

'Where's Heggi?' she cried.

'He can't be far.'

Faelan went one way and she another. Frantically scanning the stalls, she caught sight of Sigrid at an oyster barrow. Bera turned her face away at once but she was certain that Sigrid had seen her. Perhaps she had Heggi with her. Bera pushed through some rank-smelling animals and reached the barrow just as Sigrid hurried away.

'Hel's teeth!'

Faelan ran up. 'I've found him.'

Heggi was at one of the fruit stalls and had a look of concealment. Bera stopped Faelan joining him. 'Wait.'

Heggi bought a pear.

'He wants to eat it himself, not share with us,' said Faelan. 'In two gulps.'

Heggi carefully wrapped it in his neck-cloth and put it in his satchel.

Bera smiled. 'Wrong.'

They caught up with him on the ramp up to the gates and then climbed towards the palace. They passed a twitten, like the one where Rakki's dead wolf had lain. Bera stopped.

Faelan held her elbow. 'You've gone pale.'

'I'm thinking how hunting dogs have their throats slit once they get too old to hunt. No use, no life.'

'But that is not your way.'

'Rakki deserved better.' Bera made sure Heggi was out of earshot. 'I should have foreseen everything that happened and stopped Bjarni. I've lost my skern and my visions in Iraland.'

'Go and say this to Heggi.'

'He still blames me for letting it happen, and he's right. If Vallas are in charge of life and death why can I not bring him back?'

'Are they, though?'

Bera glared. 'Do not lose belief in me, Faelan, no matter that you wear the cross of Brid.'

'Then you must not make your own belief a burden.'

Heggi hissed at them to be quiet. The palace gate was in view beyond and they joined him in the shadows. No one came in or out.

Heggi took out the small wrapped pear and cradled it. Bera realised it was a gift.

'We'll wait, boykin. I'll get you in there to give it to Ginna somehow.'

Faelan met her eyes. No chance at all.

20

They dared not go up to the palace gates and knock, so they stayed in the twitten, waiting. Bera stared at the man-gate, willing it to open, Bjarni emerging, beckoning them in, and... nothing happened. She had no vision of what else she could do, nor where. She missed her skern and the sureness of the longstone and ancestors. What had they said? Bera panicked, Chaos driving all the rest of the echo from her mind. Perhaps Chaos had come, and was despair.

Through long hours she dreaded the others' questions but their kindness was worse. Their pity. Valdis watched her, too, making Bera feel a hopeless pattern of a Valla. She walked, to do something, and saw that the mortar in the stair wall was studded with bones and teeth. They did not all belong to animals and the sinister warning made her return to the shadows.

When the sun dipped behind the tallest houses Bera was shocked that she had still not been able to make events unfold. She gritted her teeth in one last effort to force the gates open, but she had lost belief in herself and they stayed closed. Soon they would be locked for the night, along with the city gates.

All she could do now was keep them safe, so they hurried back to the market, bought some cheap end-of-trading food and returned to the *Raven*, defeated. Her skern lay drooped across a barrel and Bera wanted to scream as she scraped together a rough meal with the scrag ends from the stalls. Valdis ate happily but food turned to ashes in Bera's mouth. Heggi took out the cloth from his satchel and opened it on the deck. The pear sat in golden perfection.

'It'll rot before she can eat it,' he said. 'You have it, Bera.'

His mask of manhood slipped and Bera pulled him to her and he did not resist. He was crying for the loss of so much but she did not probe the hurt, and thanked him for his thoughtfulness.

'Let's share the pear,' she said, slicing it into quarters.

Heggi managed a smile. 'Valdis can only suck her bit.'

'I'll chew it for her. Then she needs proper sleep.'

Heggi got up. 'I'll get it ready for her.'

He opened out the bedroll and then took his little sister from Bera and sat with her, feeding her small mouthfuls of chewed pear.

'I can misjudge him,' she said quietly to Faelan.

'Heggi will be a good father.' The most he had spoken all day.

Bera liked Faelan's limber grace as he weaved through the barrels, checking ropes and tackle on his way forward. Ottar would have approved of his boatmanship. All the heat of the day had soaked into the deck boards and Bera stood to catch any slight breeze. There was more chance at the bow but she thought Faelan wanted time alone, so she went over to her children. She picked Valdis up and rubbed her back. She coughed, burped, brought back some pear mash and then made sounds that Bera wanted to be 'Mama'.

Heggi's head was drooping.

'Get some rest, boykin. It's been a long day.'

'It's the heat,' he said.

Although it was already darkening this far south, Heggi never usually wanted to go to bed at all. His anguish must have tired him, for he put up no resistance when Bera placed his little sister next to him, with a blanket for the later chill. He was asleep almost at once, leaving her feeling lonely.

No. Bera was determined to be honest. She needed Faelan.

When she joined him at the prow she felt his unspoken welcome. This was becoming the place where memories were made, for both good and ill. Bera touched the wooden stem-post, thinking of Ottar, who would have carved a fine beak-head for the *Raven*. She had come to love her father. Could he hear her, up there in his ancestral hall?

'Not so many stars tonight,' she said. 'The moon is waxing.'

'Bera, can I speak with you honestly?'

'I hope you always have.'

'I think you know full well this is different.' Faelan spoke softly.

Her stomach rippled. One part of Bera also wanted their truth to be settled, but she did not yet know what her truth was, except that love brought loss, and war would only make that faster.

'Faelan, I—'

'Before this new adventure begins I want you to know my heart.'

'The new adventure for you is a heavy duty for me. So let me bear it.'

'Not alone, Bera.'

'Always, and never as myself. I had to be a Valla like my mother, a wife to Hefnir, a mother to his son…'

'You love Heggi.'

'Oh, I hated him at first!' She took a breath. 'No, I didn't, but I was unkind. I hated having no choice but to be a mother so young.'

'You were trapped.'

She almost kissed him then, for understanding. 'All I ever want is to be free; aboard the *Raven* with whales spouting and seabirds skimming the waves.'

'Your blood pounding with the beating heart of the ocean.'

'No demands.' Bera put a hand over his heart.

This close, she could smell his newly washed skin. It was barely there but a different scent since they had gone ashore. Calming and yet arousing.

'Did you buy soap in the market?'

'It's a precious oil.'

'Like your mother's rosewater.'

'Hardly…' The smile was in his voice.

Bera looked up at him, lips close enough to kiss. 'And what is this oil called?'

'Cedarwood.' It was a caress.

'Like the wind through trees.'

'Cedar is a mighty tree,' he said. 'It's precious because men die for it. Kings and Abbots have used it through the ages, but I didn't put it on to smell nice.'

'What, then?'

'Well… It stops midges biting.'

Bera laughed. 'Is it too precious to share? Am I to be bitten?'

'You won't get bitten out here.'

'So you did put it on to smell nice!'

'Bera.' The way he said her name was an act of love.

'Not here, Faelan, not now.' She dared not let feelings weaken her skills as a Valla. Or mother. 'There is only stopping this war, that's all that matters.'

Faelan was pulling his tunic up from his belt. The skin that she had once thought elfin was again pearlescent in the gloaming. Bera could not look away from the line of dark hair that began low on his stomach and led downwards. He took her unresisting hand and placed it where a killer would stick a dagger.

'Draw a rune.'

Her fingernail traced a B in pinkly raised blood.

'Your rune.' Faelan said without looking.

'My rune.'

'Then may we share one night together?'

'No!' Bera pushed him away. 'I must not give in to feelings, Faelan, for all our sakes!' How to explain her belief that the shield she had made for herself so long ago must stay raised or the pain would destroy her.

'Denying it is the danger.' He angrily straightened his tunic. 'Feelings come out as something else.'

'Like anger?'

His calm carefulness was over. This man was tense with fury. 'I would give up any freedom to marry you!'

Bera knew what her own truth was, and the pain of sacrificing such love was so much stronger. 'Whereas I can only marry a dead man.'

'What do you mean?'

'It's part of the prediction of Brid that the war can only be stopped if I marry my brother. You see, I'm trapped by Fate, because marrying Hefnir makes my brother the Serpent King.'

His face was waxen with horror, for her sake. 'But you're not Brid! And besides, that is not the Brid I recognise: the healer, the carer for the poor, just like my mother.'

Bera so wanted his comfort but this was not the time. 'If that is indeed the only way to stop the war, Faelan, that's what I shall do. I will try to find another way. Now I'm going back to my children while I can.'

Spring tides became neaps and the moon was waning. The harvest would come with the waxing Blood Moon and the Abbot was still keeping from her details of how to find the barrow or the corpse-marriage rite. How could she plan its unravelling? It was maddening to hear distant drums and the stamp of many horses beyond the surrounding hills and be doing nothing. Was the Abbot himself waiting for a sign, or for his own forces to gather? No visions gave answers and the longer she waited, the dread grew that the Serpent King would defeat her, even in death. His crew must have plotted for Bera to restore him, for no one meddled with them on their daily visit to the quay. How did things work in Iraland? What beliefs? Bera had no idea which of the various banners and shields were the enemy: all sides piled into drunken skirmishes. Faelan barely spoke, so she could not ask and add to his weight of dread.

He would give his life for you.

'I am trying to save it.'

Each night when she began the slow drift into sleep it was Faelan's face that she saw, and his deep kiss that she craved. Then she would remember Hefnir's urgency and feel hot with shame that her body responded to the memory. It was dishonest. Hefnir had never loved her, but now she needed to steel herself against Faelan's love if she was to save her folk.

And after such sacrifice... love?

'If I live.' She touched the broken line of life that she had seen in Faelan's face.

So she drove through the days, unable to return to their safer friendship. She pictured herself in armour, forceful. What made her hard on the outside also made her strong; or so she drilled herself, ignoring Faelan's warning that hiding feelings would weaken her. It worked, for then things happened fast.

It was Ginna, not Bjarni, who was waiting for them. Heggi leaped onto the quay and hugged her. He would not let go, even when Ginna beckoned to Bera.

'You must come quickly, Bera, there are new folk.'

'Who?'

'I haven't seen them. Papa keeps apart at the smithy. He is working so hard, Bera. Day and night! And the Abbot has sent for you.'

'Why send you?'

'Because you trust me. And if we don't return, they will kill my father.'

Heggi pulled her away. 'Come on, Ginna! She has to go to the palace anyway, and she knows the way.'

The pair were off, head to head.

'She being the cat's mother,' Bera said, glad to be moving. 'Wait at the steps!'

She wanted to tell Faelan how important he was to her and turned awkwardly.

'I know,' he said. 'I'll keep Disa safe aboard.'

Bera hugged her tight and passed her over. 'You know how to mash her food?'

He smiled. 'I'll bring her here to pick you up as soon as I see you.'

'Shall you be watching the whole time?'

'I can sense the moment you return.'

'I'd better not send Heggi, then!' This was not the time for teasing, when he had been in earnest. 'I will return, Faelan. If it is Heggi, you will know that I am dead and you must decide what to do about that.'

Faelan took her hand, kissed the palm and set off down the steps. He did not look back, but perhaps everything was not ruined. Bera hurried after the others. All the way to the palace her hand tingled, as if he had restored the life rune with his kiss.

Heggi and Ginna were waiting. As they climbed the steps, Bera asked for her news.

'The Abbot is so young!' said Ginna.

Heggi prodded her, grinning. 'And handsome?'

The handfasting must have made him more confident. Jealousy gnaws the bones, Ottar would say, and only laughter can put the flesh back on the body.

Ginna shoved him back. 'As handsome as the bellows-boy and I see him all the time. With his shirt off!'

'Have you seen the Abbot much?' Bera asked. You could push a boy only so far.

'Papa has to call him the Warrior Abbot. He came every day to watch him making some special weapon. I was helping, too.'

'He's teaching you?' Heggi said, surprised. 'Smiths are always men.'

'I'm not doing the smithing, silly. That's old magic. I fetch things so the bellows-boy can keep the fire hot.'

'I wonder why a smith has to be a man if Brid is a silversmith,' Bera said.

'Oh yes, we have to call you Brid now. Bjarni says so, and he was the one who told the Abbot I would keep my word, and so would you, Bera. I mean Brid.'

'What is it to do with him?' Heggi bridled.

'He's trying to make amends for—'

'Don't say it!' he cried.

'We have accepted his apology but we can never forget.' Bera was fierce. 'But Heggi, I still need Bjarni's help, so we must work with him.'

Ginna agreed. 'There's some special place he knows.'

When they reached the gate the guard winked at Ginna and let them in directly. Heggi glowered but had the sense to keep his hand away from his knife.

Ginna led them through the gardens as if she had grown up there. 'I'll take Heggi on to the smithy. If you go through that arch, Bera, then another two to the right, Bjarni will be in the scented garden. Come on, Heggi.'

The scent had made him mazedly biddable. 'I'll be at the smithy, then.'

'Stay close to Dellingr.'

Bera passed under the first arch, entwined with pale yellow flowers. She let a heavy, striped velvet bumblebee drone past her, feeling its burden. The second arch was covered in honeysuckle and the third, hanking with white star-like flowers, made her stop in pure pleasure. The scent increased when she got into the garden itself but unlike the roses, the plants themselves had no beauty. And then she understood: the garden looked uninteresting but a blind man would have been enthralled. Bera thought with tenderness of the raven master, Cronan. How she wished she could share this moment with him.

Bjarni stepped into the light. 'You came.'

'Will this special place of yours be the source of knowledge?' she asked.

'The crannog is the threshold of understanding. Only the wily may find it and the strong withstand it. It is the crib of earth, air and water that stands between sea and sky. Both here and not here. *Ultima limina.*'

'Stop copying some riddle, Bjarni, and just show me.' Bera could not keep her feet still after so many days of doing nothing.

'I can guide you, but it will take your own skill to make the final journey to knowledge.'

'That's all right. I'm a Valla.' Bera waved her beads at him and marched off.

Bjarni hurriedly redirected her to the far side of the forge, where a long structure of wood and stone had formed a lake.

'A dam,' she said. 'I think Egill tried to copy this but hers was a bodged thing that failed.'

'Sigrid told me.' Bjarni sighed. 'Egill was… unclear. One day you must tell me what happened at the end.'

Bera never would. She dipped her finger into the water. 'Brackish.'

'Fine fish are eaten at the palace,' boasted Bjarni. 'There are a series of gates that on Fridays—'

'Which way?'

He nodded at an overgrown path beneath trees. 'That will lead you to the crannog.'

Bera picked up a stick and started off, thwacking the nettles.

'Wait!' he called out. 'Ravens can fly there but humans must seek the pattern.'

'I'm a Valla, remember?'

'And it may admit you, but never me.' He studied her necklace. 'Yet I stay nearby, in case the call should ever come.'

'From the dead? My mother was never yours, Bjarni.'

'The heart will have what the heart wants.'

'That sounds like a threat.'

Bjarni rolled back his long cuff to show her the tattoo on his left wrist. 'Here is your sign to mark your path. The triskelion.'

'That's the same as the Serpent! It goes widdershins, Bjarni. How did you earn it?'

'Sacrifice. No, I shall not explain. It is the triskelion that you must remember.'

'Then mark it on my skin.'

Bjarni pressed his thumb into the centre of her palm and then used a finger to trace three coils spiralling round the thumbprint she could still feel over her life line.

Bera looked at her palm as if it were visible. 'This goes sunwise.'

'Yes. The true triskelion signifies many things but always forward movement, which suits your temper.' Bjarni tallied on his fingers. 'The main ones are: life-death-rebirth for Brid; past-present-future for Vallas; and, most importantly, creation-protection-destruction.'

Bera held out her hand. 'Again.'

'I will sign it three times. The triskelion marks the causeway but in the days to come, it will mark your passage.'

'To sacrifice?'

'Trust me, daughter of Alfdis.'

'Will it mark the path to the long dead?'

'The knowledge is in the crannog.' He drew the third. 'There. It is in your skin.'

21

The path led along the lake edge before turning inland. Bera's stick was no match for vicious, head-high nettles, which stung any patch of bare skin, while thick brambles snagged her garments and scratched her. Soon flies settled on the blood and then clegs came to feast. Clouds of midges swirled before her face and were in her hair, biting. She took it personally and wished she had used Faelan's precious oil.

None of this wiped out the feeling of the pattern on her palm. She looked at it, expecting to see its coils in raised blood like her rune on Faelan's skin. There was nothing, but the sensation remained.

The path took her to a wide clearing with several ways leading from it. Bera cast about, looking for markers. She felt she should head left, back towards the lake, but each path was choked with bracken that waved tall fronds above her head. It blocked any sight of water and after a wild search all round she lost any sense of which way was left. She collapsed onto the grass and took some breaths deep into her stomach. A clear head was needed. It would save time in the long run. Bera thought about the power of three, feeling whole with her skern. The power of a very old belief was filling her with purpose, but was its sign – the triskelion – leading her to evil? Her skern tapped a marker stone.

'How are you appearing here?'

It's liminal. Look. A triskelion.

'The pattern's back to front.'

Exactly. Widdershins.

'The true triskelion goes sunwise. This must lead to the dark.'

Or it's a trick to slow us so that the tide will be too high. Her skern waved a long arm. *We could be lost in the maze and die.*

'Cheer up.' Bera grinned. 'We can follow the sun's path.'

The true sign does look like the sun.

Bera enjoyed her skern's approval. She squinted at the sun and pictured its track away from the distant palace tower. She chose a path and soon saw the true marker stone. Her skern helpfully tapped each one along their way, ignoring others with deceiving spirals. They crossed long beds of reeds and rushes, whispering a warning too low to hear.

Pressing on, they came to a pebbled shore. Two heavy doors confronted them, studded with thick iron nails and ringed by high paling so that whatever was out in the lake lay hidden behind it.

Bera groaned. 'No one mentioned locked gates.'

These are to keep animals out, not people.

'No animals graze here or there would be no plants.'

Wolves?

She quickly unlatched one of the doors and pushed with both hands. It was unlocked but stiff and she swung it back only far enough to slip through. On the other side was a draw bar.

'It can only be secured from inside.'

Bera pushed the bar across and then turned. Far out in the lake stood a round hut on wooden posts. Its thatched roof looked like a pointed hat.

The crannog.

'Don't just use Cronan's word. It's meaningless.'

Basket, then, but it doesn't sound so impressive.

'Why are so many of their structures round?'

They believe evil hides in corners.

'That's why we keep torches lit in the mead hall. It must be an important place, to be built both round and strong. I like it. So how do we reach it?'

The causeway.

Her skern jinked away, jumping haphazardly across the water.

Look at me, I'm skimming!

Bera cursed him but when she looked closely, there were stones just below the surface. She quickly took off her boots and leggings and placed them on a sunlit stone. Bare feet were always best on wet rocks. Tucking her skirts up into her belt she followed him, digging her toes in whenever she wobbled. The water was rising.

'The sea gates open on a Friday. I should have gone faster.'

You? Faster?

'Are you sure these stones lead there? I dare not look up or I'll fall in.'

You won't drown. Yet.

She caught up and finally arrived at the foot of one of the six wooden posts that supported the round platform of the crannog, which was much higher than it looked from the shore. The post had tidemark rings of green slime.

'How do I climb up there?'

Her skern shrugged.

'Bjarni said I must use my skill, but I've lost it in Iraland.'

Scrying?

Instead of looking up in despair, Bera looked down at the still surface of the lake and saw the underside of the platform. Something writhed towards her and she wobbled.

'A sea snake!'

It's a rope.

Bera gingerly stretched out her foot to find the next stone and bring her closer. Without her skern she may never have found the path, which was completely underwater. He carefully placed her feet onto stones that first led her away but then wound back underneath the crannog where the thin rope was hanging.

'This won't take my weight.'

Thinking is also a skill.

Bera tugged it hard and a thicker rope unfurled with knots at hand-stretch intervals. 'My father said I climb like a squirrel.'

She pretended it was rigging. The knots were bear's fists, so her small feet were secure enough, but a man would have struggled. It was slow and tiring. The straw-blond rope looked unused, and at the top was a perfectly fitted trapdoor. Bera had to duck her head so that she could stay close enough to shove. Her foot skidded off a knot but she clung on, righted herself, pushed hard and the lid crashed back onto the wooden deck. She clambered through and met two gaping eye sockets.

Bera shied away, her foot met air, she threw herself forward and fell onto her knees, breathless. She faced a line of pearly skulls leading to a door. A ghost fence. Each had the reversed triskelion scored onto its crown, as did the lintel.

Sacrificial skulls to ward off enemies!

'And keep the right person safe.'

She slipped past them to the door. There was a force coming off the sunlit oak that made her unwilling to touch it and she sensed spirits were judging her. The crannog made sunlight as dangerous as darkness.

Bera held up her beads. 'This is a Valla necklace. It is a sign that our line stretches back beyond the time of your ancestors who first walked this land. I will leave one here in respect, and to offer thanks – if you grant me knowledge.'

It was true she was making this up but that's what she had always needed to do. It felt right when she said it but no answer came.

'Let me enter.'

Not even a midge disturbed the still air, nor fin the water.

At last the spirits spoke: *'Salt, wood, sun.'*

Bera glanced at her skern. 'Should I remember that?'

It goes back too far for me to say.

She pushed the door. It opened and she made sure not to trip at the threshold, which would ruin any hope.

The timbers went round in smaller and smaller circles towards the centre; it was as if a stone had been dropped into the lake and the water made wood. But ancient knowledge was to come in darkness, so Bera closed the door to the sunlight and shut her eyes. She opened them to twilight.

A pair of antlers hung from the central post, but the skull beneath was large, misshapen and human. It wore a crown of hagthorn and looked kingly.

Bera breathed in the wicker smell of safe-keeping and sleepiness.

'The crannog is no basket,' she said. 'It's a cradle of knowledge.'

The structure whispered its pleasure. It was understood.

'Stone, iron, bone.'

Bera repeated all six words. 'I shall remember this first part of the knowledge. Thank you for building this refuge and letting me share it. Warm air above and cool water below, we stand on earth that is not land.'

The air prickled. Had she shown disrespect by including herself?

Her skern's voice was shaky. *Scry quickly and be gone.*

There was nothing to scry with. Perhaps she must withstand whatever came: both as a test and preparation for how she needed to be in this liminal place...

Creaks grew louder, shrieking in a gale, thunderbolts were hitting the hut and she was driven out into steely rain...

Bera held her ground, not as a challenge but to show her mettle. She got steady, her bare soles taking the weight on every part of her foot and her shoulders dropping. This was not a fight but scrutiny of her worth. It was as if she were steering the *Raven* and a whale had risen to scry her with its ancient amber eye.

There was a shifting, then quiet. Bera had passed the test.

'Will you now grant me the other knowledge I need?' She addressed the skull king as the earthly form of the spirits. 'You know my problem. It's to do with the long dead. I don't know exactly what this means or what to do when I reach... whoever it is.'

'My guardian and shield.'

It was not the skull who spoke but a purblind humpback with twin ravens.

'Cronan! Are you here to teach me?'

Bera wanted to hug the raven master but she read a change in his frosted eyes that stopped her.

'We meet again at the edge of disaster,' he said. 'There might have been time for pleasantries on the Summer Isles.'

'You know we stopped there?'

'At the longstone round, yes.' His voice was granite. 'What did you learn?'

'That Chaos is coming and, oh, Cronan, I'm so glad to see you!'

'There is little time.' He was more icy than she remembered.

'The Abbot said I must marry my brother. Who is that?'

'You know he is the one you killed.'

'I killed no one,' she lied.

'The Serpent King, with Hefnir's sword in his throat.'

How did he know? 'I had to, Cronan.'

'Because you would never let Heggi kill anyone. But the Abbot was told it was Brid, and only Brid may give the Serpent release.'

'I'm not Brid!'

'You may be Bera in private but it will aid your cause to be Brid in public.'

Bera had no notion of private and public. 'If Brid used me to kill, I hated it. I shall never do it again!'

The ravens bated and he crooned to settle them, stroking their feathers.

'Your chest is better here,' she said. 'No cough.'

'I devised the crannog as a mutable place. A melding where spirits merge. I am here to tell you about the Serpent King.'

'He's not my brother!' Bera was terrified of melding into Heggi's birth mother, the Serpent's sister.

'Hefnir, to gain advantage over the Serpent, told the Abbot that his wife's brother was evil. Since you are now Hefnir's wife, and Brid in earthly form, you must marry your brother, the Serpent.'

'What does the Abbot truly believe?'

He touched the raven's beaks. 'These are the birds of truth and the signers of portents. And they have spoken to the Abbot.'

'Telling him I'm Bera?'

'Telling him he needs Brid to bring peace.' Cronan drew a finger across his throat. 'He has forbidden anyone to touch Brid on pain of their own death and all of their kin.'

'I think his form of peace is to win the war by any means.'

'And he must prevail. If Brid takes life away, only Brid can restore it. The Serpent King is wily and made you use his sword so that your duty is to restore him.'

'He knew I was lying about being Brid.'

'It binds you to him.' Cronan showed no pity. 'It's the only way he can return, so folk believe.'

'A Valla rides the waves of Fate; I don't rule it.'

'Chaos is coming.' Cronan swayed backwards. 'If the life of all those you love depended on it, what would you do to save them?'

'Anything.'

'So, Brid, believe in your power to restore the Serpent. He lies underground with the long dead, and will lead them into battle. It is called The Rising.'

22

Cronan was leaching into shadow. Bera needed to ask the right questions but this was not the dear man she had once known. The ancestors had given only hints and traces, smoke and water, so perhaps she was fated to represent Brid, the three-in-one, and go into the chamber alone.

'Wait! Must I raise him?'

'Brid the silversmith must restore her brother to golden sunlight when his face is silver by moonlight.'

'What does a Blood Moon mean?' she asked.

'It is a form of harvest moon.' Cronan twisted back to her. 'The Blood Moon herself only rises on the third night when the wolves run. This phase begins in three days' time.'

'And the marriage?' she asked with dread. 'Will it save my folk?'

'All folk. You must first drop pure sunlight onto his lips.'

Bera could hardly breathe. 'How can I do that?'

'By words and deeds shall the power of three be unlocked, and Brid shall know them.'

Bera had to trust herself to know the right thing to do in the moment. One thing was certain: there would be no sharing her body with the Serpent corpse.

'What is the Serpent's true name?'

'We venerate all serpents,' Cronan said. 'When he visited Iraland and wanted to gain power he began the long journey of assuming a full dragon body. He has been named the Serpent King for at least as long.'

Bera thought about it. 'I need to use the name his mother chose. Then I can pierce his dragon scales to reach the child's heart beneath.'

'It may be as cruel a heart,' said Cronan, retreating.

'It may be poisoned by time,' Bera said, 'but I scried him as a younger man, playing with his small nephew, Heggi.'

'Take heed of your smith, Brid. He has his own old magic.'

'Why?'

Bera reached out to pull him back into the light and the ravens bated. Cronan raised his arms and thrust them at her, screaming, their eyes glittering with intent. The spirits wanted her gone, fast, and so did she.

Bera ran to the door and tugged its handle. It would not open.

The skull's empty eyes drilled ice into her spine. Was it closer? In a flare of terror, she pulled savagely, putting a foot against the bottom and heaving.

Try pushing!

Bera tensed her shoulder, rammed the door hard enough to slip through the gap and slammed it behind her with her whole body. She stayed there in the sunlight, eyes closed, letting her breathing slow, the oak boards warming her back. Gradually, the red light behind her lids brought her back to herself. She was upset by Cronan and the sudden change of mood inside the crannog. It had seemed so much like a cradle and then seeing the raven master had seemed perfect. His anger was a puzzle and hurt.

Rejection. Some memory stirred about Alfdis.

Explore it.

'She couldn't love me because I was such a poor Valla.'

Oh, sweetheart.

Perhaps, being on a threshold, she could try to understand…

She was standing in a winter-bound dusk, forced there by Sigrid. Her hand was small on the latch, a child's. Inside, a haze of smoke, the smell of death. Her mother was faceless, already swaddled in her skern, cruel in her need to pass on the heavy Valla beads. And then the claw-clutch of her hand…

Bera broke away. 'Did I ever love my mother?'

He shrugged. *You fear her now.*

Was this the pattern for her own motherhood? Bera still feared her daughter as much as she loved her, because Valdis made her… spare.

This again.

'I may as well be dead. It's always about death.'

It's about how you live. And that's a choice.

Was duty a choice or a calling? She studied her beads, looking for the right one to leave behind as promised.

This is the crannog of Cronan's devising.

She thought of Cronan's frosted eyes and chose the crystal bead. Her touch brought realisation.

'Cronan's dead, isn't he? I wanted to make him my old friend again but he stopped me seeing his decay and hurting.'

Bera was sad, and although she did not blame herself, a favourite bead was a true sacrifice. She untied the necklace and carefully took it off the cord and then swiftly rethreaded the others. Her throat was cold and exposed to danger, and she fumbled with the knot. Then she held the bead to the light.

It was a very old crystal, the exact colour of sea ice as it began to melt in her home waters. She had a vision of playing with it, cradled by Alfdis, so she must have been very small.

A teething ring.

'I always thought it was a tiny sea path.'

Silly.

'But now I know she loved me once.'

That will become the important piece of knowledge.

Bera kissed the bead farewell and took it to the first skull in the ghost wall. She opened the jaw, placed it between its pearl teeth and then touched the centre of the triskelion.

'I thank the guardian of this place, and you, dear Cronan.'

She felt different, as if she were leaving behind some ancient damage, but with a rawness, like new skin.

From up on the platform, another path of stepping stones was plain. It led back to the shoreline doors, cutting straight through a reed bed. The maze-path to the crannog was a test and then a rite.

Preparing the mind to form the questions and unravel the answers.

Although the water had risen, these stones were dry enough to reach the wolf doors quickly. Bera slid back the draw bar and made sure to close them behind her. She grabbed her footwear and started off along the shoreline, squealing at the sharp stones.

Do put your boots on. Brid would hardly caper to the palace, would she?

She dried her feet on her apron, pulled on her leggings and boots, smoothed all her garments and hurried to the palace. It was time to challenge Dellingr.

Ravens flew above her, keeping her from straying onto paths she should not take, like the warders at the Ice Island Abbotry. Had their Abbot, a crumbling piece of ancient bone, started as a young Abbot here in Dyflin? Did the warders keep him safe or locked away? Perhaps death was their only freedom; these Abbots seemed as trapped as any prisoner.

Power does not mean freedom.

'Like being a Valla.' There was no escape from her duty, and now she must also step up as Brid.

Dellingr was waiting for her outside the forge, where the ravens perched, quarrelling. Perhaps they were Cronan's messengers, not palace guards.

'Do you still make the hammer sign?' she asked.

His hand went to his throat, then dropped. 'A strange greeting.'

'Old and new beliefs, Dellingr. I see you're muddled. Where are Heggi and Ginna?'

'I want to talk to you.'

'I'm here for that purpose.'

'This handfasting. They are too young.'

'We are now related, Dellingr, and old friends.'

'Our children's happiness belongs in the future, not some hasty arrangement made on the very brink of war.'

He was like a dog with a bone.

'Isn't that when these things always happen? Coupling?' She wanted to shock. 'Thorvald used to boast of it.'

'You will have forbidden that, as have I.' Dellingr's stare was steely. 'I know you, Bera. Why must you hide behind a shield of ice?'

He is your smith not Brid's, and you need him.

Bera could smell treachery as the rust of blood and iron, but perhaps her smith was caught between the two beliefs. She would heed him, as Cronan advised her.

'I need a name, Dellingr.'

He moved to his anvil. 'I thought you were Brid nowadays.'

Bera followed. 'Thorvald was Hefnir's trusted second. Did he ever talk to you about the Serpent King?'

'Why would he?'

'Because he was your friend.'

Dellingr was a man who took his time thinking. High above them, the long shrieks of swifts slashed the cloudless sky.

'He told me the Serpent King was the brother of Heggi's mother. That's why Asa and I never wanted our girl to—'

'Did he ever say the Serpent's birth name?'

'Thorvald? Perhaps, but such a time ago…' He stared at his anvil as if its runes would spell the name.

Bera had learned to be silent when she most wanted an answer, and this was a test of his loyalty, too. Somewhere behind a hedge Heggi called for Ginna. Laughter. Bees droned from a bush with long purple spikes. Distant quacking, like ducks laughing. The high mewling of buzzards, a lazy spiral. The sea breeze rustled the sunlit leaves of a walnut tree, whose smallest branches and twigs were hanked with fat, green fruit. Promise of a harvest. Time wasting with every throb of blood through her temples, in time with her skern.

Three days to go, three days to go, three days to go!

A bumblebee was choosing which flower to enter. It finally settled on a snapdragon beside her. It pushed inside but then got stuck, buzzing with indignation. Bera gently widened the petals and it backed out onto her open palm. It was covered in yellow pollen. The bee circled about, bristling like Sigrid, then rubbed its eyes and lumbered into the air.

Dellingr swore. 'I know it's important but I can't get it.'

'Is there anything at all you can remember?'

'You've been off scrying, wasn't the answer there?'

'I didn't scry. I entered a maze to find a crannog, to speak to the spirits there.'

'Oh, I could have shown you the way.'

It shocked, like walking into a ghost fence. 'You've been to the crannog?'

'Why shouldn't a smith?' He gave up. 'All right, I've not been there – but I have made that lake more powerful.'

'How?'

He patted his anvil, but then gaped. 'I've just thought of something! See, the ancient lore of iron always works. I named his sword for him, like I did yours. I forgot all this time because he turned to the axe straight after.'

'Why did you name the sword?'

'He was family, so Hefnir's gift. Mind, he was calling himself the Serpent King then and particular about the runes. Drew them himself and swore me to secrecy. I keep secrets by forgetting them.'

'Oh, Dellingr.' Her hope was dashed. 'The runes might be more powerful than his name.'

'Well, hold on. It was all new to me at the time but you see the sign all over Dyflin. That cross with a snake round it.'

'Those runes hold the power, Dellingr. It links Brid's cross with the Serpent.'

'We need the oldest magic, then.'

She had misjudged her smith. 'We must try to use it.'

His brow cleared. 'Let's get the pair of them back here.'

Bera returned to the hedge, where she had heard their voices. Heggi and Ginna were kneeling beside a pond, trying to catch fish with their bare hands, splashing each other. Their loving closeness made her hide, though she was unsure why. Bera felt ashamed and remembered listening behind the latrines when Heggi had farted and she hit her head on a bucket. The memory made her laugh and she wanted to share it with them.

Before she called out, Ginna's voice stopped her. 'Papa talked about marrying Bera.'

'That would mess up our betrothal!'

The chink-chink cry of a blackbird was a warning. Bera ducked back behind the hedge and missed whatever Ginna said.

'Ottar was full of sayings,' said Heggi. 'His marrying one went: "Them who marry blithe marry twice, but them as want them dead... something, something, wed." Anyway, they don't marry again.'

'Sigrid married twice but she's never blithe,' said Ginna.

'It's Bera who makes her crabby the whole time.'

'That's not Bera's fault!' Ginna said something else, lower.

Bera loved her for it. Heggi mumbled, so she got into a painful crouch to hear better.

'No, it's jealousy with Sigrid,' he said. 'First her best friend Alfdis, then Bera. "Sigrid's always been jealous of Bera." That's what he said.'

It rang true. Ottar told her jealousy was a rune stone of the heart. Now she understood what he meant: it was a heavy weight that pointed out what was lacking for a wise person. It made sense now: Sigrid and Asa fed on each other's jealousy. It was a canker, like red-spot. It had destroyed her father's love for Alfdis and made him warn others about Bera's own Valla passion.

Leave the past alone.

She emerged, waving. 'Come on, you two. You're needed for a bit of magic.'

They scrambled to their feet, grinning, and then ran ahead of her. Bera envied everything about them. The deep bond the young pair possessed was denied her because she was a Valla.

23

They formed a hammer circle with arms outstretched to hold shoulders, forging an unbroken link, except that Dellingr and Bera each put a hand on the anvil to make the iron part of the chain. He said it was the custom of smiths from all the North lands.

'And I shall use the mix of old and new beliefs here to make stronger magic,' said Bera.

'Like cross-iron,' said Dellingr, looking smug.

Heggi obliged by asking, 'What is that?'

'It's how to make a sword stronger. They've been doing it here since early wars.'

The words came unbidden from Bera's mouth: 'Stone, iron, bone.'

'That's only part of it.' Dellingr cracked his knuckles. 'You need ancestor's bones and then you make bone-coal so the heat for the iron—'

'I call on you, Vallas,' Bera interrupted with the new rite. 'Help this smith of ours…' Dellingr drew a sharp breath. 'Help me, Brid, to find the name in his mind that he once heard with the runes he drew.'

She placed a finger at the centre of his brow and drew the Brid cross and serpent.

This test of Dellingr could be a dangerous betrayal of your own.

'By this sign I call on the old magic of smithing. Here the one-in-three stands with the power of three. Our smith has blasted the fire within to white heat with bone-coal… and is thinking of the sword, which belongs to…'

'I have it!' Dellingr slapped his forehead. 'The spirits spoke to me!'

Was he Brid's smith or Bera's?

'What is the name?' she asked.

214

'It's you, Heggi.'

Heggi looked terrified and Bera's heart pounded. 'How can it be?'

'It's special.' The smith grew taller; he was the important one now. 'You and me need to get to my hammer pond, lad.'

'Why does he have to go?' Ginna asked, clutching Heggi's arm. Was this the betrayal?

'What is the hammer pond, Dellingr?' Bera asked.

'It's part of that lake of yours with the crannog in it. Special.'

'Special how?' Heggi stood straighter.

'I quench the cross-iron in it to make it even stronger. The water takes on the strength.'

Bera's scalp prickled. There was something besides Cronan's warning, something about Heggi and bad blood. But she already knew his kinship with the Serpent. Dellingr had no name for him, so what was it?

'We will *all* go to the hammer pond,' she declared, expecting Dellingr to argue. 'I shall scry and the Vallas will speak in the way I am used to.'

Dellingr rubbed his hands together. 'It was all of you standing here gave me the idea.'

He went inside the forge and came out with a raised sword. They made a procession to the pond, where Dellingr put the tip to his brow and then to the surface. He lowered the sword slowly, as if the water would make the metal molten again.

'You made a threesome of smiths round me,' said Dellingr. 'It has determined Heggi's future. I will share the old magic, lad, for I declare you as my successor. The next smith.'

This was wrong! Much as she loved him, something inside Bera clenched at the thought of Heggi gaining power. His eyes were fixed on the drowned sword.

'Right, lad. When I nod, you have to draw the sword from the water. As slowly as it went in.' Dellingr looked as sure as she had seen him since Seabost days.

Heggi's voice was so low Bera only heard the end. '... binding?'

'Having second thoughts?' asked the smith.

'He's not had first thoughts yet,' said Bera. 'Look, let the sword be, getting stronger while I scry. Then you can decide, Heggi. Smithing can be an honourable calling.'

Ginna took his hand. 'I shall be with you always and wherever, Heggi, but my secret hope has been that you and Papa would work together... and our son, too, in time.' Her neck flushed red.

Dellingr beamed at them. Bera suspected the 'message' he had received from the spirits had in fact been wanting to please his daughter, and talk of the sword gave him the idea. She so wanted to trust him.

'I must go where the water is still, for how long I don't know, but scrying cannot be hurried.'

'It gives Heggi time to learn what he has to say,' said Dellingr. 'Is it all right with you if we go through it, so he gets it pat?'

Heggi jumped in. 'As long as the pledge doesn't make me be a smith my whole life. If I can be out on the sea paths, not stuck in some dark and smoky old smithy.'

Dellingr's face was a gathering storm.

'The *Raven* is yours to share,' said Bera. 'She is a Valla vessel, named by me, with my mother's sail. Ottar never built a better longship and he loved you as a grandson. I shall scry now. But then, if I help make the smithing oath, Heggi, be assured that only a Valla can break it.'

The words echoed in her head while she searched for the right place.

There was a small pool surrounded by stones, holding the sky in a basin. Bera kneeled on a flat rock then lay her cheek slantwise, looking across the surface and letting her mind drift towards smithing. The scrying was a familiar vision but small Heggi and his toy horse were not there; he had not yet been born...

Heggi's mother and her brother the Serpent were young, long before his face was dragon-scaled. They were play-fighting, but his look became easy to read: lust, of an everyday kind, fully confident of success. A habit, forged over time with his own sister. She looked resigned to this recurring affront as he lifted her skirts and thrust into her...

Bera staggered away from the pool and was sick.

She was right to fear for Heggi but now the bad blood was more certain. Perhaps Hefnir had always known, which explained how he could both love his son and yet also be cold. How else could he allow his wife to be taken by pirates and cut her own throat with an obsidian knife? The Serpent King was Heggi's father – and he must never know.

It was vital that he should be bound to a man like Dellingr and his honourable calling. To deal in the safe, solid, ancient lore of iron as a protection. He must stay at the palace, even with war at its gates, and not get near the Serpent King; his father, who would try and turn him. She stood up to return to the hammer pond and make Heggi safe with his vow. The long dead awaited where she would end the threat from the Serpent forever, even if the cost was her own life.

The young Abbot was watching her with six eyes: the ravens' and his own. What had he observed? Her head was too full of horror to remember who he believed her to be. His gaze flicked away as soon as she faced him.

'Using the water, Brid?' he asked. 'It's a fine remedy for sickness.'

'I was blessing it,' she said. 'I braved the crannog and know what to seek and when. Now I need directions to the place.'

He bowed. 'I am here to show you.'

Bera needed to make Heggi safe, but he led her away from the hammer pond into another garden, which only had plants around its edges. The centre was an oblong of small white stones, with darker ones laid in varied blocks.

'Our sea chart,' he said. 'We have one around the inner chambers for each of our trading routes.'

Bera moved to the side where an arrow pointed north and it made sense. The blocks were islands, with a spiral for the Corrybrecken. She pointed at a shape, like a sack with a long neck, ending in string.

'Dyflin anchorage?'

'And there's the palace.' He gestured excitedly at rows of arrowheads. 'These mark where the enemy is gathering.'

Could she trust him to show her the right place? Bera looked up at the thickening cloud of birds. Chaos was coming; she had to.

'Where do I go?'

'Head north. Keep near the coast and you pass a large headland' – he pointed – 'in the shape of a lion's head.'

'What is a lion?'

'It is a beast made by the sun, more savage than a wolf.'

'Then what?'

'You will come to three skerries. Keep well east of them until you are clear and then head in towards the coast again. Pass one wide river mouth and later you will see two forts marking the entrance to the next, much wider. Fix a midway course between the headlands and the water will be deep enough at all tides to reach the barrows. The long dead.'

'Have you been there?'

'There was a battle and the believers of Brid recognised me as the next child Abbot. I was sold by my parents when they prevailed and was kept celibate here in the palace. It's an interesting story...'

'Everyone has a story.' Bera understood little of his. 'So we go upriver. How far?'

The Abbot shaded his eyes. 'Sharp words, Brid.'

Did he see through her? 'Time is short, Warrior Abbot, if you wish to win.'

'I will help all I can, although I have never seen the barrows, or revisited my home.'

She tried to look commanding and Brid-like.

'There are several wide bends in the river,' he went on. 'I can't remember how many. You will be passing through wolf country, so stay on your longship until you come to the barrows.'

'Explain barrows.'

'They are three immense mounds of earth with burial chambers deep inside. A maze is in each, that must be solved to find your brother. I would accompany you except that my duty as Warrior Abbot is fixed: I must remain here in Dyflin to face war should you fail.'

'I will not fail.'

'But Brid, of course, will not fail.' The Abbot was forcing her deeper into the deception.

218

'Which of the three holds my brother?' Bera swallowed bile. She could not unsee what he had done to his sister.

'Two are on the southern side of the river. They are the biggest, and blinding in sunlight.'

'And the third...'

'The oldest and most powerful is on the northern shore. It is named the Doth, in the ancient tongue of the people who devised the barrows. It means the Dark. It is where you must go, to *enter the Charnel House* as the books foretold.'

Bera would not be cowed. 'What are barrows for?'

'They are where the dead can meet the living. A melding.' The Abbot held up a small blue glass bottle. 'I have brought what you need to succeed. This vial contains the precious tears of Brid. Nearby the Dark is where once you sat and wept for the loss of your brother... your holy well? Now it is time to waken him with these tears.'

If she really were Brid she would know there was a well there. Was he always testing her? Would the vial make the Serpent King more powerful? Dare she refuse it and risk seeming as if Brid did not trust her own magic?

'My duty is to go into the Dark. What happens there is my concern alone.'

He studied her ear. 'Indeed, Brid herself may need to taste her tears. I place my trust in her.'

In Brid. He had never let her look into his eyes and see what was written there. Did he know she was a Valla and wanted rid of an enemy? Did it matter, if the ancestors demanded sacrifice to stop bloodshed? Perhaps the vial contained whatever she needed to remove the Serpent's threat, having sworn to never kill again. What was she going to do?

'Chaos will not come,' she said, and took the vial.

'Safe passage, Brid.' He cheerfully whistled for his ravens and headed for the palace buildings.

There was no time to worry about his intent when Heggi needed her. Bera ran to the hammer pond, her mind churning with horror about his father the Serpent King. Then another fear struck: would his bad blood and being given the old magic of smithing forge some terrible power?

'You've been ages,' Heggi said, glaring. 'I've pulled out the sword and everything.'

Too late. Was this the dark weaving of Fate, to make some other binding of three in the old magic the Vallas did not share? It was more important than ever to kill the Serpent, and soon.

'I'm sorry, Heggi, all of you, but I did find out where to go.'

'Will you miss me, Ginny?' Heggi prodded her.

'No!' He must not go into the Dark. 'Stay here, and learn your craft.'

'But, Mama…'

'It's so airless here, and these damn flies!' Dellingr wiped his brow. 'The lad should go with you. I have weapons to make and no time to teach. And I want no distractions for you, Ginna, slowing me down.'

Ginna went limp. 'I wish I could come with you.'

Heggi kicked a stone that skittered towards a small bird. 'Why don't you?'

'She will not break her pledge to me.' Dellingr was resolute.

'I will count the hours, Heggi,' said Ginna.

He kissed her and turned to Dellingr cheerily. 'I'll have lots of time to learn the smithing thing when we're back home.'

How could Bera stop him? Perhaps this joy was a remedy for the canker of the Serpent; she would make sure that Heggi never entered the burial chamber.

24

Once her task was done, Bera wanted no reason to return to Dyflin. If she succeeded, Dellingr could get Ginna and himself north to join them. Sigrid was another matter. Time was short but she must force herself back to Bjarni's house to make her peace and return to the *Raven* with Sigrid.

It felt like years since she had left Faelan. Bera had gone ashore and Brid returned. Would he also be changed? She could not face losing such love, which made it all the more vital to hide it from Fate that had trapped her in an ordeal she might not survive. To lose her would surely break Faelan, too.

She sent Heggi ahead. 'Tell Faelan I will be bringing Sigrid. Don't look like that, I want you to keep your little sister happy.'

'Good luck,' Ginna and Heggi said together, and then twined little fingers.

Heggi silently mouthed, 'Ginny,' as his wish.

Staying alive was too immense, so Bera failed to wish at all.

Sigrid was sweeping the yard. Bera was at once a tongue-tied child having to say sorry, as so often in the past. But when Sigrid looked up she pulled Bera into a rough bear hug and it was over.

'Bjarni's out,' Sigrid said. 'Come inside; I'm that thirsty.'

Bera wanted to hurry, but also wanted her to agree to sail. Sigrid fetched Borgvald while Bera filled two beakers with ale. They sat on a long settle, well away from where Rakki had fallen. Bera started to tell her about the crannog and having to be Brid.

'They knit different here.' Sigrid pulled at the swaddling shawl. 'Look. You couldn't cut this without it all unravelling.'

'I'm not here to talk knitting!' Bera took a breath, thinking what might interest Sigrid. 'I handfasted Heggi and Ginna.'

'Glad I showed you how, then,' Sigrid said. 'Though I bet Dellingr's not.'

'Well, he's chosen Heggi to be the next smith!'

Sigrid scowled. 'Asa would hate that.'

'Asa is dead!'

Borgvald screamed.

'Now look.' Sigrid jammed a thumb into his mouth.

'Sigrid, I came here for one thing only.'

'I'm not going on that boat and you needn't think it.'

Bera counted to ten. 'Who will look after Disa?' she asked sweetly.

'I know your game.' Sigrid held her son up like swag. 'I'm not taking poor Borgvald out to sea and drowning.'

'Oh, come on, Sigrid, listen to yourself! Overcome your fear, like I have to!'

The two women glared at each other. Had Sigrid crossed some hidden line? Distance can build walls of stone, as could belief.

'Brid!' Sigrid scoffed, rubbing her nose. 'Yes, I heard you. Another excuse to leave me holding your baby. Big talk of courage, just like your mother, but I'm the one picking up after you both.'

'You crib yourself, Sigrid. This is your last chance to break free.'

'And I said I won't go!'

Bjarni strode into the hall. 'You can cut the air in here with a knife.'

Sigrid got up. 'Bera wants me to join the crew.'

'You?' Bjarni snorted. 'The wife who used to beg me – a fisherman! – to never go out on a boat. Of course you won't go. Besides, I bought you. Your place is here with me.'

Sigrid's lips were white.

'Come with me to the *Raven*, dearest,' said Bera quietly.

Bjarni smiled. 'I have something for you … Brid.'

Bera wondered if he had told the Abbot she was a mere girl from Crapsby. How far would his love of Alfdis protect Valdis?

Sigrid made a sound like a sob. 'See? Just like your mother, even now. Making Bjarni…' She put her hand in her mouth.

'Oh, Sigrid.' Bera tried to hug her but Borgvald was in the way.

'Stupid as ever,' said Bjarni. 'I'll be outside.'

'I can't do it, Bera. I'm afraid to stay with him, but I'll die for sure on that boat.' Sigrid breathed deeply into her son's neck. 'He smells like his father.'

So she did still love the man she had lost. Loss had made her fearful, not strong, and now Bera understood such love.

'Better you keep safe here, then, with his son.'

Sigrid nodded, and left before she cried. Parting was always hard but this time it seemed they both knew it might be forever.

Bjarni was waiting further down the street. 'I'll make sure you get through any ruffians.'

Bera walked straight past him and they kept apart until the quay was in sight. Then he stopped her, waiting until no one else was nearby.

'Look, I need to speak to you before we reach your little friend.'

'If you mean Faelan, we have no secrets.'

'Oh, I think you do. The Warrior Abbot gave you something, didn't he?'

'For my use alone.'

'For Brid's.' Bjarni stressed the name. 'The Abbot told the council that it is one of our most precious relics and is to be opened in the final chamber of the Dark at the chosen time.'

'How would you know about any chosen time?'

'Fishermen know the stars but here I have studied how the ancients, who built the Dark, used them.' He raised a finger. 'When the wolves run, watch the sky.'

'Well, I know where the sky is, Bjarni,' Bera said. 'Watch the sky for what?'

'Bifrost, we would say. The Shimmering Road.'

Bera closed her eyes, remembering the vision in the waterfall, and picturing the real night sky with its milky bridge of stars. 'This time of year it's straight as an arrow.'

'In the burial chamber you are on its threshold.' Bjarni watched her closely. 'Here, it's known as the Road to the Dead.'

Bera refused to show any fear. 'How does this help my task?'

'You're the Valla – I expect you will touch a bead and devise something.'

'Did you insult my mother this way?'

'No insult. I loved to watch Alfdis work.' Bjarni caught her wrist. 'I loved her!'

She glared at him and he let go.

'I envy you, Bera. I would follow the Road to the Dead to find her.'

A love that lived on beyond the grave. Bera sat on a pile of planks, untied the leather thong of her necklace and set it down on her apron. Her neck and scalp prickled as she passed the beads across, hands trembling.

'I don't know why I'm doing this, Bjarni.'

Bjarni sat beside her. 'The order matters, I know.'

Bera came to the B rune bead. She carefully took it off, put it in her mouth and did the process in reverse. Then she held the necklace up to her neck for Bjarni to retie the cord. When it was secure, they both released a breath.

Bera cupped her hand to receive the bead and studied it on her palm. Bjarni reached for it and she closed her fist.

'You know I gave it to Alfdis?' he said.

'I always wondered why it was not an A. When we were small Bjorn and I used to fight over whose bead it was; we'd make up stories. Well, this is a new story; I believe it is important that you have it. Perhaps my mother is willing it.'

Bera opened her hand and let Bjarni take the bead. His face softened as he kissed it, then placed it in a leather pouch.

'I mean you no harm, Bera. I never have. If I sound bitter... Well, that's between me and Sigrid. In gratitude for this most precious gift, I shall warn you. If the Abbot's relic is something you must swallow, do not. This is the land of wolfsbane.'

'When the wolves run.'

Bera could feel the vial against her skin all the way to the market, which was so crowded that it was hard to stay on her feet. There were new, sinister faces and Bera kept a hand on her necklace, hidden beneath her garments. Bjarni went slightly ahead, taking her elbow to guide her through the jostle. She liked it because somehow it was both helpful and respectful.

How hard it was to judge anything in Iraland, the place Egill loved. Bera wondered if Egill was right about her seeing things too black and white. People were a mix. Take Sigrid: Bera knew full well she got most angry when really she was most afraid. Bera often sounded cruel when she was closest to tears. Only dogs were simple souls… She packed grief away.

And there was Faelan at the steps, with his back to them. She could not hide from herself the sudden joy and wished he had seen her coming.

'I'll be safe now. Thank you, Bjarni. Be kind to Sigrid, and to Borgvald.'

'Farewell, Bera. May the Shimmering Road light your way.'

Bera started to run, wanting to reach Faelan and surprise him by putting her hands over his eyes. Perhaps to kiss him.

He turned before she got there. 'Bera! How could you? Did you consider for a moment how I would feel, rowing ashore and seeing Heggi waiting here alone?'

'What?'

'You promised that only death would stop you returning.'

She had completely forgotten. 'Heggi must have told you at once I was with Sigrid.'

'Don't blame him!' Faelan was working himself into anger. 'I don't suppose you thought about me, seeing the slaves, remembering…'

'Is this about me or you being a slave?'

'Well. I shall never suffer like this again.'

'It's dangerous to argue here.'

'So get in the curricle and let's leave this pitiless place. I shall never come back here, ever.' Faelan glowered, pulled his hat low, and as soon as she sat, rowed away fast.

Bera fumed all the way out to the anchorage. There were more dragon boats in the war fleet, a reminder that her duty was with the dead, to stop the coming storm. How dare he be so angry when she was trying to save everyone's skin?

The tide was fair and they prepared to leave as soon as they got back to the *Raven*. Heggi asked Bera if she was ill, took one look at Faelan and went off to weigh anchor. Bera took the helm, loving the moment when her boat twitched to the wind. They passed through lines of empty knarrers and then were out in the wider channel, heading for the harbour entrance. The wind freshened and the water was chopped by heavily stacked traders, rolling fishing boats and big oval curricles, crewed by up to ten men. Swans smoothly skimmed away from passing hulls and terns splashed through the fleets, coming up with silver in their beaks. Clouds of gulls followed the fishermen who were coming back in with their catch, squabbling over the guts being flung behind the vessels. Bera was reassured that daily life was carrying on for these folk.

So far, so good. Her skern danced a fisherman's reel.

Out in clear water they trimmed the sail and boat sounds lessened. Heggi was singing to Valdis, rocking the small hammock Faelan had made for her. Perhaps his love for Rakki was shifting to his sister. If only loss was so simple.

Time heals all hurt.

For now, at least, her two men were on the *Raven* where she could keep them safe. They stood together, looking out towards the whale roads whose darker streams and long waves swept through her like coming home.

Later, Heggi joined her at the helm. 'He was sure you were dead.'

'Are you growing up, boykin?'

He cared, which was a good sign, and grown-up enough to ignore her.

'I forgot, about sending you alone.'

'So you have to make it up to him,' he said. 'Don't be prickly.'

'He won't want me near him.'

Heggi's stare was steady. Yes, his dog had died but he had forgiven her and they must all go on, as one.

She nodded. 'If you get him here, I'll think of something to say.'

'Remember his name means wolf.'

While Heggi fetched Faelan she thought about the wolf pack on Ice Island and hoped they were thriving.

Heggi came back with him. 'She wants to know what does it mean when the wolves run.' He thumped Faelan's back and left them to it.

'Ah. Now I see Heggi's tactic.' There was a smile in his voice.

A big wave was coming and Bera pushed the tiller hard over. The swell rolled away beneath them. The breeze whipped the hair away from Faelan's scars. Bera wondered if he no longer cared what she thought of his face. The sail filled and they picked up speed. She scanned for dangers but she was taking them well out to sea before heading north. Some distant boats on the steer-board side would pass by safely as they headed for the entrance to Dyflin.

Faelan's browned and freckled face was healing, though the hair at his temple and half an eyebrow would probably never grow back. Her feelings about the scars had changed. Once she had almost feared his elven good looks: the line of brow, nose and jaw flawless by moonlight when they rode Miska together. Now he was blood and bone. More a man who could be loved.

Except you deny yourself.

'I am truly sorry, Faelan.' It was easier to say it while looking out to sea. 'Meaning, I'm sorry for all of… this.'

'It was fear that made me shout.' He carried straight on. 'I would be lost if you were dead, Bera.'

'Then you know why I dare not let friendship become passion.'

In case you are the one who must die.

That was the change. Bera wanted to explain but she was having to steer with care. The longships she thought were distant were in fact low to the waterline, sleek and fast, coming up from the south. The nearest began to turn for the harbour mouth and their long hulls were studded with shields.

'Warships!' Faelan growled. 'Biggest yet.'

Heggi ran to the helm. 'All those shields!' he said. 'I reckon each boat could carry forty men.'

'Count the helmets,' said Faelan. 'Could be more than sixty.'

The warships sliced through the water, powered by huge striped sails.

'I wish I was on one of them!' Heggi was on fire.

'I'm glad you are not,' said Bera.

'But look how fast they go, Mama!'

'The first battle will be coming fast, too,' said Faelan.

'Will it be land or sea?' Heggi was too eager.

'Nowhere.' Bera was firm. 'I am going to the Dark to bring peace.'

'There are many battles before a war is over,' said Faelan.

'Can I take the helm now?' asked Heggi.

Bera moved over, glad her boy had no forebodings. She beckoned Faelan to the bow.

'Do you recognise any shields?' she asked. 'If they are the enemy, it is already too late.'

'Who can tell which side any man is on in these troubled times? They could be from the far south, or Marsh Lands. Even then, how can we know if they are for or against the new beliefs?'

'War seems to be about power.'

'And money,' agreed Faelan. 'Still, we have escaped Dyflin. All we can do is to get to the Dark before the Blood Moon rises.'

'When the wolves run,' she prodded his ribs.

'Yes, all right,' he smiled. 'It may be what my name means but I have no special understanding. Some say that they form new packs. Young males choose to leave their cub packs or stay. I think they run to find out who they are: to scent blood and cower from it, or to let it fill them with lust for the kill.'

Your own fear for Heggi.

What might he discover about himself? Bera decided to share the secret with Faelan as a gift of trust.

'Faelan, I was given knowledge when we were apart. It must never be shared with Heggi.'

He lightly touched his lips and heart. True, then.

'It's about his bad blood, which we have spoken about. It comes from both his parents.'

Faelan frowned. 'Hefnir? He was no monster, you said.'

'Heggi's true father was the Serpent King.'

'With his sister?'

She hated causing the shadow that passed over his face. 'Perhaps I should not have told you. Please don't doubt Heggi.'

'Never regret it, Bera. It makes me more determined to guard the poor boy against its corruption.'

'Can any of us escape what our parents hand down and the Vallas weave?'

'You're thinking of yourself.'

The softness in his voice made her eyes prickle. 'Can any of us change?'

He met her eyes and they stayed in an easy silence. Perhaps they shared the same memory, as folk did dreams. Bera was thinking about the day she met him on the beach in Ice Island. Fate had stolen his good looks but never spoiled his kindness. Animals trusted his gentleness, Rakki from the first.

'I had a good mother,' he said.

'Is that what counts?' Bera looked back to Valdis in her hammock. 'Do we follow a pattern?'

'Meaning?'

'If you have a bad mother, or one who dies when you're very young, does that make it certain that you can never be a good mother yourself?'

He ran a hand through his hair. 'You're asking the wrong person. Are we talking Heggi – or you?'

Bera pushed the question away. 'I didn't know his mother...' Except as the worst Drorgher, furious at her betrayal. 'In my visions of her as a young woman she was kind.'

'Then there is hope for Heggi, isn't there? We are known by the company we keep, my mother used to say. Perhaps it's more than that. Perhaps what shapes us is fellowship and a pattern of what a good life looks like.'

Bera held her beads. 'We can keep him strong, we three, if I bring him safely home to Ginna.'

'And you?'

Bera liked his gentle probing of her heart when it was not about him.

'Other people have their own versions of my mother. I gave her bead to Bjarni, before we left. His part of Alfdis.'

'You regret it?'

She shook her head. 'I think now that the beads hold all our Valla stories. I made room for new ones to be added, and I shall make them the best I can for Disa.'

'It's all any of us can strive for, Bera. To be the best we can be for those we love.'

Bera left him, tugged by the cord that bound her to her tiny Valla. It came from the deep place where she hid her feelings, but surely this was one love she could permit herself?

Yet you will abandon her. Her skern shrivelled. *If we must sacrifice ourselves.*

Valdis was sound asleep, lulled like her mother by sea air and boat song. Cloud shadows kissed her sweet face. It was easy to love a sleeping child, making leaving harder. Faelan thought she was at her best, but had she sacrificed her Valla powers, by accepting Brid's duty? What if even death itself could not stop Chaos coming?

25

Bera wanted time with Heggi, so they spotted landmarks while Faelan steered. The headlands and islands were exactly as the Abbot described and Bera refused Heggi's pleas to enter the first river mouth. Valdis woke and Heggi played with her, cheerfully burbling, while Bera's guts were shrinking with dread. She wanted to grab the tiller and head north, back to the Summer Isles, willing it so strongly that she was shocked to see the yawning river mouth ahead. They had arrived.

Her skern was mournfully chanting. *Long dead, long dead, long dead!*

The sun came from behind a cloud and they cried out, blinded. Bera shielded her eyes, squinting as sunlight flashed back from the whiteness of stone.

'I can't look. It's like two big suns,' Heggi moaned.

'Look away,' said Faelan. 'It could burn your eyes.'

Bera silently vowed to her true self, 'I will face my foe as a Valla.'

Her entire acceptance of that duty released the iron bands of her ribs. She drew deep breaths. Whatever she found in the Dark, whatever form the Serpent King had taken, she would blast him from the earth for all he was and for all he might do. She closed her eyes to let the blaze of light fill her with the power to do it.

'I thought we would be ages looking for the right place,' Heggi said.

'Or never find it,' Faelan agreed; both trying to sound bright for her sake.

The *Raven* slipped through tarry water as the wind died to nothing away from the coast. Faelan and Heggi took up their oars and Bera swaddled her baby about her waist while she steered. Valdis mewled and struggled, glaring at her mother for bringing a small Valla into danger.

'You're getting too big for this.' Bera spoke loudly, hitching up the bundle so that the others would not grow more afraid.

They already are.

Her daughter stayed alert, rigid with fear. Bera gripped the warm wood of the tiller to ward off her first sight of the Dark. Surely, in this strange flat land, it should be easily seen? But there was only the long sway of reeds and the forlorn cries of mud-skating birds. She gradually allowed herself to relax, humming a lullaby, and her daughter dozed. The river wound its slow way, each wide loop taking them further from the sea. The thud of her heart against her ribs marked time: they could be passing through the ages, back to the forming of the ancient barrow, as the day was dying. Night clouds were gathering to smother the sun.

And then, after the broadest bend, the Dark was suddenly ahead of them, crouching to swallow them. Bera quickly looked down at her knuckles, white on the tiller.

'Wood, bone...' What was the other?

Valdis woke with a small gasp.

If the other mounds were the sun, this was no moon. It was rather the vast blankness of space that Bera had scried in Obsidian. It soaked up daylight, returning nothing. She wanted to have living beings around her and called the others to ship oars. They stood together as the *Raven* drifted, her beak-head prow being sucked into darkness.

'It's a lodestone of sunlight,' said Faelan.

Heggi seized the tiller like a shield. 'I'll steer.'

His jaw was stubborn, so like his father's when his mind was made up. So like Hefnir, rather. Was the pattern set by the man who raised him or his real father's nature? In any case, he must not go into the Dark.

'I'll get a pitch torch ready; we'll need it for sure in there,' said Faelan.

'I'll help,' said Heggi.

'No, fellow, you made your choice,' he said, firm but agreeable, and went off to a locker.

'It's not fair,' Heggi muttered.

'It's completely fair,' Bera said. 'You can have your sister while I get her something to eat.'

'I'm starving,' he moaned, but kissed Valdis as soon as she was tied to him and stayed at the helm.

Bera went off to mash some porridge and then took the baby off to her hammock to feed her, keeping her calm. Faelan clattered some stores onto the deck and shocked Valdis, who screamed. He put a finger to his lips and rubbed his heart, signing 'sorry' and then quietly sorted what he needed, stowing the rest.

Afterwards, Bera started to sing the raven lullaby and when Faelan joined her she liked how their voices blended. Her baby's dark lashes were losing the battle to stay open.

'Should babies say clear words by now?' she asked.

Faelan stopped singing. Too late, Bera remembered his baby brother had died. She rubbed her heart, a new sign, truly sorry.

'We might have fought if he had lived.'

'Come on, Faelan, you and I shall row upriver and find a good place to tie up.'

'I'm hungry,' said Heggi, drooping over the tiller.

'We'll eat before—' began Bera. 'Soon.'

They went forward and stepped over the dropped sail.

'We won't need that for a while,' said Faelan.

They folded it neatly on the yardarm, lashed it in its place and he kissed her lightly on the cheek.

'Thank you, Bera.'

'What for?'

'Stopping me sulking or grieving. Your good example. How you know your duty and press on. How you won't let worry… make you smaller.' He shook his head. 'I can't explain properly.'

'I don't deserve you, Faelan.' She meant it. 'Now, come on. We'll ram the riverbank soon.'

They put out the oars. Bera gave the stroke and then carried on counting; a swerve away from brooding for them both. Heggi steered, finding a rough wooden jetty that jutted out beyond dense reed beds. They shipped oars to let the *Raven* glide to her berth alongside some mooring stakes.

'Right,' she said. 'Eat first, or Heggi will be gnawing his own arm.'

A gloom settled over them as they ate, and no one spoke. The Dark overshadowed them and sucked in thought. Bera had to keep dragging her eyes away from its mass. The others kept glancing slantwise, as if looking at it direct would suck them in like iron shavings to a lodestone.

Valdis woke and broke the spell by cheerily eating her very own unsoaked rusk. Faelan filled their beakers with more ale, which Heggi downed in one, tore off a lump of cheese and took himself off to the bow.

Faelan got up. 'I'll go and keep him company.'

'Wait,' Bera said softly. 'I think he needs to cry. He misses Rakki most when we land.'

'As I do Miska.'

Bera touched her scraps pocket. 'It's the first time this has ever been empty.'

Faelan turned away and spat something out. 'A fly. It's as if that barrow is filth that draws them.'

With its rotting corpse. Her skern's teeth chattered.

Bera reminded herself that bravery was not the same as being fearless.

She ought to scout out the start of the maze to be quicker when the wolves began running. Instead, she watched her growing daughter kicking her legs in the air. Bera's heart clenched with the thought of leaving her. She was glad to have Faelan close, giving her the time to feel her sorrow without trying to mend it or talk it away.

'I wish Ginna was right about me.'

'In what way is she wrong?' asked Faelan.

'It's what you think that matters to me.'

'As a true friend, I have told you before.' He held her gaze. 'I see, my dearest Bera, that you feel too much, and you seal it off to avoid being crushed.'

Bera liked being known, stripped of her Valla casing. But he was right: she dared not let the flood of feelings make her smaller. She had to be bigger than other folk.

'Now it's more important to— Oh!'

Valdis was sitting perfectly upright. She waved her pudgy fist when Heggi peeked out from behind a barrel. He bobbed back again, and then she chuckled and waved every time he said 'Boo!'

Another step of her growing that Bera had had no hand in, and that hurt. So, too, did the joy on Heggi's face that she had never given him. Was every mother this mix of joy and pain?

Faelan was watching her with tenderness. She longed to give in and have him kiss away the sadness. He crossed his arms over his chest: hug.

'I'm going ashore.' She moved away. 'Don't come with me, not anyone. I need time to think.'

The Dark crouched, a sullen spider in its web of unseen threads. Bera looked for their glistening in dipping sunlight but then caught herself being stupid. The only weaving here was by her Valla ancestors. Obsidian had given her the knowledge that their dark side existed and she must use that power to bend them to her will. She was the living Valla. The test would come the very next night, for it was the third harvest moon and the wolves would be running.

'Will you be with me, Mama?'

I am! Her skern was at her neck. *Rely on the power of three.*

'Do we count as two or one?'

He faded with a question he could not answer.

Bera hunkered down behind a large rock so that the barrow was hidden and sat with her back against the stone, which had soaked up the warmth of the day. A trick Sigrid had taught her when she was small. Was this what lay ahead? Each new place not an escape but a prod to bring up painful memories.

Her skern was back, chewing a piece of grass. *More special is the care of folk who don't have to love you through kinship.*

'And animals.' It hurt.

See why I never deal with the past?

'The past is who we are. I am trying to make sure we have a future.'

Oh, sweetheart.

'Now I'm so close, the task is real. What if the Serpent could only die if he truly believed I was Brid?'

You must believe.

'This is the land of shifting beliefs to suit folk. I'm not Brid. What did the Serpent King end up believing?'

Why was she in a cowardly sweat here instead of scouting out the Dark? Were the Vallas somewhere in the darkness of space, the whole long line going back into nothingness, scorning her?

You are your mother's daughter. Understand that fully and you will find your Valla strength.

'I've grown up knowing it!'

And still resisting.

A small bird began a piercing song, going early to its roost. It was telling the world that it had made it through another day and would face the morrow with joy, if it lived to see it. Let tomorrow bring what it may, tonight Bera needed the *Raven*'s protection.

On her way back, she met Faelan, carrying a spade.

'I've dug a field latrine,' he said. 'You can be first to use it if you like.'

'That's a good gift, Faelan. Thank you.'

Body and spirit.

He tipped his hat, took her to the place and then left her alone. His practicality made Bera feel workmanlike about her Valla duty. It simply had to be done, whatever it was, and she would be skilled enough for the task.

Bera woke from a deep sleep, filled with purpose. After feeding her lively daughter, she wanted to prepare. This time she told the others to go ashore so that she could draw strength from the *Raven*, where she felt love and hope.

Faelan hung back, telling Heggi to wait at the end of the jetty.

'I would rather we stayed together, Bera.'

'We are safe until the Blood Moon starts to rise. Promise me you will keep Heggi away from the barrow, though.'

'Gladly. I think the Dark might suck us in if we get too close.'

He tipped his hat and then walked out of view.

Bera went forward with Valdis happily crawling beside her. She lifted her child and placed her small hand on the prow. Every time she went there she gave more power to the spirit of the *Raven*, and it was returned twofold.

You are planning to take your daughter with you.

The thought shocked her, but then it was true. 'I'm giving her the strength, for the past draws nearer to the present and future Vallas.'

Valdis made small mews of understanding and bit a Valla bead.

'They will all be yours one day.' Bera kissed her, sealing their mutual Fate.

Faelan came back, alone.

Bera's mouth went dry. 'Where's Heggi?'

He held up a hand. 'No danger. We found the start of a marked path and Heggi is waiting there to show you.'

'I don't want him near it!' She picked up Valdis.

'He's promised to stay put.'

Bera headed for the midship step. 'Best get to him.'

'Mamama!'

'What, sweetheart? Say it again for your Mama.'

She smoothed the silky hair from Disa's forehead and kissed it, drinking in once more the smell of love. Disa cooed. A small bubble of spit popped and she chuckled.

'Did you hear that?' Bera asked.

'Laughing?'

'Before that. She said "Mama".'

Bera cleaned the baby's mouth with her muslin cloth, hoping she would say it again, but then let Faelan take her so she could step out onto the jetty.

'I'll keep her on me,' he said. 'You're getting heavy, my sweet.'

They followed the rough trail their feet had made through the grass before. Bera looked up at the cloudless blue sky where swifts made a V rune. It filled her with determined hope. Surely it was a message from the Vallas that all would be well.

'I will be a better person when this is over, Faelan.'

'You won't be going into the barrow yet?'

'Only to scout out the entrance.'

Disa squirmed and Faelan held her tight. 'I'll keep you safe, small one. Your mama won't be long.'

'For now. Later, she will be coming with me into the Dark.'

'No!' Faelan's eyes sparked with anger. 'Stop this, Bera! You cannot take a child in there.'

'We are Vallas, stronger together.'

'I don't want either of you to go, but please, leave Disa outside with me and her brother.'

'No.'

He flung off his hat.

'I won't be long down there.' Bera crossed her fingers.

'You don't know that!'

'I can't start until the wolves are running and must end this when the stars point on… its face.'

They stared at each other in horror, and then Heggi arrived.

'I got fed up waiting.' His bloodless face told another story.

'What did you see?'

He kept flinching, as if a wasp was attacking him.

'You don't have to be brave, boykin.'

'There's something about it, Mama. It puts ideas into your head. Sort of… summoning.'

Blood calling to blood.

If the Serpent King was summoning his son, she would keep them apart until it was ended. Her anger gave her power to do anything.

'Don't go near it. I shall scry instead.' Bera closed her eyes…

She soared upwards to hover above the paths that led towards the barrow. They formed a true triskelion but not a maze, for whichever she chose was a tentacle that would cram her into the mouth of the Dark …

'It knows I am here,' she said. 'And I am ready.'

It was as warm as high summer. They rigged up a better shade and drank some ale while the baby dozed, but the afternoon heat cast a weight of dread on Bera. She could smell it in her sweat and angrily switched flies away.

'I'm so hot.' Heggi flapped the neck of his tunic.

'The reeds and grasses keep the air too still here.' Faelan wiped his brow. 'Come on, fellow, we'll launch the curricle and scrub the *Raven*'s hull.'

'Can't we row upriver?'

'No,' said Bera. 'We stay here together.'

'It needs doing,' Faelan said. The *Raven* will have a beard of weed by now.'

Heggi dragged himself to his feet but as soon as they got into the curricle with brooms he brightened, and started waving long green strands at Faelan, who splashed him. Bera admired Faelan for his practical way of taking his mind away from the Dark. Ordinary life.

Bera sat beside her happy child and took her hand. 'See this, Disa? It's a life line and yours is very long.'

'Mama!'

'Your mama has the power of three.' Bera touched her beads, but she was wrong somehow.

'Mama, Mama, Mama.'

'I'm here.'

She is calling across the chain of time, to Alfdis.

Bera bowed her head, recognising that summoning her mother to complete the three would bring power if she came – but would that make her own death sure?

It was time to go. Bera dreaded the cold of the grave, so she draped a thick shawl round her shoulders, swaddled her child and felt too tired to move.

Fear is leaden.

Faelan lifted Disa. 'Will you take her ashore, Heggi? I want a quiet word with Bera.'

'We'll stay close.' Heggi swung over the rail, taking his sister.

'Don't leave the jetty!' called Bera.

Faelan returned to her. 'I want to give you something to have in there with you.'

'I have what I need.' Bera dreaded his offering the cross of Brid. 'Except …'

'Anything.'

'I have to pour "pure sunlight" onto his lips.'

'I'm not helping you wake him!'

Bera punched his chest. 'Can't you see? I need to get everything right this time, for Heggi's sake. I will not lead the rest of my life looking behind for that… creature.'

'If you live that long!' Faelan pulled her to him.

Her mouth prepared for a hard kiss like Hefnir's, her lips tingled and her breath was short. She had wanted this for so long. What if this really was the last time they would meet on earth? Bera lifted her face.

'I'm coming with you,' he said.

'Never.' She pushed him away. 'Only Disa and I are going.'

'You drive me to distraction once your mind is made up.'

'Do you trust me?'

The question held their future, if there was to be one, and his eyes showed he recognised it. Faelan took her hand and entwined their fingers to seal it. He gently drew her close but her body felt like a taut steel wire. Her guts clenched, but when she stopped resisting, the heat from his face was like a promise. Bera yearned to keep him with her, but Heggi must never enter the Dark and the Wolf must protect her boy.

Love and loss.

Bera stepped away. 'The Dark is no place for anyone who is not in charge of life and death, as the Vallas are.'

'Are the Vallas good or evil?'

'My daughter and I are bound to the wheel of Vallas, Faelan, whatever Fate brings. We bear the weight of our own belief, which is not a choice but a duty. I believe if she is with me, we can succeed. But if I am to die, we will all be together.' She was thinking of Alfdis but he did not notice, reaching inside his shirt.

'Then take this.'

Bera was stricken. It mattered so much to him, but she had to put Brid aside and be her true self in the Dark.

'Here.' He took out his fire-striker and put the leather thong over her head. 'You know how it works.'

She smiled with relief. 'No sun to use my fire-glass, of course!'

'Light a torch at the threshold and keep your hands clear. I made one with enough pitch on it to burn until dawn, I reckon.'

He helped her off the boat. 'I'll leave you alone with your children.'

'Thank you, Faelan.'

'Wolf,' Heggi said, bringing Disa.

His eyes were red and as he helped tie her to Bera, she forced back sobs. She dared not hug him or she would never let go.

'Guard the boat with your friend Wolf. He will keep you safe when the wolves start running.' Her voice cracked.

Heggi climbed aboard and she set off inland, taking the nearest path up to the mound.

Before them was a wall, dull with black stones that drank the fast-dimming light. Birds shrieked the approach of night as they flocked to their roosts. Sunset was coming and so was the Blood Moon, hidden as yet by the sky rim. They faced the Dark.

26

Sound was hushed the moment Bera crossed the high threshold into a cobwebby twilight.

She rested the unlit torch against the lintel and turned to let the long dead reckon her.

Valdis cooed, unafraid, and Bera was defiant. Let the unseen dare try and shred her for breaking their bounds.

There is no sense of anything. Her skern's voice drifted, aimless and forlorn.

The very blankness was frightening. Even winternights had the North Lights and stars. Bifrost, the Road to the Dead.

Valdis announced herself to the Dark. 'BBBBB!' And the echoes shouted back.

Bera tied the swaddling shawl tighter and higher, so that her daughter's head was at her heart. So heavy now. 'We shall stay close as skerns, dear one.'

Was the particular scent of Bera's skin as comforting to Disa? Was the smell the cord that bound them, so that her mother's presence was all her child needed? Instead of standing outside herself and finding herself lacking, Bera let love fill her completely until they were one body. She had never felt about her daughter like this before. It had all gone wrong at the birthing.

Are you going to dwell in the past all night?

Disa twisted away towards the deeper darkness, arms outstretched. All the hairs stood up on the nape of Bera's neck.

'Mamama!'

'I'm here.' Bera's voice was shrill.

Nothing came out of the darkness but the child was fixed on the same place. Bera had to see. She pulled out Faelan's fire-striker and after a few attempts, it lit and small flames licked the torch. As she walked around the chamber it threw a flickering light on to the huge slabs of stone that made it a rough circle, with three passages leading off it. Bera decided she must take whichever made her feel most afraid.

Two were wide enough to see that one led left, one right, perhaps making an inner circle of the mound. The third was the one Valdis had stared at. She held the torch up and took a few steps. The stones were tall but set like a stockfish drying rack, an inverted V, leading inwards and downwards. Her scalp prickled. It could only be this one.

Would there be enough air? What if the ancient dust held some poison that would kill them? What if the ancestors were not accepting them but luring them on to some worse horror?

Worse than the Serpent?

How could she think of taking her baby in there? What to do? She needed to breathe.

Bera backed away and rushed to the entrance where the greying light shone like a beacon of life and hope. The air was so still that the torch flames did not flicker. The sky was the ink-blue of the deep sea and on its rim the moon was rising, like a strip of red sail. The sun was behind a stand of trees, so there was a little time before starting out. Too early yet for Bifrost. If only she was seeing it on the *Raven* with Faelan.

This is your moment, your calling.

The summons was in the blood and bones, binding her daughter, through Bera, to her mother Alfdis, and back to the fathomless Vallas, whose echo was clear …

'… *from deepest black through blood-red, scorched by the blue flash of an exquisite trail of dying stars, we are in space and time, until we reach* …'

'You told me that was an ancient summons. Of what?'

Her skern shifted. *It's an echo, that's all I know.*

'You said it repeated until the end of time.'

Did I?

243

'Is that time now upon us? Is it the end of time?'

His wan face melted into the milky sky where a handful of stars appeared. A long, lonely howling came from far away inland. It was beginning. The wolves running was not her concern but Faelan's, who would protect Heggi with his practical skill. Disa squirmed, like one of her kicks in the womb. She would not be left behind, on this Valla duty, and she was right. Bera took a last look out to the sea paths, then turned her back on them forever.

She returned to the V tunnel that would take her below the earth.

'Stay close.' She spoke to daughter and skern.

Always forward.

As she went deeper, Bera fancied her heartbeat was echoing off the walls in a rush of blood, like the wash of waves on a shore. Was it her own, or was her mother close? Was this what the passage was about, except that instead of a terrible journey ending in screaming light it would force her back down into suffocating darkness? Or drowning, unable now to breathe in the tideless water of the womb. Bera had the strongest feeling that some bargain had been made before time: that her daughter would be safe, but that she was walking into her grave.

One foot in front of the other.

The stones narrowed above her head and pressed down, making her walk with knees slightly bent. One arm ached from supporting Disa's weight and the other from holding the torch. Was there enough pitch to keep it alight? How long would she be down there? What if they were left in darkness?

'I will grope my way back, Disa.'

Bera regretted speaking; she sensed some presence ahead that she did not want to waken. She pressed her lips against her baby's head, feeling ever closer in this darkest place. Her skern wrapped around them, especially comforting for her daughter's small and silent skern, apparent now, trying to protect its baby Valla.

'I was afraid you skerns would disappear in here.'

The space was made long before our banishment.

Bera listened. Somewhere outside, in Valla deep time, the ancestors were urging the wolves to run beneath the Blood Moon.

She was trapped, stifled in a place where she must hurry away from light and life.

On, always on.

As she stumbled forward Bera begged them to slow the moon's path. The torchlight flickered. Was it her mother's breath? Bera's heart thundered in her chest. She carefully took a step and the rock walls vanished. The torch was struggling to light nothingness. Had the Vallas brought her to deep space?

It's a ledge.

'We could have fallen.'

Bera got Disa's weight further back and peered as far as she dared over the edge. The tall brand became a thin taper in the dark void that it could not reveal but only suggest.

An abyss, like the deepest ocean.

There was no way down. This was the wrong passage.

'BBBBB,' shouted Disa, an echoing call to the dark spirit of the place.

'Shhh, small one, Mama's sorry, but hush, now.'

Bera wedged the torch between two rocks, untied Disa and put her down on a shawl. At once she felt better for losing the weight, and stretched out wide and high. The child hardly took her eyes off her.

She stroked her cheek. 'My own tiny girl.'

Did this fierce love risk losing her? Or her skills? Was that the heart of it? Did a Valla mother never give her whole heart to a daughter because she might lose her own powers?

You need to use them properly to choose the right passage. Her skern tapped a rock near the torch.

A single drop of water was poised above the bowl it had formed through the ages. It was perfect for scrying and to Hel with doubt, Valla lessons would begin.

'Watch, Disa.'

It was hard to get into the right position and knobbled rock dug into her knees. She lowered her cheek to the stone and then reared away, remembering the longstone round.

'It smells of blood.'

You don't have to taste it to scry.

Bera gazed across the surface. One day her daughter would do this by instinct, gaining real insights, not following by rote. Then her mind drifted across a deep darkness that slowly became greyer, thicker.

Bera jerked upright. 'This is the right place but there's something I don't understand. A kind of sea fret here, underground.'

Smoke?

'More like... despair, a forlornness you could drown in. It's where we must go.'

But how? There was no rope, no ladder, no steps. No hope.

Don't make me unclench to find out.

Disa had wrestled out of her swaddling. She waved her arms, rolled onto her back and kicked her legs. Her laughter echoed in the vaulted darkness and this time Bera was proud.

'Most babies would be terrified down here. I think you like the dark!'

Not a clever thing to say.

She made the Thor hammer sign at her throat. It felt empty. When had she last made it? Had she only made gestures since leaving Ice Island? No, earlier than that there were new beliefs. Claiming to be Brid had distanced her from the old beliefs when she most needed them.

Where had her skern gone? Had he found a way down?

'Wait there, Disa. I won't be long. Don't move, sweetheart.'

Bera went along the edge in another direction but there was still no sign of him. Her scalp felt odd: not a prickle but as if a comb was going through her hair. Disa was too quiet. She pictured her baby slowly tumbling through the limitless air and ran back to make sure she was safe.

Fear numbed her in its spider-bite and one by one the hairs rose from the nape of her neck to the top of her scalp. The presence she had sensed was here, somewhere in the dark. And then Disa waved at a shadow flickering in the torchlight.

'Mama,' whispered Bera, and Alfdis came fully into being.

Her face was as Bera had last seen in life: eyes deep and dark as scrying pools, bruised beneath a sweep of eyebrow. But now, as a woman and a mother, Bera saw so much love that she could not look away, not even from the pain and death.

'Are you here to guide me to the grave?'

'Mamama!' cried Disa.

'*Mamama, mamama, mama, mam, ma…*' echoed the Vallas through time. So many mothers… and daughters.

The shape of her mother was losing its form.

'No! Mama!'

'*No, Mama, no, no, no…*'

'We are the three!'

'*We are the three! Three, three, ree…*'

The shadow was all that remained of Alfdis, flickering against the rock face as the echo died, before passing through the solid stone. She was right: they needed to move on quickly. Bera grabbed the torch and followed. It revealed a cranny, hidden from the front but too narrow to get through with the baby. Faelan should have kept Disa and she would face her duty alone, as it had always been. But hadn't there been the need for three? Or was this some Brid trick?

Her skern tapped his head. *You Vallas bring true belief with you.*

'In this vastness all beliefs are too… small.'

So you need to form a circle of light.

'Not a ring of skulls!'

Scuffles and shouts echoed through the passages. It sounded like a rumpus of bears and she recognised the voices. They had disobeyed and Bera loved them for it, relief like hot gulps of mead.

Heggi emerged first, peering beyond his torch.

'Boykin!'

Faelan appeared, with a big burning brand. He raised a hand in surrender of their wrongdoing but his smile, quicksilver in the flame, made her heart jump.

'Did the wolves chase you in here?' Bera laughed. 'I am so, so glad to see you both. Look, so is Disa.'

'I have some mash for you, baby girl.' Heggi swept her into his arms.

'Then she will be even more delighted. Now, I must go. I have taken too long already.'

'Wait,' Faelan said. 'There's something else you need.'

'If it's fire, I'm holding it.'

'Pure sunlight, remember?'

'Not possible.'

'It was my idea,' said Heggi. 'I used to do riddles with Thorvald.'

The reminder of his boyhood chased away the joy. Had Fate driven them into the Dark to expose them to whatever evil the Serpent had spread?

'No, you—'

Faelan winked at her and took out a small jar. 'Honey!'

They were back in the garden together, the lazy sound of bees in warm sunlight. The wholesomeness of their love and his mother's healing care. Perhaps this was a repeating pattern of three, wherever love made it complete.

Heggi groaned. 'Stop all this stuff, you two. We need to crack on.'

'There is no "we", Heggi.' Bera chopped her hand, unyielding.

'The time of being alone is over.' Faelan swigged from a flask.

'Do you know what is down there? What sacrifice I may have to make?'

'You left me for dead.'

It seemed so small now. 'It's not you I am afraid for.'

'No, Bera, I meant… be ruthless again. You go forward and I will have your back.'

Flooded with feelings, Bera sank to her knees. 'I cannot take another step.'

Her children looked at her with such love that she wanted to have nothing change forever and ever. Even if it meant staying beneath the earth. She was so, so tired.

'The wolves are running,' Faelan said softly.

Her summons to move.

'I can't take Disa.' Bera's tears were scalding.

'It's all right, Mama.' Heggi kneeled beside her, taking Disa. 'I will stay here with her. Dellingr must have seen something in me to make me the next smith. I will keep us safe with iron and the old magic.'

'You haven't learned it yet.'

'But I have chosen my true calling.' He took out a horseshoe. 'Dellingr says this goes back to ancient times.'

Bera understood. 'In this place the ancient lore needs only to be. Keep it close.'

'There's something else you can take.' He pulled out a handful clenching nails.

For boat repairs. The old lore and the sea paths: her father and Dellingr, the father Heggi had chosen to follow. The truest three. Bera pocketed three nails, kissed her children and let Faelan pull her to her feet. It marked her acceptance of help.

'I'll leave you my torch,' she said. 'The wolves will not come inside.'

She hurried to the start of the cranny, stronger with Faelan beside her. It was possible that she had been wrong, and she was learning fast. Perhaps she could have the spirit of Alfdis and Disa with her, like skerns. She took a last look at Heggi, who gave a kind of salute, with Disa's hand, too.

Faelan held the brand inside the cranny. 'It's too narrow. We'll be burned alive with it lit.'

Blindness was terrifying. 'I will feel my way.'

'I'll go first and you can hold on to my tunic,' he said.

'If you get stuck, I won't be able to get past. Let me get inside the opening before you smother the flame.'

Opening was too wide a word, suggesting light, when ahead was utter darkness. Bera went on alone until her touch told her the cranny was narrowing and she stopped. Faelan scuffled stones at the entrance to let her know he was coming. He bumped into her in the dark and backed off to give them air.

Bera cautiously raised fingertips to the roof to check headroom and then set off again, trailing them on either side. It was a closing gap and she soon had to turn sideways, with her back against one wall and crab-walking, arms outstretched to touch the opposite side. Then it became so narrow that her hands ended up close to her face. She stopped. Her skin smelled flinty. The roof was less than an arm-span away. Bera pressed her heart to keep it in her chest. Her warm breath came cold and wet off the stone. Constant drips. Panic was rising; she had to find air. She began and something sharp jabbed the arch of her foot but she could not rub the pain away because the walls were too close. A scream was building, except her lungs were empty.

'I'm coming,' said Faelan.

Too tight. No air. She was going to die. To Hel with it! Bera pressed her hands against the stone, teeth gritted, as though she could force back the wall with rage.

And then the comforting smell of Faelan's nearness.

'I'm all right,' she said.

'I'm not.' She heard the smile in his voice. 'I may be stuck.'

'Then we'll be stuck here together forever.'

'There are worse ways to die,' he said. 'I shall lie beside you.'

'You told Heggi once.' Tears were salt in her mouth. 'You said a dog would lie beside you when you lie exhausted in the snow.'

'That was the day we met, Bera.'

She nodded, although he couldn't see it, and her eyes were smarting. Too many feelings, too late and dangerously weakening.

He went on. 'Then Heggi said Rakki would stop you dying and you said—'

'I said if you die, you go together.' Her throat closed.

So much loss. Fate had wasted their past, too, when they could have been together and their future was shrinking with every heartbeat.

Without sight, Bera's other senses quickened. She was aware when Faelan angled himself to face her but then kept still. He was letting her come closer only if she wanted to. That freedom allowed her to test her feelings in the present. Her hair rose slightly, as it did before thunder.

Bera reached out for the scratchy weave of his tunic and then gripped it, never wanting to let him go. Wedged tight, grubby, clumsy and blind, they bashed noses. She rested her cheek against his and shared his smile. It was not only hearts that stored the truth. Bera took her time, tracing the crease in his cheek, the line of his jaw, hearing the rasp of stubble; she softly traced his mouth with her fingertips and then, letting her lips be true at last, they kissed.

27

Bera had felt Valla passion before, but that was all about the body. This time, her heart and mind were singing. She must not be distracted... and yet going forward might be the end of them both.

'What if this overwhelms me?'

'This?'

'All right, you.' She flushed with heat. How to explain that his kiss did not satisfy a craving but made her desire more.

'What might overwhelm you, Bera?' He was gentle.

She dared not risk saying it. 'The Blood Moon must be high by now.'

'And the Shimmering Road.'

'Then I must move quickly. And I alone fit the cranny.'

He let out a long breath. 'Bera, have you thought love might make you stronger?'

She might, with him here.

He took her hand and placed the brand in it. 'Keep it dry. I will wait here in case you can't get through.'

'Don't wait, it's like being buried alive.' Bera made sure the fire-striker was round her neck. 'My children need you and I don't know... how long I shall be.'

The silence prickled with the possibility of her death.

'Faelan, I do—'

'No need, my own darling.' He kissed her palm. 'We have a lifetime for such words.'

She pulled him to her and they kissed, sealing love and trust for all time, beyond the grave.

Bera moved off into the narrowing dark, counting each step. It was better to keep her eyes shut and it allowed her to sense that her skern was off on a search. She prayed to her mother to guide her and afterwards it seemed that Alfdis was slipping through the cranny ahead of her. Like scrying, Bera let her mind drift and was able to follow the slender shadow. Only small women like her could have passed here, or children. She froze. The small skulls in the Abbotry well, with a hole drilled in their crowns. Hefnir had said children were closer to the spirits and the skull was the house of the soul. He knew of sacrifice. What evil had killed those children? Brid. Bera pictured a file of children being led to their slaughter.

'Mama?' She held her beads. 'If Disa is in danger, go to her. I will manage alone.'

Her skern should have been with her; had the long dead seized him? She began to panic and tried to picture bright light and salt air, a distant sea rim. But she was squeezed in the dark beneath cloying soil and truly alone. Buried. Lost. What if other passages led off this one? What if this one spooled away into a void?

She pressed on; she had to find her skern. But then what?

Slowly an idea came to her. Her skern had told her thinking was also a skill, and thinking was what the Dark was for. Its nothingness was not the danger; it was like the long blankness of sleep. What happened could be a dream or a nightmare, but answers came in the night and calls from the long dead ancients.

She repeated it aloud: '… *the scantling mote shall split.*'

The echo rang true and at last she understood it. The very least thing, too tiny to take up space, or lost in the deep reckoning of time, must be split into three. Even unseen, the triskelion always marked the pattern, repeating like the echo itself. The sun's daily path. Neither good nor ill, but a power to be used.

Bera started off and was pulled back. She wrenched away, hit her head on stone and thick hotness trickled down her face. It tasted of iron, as if the underearth smell had been compressed into blood by the weight of rock that was crushing her. She stifled a scream, or it would send Faelan mad to hear it.

Bera gripped her beads, picturing herself aboard the *Raven* with everyone she loved out in clean air, free.

Her cloak was caught, that was all. She pressed her cheek against rough stone, her fingertips at full stretch, groping for the cloth. Perhaps she needed to believe that love did make her lucky. She tugged and was free to follow her mother towards her skern.

She was guiding herself in thought as well as action. She had believed that being Brid was the power of three but since Alfdis had come the Valla kinship was strong. Mothers, daughters. The blood thrummed and Bera was being born in a crammed push towards the distant dream of a mother. In a birthing, was the baby urging towards the idea of a mother she created for herself? Had she created a Valla mother who made love a duty, set in darkness and stone? Well, she and Disa had called Alfdis into being; this was the chance of rebirth, which would make a better mother of herself, too.

'Love sets us free.'

Every step felt as if she was sinking deeper into the earth. Bera put down the torch to wipe the blood from her face and then could not find it. She flailed about, knocking it over. Once again, she had to stoop, her face pressed against rock, tasting of salt. The salt was tears.

...Out on the sea paths again, with the shriek of gulls and the deep song of whales. Hissing hull and rattling rigging of her father's boat. She had his blood for sure, and could love him properly now. In the bones...

> *In the bones, in the bones*
> *Feel the east wind in the rigging*
> *And the boat-song in your bones.*

Bera grasped the torch. The song gave her strength to move forward, and a measure.

> *In the blood, in the blood*
> *Feel the rumble and the tumble*
> *And the boat-song in your blood.*

In the heart, in the heart
Feel the pulsing of the whale road
And the boat-song in your heart.

The last verse rang in her head as she stepped into space. There were no walls, no light, but she had a full heart, and fire. Bera hunkered down, pulled out the fire-striker and struck it a few times. Sparks lit nothing more than the stones around her.

At last the brand caught and when the flames were certain, she held it up. A gnarled monster reared at her and she fell back. So did the monster; it was her own shadow, thrown on to the rock face.

A shaft of moonlight coming from above gave a dim light. Bera took stock of the space, catching glimpses of flickering shapes: a huge antlered head, triskelions... The true sign was carved into nine granite slabs that made the burial chamber a perfect circle, like the longstone round. Circles within circles.

A ring of small skulls protected the real monster, lying on a raised bier at its centre. Children brought here to die for his filthy purpose. Their poor eye sockets flickered with a message: *'The stones want blood.'*

The longstone circle had oozed blood. Was she right after all, and this was a trick to make her the sacrifice? As Bera or Brid? There was no movement from the corpse but she could not bear to look at it directly. She would take the Serpent with her to Hel as a Valla, if she had to.

How long did she have? The passage-marker of her duty was the thin shaft of light coming in through some unseen gap high in the vault and slowly creeping towards the bier. Her thoughts scrambled. What was her true purpose? The Serpent's life was hers to take – but for the greater good. This was war and Chaos. Even if she died, she could not leave her children in such a world. Here, underearth, belief was found and then crushed. Had her whole life come down to this: kill or save?

Faelan's voice drifted into her mind: *'Trust what is in your heart...'*

'Nothing is in there. This is a place too remote.'

The ultimate reach...

Her skern's voice brought a burst of joy, until she felt his misery.

It came from within the shadow-fret, a forlorn milky greyness: a host of banished twin spirits.

'Get away from them.' Her voice trembled.

I had to try and rally them, but they are lost.

'Get away, please, before you are lost, too. I need you.'

Her need was a spur and he pulled away from the fret. A few thin trails wisped with him, but then were sucked back into their shadowy despair. Her skern nestled into her neck, growing stronger with her belief.

Bera's glance skittered round the chamber until an iron sconce steadied her with the smith's craft. She recognised the whole formed a triskelion: a mix of old magic and simple practicality. Bera set the torch in place and was glad to leave behind its heat and tarry fumes. The air was salty but carried other smells, something of the forge and metals, which held the creature between life and death. She pressed the sharp points of the clenching nails against her thumb in turn.

'This place is to make folk afraid. It's a weight of belief set in stone from the ancestors, who envy the living.'

Her skern whispered, *It is a dark threshold. We stand within stone: under the earth and yet between water and air.*

'And I brought fire.'

Bera went closer to the antlered head. Unlike the skull king from the crannog, this head was not human; perhaps it was some immense creature from a time before man. It guarded the chamber and demanded respect. There was a murmur of spirits that began at the crannog, but stronger now. Well, so was she.

'I will not be buried beneath earth and stone with this evil!' The boundless crannog had given her the words. 'Salt, wood, sun.'

Bera passed through the skull circle.

She would not bow before the monster, but could not raise her eyes and face evil itself. Starlight poured in from the round opening above the body. There was little time. Bera looked at the Serpent's scaled throat. The sword was gone and the slow beat of its undead heart made her own quicken. She wanted to run. Instead she moved closer. He had made himself appear grotesquely misshapen with blood, dyes and pain; his was a full dragon body with no decay but not yet breathing.

Bera needed a Valla's full strength and knowledge. She closed her eyes and pictured her mother after the birthing, near death… in a winter-bound dusk, the crackle of the fire, the sharp smell of new firs and a voice calling in a smoky haze. 'Bera? Come to me, I need you.' Fumbling with the knot, the weight of the beads. 'It's our life line…' and the Valla necklace passed to her small daughter…

… and Bera was in a burial chamber, clutching it. 'The giving of it killed her!'

Death and release. And knowing that, find peace. Her skern drifted to the far side of the creature. *In the pain of leaving you, I did rally one that might help.*

There, beyond the body, was the Serpent's frail, long-banished skern, supported by her own. Bera scanned the dragon face but it was unchanged. Her Valla beads could be read as the pattern of all their lives, somehow. A life line, even for the one she now addressed.

'If you need to live again for some purpose of the Vallas, you must be tamed. I don't know if you raised the war or can bring peace, but alive or dead, I command you to let Heggi be his own self.'

Her skern smiled and gently blew the other towards the body. The Serpent remained in the borderland and the light from the Blood Moon was creeping towards his face. Every fingernail advance numbed her reason. Kill or save?

Bera asked his skern. 'Why do you not cleave to his body? Is it alive or dead?'

His skern's voice is lost.

In desperation, she tried the next words from the crannog, directed at the huge antlered head. 'Stone, iron, bone.'

These were solid words, grounding, and Bera pulled out the clenching nails that Heggi had given her. Her son had already chosen a better self, and this was the proof. Perhaps his father could be saved and cleanse their blood. She held her beads in one hand, the nails in the other and connected with the respect she had for the crannog.

'I had visions of the youth the Serpent was before he sent this skern away. I hoped that sweeter self was already with his ancestors:

can you help me now? Let his skern cleave to that person who could have chosen an honourable path.'

The skern cannot join an unbeliever.

Bera read the beads with her fingers. Had she weakened them by giving some away? She had tried the old lore of iron, too.

Power of three?

'All I have left is the relic the Abbot gave me.' She took out the blue vial. 'Gave Brid.'

Her skern paled. *It's the Serpent's belief.*

'Is this Brid's tears or wolfsbane?'

Might be the same thing. Don't drink it!

'Bjarni warned me not to trust the Abbot.'

You don't.

'What else can I do? When the Blood Moon touches his face the Serpent will grow strong.' She was suddenly sure of one thing. 'It cannot be right to defy nature. I will not drink Brid's tears. I put my trust in love.'

She swapped the vial for the jar Faelan had given her and broke its wax seal. It was the smell of summer.

'Honey!' She laughed. 'Pure sunlight.'

There's something else in there.

At the bottom was a small piece of honeycomb, like a pocket-sized volcano. Bera delved in and gently bit off the top. Inside was liquid mother-of-pearl, with a tiny curl of a queen bee skern. She popped it on to her tongue. Lavender honey – but then a new taste. Should she use it on the Serpent?

Hurry up!

The starlight had reached his chin. Whatever she was going to do, it had to be now.

Kill or save?

She thought of his earliest self: a baby, born without stain and loved, as was natural. As a mother, Bera could love that child, sweet as honey, as she did her own. Even if in giving life, it also brought death.

Yes, sweetheart. It's the pattern.

Bera understood that her mother had been ferocious in her struggle to stay alive, not through some Valla jealousy or fear, but every woman's determination not to leave her child. She recognised it herself in the savage love she felt for Disa – and Heggi, and she had not birthed him. Whatever it took to save them: a sacrifice.

She unstoppered the vial and her eyes stung. Brid's tears were like a bitter distillation of the Abbot's scorn.

You can't drink it!

'I mean it for him. One drop will burn through that dragon skin and kill as it purifies.' She held it above the Serpent's lips. Her hand shook badly and she could not bring herself to pour.

Bera replaced the cork. 'I cannot kill the Serpent King but he must never return, as man or Drorgher.'

She looked up in anguish. What to do? The round opening above them was perfectly placed to form a gateway to Bifrost, the Road to the Dead. It was leading from underearth straight up into the night sky. Moving the way of the true triskelion.

'What does the Serpent believe?'

Her skern pointed to the triskelion on his brow: widdershins. He had sacrificed others and was poised to do so again. She had to stop The Rising; he must not lead an army of the dead.

Death, birth.

He was lit by starlight. Perhaps Bifrost brought life and then carried the dead away at its end.

'We are all born into this world so pure that we need no name, but our loving parents see our character and name us. Later, we choose to live up to that name – or be what we shall be. I am not Brid of the Serpent's belief, so could not give you peace. But I am Bera, a Valla come to give you rebirth with an unblemished name.'

But what name? What if you restore him and start The Rising?

Was she already too late? The naming had to be done the proper way, with the Thor hammer traced on his brow. She would have to touch him and cover the reversed triskelion. Did that mean she had to sacrifice herself to free him?

Bera reached out a finger... and dropped her hand.

Look! The Blood Moon is making Bifrost fade. Hurry!

She dared to touch his face and loathing struck like a thunderbolt. She staggered, fell and retched... That skin, pressing hard, smelling foul, the writhing snakes, the smell of his armpit with its all-seeing eye as the Serpent tried to force a scaled hardness inside her...

Dearest, act quickly!

Bera beat the memory away but stayed rocking. What name? Her heart was skittery and she tasted iron and salt. Blood and tears. To think she and Sigrid had laughed at him as he rode away with snow falling. Ottar always said what begins with laughter ends with pain. Snow did not cleanse but cloaked. Drunken men buried all winter returned as Drorghers. Only sea paths and sunlight purified, and sacrifice. It had to be her own, and she wished it was not in the furthest dark.

She got to her feet. 'I call you now, child born of sunlight and seafaring. I share that love, and bring it forth in you with pure sunlight.'

Bera's gorge rose at the thought of what she was about to do. A true sacrifice must cost, and this was hers: to make a ritual of sharing love. She wiped Faelan from her mind, refusing to link him to this horror. She took a fingerful of honey from the jar, placed it onto her tongue and gagged, then steadied, for the sickness to pass.

She forced herself to part the Serpent's stiff, blackened lips. Her finger scraped his notched teeth and she moaned, trying not to lose the honey as a wave of revulsion swept through her. But she gagged again and it spilled over the lips, as if the corpse had drooled.

'I can't do it.'

You must. Go faster. Think of a name.

Bera took more honey, moving fast against revulsion, set her lips on his and let it flow into his mouth. She fell back and screamed in the awful horror of it. She called on Alfdis and Valdis to lead all the Vallas to her back, to let her live long enough to name him.

Hurry!

'I rebirth you with a living Valla's precious blood and tears in the mark of your faith as a child.' She dabbed her finger in the salt wetness of her face and drew the Thor hammer on his brow.

'I name you Sumarliði.'

Summer Farer. Clever.

To be seafaring in summer, hearing the pulsing of the whale roads. Would he feel the same and be at peace? Sumarlidi's face had softened beneath the tattoos that were, after all, only plant dyes and ash. Under that skin his blood was a man's, warmed by sun he would feel restored to his ancestors. His skern was cleaving to him.

'Hear me, Summer Farer. The Vallas are older than time and I am here with the spirits of the Valla before me and the Valla that will follow: the true power of three. Chaos is not ours. It is summoned by living men with new beliefs. There will be many such wars throughout time, until no man will be alive to see the waters close over the earth. This is my gift to you, Sumarliði. With this name, I return you to your mother and all those you truly loved. Go in peace, while Bifrost lights your way. I, Bera, free your spirit.'

The light went out.

28

Bera blinked awake. The brand had grown dim but her sight had failed, not the flame. Her skern was crumpled beside her, a reflection of herself.

Our heart is too fast.

She could see the small rise and fall of her tunic. Bera cupped her left breast and the heartbeat flapped under her palm. Had the strain broken her heart? Had love been snatched at the point of understanding that it made her stronger?

The weight of air felt as heavy as water. She was drowning, tumbling into the deep and her sight was a pin-point. A Valla's hair a narwhale tusk.

You keep fainting.

Shifting in the shadows. Had she been utterly wrong and made the Serpent more powerful? ...A monstrous form was crouching, ready to spring, with huge antlers on a giant's shoulders...

When she came round again her skern had an ear to the Serpent's chest.

Stone dead.

Her senses were keener. The top smell was of mead and unknown spices and beneath it the sulfur of Hel. Bera stood over the body. The blackened skin was tight over the nose and cheekbones.

'I think his crew used something to stop it rotting.'

The air down here, too. Her skern sneezed. *We have to get out, now.*

The brand's flame was lower and finding the right way back through an unlit cranny was unbearable. She needed to go while she could, yet her final duty to Sumarliði and his son was to free his earthly body in the proper way, by burning.

The ring of skulls stared back at her. It was impossible to carry babies through that narrow channel, or force small children.

'There must be a wider entrance.'

The triskelion.

'That doesn't help at all.' And then it did. 'So it's like the crannog. Find the key to the right path and then once you're inside and have passed the test, the way out is simpler.'

He capered. *It keeps fools away.*

'I know what will be guarding it.'

Bera lifted the brand from its sconce and took it over to the antlered skull, guardian of the chamber. Sure enough, behind it a tall longstone shielded the opening to a passage. Her skern tapped the triskelion's three-legged spirals, sunwise, marked the passage to light.

It keeps on going, round and round.

'So I was going round, not downwards?' she laughed.

Bera quickly returned to the body with the brand. The skulls were sacrifices, too, the same age as Disa.

'Are their skerns in the fret?' she asked.

Don't send me back in there.

'I don't need to. As a Valla I summon you,' she cried. 'I cannot restore all that had been lost but you shall cleave with your small humans again and be freed with the one they protected.'

Then, like all the North folk through time, Bera set the wooden bier alight and the flames quickly took hold. A grey mist swirled around the skulls and soared upwards with the smoke of Summer Farer's leaving.

Quickly!

There was enough light to get through the passage and then the dying flame flickered in a slight breeze. As the brand died, Bera reached the opening and breathed clean air at last.

She felt a hundred years old.

The moon lit a silver landscape, bright enough to see the *Raven* completely still on the water. Bera took time to recover, drinking in the sweet air. Distant fields of stooked corn were white so that trees seemed to be floating amongst dancing skerns. Perhaps it was the freed skerns. Let it be so. She had restored the natural order of life and renewal. Vallas were women who were tied to nature, who understood the moon's pull of tide and blood. No matter what lay ahead, this must be her yardstick. Let the dead stay dead so that others may live. Babies be born. She set off to find the others, knowing they would be safe.

A quicksilver stream of shapes silently running passed below her. Wolves. These creatures were as beautiful as a wave train and as elemental. They made no move towards the mound, for her man stood at its highest point, arms outstretched. Wolf. Protecting them all.

They were alive, but how changed? Like coming out of a long dream, Bera had obeyed a summons to travel into the farthest Dark that any living being could go.

Faelan turned and made the sign for love. He was calling her home.

Every small piece of life, its jumble of happenings and feelings, came together in a single moment to make the world whole. Whatever the changes, Faelan was her world. Bera returned the sign, making it their own, and walked into her new life. They held each other tight as skerns, and Heggi ran to her then, bringing her daughter. Complete.

'Disa. Thank you.' She breathed in the smell of love, and then stood back to scry their changes.

'Can we eat now? I'm starving!' Heggi's grin marked a difference: he had the self-knowledge of a man.

Bera could only see happiness on her small Valla's face and knew she had been right to send Alfdis to her for extra protection. The new world was a flood of feelings, past and present. To let them in and share them might hurt greatly, but that was for later; for now she had her family to hold tight.

Her skern pointed to where a pale sun shimmered. *Moon and sun in perfect balance.*

'Is that part of the prediction?'

No matter; Bera had determined her own path – and succeeded. There was one last reassurance to give them, and then she would speak of the Dark no more.

Faelan jerked his head towards the trail of smoke. 'Sending him to his ancestors?'

'A proper burning.'

'I'm glad he's dead.' Heggi said. 'He used to be a nice uncle, before—'

'Let him go, Heggi,' Faelan said.

'He won't return,' Bera said. 'I gave him a new name.'

Heggi was eager. 'What is it?'

'It's whispered in the smoke for only his ancestors to hear. I returned him to that better person you remember, boykin, so the blood you shared is cleansed. I will tell you when we are safely aboard the *Raven*.'

'We can go now,' Faelan agreed. 'The last wolf has passed.'

Bera swung Disa onto her hip. 'I'm starving, too, Heggi!'

Drunk with tiredness and relief, they laughed like fools, jostling and stumbling towards the boat, swinging Disa between them. When they reached the jetty, sunlight burned off a slight mist and Bera held her small daughter to let its heat and light renew their Valla strength.

'Thank you, Mama,' she whispered.

'Mamamama!' Valdis joined all three in a word.

Would that be her Valla skill: to meld? She looked wise beyond her years, but then she burped and chuckled, and was Disa again.

After visiting the latrine, Bera went off alone and washed her face over and over, scrubbing her lips. The Valla was strong but the woman felt defiled.

Pure in heart, dearest.

She began again, until her skern wrapped her tenderly so that her hands were still.

They washed and changed all their undergarments and after a rough meal, Bera finally got the overtired and grumpy toddler to sleep.

'Now, I want to know everything,' said Bera.

Heggi shrugged. 'Disa kept staring and I held the horseshoe. That's it.'

'I was half-stuck for ages, then found them fast asleep,' said Faelan, stopping Heggi's protest. 'So your story, Bera, please.'

It will help you recover.

So Bera closed her eyes and let her hand choose a bead. Unexpected: pure green glasswork. She began in the clenching horror of the cranny and from the ring of skulls onwards they were completely gripped by her story, even how she used the honey.

Heggi clapped his hands. 'That was really clever of you, Bera, to make him a new person! I expect it was a good name, too.'

'Stop fishing,' said Bera.

Faelan smiled. 'You are clever, Bera. The more I think about it, the better it is.'

Praise made Bera's cheeks burn. 'What was in the honeycomb, Faelan? Small and milky.'

Heggi pretended to be sick. 'A maggot!'

Faelan laughed. 'It's to give you the strength of the Queen Bee and protect you. We call it Royal Preserve.'

It really was over, and weariness struck. The Queen Bee Disa drew Bera's attention and she was struck by her baby's downy cheeks. Their breathing slowed.

Heggi nudged her awake. 'Faelan asked you about the war.'

'The war?' It was an old nightmare. 'That's over.'

'So what has changed in Dyflin?' asked Faelan.

'Shall we talk about what you want, instead?' Bera clung on to happiness. 'How would you like to shape your lives?'

'That's new,' said Heggi. 'You've never asked anyone what they want before.'

'Because I have never had a choice!' Bera swallowed hard. 'Oh, Heggi, boykin, I'm sorry. I am bone-tired of bearing the wretched weight of Valla duty my whole life. The sacrifice I just made to keep you and everyone I love safe!'

'I know, Mama,' he said quietly. 'I was only sort of teasing.'

Her skern stroked Bera's neck. *It's not over.*

Bera let anxiety back in. 'The trouble is, I didn't do as the Abbot commanded. What if I haven't brought peace? Now I must fear what he might do to everyone I love.'

'Fear is at the root of everything bad,' said Faelan. 'Anger, despair, jealousy, revenge, wars: all begun by fear. We can be better folk than that.'

'We chose better on Ice Island,' said Bera. 'We became kin.'

'We tried,' said Heggi. 'Then look what happened.'

'A volcano.'

Faelan smiled at her. 'You can be blown off course by a storm but always know where you are headed.'

'With a true compass.' Bera took a deep breath. 'There's something I need to say.'

Heggi laughed. 'No need, Mama. Even I noticed.'

'When?' Bera was slightly aggrieved.

'Ages ago. The way you look at each other.'

Faelan touched his lips and shook his head.

'Ginna told you, Heggi,' said Bera. 'So she will also tell Dellingr.'

'She already has.' Heggi tore off some bread.

'What did he say?'

'That me and Ginna would be wed for sure, then.'

'Dellingr dislikes me, Bera,' Faelan said, 'as much as I have never trusted him.' He got to his feet. 'Since you ask what I want, I say we set sail at once. For the Summer Isles.'

'North,' she breathed. The word filled Bera with longing.

'I want to keep us safe,' said Faelan. 'Our small family.'

How she yearned to take her children away from danger, but she would not break her word, and Heggi, staying silent, knew it.

'Ginna is kin, and Dellingr. Sigrid and her son. I will not leave them behind, Faelan.'

'As you left me?'

Bera was icy. 'I gave my word to the Abbot.'

'That you would marry a corpse and return with an army of the dead!' Faelan's anger throbbed. 'How will you explain returning alone?'

Heggi squared up to Faelan. 'We have to stay and fight, not run away like cowards!'

'Your head would be off before you could say axe.' Faelan's hand chopped his own neck.

'What do you know?' Heggi sneered.

'Stop it, both of you!' Bera stood between them. 'We work together.'

'I don't want either of you near war.' Faelan ran a hand through his hair. 'I've met warriors in Smolderby. When they have drunk

266

themselves truthful, they talk about the bloodbath, the mad lust for killing. The smell. Forget the glory of the brave, Heggi, it's spilled guts and torn bowels. They can't get the stench out of their nostrils, no matter how much they drink, no matter how many years pass.'

'I don't care!' Heggi spat.

Faelan cursed and went forward to the bow.

'Oh, Heggi.' Bera spoke softly. 'You have hurt him. Faelan has already suffered to keep us safe. And who looked after Rakki before we got back? Words can strike as deep as an axe, especially when we all fear what comes next. No, boykin.' She put up a hand. 'You are as torn about staying or going as we are. Not being honest about your fear is making you behave badly.'

'I'm not. I'm showing courage.'

'True courage is doing what must be done despite the fear – which you must first own and only then can you be strong. We could start by making a pact of determination. To be a team.'

'I want to go home, really.' Heggi's eyes trembled with tears. 'I mean Seabost, with Ginna, and Papa arriving with honey and Thorvald wrestling me and going puffin hunting with Rakki.' His voice broke, and Bera drew her boy close.

'I understand, boykin, and I think Faelan does, too.'

Faelan rushed back. 'I want a home for us all. Come, Heggi, let's rig the sail.'

They were friends again, preparing to cast off, seeing who dared wait the longest to leap back aboard. Bera got the hammock ready for passage and Disa sat on the deck, watching her every move.

Faelan left Heggi to steer. 'He's at a hard age for a boy. I think he was testing me, to see if I deserve you.'

'Oh, Faelan, I long for home, too.' She picked up her daughter.

'Which home would you choose?'

Home is wherever you belong.

'I wish we were free, all of us, out on the sea paths. That's where I belong.'

Faelan smiled. 'It's simple for me. Home is wherever you are.'

'Don't let's talk about it now.'

'Why not?'

'You know why! I have to return!'

'Bera, don't cry. I'm sorry.'

A tear fell onto Disa's lip and she brushed it away with the tip of a finger. 'This girl and I were stronger Vallas when we were together with Alfdis. The power of three, Faelan. Do you understand?'

'Only two are living...' He scratched his head. 'Is your fear that one must stand alone above ground?'

'I think the Abbot always meant for me to die, as Brid or Bera.'

'That's my fear! He will kill you, and the Vallas already have the next in line.'

'Too young to stop Chaos.'

Bera willed Faelan to go so that she did not have to look at his dear face, because she was too tired to move. Sitting forlorn on the rail was her skern, who would not look at her.

Faelan got his breathing under control. 'If that is what the Vallas are weaving, I defy them. We are a team, Bera, you said so. We can stop Chaos coming to Dyflin.'

'With our smith. Whether you like it or not, Faelan, we need the old magic, too. The lore of iron.'

Bera hated turning back. Out on the whale roads, she had an urge to keep heading for the sky rim. Heggi watched her, his own desire to both go north and keep his word to Ginna plain on his face.

The return to Dyflin seemed faster. As they passed the lion's head Bera smelled a storm coming, and when they turned for the harbour entrance it broke. Soaked, weary and with a dull dread, they eventually found a place to anchor among fleets of dragon boats. They could have walked ashore over the decks. All empty, the only sound the rigging slatting in the wind gusts.

'Can you hear a battle?' she asked.

Faelan shook his head.

Heggi pulled his cloak tighter. 'I think our summers are warmer.'

'I wish I had my woollen cloak,' Bera said. 'I'm never let into the palace.'

'Take mine,' Faelan offered.

'It's too cumbersome.'

'Ginna's is here.' Heggi opened the stern locker. 'You're small enough to fit.'

'Stop fussing about a cloak!'

'We don't fuss, we care, Bera,' said Faelan. 'And you are frightened and won't say so.'

Heggi threw the cloak over her shoulders. 'Stop fiddling with the pin!' She was desperate to get it all over with. 'Sorry.'

'I want—'

'No, Heggi. I'll go alone, but I will send Ginna ahead, so watch the quayside.' Bera kissed his anguished face. 'Let's make a new ritual before I go.'

The men looked at each other. Bera showed them her three clenching nails.

'I'm not very good at it yet,' said Heggi.

'We'll use the horseshoe. Can you hold Disa, Faelan?'

They stood at the prow for Valla protection from the *Raven*. Each held something precious in their left hand: Heggi the things of iron and Bera her necklace. Faelan cradled a small Valla but one hand was on the cross beneath. Bera let it go, deciding the new mix was apt. When she closed her eyes it was Dellingr she saw, the smith of Seabost, as straight and true as an ash mast. Strong in the old magic. With his knowledge and Faelan's courage, there would be an earthly power of three. For the war was waged by living beings of all beliefs.

Bera hammered on the palace gate, determined to be heard. She waited, shivering. The rain had become a drenching mist that soaked through the thickest wool and Ginna's cloak was a summer one. There was an eerie quiet as the world was poised for war to begin.

The guard slid back the grille and let her inside. 'He's waiting in the scented garden.'

'The Warrior Abbot?'

He kept walking.

It was Bjarni in the garden alone with the ravens. Both birds glared at her, then returned to pecking crumbs from the grass.

'It never stops raining here.' He put a hand down his collar. 'That branch just dropped a gallon down my neck.'

'More importantly, Bjarni, I'm back. In time to stop the war.'

'The Abbot says you will bring a sign to show our side will win.' He shrugged. 'Except… in private, I think he doubted that you would return.'

'I think he tried to make sure I did not.'

'As Brid or Bera?' He stroked his chin. 'I did tell him Brid would succeed, meaning Bera. I am glad to see you.'

'I am not being Brid ever again. Is Brid even the Abbot's side now? What did he say to the council?'

'It did not sound as if he wanted you – or the Serpent – to return.'

'The question is, why?'

The ravens clattered up into an apple tree and began stamping on the boughs to loosen the ripest fruit.

Bera pressed him. 'You know, don't you?'

The birds jumped down onto the grass and began stabbing the apples with their obsidian beaks. Bera used the pressure of silence, and watched Bjarni rolling the answer in his mouth like a pebble for thirst. He tucked a wet strand of hair behind her ear.

'This is just my own view. I think the only thing he feared was The Rising. An army of the dead is unpredictable. So now he is waiting to see which side looks stronger and he will switch beliefs.'

'How will he decide?'

'The armies are in the field' – he waved a hand towards the inland side of the palace – 'but there are many opposing sides, and which belongs to the Abbot is in doubt. This war is a welter of beliefs. Old, new, a mix of them to gain power. We are told to believe one thing one day and another the next.'

'To Hel with this! I'm going to confront him.'

'I paid the guard well to make sure I saw you first. I think it best that you should stay away from him until matters are clearer.'

'About what?'

'Chaos is coming,' said Bjarni. 'Or it may already be here, in the hearts of folk we should trust.'

'Do you mean me? I've come back, haven't I, when I could have sailed north!'

Bjarni touched his heart. 'You should trust me, Bera.'

'For my mother's sake, I do.' Bera pulled out the blue vial. 'This relic contains the precious tears of Brid, according to the Abbot. He said if I felt the need, I should drink it.'

'And I warned you about him,' said Bjarni. 'What is in it?'

Bera dripped the holy water onto the grass, which shrivelled and smoked. They reared away from the smell.

'Acid of sulfur,' he croaked.

'As you see, I trusted you and did not drink it.'

'What happened to the Serpent?'

'I gave him a new name with the hammer sign on his brow.'

'The old belief.'

'He is dead but reborn with his ancestors. Now and forever.'

Bjarni was thinking. 'The Abbot will not share power. He wanted you to destroy the Serpent forever, not return as Chief Warrior. He might enjoy having Brid on his side if you bring him power.'

'I said I've finished with pretence.'

'Then let him think you are dead, or have flown. Go now, quickly. I'll pay the gate guard to keep quiet.'

'Not without the others. Is Dellingr at the forge? And Ginna safe?'

'The Warrior Abbot would not harm him. Yet. He needs him to work, so Ginna is also safe.'

'I'll go there now.' Bera went to the arch.

Bjarni stopped her. 'The Abbot may be true to Brid or not; Dellingr may be true to you or turned, but be careful. The palace has more wealth than you can dream of, and power, which can corrupt the most decent of men.'

Her smith was inside the forge, working the bellows on his own. Bera was glad his bellows-boy was missing and took the chance to get warm. Dellingr was again the man she had pictured in the new ritual, and she admired the strength of his muscles as he whumped the flames into white-hotness.

When he stopped, she spoke his name with the ache of something lost.

Dellingr took two strides and pulled her to him. Her face rested against his filthy leather apron, smelling of walrus and burning. Home.

He kissed the top of her head and then held her out to look at her, like a father. 'I fashioned that brooch and she got that het up.'

'I forgot this is Ginna's cloak.'

'Her mother dyed the wool special, and it was the last thing… Well, you know all that.'

Bera wanted to tell him how she faced death to stop war and Chaos coming, but said, 'Heggi is impatient to see her,' and pinned on a smile.

'A guard took her down there. They've been watching the harbour.'

'If he let Ginna go, the Abbot must know I am here?'

'That's the deal. He's charged me to get you to the crannog.'

'Why?'

Dellingr shrugged. 'No woman is allowed inside the palace.' He offered his skrim rag. 'Your face. Better clean it before…'

'That will only make it worse!'

He wiped his hands. 'I forget how young you are, Bera.'

'And yet you all depend on me. Now, I shall go and keep us all safe by telling the Abbot the Serpent King is dead.'

'Stay away from the Warrior Abbot, Bera. He is dangerous.'

'Why tell me to go, then!'

'He did, I didn't.' He shook his head like an ox at its stall. 'He's got me to do stuff… Keep away from the crannog is what I'm saying.'

'The crannog itself will protect me. It sits on your hammer pond.'

Dellingr drew a large cross on his chest.

'A Brid cross? Oh, Dellingr. Has the Abbot muddled your thinking?'

'Don't mock me, Bera. I'm a plain smith, but our magic is older than we know. It may keep you safe – or the Abbot's new belief is stronger. You weakened yourself by being Brid.'

'I have returned stronger, and the power of three—'

'Leave now, and keep my Ginna safe.'

'The power of three includes you.' Bera took his hand. 'Whichever side he chooses, the Abbot is scheming and I will not be his new god to bring Chaos.'

Dellingr rubbed his face. 'The working with metals brings me joy but now…'

'Come with me, then, after I meet the Abbot.'

'Don't go to him!'

'I must prove him a liar. Then I will stop the war, with you and Faelan beside me, and then we can go home.'

'What home? I will not defile the old magic by standing with that elf-believer Faelan. Get back to the *Raven*, Bera. I sent the bellows-boy down there with swords so you could fight.'

Bera was furious. 'How could you be such a fool? I left our folk aboard to keep them safe but now you have dragged them into danger!'

'This is the time of war.' Dellingr's lips were white. 'Do you think we can keep anyone safe without arming them?'

'And you may have killed your bellows-boy if they are watching the *Raven* and the others, too!'

The light went out for a moment as someone stepped through the doorway. Bjarni.

'Keep your voices down,' he said. 'The Abbot is waiting for you, Bera.'

'And I shall meet him.'

'Wait!' Dellingr stared at Bjarni. 'I will leave with you, Bera, if we go now.'

'You have one last task, Dellingr,' said Bjarni. 'If you don't do it, none of us will be safe. You know this.'

'Chaos.' Dellingr's shoulders slumped. 'This is the last, Bjarni, I'm telling you.'

Bera's thoughts jangled with riddles, and she went outside to be alone. Her first task was the Abbot. What did she owe to a dangerous boy who lied and cheated; who rabble-roused his people by threatening Chaos because he wanted the spoils of war; who pretended the Serpent was her brother who would return with Brid when he tried to get rid of them both with sulfur?

A blackbird sang, celebrating the end of one belt of rain, though another was approaching on the sky rim. A light breeze ruffled her hair and thin rays of sun dappled the singing reeds. She went to the hedge where she had overheard Heggi and Ginna. If she stayed this side of it, she could imagine them still trying to catch fish, laughing, kissing. Full of life. If it meant she could save them, she would die – but die as Bera, a Valla, not Brid.

Dellingr joined her, his face grim. 'Chaos is coming, Bera, but I never thought I would be the one to bring it.'

'This is Bjarni's doing, making you feel guilty. Fetch your tools and go down to the quay, to your daughter.'

'And leave you here?' He punched his chest. 'Besides, I gave my word.'

'The Abbot is using you, Dellingr. His word is worth nothing!'

'The truth is, I wanted to do it and now…' He watched Bjarni walking away. 'And I wanted you to see how well I devised it.'

'Devised what?'

'That's why, in a way, I wanted you to stay. But go now. Look after my daughter.' He strode back to the forge.

There was nothing for it. She would have to save her smith herself, and that would start at the crannog. It lived in her heart, since the long dead, as a place of protection, which would give her truths to confound the Abbot's lies.

29

Bera went the quicker way from the hammer pond, intending to summon Cronan's aid. She wanted to save his crannog from the Abbot, who was in there now, staining it with dishonesty. Perhaps he even meant to spill her blood there.

Of course! And then he would place her skull in there forever, so simple folk could look on Brid with awe and make him even more powerful, sweeping up the Brid cult with any new belief – along with any other festival, like Sowun. Control the folk in Iraland. Kill the wolves! Poor Dellingr, taken in by his lies. What did Bjarni believe? Was this what Chaos meant?

What should she do? Without her skern her confidence flickered. He had not spoken at the forge and her last sighting of him was a picture of misery. This new belief in Iraland talked of peace and did nothing but make war. She had heard it from traders and quayside brothels: whorehouses and warehouses. New words, new understanding. Trade of every kind, and trade was all. Bodies were a commodity, and slaves brought from all over the Known World to be sold at market.

Was this why the Vallas had sent her? To end a war about trade and power, not belief? If only she had Obsidian, then one woman could make peace certain.

She staggered. Was the black stone making her think like this, now she was near the Abbot, who craved it? She knew its terrible danger. She had to get away with her mind intact.

'Wait!' The Abbot was stumbling along the shore under a heavy sky-blue banner. 'The enemy has advanced!' He sounded elated.

'I hear no battle,' she said. 'Is this another attempt to fool me?'

'Who could fool Brid?'

'We both know I am not Brid.' Bera wanted him to crumble under the weight of her truth.

Unconcerned, he cocked his head towards the outer wall. 'They think you're Brid. That's all that matters. I've been in the crannog trying to get this blessed. Seems I need you after all. I promised to make the banner of Brid more potent.'

'But you alone could not.'

'Look.' He fingered the flag, smirking. 'It's Brid-blue and depicts Brid joined with the Serpent in... let's call it holy union.' For the first time he met her eyes to savour her revulsion. His own, dull stones of greed were the Serpent's. 'Come on, *Brid*, time to be potent and fulfil the prophecy.'

'You made sure that couldn't happen.'

'They don't know it didn't.' The Abbot laughed. 'Oh, come on. If you want peace all you have to do is let them see you.'

Her word had been given with no true understanding, but it was her word. The Vallas had given her their warning of Chaos, and she had gained strength. Surely if she appeared, a true Valla, then the war would be stopped.

Bera followed him to the thick outer wall, with its small room inside at the base of some steps. A guard came out and carried the banner ahead of them, onto a wide wooden platform. He rested it against the wall and Bera went to the edge, high above an open plain. How would the armies notice her? She had pictured herself addressing them. She needed to connect with the land and draw strength from it, knowing that when her hand had chosen the green glasswork bead it was a sign of this.

Any lasting trace of the Serpent, even memory, had to be cleansed. Bera let the colour wash over her: green, purest green, the colour of unfurling spring leaves, as healing as Faelan's garden. It was right that she was here.

In the distance lazy columns of rain slanted across the silver landscape. The circling hills were clouded with forests of ancient trees, not spiky firs, but still the lair of bears and wolves. There were some dotted farms but no sign of livestock in the pastures. The nearest wood was only a collection of hagthorn and brambles above old quarry workings. Perhaps this was where the ancients got their stone. Bera felt a deep connection where past and present would join to make a better future within herself, not the land.

The hill that the palace was built on dipped slightly on this side and then rose to a lower point, where three riders in Brid-blue were looking down the slope to the broad valley, where a river snaked in long coils.

'The Serpent's Plain,' said the Abbot. 'Older than time.'

A serpent was also a sign of healing, Faelan once said of his cross. All might still be well, as long as she used the same creative thinking as the long dead had taught her.

'Are all the groups this side fighting for the Warrior Abbot?'

'*Chief* Warrior Abbot.' He started, swatting at his face and spitting. 'Thunderflies! I hate them.'

So he had taken all that power for himself, but scorning Fate could be his undoing. As a Valla, she would show pity; for if you caged any child inside these walls with absolute power, who would be strong enough to resist?

Bera took stock of the war, to form a plan. The flat plain was divided into two main groups, thronged with spiked and armoured fighters, horses and war dogs. Within each were factions with their own banners, booths and shields, as seen in the war fleets. Other beliefs. Small fires were dotted around both camps, dancing bright against black clouds that were swarming upwind.

'I can see Brid-blue,' she said. 'Who else is here?'

'Most of our side are from the Marsh Lands and south and east, through to the Golden Horn. They'll be the ones shivering round the fires.' He was sneering at his own army. 'You Northmen are mostly on the other side. Too many gods, I'm afraid. Who are you going to call on?'

'Myself.'

The Abbot shrugged, making Bera doubt herself. What was she fighting for? She had found the way to both save and dispatch the Serpent King, but who was the enemy here? There was only the gathering of strangers, and the calling of blood.

Thunder. Bera counted between the rumbles; the storm was getting closer, and fast. Rain smudged a grey sleeve across the land. The hills shivered and the stone walls of neighbouring fields bounced and blurred. It reached Bera, drumming a hard, plastering beat on her scalp. Loose strands of hair stung her eyes. Bera groped behind her head and found a hood and gave thanks to Ginna and Asa, feeling safe in the wool's protection.

'Curse this cursed weather!' The Abbot's face was ugly with rain and spittle. 'I said wait until tomorrow, but no, the council said it would be dry. Curse you stupid Northmen with your idiot god of thunder. The day is ruined!'

'Men kill in rain just the same,' said Bera.

He rolled his eyes at her stupidity. 'It's not about killing. It's about winning. It's about them bowing down to the Chief Warrior Abbot, so that I can bring peace to the Known World!'

Bera could taste his madness. 'Mad for power,' she said. 'You can't even hear the mismatch in your own name.'

He seized the banner from the guard and sulked with it, leaning against the back wall. The guard left and Bera wanted to follow him, to get away from this unstable youth. Why was he so upset about a storm? He didn't believe in Thor. He blamed the Northmen, but only their children thought Thor played with thunder. Perhaps he feared the belief gave them the upper hand. There's no leeway in battle, so better steer hard, Ottar used to say.

She thought about Faelan's board game and getting the King back into his fortress by going round the back, not kicking all the pieces over. The ermites that taught him must have learned it here. How like men to think killing would play out by rules.

The rain had eased but the air was thick with worse to come. Bera pulled the sodden cloak around her neck and refastened Dellingr's pin. A fat drop spat onto the wooden planks, then two, three. Out on the smouldering plain, the groups were thinning and the distant tinny hammering stopped.

Thundercrack. The noise was a flattening hand, making Bera reel. Ashamed, she checked to see if the Abbot had noticed but he was sheltering behind the banner. A heavy stillness settled, waiting for the next crack of thunder, but there was only a distant rumble. The camps filled again with noise. Some bolting horses careered away from shouting men, or reared up amongst barking dogs. Women chased, screaming, after children and Bera was shocked to see how small they were.

She pulled the Abbot round. 'Stop this madness! Look down there, both sides suffering exactly the same! Children, mad with terror, and all the animals!'

His eyes gleamed. 'Chaos is coming.'

'Not under my banner.' Bera tried to seize it.

'Not yet!' He put his full weight on it. 'Anyway, it's not yours. Watch for the Serpent King!'

'No! That's not possible!'

A white veil was blanking out the valley and ahead of it, folk were running for shelter, or huddling under already crowded booths. The squall hit Bera like a flint wall, driving her back. The wooden platform jumped and sparked with hail. She had a headache from the pounding, even under the hood; it was weighing her down. And so was fear. She had renamed him and freed Sumarliði – but had that somehow made the Serpent King stronger? Had the Vallas intended this, or had her own terror formed the crouching, antlered monster that had shifted in the Dark? She dreaded seeing the Abbot's side advance with the Serpent at its head, a Drorgher in full dragon body. And The Rising?

Hail turned to rain and Bera found she was turning over and over in her hands something that felt like a pebble. Cool, smooth, round and now wet. All around her wood and stone glistened, black as iron. The three riders had gone, the small mound like a desolate skerry amongst blue hills that swayed forward and back as showers passed in waves. The platform was adrift, the deck awash, no one at the helm.

A pale sun lit the dismal scene, ghostly in the misty rain. Bera pushed back her hood and coldness trickled down the back of her neck. The storm had doused the fires, leaving behind slow-moving, bewildered people in a wreckage of shelters and trappings of war. Brutish dogs that loped like wolves were hunting in packs, lunging at the armoured war dogs, or at horses with glistening flanks that stamped and snorted.

All suffered the same; no side had 'right' on its side. Even if she could have made herself heard over the din of battle, no one would care, for the leaders were stoking the blood-rage to white heat. This was an unstoppable lust for killing that longstones recorded. The ancients had known it would go on, with their echo, throughout time.

There was nothing for her here. Bera made for the steps.

The Abbot moved to block her. He was glowing, as if he had personally seen off the storm. 'Running away?'

'I hoped to bring peace,' she said. 'I see now that there is no such thing, only an unending struggle for wealth and power. I will not be used in it.'

'Poor little Bera, nobody cares about you.'

'Then let me pass.'

'I shall wave this banner soon and my side will charge… and win.'

'By killing.' Bera scraped back her wet hair. 'You said Brid brings peace. So what is the truth?'

'Well, you see, there's your truth, my truth – and their truth.' He looked down. 'They all look like ants from here, don't they?'

'No. They look like the living beings they are, hoping for a better future for their children.'

He laughed. 'The ants believe you married your brother to gain huge power. We're all after the same thing.'

'Your lack of years misled me once into thinking you were innocent,' Bera said. 'I see now that you despise everyone except yourself. You have no honour.'

'Depends what you mean by honour.' He shrugged. 'And as you know, if you lie often enough it becomes the truth.'

Bera smarted with the shame of her pretence. 'My truth is…'

A horn blew three loud blasts below them.

'Behold the Serpent King in all his arisen glory!' The Abbot spread his arms.

Bera's cheeks prickled and spiralling rainbows were closing her sight. She bent over, desperate not to faint. It was her forfeit for failure, to bear witness; she dreaded what it would be. The sound of a deep, slow heartbeat struck like blows but she willed herself upright. Coming from the rear of the palace was the antlered giant she had glimpsed crouching in the Dark. Now it stood proud, towering over the Abbot's men. Had she summoned it by mere thought? Bera turned away, shutting out that monstrous head and body plated in shining black scales.

'The Rising! Pay homage, for Chaos is come!'

'What have you done?'

'Look – I knew it! Your side is already running.'

'I don't have a side.' But he had made her turn.

'Watch! This is the best part.'

Drums marked the slow heartbeat. The Abbot's side parted to let through a team of men, sliding in the mud. That was why he had been furious at the rain. Boys ran to the front, laying brash along their path. They got going again, straining on long ropes, leading back to a heavy trolley bearing the monster.

A ray of sunlight pierced the clouds and revealed the beast to be no living creature, this was some iron monster forged by Hel... Or, worse, by someone she loved.

The drumbeats stopped and the creature glowered at the enemy from the head of the Abbot's army.

'You see, this isn't my belief at all but yours.' He was spinning, whirling his arms, a hideous, triumphant child. 'You Northmen created this monster to kill your own side!'

Bera's ribs juddered as the monster thundered, filling the valley with deep sound, like a diving whale. People ran on all sides. Others were too stunned to move; children cowered alone. She could smell sharp fear as the bellows of Hel whumped, whumped, and a burst of flame roared out of the mouth of the beast. Whoever was before it, no matter what side, became a black brand before melting. There were screams, yells and confusion. The foul breath of Chaos, like the gateway to Hel, repulsed Bera. She retched, a thin yellow bile like sulfur.

She had to get away. and started down the steps with death at her heels. Could she ever forget the sound? She kept running, like a child wanting the comfort of fatherly Dellingr, telling her she was wrong to doubt him. But that man no longer existed and the forge was deserted. The gardens were silent: no bees, no ravens; no life. The main gate was unguarded and she went straight through the wicket and headed through empty streets for the quay. What would Faelan say when she told him she had run away?

Bera pulled up.

She was not that uncertain child but a Valla. She faced the living and undead. It was guilt that had made her think she had failed. She had done her Valla duty and removed the Serpent, and in his destruction, created a new life. Not some monster, but safety for the ones she loved. Into her mind came the triskelion, seen properly. It not only marked the power of three but it was her own sign of forward movement. On, on. Sunwise. She was her own Valla and woman. It was love that had triumphed in the long dead, and the proof that it always would was close at hand.

Sigrid, when she got there, was in no mood to hear Bera's account and cut her short.

'I know what you're up to.' She swung Borgvald like an axe. 'You're running away again, like you always do.'

Sigrid always poked the quick of any sore.

'Be quiet, Sigrid! Stop telling me what I am about to say and start listening.'

Quiet clapping came from a corner. It was not her skern but Bjarni who stepped out.

'You sound so like your mother,' he said.

'Doesn't she just!' spat Sigrid. 'As you'd know only too well.'

Bjarni slapped her. Sigrid put a shocked hand to her cheek.

Bera stood between them. 'Don't you dare touch Sigrid. I owe her my life.'

But the slap gave Sigrid the anger for truth. 'You do nothing but cause trouble with folk, Bjarni, always have. Why do you think our fishermen left you for dead? They couldn't get away fast enough. We all hoped they would kill you if the sea didn't.'

Bjarni let a shadow fall across his face. 'I drowned.'

'Stop trying to look like a Fetch,' said Bera. 'You may have fooled

Sigrid at first but I have been in the Dark and know what the half-living look like. You can't rule by fear. Sigrid, there is a place for you and your son aboard the *Raven*. It honours my debt to Thorvald, so I ask you again to join us. I'll help you down to the quay.'

'Best be quick.' Bjarni turned at the door. 'I'm not a bad man.'

When he was gone they let out long breaths.

'I didn't mean the bit about your ma,' Sigrid told the roof beams.

'You did. But we need to get away. Come on.'

They went through to the billet, where Sigrid's few belongings were in a chest.

Sigrid listlessly pulled out a shawl. 'I suppose he's gone back to the palace. What if he dies? Or says we're leaving?'

'It doesn't matter either way: you're coming with me, but hurry.' Bera stuffed some undergarments into a bag. 'Is there a bedroll we can take?'

'Iraland muddles things. Too many folk from too many places with too many beliefs.' Sigrid twisted a loose thread round and round her forefinger, making the nail blue, then white. 'Like it's made up to suit folk, not something true, passed down through time.'

'Get Borgvald ready.'

'You know I'm not coming, don't you?'

'You are, Sigrid,' Bera said. 'We are leaving right now. The Abbot is winning the war and he will slaughter all Northmen in a show of power. Think of your son. What would his father tell you to do?'

'Fly,' Sigrid whispered.

30

Bera ran ahead to the city gate to warn Faelan. He had the *Raven* at the quay, with the lines ready to slip. Judging from the mast height, the water was low. There was little time. She ducked through the market, where the last few traders were wheeling away their stalls, and scrambled down the ladder. Her skern gave a feeble wave but it helped.

'Get your breath.' Faelan passed her Disa.

Bera snuggled into her. 'Sigrid's coming soon.'

'She'd better be quick if we're to catch the ebb.'

'Where's Heggi?'

'With Ginna, along the quay.'

'They should be here!'

'I've kept my eye on them. They need time together, just to be.'

Bera's scalp flared. No enemy was in sight but Heggi and Ginna were alone on a deserted quay. Last time it was Rakki who had caused her boy to be ashore. Then Ottar... Was it happening again?

She tied Disa into her hammock. 'Did the bellows-boy come?'

'What?'

'So we have no war swords. You were right to never trust Dellingr.' She made for the ladder. 'I'm going to get those two!'

He stopped her. 'I'm faster.'

Faelan scaled the ladder as neatly as he had once climbed a cliff face with a lamb on his back. She had stood back last time; now she was sure Heggi's life depended on her. Her scalp was on fire. Bera pulled the back of her skirts through her legs and tucked the folds into her belt. If she had helped bring The Rising, it was her duty to face Chaos.

Her skern was at her neck. *Valdis would be safer if her mother stayed with her.*

She batted him away and started up the slimy rungs of the ladder. Time did odd things again. It shrank and stretched as she climbed up to the quay, both past and present, too; mother and child. Feeling the fear more keenly, with more to lose, and yet facing it. That was courage. She reached the top and summoned the Vallas to her back, ready to face a foe she didn't understand.

It's c-coming. His teeth chattered.

The ones she loved were running back.

'Get them aboard,' she shouted.

'You go with Bera, Ginny,' Heggi said, pushing her ahead.

Ginna's eyes were wild. 'Where's Papa?'

Bera was steely. 'Get aboard and stay there.'

'Please come, Heggi,' Ginna said, terrified.

He was chewing his lip hard enough to make it bleed but he helped Ginna to board.

'What is it?' Faelan kept his eyes on the gates.

'My scalp is on fire and I am ready.' Ready to splinter Drorghers.

Faelan backed away. 'You have terrified the young ones.'

Steady. It's the living you have to fear.

Beyond the gates was a rumble like thunder, the clank of metal.

'Bera…' Faelan was serious. 'If I die…'

'You won't.'

'The burns on my face say otherwise.'

The rumble was the approach of many feet.

You know the truth about the Abbot's new belief. He will kill you.

'All victors wipe out the enemy,' she said.

'I know.'

Bjarni rushed through the gate, pushing a handcart, which carried Sigrid and her bawling baby. Dellingr was not with them. Still unseen, the tramp of feet stopped to a well-drilled silence. These were trained guards, under close command.

'Why have they stopped?' Faelan muttered.

'They are waiting for the horror to come.'

The cart rattled and jolted over the cobbles and Sigrid was clinging on to both sides.

'Get on the boat!' yelled Bjarni as he ran along the quay.

'Where's Dellingr?'

'Get on the boat!'

The cart tipped and Sigrid clambered out. 'Will you for once just do as a man says?'

'Get aboard,' Bera blazed. 'My duty is to protect you.'

'I'm here, aren't I?' Sigrid blustered, tying Borgvald to her. 'Hel's teeth! I'm getting on the boat! For Frigg's sake and every decent power, Bera, even you can't fight a whole army!'

'Is the Abbot leading?' asked Faelan.

'Do you think he would risk his own fair skin?' Bjarni's scorn was blistering. 'He has just named Brid as leader of an enemy cult and out there are trained soldiers come to destroy all her believers.'

'He knows I'm not Brid.'

'It suits him to kill you, Bera, in public. He lies to suit himself about belief. All he ever wants is land and money, grabbing everything owned by old beliefs. It's how he pays his army, who fight for whatever is the latest "true faith". And you will speak the truth if you live.'

Faelan gave a nod. 'Power.'

It was clever: if she exposed the lie she would be killed for her own deception. How deep was her smith's betrayal? She needed to know, for her sake, and Ginna's.

'Where is Dellingr?'

Sigrid was frantic. 'They will kill any woman standing here once they've finished with her, if she isn't dead already. Please, Bera, for the love of your ma, it's nothing a Valla can defeat, let's go now.'

'I will not leave without Dellingr.'

'You'll have to,' Sigrid said. 'He's changed sides.'

'But which side?'

'The Abbot's,' Bjarni said. 'They're waiting for him up there.'

'I knew it,' Faelan said. 'Come on, then, Bera. Fast, now.'

Bera still could not fathom the betrayal. 'It was Dellingr who fashioned the monster. Dellingr brought Chaos into war – but why would he bring it here?'

'He's coming for you,' said Bjarni.

'Never.' Bera shook away the words like flies. 'Get Sigrid aboard.'

Sigrid shoved Faelan away. 'Throw her onto the frigging boat!'

'If you go, she will follow.' Faelan took Borgvald.

Sigrid struggled down the ladder, cursing. There were more rungs to get down.

'I hope the *Raven* can get away,' Bjarni said, taking tool rolls out of the cart and throwing them down to Heggi.

'Are you mad? There's no time for this!'

'Dellingr made me take them for the next smith.'

So he knew he would die once his evil work was done.

'We need to slip the lines,' Faelan shouted. 'The water's going fast.'

'Heggi! Help Faelan!' Bera shouted. 'Leave those tools, Bjarni, they are tainted by Dellingr.'

'Tools can't be blamed for the hand that holds them.'

'But the power of iron can be corrupted. I will not risk my son.' Bera made for the ladder.

Both city gates crashed open and the enemy appeared. At its head was a rider, naked to the waist. His chest was glistening with fresh blood, with a dragon body beneath. His face only had one coil around his eye and when he raised his arms to signal the men to stop, there was no all-seeing eye. This was an everyday serpent. Perhaps there would always be other serpents. Knife, ash and dye – that was all they needed, but the real Serpent was hidden, coiled inside those who lusted for blood.

'Stop there, Whore of Babel!' shouted the rider.

'Go,' said Bjarni. 'The ones you love need you, Bera. This is not your fight.'

'Come with me.'

'I belong here.' Bjarni pushed something into her hand. 'Sorry to say, I blow with the wind.'

More riders joined the leader on the quay, jeering. This was her fight now.

Bera took a step towards them. 'I will be shown respect as a Valla. I will not deal with unruly brats.'

They laughed louder.

Beyond the gates was a grinding and graunching, and then Chaos arrived without drumbeats. The cartmen held the trolley steady at the top of the ramp leading down to the quay. Seen clearly, this creature, plated with shields for scales, was a device made by a man. Her smith corrupting the lore of iron. The same harsh smell was in the air that would bring fire: not to cleanse, but to kill.

Bera looked for Dellingr, hoping that Ginna would not have to witness her father's evil. She could not see him, and wanted to be wrong, but she was not. She hoped Ginna had not been infected by getting too close. Yet even when the bellows began she could not believe the smith had meant to kill her.

The horses snorted and stamped as their riders backed them away from the coming flame.

'Stop!' Bjarni seized Bera from behind, ramming her arm up her back. 'I was sent with new orders from the Chief Warrior Abbot. This woman is an imposter. She is not Brid, and must be taken to the palace, alive.'

Bera wrestled to get away. 'Whose side are you on?'

'The winner's.' His grip was tight as the grave.

She despised this person all over again. He had killed her truest Rakki and would never understand loyalty. The riders advanced, their horses smelling of swagger and death.

'Slip the lines, Faelan!' Bera yelled.

Ropes snaked off the mooring posts, but the *Raven* did not drift off.

'Mama!' Heggi and Ginna were keeping the boat near the ladder.

Bera struggled. A bellowing war cry came from behind and Bjarni thrust Bera away. Dellingr charged at him, knocking him over.

'Bera! Jump off the last rungs!' Faelan shouted.

'Too late! We're all going to die!' Bjarni pointed up at Chaos, poised at the top of the ramp. 'That is your making, Dellingr!'

The monster was clanking, stoking up its flame-breath. It would burn the flesh off their bones, then hurtle downwards and crush them. All. The riders shouted, unable to control their terrified horses. Some were thrown.

Bera was frozen.

Dellingr swung her up and hurled her towards the stern. Faelan grabbed her and ran to the others, already pushing off with oars. Dellingr was halfway down the ladder and took a giant leap onto the *Raven*. Bera took the helm, as the men put their backs into rowing, desperate for steerage. Bjarni made no attempt to board, and when she turned, he raised a hand in farewell.

Without its fire-master the monster had no flames to torch them but it was making a last stand. The trolley-men let go. The iron-clad beast charged down the ramp, crushing a screaming rider as it thundered onto the quay. Could it reach them? Terrified, they had stopped rowing. The beast flew off the quayside, heading towards them but with a mighty splash it fell, its leaden weight taking it down fast, with hissing rage. The wash rocked the *Raven* but freed them from danger and they pulled away strongly.

Bjarni was still on the quayside, watching them. Bera wondered if he had lied to save her life, but even if he was still the Abbot's man, someone had to pay for failure. The serpent rider was off his horse and moving towards him, his sword raised. Perhaps Bjarni welcomed death.

He mouthed a word at Bera and put both hands over his heart.

Gulls screamed their warning and before he could turn fully, the serpent's sword slid in, then up, from groin to throat. It caught for a moment on his jawbone and then Bjarni fell. The serpent swung up onto his horse, leaving the body to be scavenged. He cared nothing; they would get paid, and it was not their fight.

Bera held what had become his parting gift. It would be the bead. She opened her hand and looked at the B rune. He had saved her for her mother's sake, still loving Alfdis.

And respecting you.

Ginna must have known her father was the maker of Chaos, but she was hugging him, full of love, which Bera used to share. Her strong smith. Trust, like belief, was a decision.

And you trust Bjarni.

'He never doubted me as a Valla, and has paid any debt of dishonour.'

They raised the sail in the outer harbour. Sigrid was at the rail, sobbing into her apron. Faelan steered so that Bera could join her.

'Why are you so upset, Sigrid? I thought you hated him?'

'I don't, then. He was my husband for years, wasn't he? And Bjorn's father. He was an honourable man.'

Perhaps Sigrid had always told herself stories about the past that would let her go on living.

Deception keeps her strong.

Bera rolled the bead in her pocket. 'Did you hear Bjarni say something? One word, at the end.'

'My name, of course.' Sigrid slipped away.

Bjarni's dying breath had been 'Alfdis', and she knew it. Bera took out his bead, kissed it and carefully threaded it back on to the necklace. His story was over, but their love was stored inside.

31

Faelan steered for deep water, away from coastal dangers. Bera stayed close to him and hoped he could not see her shaking. Sigrid was at the rail, losing her last meal overboard, with Dellingr holding her garments. Ginna looked after the hammocked babies and Heggi was weather-proofing the boat stores. No one was speaking. Perhaps their earlier courage and relief had given way to shock.

When they were clear of land, Faelan changed course to head north and they sailed into a sea fret that muffled sight and sound like falling into a snowdrift. Bera sent Heggi to get out the longship horn and go to the bow as lookout, leaving them in their own, secret world.

She dropped her guard. 'When I am most scared I will do even more than is expected. Perhaps I should have listened to you. If we had not gone back to Dyflin none of this would have happened.'

Faelan looked at her.

'Well, say something. Tell me I did my Valla duty.'

'You did your Valla duty.'

'I want you to say what you really think. Say anything. I hoped for some comfort!'

'Did you, though?'

'Meaning?'

'Pointless telling you things you already know.' Faelan softened his voice. 'Bera, my sweetest love, there are some things you have to accept in yourself. If you don't, you will never find peace.'

'Ottar used to say that true peace only comes when the battle is won.'

'You know what I'm saying. You can be afraid and still do the right thing if you trust your own feelings.' He patted his heart.

'Finding your own true nature is the battle. You don't need me, Bera, not anyone. You had too many folk telling you what you should be, how you have failed.'

The familiar swing of his black hair, the shadow of beard over the crease to his mouth, the arch of his eyebrow, all the places she had always longed to kiss, all his white skin. Could she ever tell him she no longer wanted to be alone?

'This fog is getting thicker!' shouted Heggi.

Her face was hot. Bera went forward, as if it was the fog that was dangerous.

It was time to feed the babes. Ginna was preparing their food and dropped the spoon when Bera was close. She muttered something about helping Heggi and left.

She is afraid of you.

Puzzled, Bera took over mashing.

'Their meal is ready, Sigrid,' she called. 'You'll feel better if you eat something, too.'

Sigrid made her careful way aft, helped by Dellingr. She was less green now the fog had flattened the sea but she shared every detail of her sickness, which sent her back to the rail, dry-retching.

To Bera's dismay, Dellingr stayed back. 'You and I are kin now, Bera.'

'Pass me that other beaker, would you?' She began to feed Disa.

The smith spooned some mash into Borgvald's open mouth. Bera kept making baby talk, to silence him. They needed a smith, but she did not yet know how to live with a man who had made so monstrous a killing machine.

'Bera, I will speak.' Dellingr held up the spoon. 'I am a man who has followed you without question, at the loss of the ones I loved, at the loss of my ancient craft.'

'Don't try to force me to forgive you.'

'That's not it.' Dellingr cast about like a baited bear. 'I want to explain.'

Bera waved the spoon in the air until Disa laughed, then swooped it into her mouth. Borgvald shrieked.

Dellingr gave up. 'I'd best help Sigrid.'

He was a kind man, holding Sigrid's plaits while she leaned over the rail. Did that excuse what he had done?

You don't have to weigh everything. Just feel it.

'I can't feel it if I can't reckon it.'

Her skern tapped his nose and settled on a barrel.

The fog blew away. There were shapes of islands on the steerboard side and sea birds dived all round the boat. Heggi threw the horn into a locker and took over steering. He whooped as the sail filled and the *Raven* picked up speed.

Faelan swung Disa into the air and she was sick on his shoulder.

'That's the meal gone.' Bera sat her down again to wash her face.

Faelan wiped his sleeve with a stiff boat rag. 'She's growing.'

'Now you'll smell of fish as well as sick.'

He held the rag to his nose and made a face.

'Where are we heading?' she asked.

'North. It is in you, Bera, like the blue heart of an iceberg.'

She gave him a long look. 'I suppose you'll say it is my choice.'

'It is. What did Dellingr want?'

Bera sighed. 'Our trust.'

'He never had mine.'

'He's kin, because of Heggi and Ginna. And making him a smith.'

'How do you feel about that?'

Disgust, if she was honest. 'It's a man's choice, how to smith. Heggi can fashion goodness if he chooses, so he needs a good pattern more than ever.'

Faelan agreed. 'And here's me, look, covered in baby sick and fish scales.'

With a following wind and calm seas Sigrid found her sea legs. She enjoyed her food, which she declared made her even guiltier about leaving Bjarni to die.

'When I think—'

'Then don't!' the others cried.

She kept watch over the children as they crawled about the stern platform at high speed, pulling themselves upright on spars and barrels and falling onto their bottoms with screams of laughter. Bera and Ginna blocked off the bilge and tied lines to them as a kind of harness.

Heggi poked fun at them. 'Just like piglets off to market!'

It wasn't his best joke but they laughed a lot, and afterwards they all chatted as if they had not left death behind them. Ginna had seen Bera in full Valla fury, but was it fear or shame that made her sit apart? Heggi happily joined her.

For the first time, Dellingr acknowledged Faelan. 'Give me some work to do. I need to use my hands.'

'Better ask Bera or we'll both be in trouble.' Faelan was being carefully agreeable.

Then he looked at her. His smile was only for her and warmed her.

'Help me with the sail, Dellingr,' she said. 'There's a patch that needs mending and it's hard for me to get the needle through.'

It was true that it hurt her to sew cloth that was toughened by age and grease but she recognised that Dellingr needed to tell his story for the good of them all. They pulled out the spare sail and Bera got ready the walrus needles and thread. She fetched Ottar's 'bag of bits' and rummaged, pulling out some short lengths of rope and scraps of sail that he collected for repairs. His leather palm was in there and she pushed her thumb into place and tried to tighten it.

'What's that?' Dellingr asked.

'Ottar's old sailmaker's palm. You push the needle through with the pad, look.'

The pad kept twisting round her hand, and then blurred when she failed to make her father's palm fit her. Tears fell off her nose, running crookedly over the wrinkled leather.

'It's hard to tighten it yourself.' Like a father, Dellingr threaded the long tie through the buckle but then looped it up inside the thumb piece and around her whole hand, securing it with a knot. 'There. I'm guessing the wooden pad is where you push the needle, with all those dents.'

Her smith knew that being practical eased sadness, and she was grateful.

'Ottar made the dents so the needle-head won't slip. He used to say, "More control means less injury." I'm sorry there isn't a palm for you.'

He studied his hands. 'My skin's tougher than walrus.'

He's baffled by what those hands can do.

Bera found a worn place and they sat with the sail over their laps. They worked together well, picking up a rhythm, like weaving with Sigrid.

'I don't feel a storm coming,' Bera said. 'But my father said you always need the spare sail good and strong.'

'Like fellowship aboard.'

They were companions, a team, like the early days of the settlement. She enjoyed the steady flow of push and pull, glad to let him stitch the thickest pieces. Those big hands of his, capable and strong, so like her father's, had always been attractive.

And made a killing machine.

Bera hoped Dellingr would start to explain. She sorted through more sailcloth scraps and they began smaller repairs. Then he stopped. The needle had gone through his thumb.

'Let me see,' Bera said.

He hid it. 'A scratch.'

'You're dripping blood. Let me clean it.'

'It's only an old patch, Bera.'

'I'm not worried about the sail.' She called to Heggi to fetch a pail of water.

'What happened?' Ginna came running as if her father lay dying.

Perhaps they were all expecting disaster. Except Heggi, who was carefully lowering the bucket, his tongue sticking out.

'Hold Heggi's legs, Ginna,' she said, for lightness, 'or he'll follow the bucket.'

As they tended Dellingr, the two women became friends again and Bera began to hope forgiveness might be easier. Ginna kissed her father and let them work on alone.

'I like it when you sing,' Dellingr said after a while.

'When do I?'

'When you're on a boat, whenever you're happy.'

'Was I singing just then?'

'Humming.' He put down the sail. 'Bera – I... I don't want to ruin our future.'

'Then don't.' She was suddenly afraid to hear his excuses.

'I'm not asking for forgiveness but Ginna says it's best to have it all in the open, before we land.'

'Let's keep working.' She did not want to see bloodlust in his eyes.

'I did not ever change sides.' He shifted to face her. 'But, oh, Bera, the joy of iron! You'll understand that, you and sailing. To be using my skills again, with every tool, every metal I could ask for! There was a trader from the Golden Horn with so many ideas, new to me, and that burning, like molten pitch, but the price of gold...'

She looked up. 'What?'

'The flame. They use fire in wars in the east and when the Abbot wanted Chaos; we devised it together.'

'But you built it, Dellingr. Why would you make a device for terror?'

'Because the Abbot said if I made it truly terrifying the enemy would scatter and there would be less killing. And most of them did run away. Chaos brought peace.'

'You poor fool, Dellingr. You had a lust for self-glory, to dazzle the Abbot and his council with your skills.'

'You're wrong.'

'But I shall be honest with you now. I got muddled in Dyflin, too. I claimed to be Brid when it suited but that had costs. I only found my true Valla self again in the Dark.'

'You're always true to yourself.'

Bera touched his hand. 'Listen. I took you away from your true self, Dellingr. I robbed you of iron and respect for smithing. We must both promise to do better, and then Chaos will never come again.'

Dellingr was moved. He could only nod, but gripped the iron on his belt. He had sworn.

Next day, a constant mizzling rain blew in. Sigrid rubbed her nose hard.

'Look at those poor babes, stuck under an old greased cloth all day.'

'We will soon be at Faelan's Isle.' Bera left before Sigrid could find more fault.

Ginna was sitting with the children. Borgvald was happily wrestling with Disa. Did children truly follow their fathers? She kissed his nose and passed him to Ginna.

'Did you know I came of age, Bera? When Papa was building Chaos, it was my birth day, the first one without my mother.'

'That hurts.' Bera squeezed her hand. 'Your father is a good man, Ginna.'

'What lies ahead for us, Bera? Can you scry my palm and see how it all turns out? Or do you already know where our home will be?'

'In truth, Ginna? Not yet. I have seen how Ice Island sits at the crossroads of ruin, where the Known World splits.'

'I am so tired of being afraid,' Ginna said.

'Be safe, then.' Bera kissed her. 'We can choose, now, to be safe.'

It was her turn to steer. Heggi was fishing off the stern. His pail was empty. She kissed the back of his caffled, salty hair and he rubbed the place absently, letting out more line.

Faelan stepped away as she took the helm and watched as the *Raven* quickened under her touch.

'I must do some boat chores and take that wastrel son of yours with me,' he said without moving. 'He'll catch nothing with this boat speed.'

'He could get the curricle ready for going ashore.'

'There's a snug harbour where the *Raven* will be safe from gales.'

'And you were steering for it.'

'So are you.' His smile warmed her, toe to head.

Returning home always seemed shorter but this time the following wind made the passage faster towards Faelan's Isle. When it appeared in the distance the clouds parted and it was outlined in silver. Faelan knew the leading landmarks and took over from Bera to steer them into the harbour, where he told them the *Raven* would be safe. For how long? Sigrid hung off the rail, desperate to get ashore, and they all needed some rest.

He brought the boat alongside a rough jetty, then sorted through lengths of rope before they went ashore.

'This matters to you, doesn't it?' Bera said.

'I want the boat to be safe, that's all.'

The island's autumnal scent was rich and heady, like ale-apples. Sigrid wobbled onto the landing stage, threatened to be sick, reached the grass and fell over.

'You see?' she accused Bera. 'You drag me onto that boat of yours and now I'll never walk straight again!'

Bera pulled her up. 'You stay strong over your big losses, Sigrid, but Hel's teeth you moan about trifles!'

Sigrid drew a finger to seal her mouth and set off, making her legs buckle to overplay the weight of Borgvald. The others smiled at Bera. They all knew Sigrid's game, yet cared for her.

Faelan called, 'I'll catch up with you.'

'Where are we going?'

He pointed towards some rough stone buildings. 'Up there's a croft. I gave Heggi and Ginna some food and there's an orchard behind. Maybe other crops.'

'You go on with the others,' she said to Dellingr. 'Can you take Disa?'

He swung the toddler onto his shoulders. 'Are you scrying, then?'

She nodded, and went over to a rocky outcrop. There was no need to scry: she could plainly see that Faelan was letting the *Raven* drift back out into the harbour. He had lines coming off the bow and must have another attached to something heavy underwater to keep the boat safe in a gale.

He was planning to stay.

Bera felt the shock of a different betrayal, and for the moment did not know what she would do about that.

32

Sigrid was trailing behind the others, even though Dellingr was striding ahead with a baby on each shoulder.

'I'm that tired,' she said.

'Let's sit here then.' Bera kicked some pellets away.

'It's wet.' Sigrid put down a greased cloak. They sat close and she held out her hands, showing their brown spots and lumpy knuckles. 'They've gone to look like my mother's.'

It seemed extraordinary to Bera that Sigrid could have had a mother.

'Died my age,' Sigrid went on. 'Northwomen get worn out early.'

'Don't say that!'

'I'm not leaving you.' Sigrid stroked her cheek. 'Will you say some words for the dead? All the mothers. Go on, ask the Vallas. They're all mothers.'

Surprised, Bera held her necklace and named them. 'But also protect the men we hold dear, and animals…'

'You and that dog.' Sigrid rubbed her back, but Bera was no longer a child and there were decisions to be made by them all.

'It's starting to rain again.'

She pulled Sigrid to her feet and they held the sea cloak over them while they walked. The sun was still shining and the rainbow bridges appeared.

'I'd forgotten it, but when we called in here before I took them as a sign of belonging.' Bera wanted to share it. 'It's as if the place has chosen me.'

'You and your notions.' Sigrid shook her head. 'You're more likely mazed with hunger.'

Bera looked round their makeshift longhouse. There were puddles underneath blackened roof spars and the other end of the mud floor was full of mouse droppings and dead leaves. They were disheartened, cross with hunger and exhausted but it was late in the day and shadows were thickening. Bera got them to clap hands in every corner to chase out evil and warm themselves.

'Now we need a raised place to sleep, off this filthy floor. Dellingr, could you build a platform with whatever you can scavenge?'

He went off, muttering. Faelan sorted through some flat stones to remake the hearth. Heggi and Ginna headed for the door.

Sigrid called out. 'Cut some broom, so we can set to sweeping. I've found a dry place for the babes at the back.'

'We were going down to the boat,' said Heggi.

'What for?' Bera asked.

He screwed up his face, failing to think of a reason.

'I'll help Sigrid,' said Ginna, giving in.

Better choices are made with a light heart.

'Go on.' Bera nudged Heggi. 'Fetch the broom, then you two can bring the spare sail back. We'll make a booth in here.'

'When you're ready, I'll help you get it off the boat.' Faelan coughed. 'The *Raven*'s at a deep water mooring.'

Bera kept her face blank, but was pleased it was no secret and the boat was reachable. Sigrid showed her the back of the hut, where the children were in one big hammock, chattering nonsense to each other.

'Most of the roof's left, look, though some burned stuff has fallen.'

'If it's cleared, we could all sleep here,' Bera said. 'These spars look torched.'

'Not recent.' Sigrid sniffed. 'Maybe when Faelan was snatched by slave traders.'

Bera made a start, ignoring Sigrid's prod about her own capture.

Heggi was soon back with the broom twigs. 'Faelan says we're to wait for him at the jetty.'

Faelan was giving them time to be alone, and Bera was pleased for them. She and Sigrid wrapped cloths over their nose and mouth and swept the floor until it was level. When they laid out some rugs and furs it was a small home.

Disa screamed. Borgvald was tugging her hair, and she pushed him over, making her skern jump.

'They are as bad as each other! Sigrid, go and wear your son out.'

'I've cleared all around the hearth,' said Faelan. 'Let Disa crawl to me.'

He kneeled and opened his arms. Bera set her daughter off towards him, crawling fast but then she tried to stand. She tumbled, chuckling at the new game. Bera stopped herself from rushing to help. Faelan shuffled closer, coaxing her. Valdis stuck her bottom in the air, got upright and took three fast steps before she began to wobble. He reached out, caught her hands and walked her into a hug.

Bera clapped.

'Go on, poppet, back to your mama,' Faelan said.

Bera closed the gap. Disa's sweet face was full of joy and determination, and in a few steps she was walking.

Bera hugged her. 'I love you,' she whispered. Her heart was healing – and it was bigger.

A mended boat is stronger for its clenching, he informed Disa's small skern, who looked impressed.

Sigrid walked Borgvald towards them. 'We need hot food inside us.'

'The stewpot is somewhere in the tackle. I'll collect driftwood while there's some light left,' Bera said. 'Dellingr will be back soon.'

Faelan was at the door. 'I'll get down to the boat. There are more rations, to come ashore.'

'Don't bring too much.'

He shrugged, but left without making her explain. Bera wasn't sure she could. She left Disa behind, needing time to work out how she felt, hoping her skern might help. As she headed for the small beach, she met Dellingr, who had found some fine planks.

'We'll be snug as bugs,' he said, without stopping.

His mood had lifted, while hers had darkened.

*

Twilight, and the sea shone with its memory of sun; too bright to see the waning Blood Moon. Bera stood for a moment, remembering how she had once bathed in a moon's path on a brittle white beach of bones and shells. From that far off place and time, Egill's voice came to her again: *'You see things so black and white, Bera.'*

'I don't anymore, Egill.'

Was it better or worse to live like that? Growth, decay: it was all around her.

Life isn't twofold.

Puzzling her skern's riddle, she went up to the highest tideline and was surprised to see Ginna gleaning in a field. How sensible she was to gather grains for the stew. She would like to teach her some remedies, make a healing garden together. But where?

'The only decision is twofold: stay or go, so why am I not choosing?'

You fear the war is inside you now, echoing with the Vallas through time.

'I've seen it can be caught, like the red-spot sickness. What if it infects the others?'

Could she bear to lose the new small family she had made? If she stayed, with two Vallas and two smiths, how much stronger they would be.

Bera was surprised by how dark it was. She had enough driftwood and headed for the croft, but then worried about finding it. The twilight blurring of features was over and the blanking out begun. Land, so welcoming by day, always turned hostile by night. Strange shrieks and calls echoed around her. Folk had lived here for years; were there Drorghers? Was that shuffling? She kept turning and then lost her direction.

A cough – one she recognised.

'I'm over here, Faelan,' she said.

'By the apple trees?'

'Come and help.' She threw down the bundle, already happier.

He soon appeared and put a shawl over her shoulders. 'Sigrid says you'll catch your death.'

Faelan picked up the driftwood and they walked on, the darkness thick with a feeling that she could not name.

'You talk a lot about duty,' he said.

The swerve took her off guard. 'My Valla duty?'

'I've had a lot of time, waiting for you, to think about things. About what happened in Dyflin.'

'Is this about Dellingr?'

'What?' He stopped. 'This is about you. There's a darkness in the Vallas that I have seen in you, Bera. Perhaps you can only love me when you are afraid, as we were in the long dead. I became your hero and not the plain man I am.'

'No!'

'I worry that you like the fear, Bera. Do you draw horror to you because the rush of facing it makes you feel alive?'

That's your worry.

'It's my duty!' She rubbed away furious tears.

'You like anger, too, it crackles like a storm at sea.'

'So you've been storing this up!'

'Is love enough, Bera? Can you see yourself in my mother's healing garden, really?' He quickened his pace, before she had an answer. But the loss in his voice was echoed in her heart, and what was the sign for that?

Sigrid had her end-of-passage stew ready and they sat around the fire with their bowls, declaring it the best ever, thanks to Ginna's gleanings. The others had second helpings and Heggi a third. It was ashes in Bera's mouth. Faelan's choice had been made, and now it was time for honesty, spoken aloud by them all.

Folk always make better decisions on their feet.

Bera took her place at the hearth. 'I call a meeting.'

Memories of bright flame in a home lost to them all. Thorvald beside her, calling the ranks of Seabost folk to order.

Stop looking back and get ready to talk of the future.

'It is our tradition to make decisions at the hearth in a mead hall. Well,' – Bera gestured around the patched-up croft – 'this is our hall and here is a hearth.'

Sigrid shifted, a warning sign that she should crack on.

'I stand here as a Valla and leader of our small band of settlers. I will ask you all for your view before we decide.'

'Stay or go, then,' said Dellingr.

'You are the eldest and our smith, so you start.' Bera hoped hearing their views would persuade her one way or the other.

You must lead.

Dellingr came to stand beside her, to claim his rank. 'I never deal in what-might-have-beens. I was thinking, on the boat: the Vallas know best and have woven Fate to be the six, here, now. And the two bairns. I say we make the best of what we have, make this our home. Stay.'

'It's not my turn but you know what I'll say, all of you.' Sigrid stayed sitting. 'I'm never getting on a boat again as long as I live. Home is what you make it. I'm staying.'

Bera's stomach griped. 'Faelan?'

He took off his hat. 'This is my home and my mother's home. I hear her on the wind, in the waves of the storm.'

Dellingr snorted but made it into a cough.

'The word-song returns here, Dellingr,' Faelan said. 'It's in my blood, like iron is in your bones. I am more the man here.' He looked straight at Bera. 'I stay.'

Blow after blow.

Bera tried to find her truth as she spoke. 'I was wrong to make it sound as if going into the Dark and escaping from Dyflin would make our future safe.'

'Won't it?' Ginna looked at the door.

'I meant that no faultless world awaits us if we only make the right choice. Wherever we go, we face hardship. If we all pull together as a strong team, we can be content in the knowledge that we have done our duty.'

'We can't decide yet,' said Heggi. 'Ginna and I haven't had our turn!'

'You're right, boykin.'

'I'm not a child!'

His anger knocked Bera off balance. She fell to her knees, clasping her head to hide such weakness. The shame of longing for things she could never have because she couldn't both stay and go, or even love and be loved it seemed. She deserved to be alone forever, and could never tell them. How could she protect them and not be that strong Valla?

Bera sat up straight. The others were in a ring around her. Standing close, keeping her safe. Ginna's face was stricken. She came and laid her head in Bera's lap, needing her hero back.

'I'm all right.'

'No you're not.' Faelan hunkered down in front of her. 'This has been brewing a long time, Bera.'

'We all take loss differently.' Sigrid made the hammer sign. 'Grief is anger and don't I know it. I say we stop making decisions and take life as it comes. One day at a time, one task at a time. You don't have to lead, Bera, just do your share of the work.'

'That's not—'

'Let us bear the load, Bera,' said Dellingr. 'I urged you to rest when you were near birthing, remember? You should have listened.' He also was wrong but unstoppable. 'We know what must be done. At first light we shall find better shelter and then I shall start smithing with Heggi, and I shall teach him the old ways, as promised.'

'And then Ginny and I can have a proper feast!' said Heggi, and Ginna stood beside him.

None of them understood. 'I must decide.'

'Hush, dear one,' said Sigrid. 'Life doesn't need to be forced or Fate-woven, as you Vallas would say. Let's wait and see. I met a woman earlier, she was out looking for windfalls, and she says she will show me where most folk live. She could be a friend.'

'You're good at making friends, Sigrid,' Ginna said.

'I may have kin here,' Faelan said, 'but in any case, island folk are strong on hospitality. Never turn away a stranger is written in our blood.'

'Like ours,' agreed Dellingr, patching up their fellowship and Fate.

They went cheerfully to their bedrolls, believing the decision was to stay. Bera was only certain that as Vallas, she and Valdis were stronger together. As a woman and mother, she should stay with both her children. Could she make a choice for herself that did not affect the ones she loved? Faelan had, without discussing it with her.

She nudged Sigrid. 'If I die, you would look after Heggi, wouldn't you?'

'What nonsense is this? You know the answer. Now go to sleep.'

Every time Bera drowsed, she woke with the remembered pain of hurting someone she loved. Body and mind. The deaths. Was it the fault of her duty, or her poor choices? She was too tired to decide anything, ever again. Her skern had no answers; he was half-cleaved to her. She reached a numb listlessness, like Hefnir on the *Raven*, deep in wolfsbane.

The beads were blood-hot at her neck, like another skern. It had all begun with the necklace. What if she buried it or threw it into the deeps? It was tempting, to save Disa from such a load.

The necklace would retain its power.

Bera pictured the beads, starting with the returned B rune: a token of passion and betrayal; Obsidian, made by fire, next to wolf-eyed amber. The sea-change glass bead. Others familiar in form but without meaning. Yet.

'The beads are stories, but can't make things happen.'

Fate sealed in stone.

'And precious because all our Valla pasts are stored in them, which skerns can't tell us. The past shapes who we are today. How Disa will be. The other beads will be new stories made by her.'

So you cannot destroy them.

'The old ways are changing. I can choose differently and change everything. I could give my daughter the necklace now.'

Your child cannot wear it until she can bear the weight.

'I remember the weight. It's all I truly remember of that day. The weight of it.'

And you must bear it.

'I can't, not anymore.'

Bera lay, aching for the *Raven*'s cradle-rock, listening to the night noises, snores and rattles and the rustling of the spare sail in the night breeze off the sea.

A blackbird greeted early dawn. Bera collected her daughter and slipped out without waking the others. Disa did not cry, as if she knew what they were about and that it was the right thing.

There was a low mist in the orchard, where Alfdis was waiting to accompany them. She nodded at Bera and they went down together, three generations silently about their Valla business.

The light was clearer near the sea, showing the full sweep of the bay. The *Raven* was stirring at her mooring, pointing out to the sea paths, impatient to set sail with the dawn. Alfdis raised her hands in blessing and stayed on the headland, guardian of their leaving, like one of her rune stones.

Bera hurried towards the dock. 'If anyone catches us too soon, I can say we came to check the mooring.'

She could not resist looking back, but unless Faelan was hidden in the mist, he had not followed. She thought he knew her better than she knew herself.

Bera studied the mooring post, which had two lines and a loop. 'See, Disa? Clever Faelan has her on a running line so we can pull her in. Here's your first lesson in boat-handling, dearest.'

She released one of the lines and hauled the other, praying the boat was on a long loop. It was, and easy to pull the boat back to the landing.

'The *Raven* is coming to fetch us!' Bera waited for a swell to lift the boat, then quickly took some turns around the post. 'That's the bow line. Now we'll do the same at the stern.'

Bera threw her bedroll on deck and lifted Disa over, who held the rail and stood sturdily while Bera got aboard. A good sign. Bera admired the silver-scrubbed boards that ran the length of the boat as they walked them, the well-made deck strong and sure. She stopped at the prow and picked up Disa. The *Raven*! A freshening wind whispered the lure of the sea paths, haunting whale song and the crash of waves. Bera's mind snapped open and she was truly alive in this moment with her child in her arms.

She carried her to the mast. 'Touch it, Disa. Your grandfather chose the tree, and fashioned a fine mast. '"*The mountain ash is the strongest and the whitest wood comes from the north face.*"'

One woman and a baby cannot manage this alone. Her skern was afraid, too.

Ottar would never have allowed it, and with no spare sail.

307

Disa squirmed for freedom and then did such a fast crawl that Bera had to run to catch her before she fell into the bilge. She tied her determined child to her belt on a long line and was satisfied.

Madness.

'I can do it.'

Her fingers ached and she looked down, expecting them to be purple with ice-bite, her face stinging in scouring hail and her cloak stiff with rime, as if she were already at the Ice-Rimmed Sea. One woman against all the ocean could hurl at her. It would be the most honourable battle, and when it was done, there was honour in dying on her father's longship; losing was certain but it would be a proper passing, like the old days. The *Raven* was strong enough to sail on forever, keeping her dead crew safe. Bera slipped the running line and let the boat drift out into the bay.

You would not sacrifice your daughter.

'I can't go back. I have to think.'

She hauled them out to the underwater mooring and made off the line, so that no one could pull them back to shore. She untied a fur bundle and crawled beneath it with her child, desperate to sleep, staring dry-eyed. High mare's-tail clouds whipped across the red sky.

Red sky at dawn
Fishwives mourn.

She longed to drift upwards, ash in the wind, not having to feel anything ever again. Untethered. If she lay here without drinking she would become as brittle as an ice shark's egg-case blowing on a windy shore. Then Disa caught her mother's forefinger in her tiny, mighty fist and held on for both their dear lives.

A low whistle woke her, and it was Faelan's. It was always going to be him but she was still not ready. What did she want him to do? She had made a decision in the night and now he was going to confuse it all again. He was standing at the dock, not able to pull her back to him unless she untied the *Raven*.

It was like King-Maker, whatever the move was called. They watched each other, unmoving.

'Rucka, Mama!' Disa shouted. 'Rucka, rucka!'

A new word. Bera gave her a rusk. 'Hard tack, small one, to cut your teeth on.'

When she looked back, Faelan was gone. Heartache was a bodily pain. Bera pressed her palm against her chest to stop all her feelings bursting out and cracking it open. Why had he made no effort to stop her? Did he respect her too much? To Hel with all that.

Bera went forward to cast off and saw the curricle merrily bouncing towards the *Raven*. Was he going to stop her? Let him try! Still, she waited for him to tie up alongside.

There were some bundles in the curricle. 'I've brought blankets and food.' He waited for her reply, then pressed on. 'Can I come aboard? A curricle is not the easiest place for a serious farewell.'

She stepped away.

Faelan neatly swung himself up onto the deck and surprised her by holding her tight at once. The smell of his hair, his face, so familiar, so matched. Their bodies fitted together like human and skern. Cleaved.

She pulled away. 'This is no answer.'

He grew serious. 'We all knew you would go.'

'You think this is easy? I feel ripped in two, Faelan, so don't say "everyone knew" as if you are Sigrid, as if I always let folk down. I never do!'

'Oh, sweetheart, that was not what I meant.' He reached out but she ducked away. 'I was hoping to show we understand; to make it a kinder parting.'

'How could a parting ever be kind!'

He looked past her to the sea paths. 'You long for the Far North, that's always been clear.'

'But why do I? Do you know what it's like to be over the Ice Rim, with dread cold seeping into the keel? Listening all night for the crackle of bergs and growlers? Blackened toes, fingertips dead as iron, scraping away sea ice from every spar and sail before it drags the boat under.'

'Why go then?'

Bera tugged her hair from the roots. 'I don't know!'

He went to take her hand but stopped himself. 'Do you think being buried alive has made it worse?'

She turned the idea over. 'It was a kind of death to be under the earth. Being on the *Raven* is the very opposite. But when I'm out there I miss kinship and the hearth.'

'You long for home?'

'My home is out there, on the whale roads and with the beasts that travel them.'

'Are you saying this to give yourself enough courage to go?'

'I'm scrying what's in my heart.'

'Listing the things in your heart does not mean you must ignore your head. Wait until the spring and go out when the weather is fair.'

'The *Raven* is no fishing boat! Besides, ice will crush her if she waits in harbour.'

'The sea does not freeze here.' He gave her a long look. 'Hefnir must have told you that. It's why he overwintered here.'

'So I'm lying?'

'I think you are making excuses to go off and die.'

Bera punched his chest. 'Stop it! Now I have to go even more!' She hit him again. 'I can't stand all this back and fore in my mind. I made my choice!'

'Enough, Bera.' He held her wrists, hard enough to hurt. 'Who are you trying to impress? Heggi? Ginna?' Faelan spun her round towards the shore. 'Look.'

The sky was a rose dawn beyond the headland where Alfdis stood with four black figures. Bera knew their outlines as well as she knew her skern. The smallest was Sigrid, unknowingly standing beside her childhood friend. The next in height was Ginna, then Heggi, nearly as tall as Dellingr.

'They came.'

'As they always will,' said Faelan.

'Trying to stop me, like you?'

'I have not come to stop you.'

'What, then?'

'Look at me now, Bera. No, straight at me.' He gave their sign for love. 'You have to trust me.'

'I do.'

'No you don't, not completely; there's a part of you that always flinches away. What do you fear? Being trapped?'

Bera let out a long breath. 'Not by you.'

'But?'

'But… I will never settle to be an ordinary woman. Who knows what trouble I may bring to you, to all the ones I love so deeply.'

'We all fear something, Bera. We must contain it or it can bring about the very thing we fear.'

'What is yours?'

'That you may never love me as I love and treasure you.'

How she had longed to hear this, once.

'It doesn't matter now, does it?' Bera pressed against the mast. 'I have lived among folk my whole life, but always been alone.'

'You're wrong, Bera.'

'You have come home to this island, but I do not belong. When I am old, the sea will have me.'

'Leaving your baby? Or making her suffer, too?' Faelan nodded towards Disa, happily playing by herself.

'Oh, let me be!'

'I'm not trying to bind you to me. Be free, Bera. Belong only to the sea – but let me come with you.'

Hope kindled a small flame while she tried to think of reasons it could not be. 'You'd leave your birthplace?'

'Could you leave me behind again? Or any of us?'

Bera's heartbeat throbbed the truth.

You can both love – and leave. Have – and hold.

Her folk had not moved. If they tried to stop her, she would cast off and be gone.

'They are still here,' she said.

'So are we.' She heard his smile, the one that crinkled his eyes.

It was that light touch of his that freed her. Bera pointed at herself, crossed her hands over her heart and held them out towards him. Faelan replied with the same sign, crossing his fists for passion.

'You are the only man for me, Faelan. The only one I have ever loved. No, wait. Love itself solves nothing. I need now to find out who I am. I know how to be a Valla. Now I must find out how to be whole as a woman. Then, if I can be at home in my own skin, where home is will not matter.'

'And so…'

'And so… until then I owe my life to you and my folk, up there. Perhaps a body can become whole in all the different ways folk see the best in her.'

'Meaning… ? Will you stay?'

She took his face in her hands and kissed him as tenderly as a child. Perhaps it was part of her to never be certain, or perhaps that was what all women felt.

Never black and white.

Conflict with heart, body and skern. And the Vallas. But then the kiss itself became all that was urgent. Something crashed into her shins and held on. Disa was determined to join in. Faelan swept her high up in the air, never letting her think she may be dropped.

'We winter here, then,' said Bera, 'and each spring, we will let the *Raven* take us wherever the wind blows.'

'With all our children.'

It was that simple after all.

THE END OF THE BOOK OF BERA

ACKNOWLEDGEMENTS

The Book of Bera: Sea Paths was published in 2018 but the story began long ago in a second-hand bookshop in Southsea, where I liked to mooch on a Saturday morning with 2/6d pocket money. One day I found a chunky, sage-green book with golden page edges and title lettering: *Myths of the Norsemen*, 1908. Now I see there are two golden ravens on the cover! I grew up with the *Mabinogion* and various other legends but was shaped by a visit to Beddgelert when I was twelve. Somehow it all trickles through.

Every single supporter has my thanks, for without you these books would not exist. I've gained so much professionally from Iceland Writers Retreat and with the support of fellow authors, especially the Hairy Godmothers! Bera is a great character and my special thanks go to Elizabeth Garner, whose creative editing unravels themes and purpose from jumbled early drafts with the genius of total understanding. I've also had the same insightful copy editor each time, and trust me, her job is essential. The whole team at Unbound is keen, kind and genuinely happy for every success. I live to write and couldn't do it without my small gang at home. And a big hug for all Labradors. Thank you.

A NOTE ON THE AUTHOR

Suzie Wilde is the author of the previous two books in the trilogy, *Sea Paths* and *Obsidian*. She has an MA with distinction in Creative Writing and is a member of the Society of Authors. She writes full time with her dog beside her, when they are not walking the South Downs. Her weekly podcast, *Wilde Walks* and monthly *Talking Books* can be found on Shine Radio, Petersfield. She is married to the man who took her off sailing for five years and they now live in Hampshire.

www.suziewilde.co.uk
Twitter: @susiewilde
Facebook: @suziewildeauthor

Unbound is the world's first crowdfunding publisher, established in 2011.

We believe that wonderful things can happen when you clear a path for people who share a passion. That's why we've built a platform that brings together readers and authors to crowdfund books they believe in – and give fresh ideas that don't fit the traditional mould the chance they deserve.

This book is in your hands because readers made it possible. Everyone who pledged their support is listed below. Join them by visiting unbound.com and supporting a book today.

Clara Abrahams
Eli Allison
Michael Auger
James Aylett
Susan Bain
Jason Ballinger
Mike Barnett
Liesbeth Bennett
Fran Benson
Jonas Bergstedt
Karen Boxalll
Stephanie Bretherton
Struan Britland
Sarah Broadley
Richard Brooman
Guy & Pam Cheeseman
Harriet Cherriman
Camilla Chester
Meagan Cihlar
Anthony Clark
Corrinne Cload
Dom Conlon
Alan Copsey

Robert Cox
Nancy Crosby
Lydia Cunningham
Lesley Dampney
Margaret Dascalopoulos
Gill Davies
Linda Davies
Steve Dew
Miranda Dickinson
Colin Dixon
Abla El-Sharnouby
Julia Elliman
James Ellson
Richard Emlyn Watkins
Kathryn Evans
David Fennell
Gladys Ferns
Philippa Francis
Karen Galley
Lynn Genevieve
Julie Gilmour
Clare Glancy
Bill Grimwood

Geoffrey Gudgion
Julie Hart
Maximilian Hawker
Andy Hawkins
Peter Hawksworth
Thea Hawksworth
Susan Henderson Miles
Anita Heward
L Hockley
Kim Howard
Paul Hudson
Ivor Humphreys
Mike James
Frank Jennings
Colleen Jones
Tiffin Jones
Dave Joyce
Hilary Julian
Priscilla Jutton-Holland
Liz Kent
K. L. Kettle
Dan Kieran
Jonathan Kim
Lizzie Ladbrooke
Ewan Lawrie
Jon Lawson
Sam Learmonth
Jude Lennon
Susi Lennox
Jonina Leosdottir
Jean Levy
Kim Locke
Bridget Lubbock
Jon Mackley
Ferran J Mari Rivero
Jessica Martin
Steve Martin
Abigail McKern
Alice McVeigh

Mike
John Mitchinson
Wendy Moir
Alison Morgan
Cass Morgan
Chris Morgan
Patrick Morgan
Iain Morrison
G C Mosse
Tim Mudie
Carlo Navato
Linda Nelson
John New
Ivy Ngeow
Tim O'Kelly
Kevin Offer
Louise Parker
Justin Pollard
Jacqueline Potter
Samantha Potter
Mandy Rabin
Sara Read
Andrew Reed
Caroline Ritchie
Jan Ritchie
Janet Ritchie
Peter Rossiter
Matthew Rowe
Jenny Schwarz
Harry Scott
Bri Seares
Linda Sgoluppi
Ste Sharp
Victoria Simkin
Nicole Small
Susan Smith
Heather Sorrell
Glynis Spencer
Valerie Spencer

Bob Stone
Tim Stretton
John Surace
Claire Swift
Charlotte Teeple Salas
Maddy Templeman
Lesley Thomson
Nick Tigg
Adam Tinworth
Robin Townsend
Wendy Townsend
Claire Vennis
Mark Vent
Marina Vundum
David Wakefield
The Wakefields
Steve Walford

Sue Wallman
Tanya Walters
Helen Watson
Louise Weller
Jan Welsman
John Welsman
Laura Westmore
Ian Wheeler
Andrew Wilde
Peter Wilde
Suzanne Wilkins
Sarah Willett
Derek Wilson
Kate Wiseman
Matthew Wood
Clifton Wray